UNDER A CORNISH SKY

On the sleeper train down to Cornwall, Demi can't help wondering why everything always goes wrong for her. Having missed out on her dream job, and left with nowhere to stay following her boyfriend's betrayal, pitching up at her grandfather's cottage is her only option . . . Victoria thinks she's finally got what she wanted: Boscawen, the gorgeous Cornish estate her family owned for generations, should now rightfully be hers, following her husband's sudden death. After years of a loveless marriage and many secret affairs of her own, Victoria thinks new widowhood will suit her very well indeed . . . But both women are in for a surprise. Surrounded by orchards, gardens and the sea, Boscawen is about to play an unexpected role in both their lives, as long-buried secrets are uncovered and a battle of wills begins . . .

UNDER A CORNISH SKY

LIZ FENWICK

LARGE
PRINT

First published in Great Britain 2015
by
Orion Books
an imprint of The Orion Publishing Group Ltd.

First Isis Edition
published 2016
by arrangement with
The Orion Publishing Group Ltd.
An Hachette UK Company

A catalogue record for this book is available
from the British Library.

ISBN 978–1–78541–198–4 (hb)
ISBN 978–1–78541–204–2 (pb)

Published by
F. A. Thorpe (Publishing)
Anstey, Leicestershire

Set by Words & Graphics Ltd.
Anstey, Leicestershire
Printed and bound in Great Britain by
T. J. International Ltd., Padstow, Cornwall

This book is printed on acid-free paper

For Andrew

One does not jump, and spring, and shout hurrah! at hearing one has got a fortune, one begins to consider responsibilities, and to ponder business; on a base of steady satisfaction rise certain grave cares, and we contain ourselves, and brood over our bliss with a solemn brow.

Jane Eyre — Charlotte Brontë

Prologue

The eyes look at her and Demi laughs. She turns to the child next to her, the one she has played with all week, but the boy is not there. Nor is the girl who is looking after them, nor are the other children. She is alone with the butterfly and the sunshine. It is so beautiful. She steps closer to it and it flies away to stop on a purple flower. Looking around, she decides to follow the butterfly. It must be flying the way the others went. Maybe the butterfly was really a fairy or even a Cornish pixie. Mummy says pixies are naughty, like Demi is when she doesn't eat her carrots.

The butterfly holds still only for a moment and then the next it is gone. Demi tries to catch it, but can't. When she is back at the hotel, she will draw the butterfly for Mummy.

The purple eyes flap and move, setting off again. There *must* be a fairy on its back. It goes up then down, stopping to rest but then moving on towards the woods and the bluebells. Grannie has told her all about the bluebells. She has been to bluebell woods before. This is where the fairies live and she must never go into a bluebell wood without Grannie or Grandad because the fairies will trap her. Grannie told her that long ago when she was really small. But the butterfly with the purple eyes flies into the woods and Demi follows. She is big now and the fairies can't catch her because she can run fast.

The path twists and turns. Demi skips, singing a song Grannie taught her as she goes: "Bluebell, bluebell, what a pretty bluebell. Bluebell, bluebell, will you really true tell? Who will love me bluebell? Do tell?" She stops and listens. Will the bluebells tell her? Mummy loves her, Grannie loves her, Grandad loves her, and Charlie loves her. She doesn't need the bluebells to true tell.

Sunlight falls through the trees colouring the ground blue and purple. Demi takes out the crayon in her pocket and pretends to draw the trees and the flowers. The sun is high and her tummy rumbles and her head hurts. Spinning around and around, she falls to the ground. The butterfly disappears and she is alone.

She is in the fairies' wood; she knows she is. She can feel their magic.

A butterfly passes in front of her, cutting the sunlight in half for a second. Demi shivers as a breeze moves the bells. Will they ring? What was it Grannie said? If you hear the bluebells ring, something will die. Mummy told her to stop telling her these old super-somethings. Demi puts her hands over her ears, but she can hear ringing. She stands up. The wind blows stronger and she shivers. She must get away. A twig snaps and Demi looks around. She can see nothing but flowers and trees. She runs and she stumbles. Throwing her hands out she lands. Pain. Blood. Tears. She gets up. She must keep running but she can't get her breath. "Mummy!" she cries. Her voice is taken by the wind. Mummy won't hear her call.

A shadow darkens the path and fear tightens her tummy. It must be the Kowres, the scary giantess that Grannie tells her will eat her if she strays out past the end of the garden. Granny showed her the one that had turned to stone in the field near where Granny grew up.

Her knees, hands and head hurt, but she must escape the Kowres. She will eat her. Grannie says the Kowres like to eat children who don't do what they are told!

The stone Kowres looms in front of her. She runs to it and away from the giant behind. She tries to hide but the giant grabs her. The Kowres have caught her! She can smell ginger. Will the Kowres eat her? Was it because she heard the bluebell ring?

Spring

A son can bear with equanimity the loss of his father, but the loss of his inheritance may drive him to despair.

Niccolo Machiavelli

CHAPTER
ONE

The scent of honeysuckle drifted through the open window and late afternoon sunshine fell on the tangled sheets. Victoria smiled. She could still smell Adam's aftershave. She pulled the duvet over the bed and plumped up the pillows. It was all well and good to have a lazy afternoon of sex with her toy boy, but it would be decidedly unpleasant if Charles walked in to see the evidence and she'd heard his car come up the drive a few minutes ago.

Removing the green silk shift from the hanger she pulled it over her head, enjoying the feel of the fabric as it slid across her nipples. She shivered. It was a shame they had this party. Charles might well have stayed in London for longer and she could have enjoyed Adam for the whole evening and not just the afternoon. He was training up satisfactorily. Property, old houses and sex . . . total bliss.

Victoria ran her fingers through her hair. Despite the fact that it had turned grey a few years ago, it wasn't any old shade of grey but gleamed like polished steel and the texture had held up well. She slipped earrings on then picked up her pearls. Charles had given her these for her fiftieth birthday. She, of course, had chosen them and they were exactly the right shade for her skin tone. Pearls reflected such a wonderful radiance on to the face. She touched her neck. Considering her sun exposure over the years her skin was good. No need to resort to a surgeon.

She straightened her back as she tried to fasten the clasp on her pearls, but couldn't manage it by feel alone. "Where are my glasses?" she said aloud as she scanned the surfaces in her bedroom.

"On your head." Charles stood in the doorway. He wore a dark suit, which, despite the clever cut, didn't disguise his paunch.

"Thank you. Why the suit?"

"Business." He shifted on his feet.

"You haven't un-retired have you?" It would be excellent news if he had.

"No." He walked up to her and took the pearls from her hands. She let him drape them around her neck but his fingers struggled with the clasp and his aftershave filled the air around her; she wished he'd put on a bit less. Her nose was far too sensitive to the fragrance after forty years. He rested his hands on her shoulders when the pearls were finally secured and rubbed gently. Victoria tried to enjoy the sensation, but it didn't work, and as he kissed the side of her neck she watched the displeasure cross her face in the mirror. She changed her expression when Charles's blue eyes looked up to meet hers.

"As always, you look beautiful, Tori."

"Thank you." She turned around in his arms and adjusted his tie. He was a good soul — she must remember that.

8

"Remind me what the Smiths are having this do for?"

"An engagement party for their daughter." She swallowed. That was something *they* would never be able to celebrate.

"Ah, yes." He turned from her.

"I hate it when you sound that way." Victoria ground her teeth. Even the view of the garden out of the window couldn't fill the emptiness inside her.

"What are you talking about?" He shook his head and then puffed before he said, "I have something I need to discuss with you. It's important."

She spun round. "You know exactly what I mean." Oh, she loathed him. The sadness she'd heard in his voice irritated her and now he looked like a hurt puppy. It was absolutely not the way a sixty-two-year-old man should look.

"Tori, there really is something I need to discuss with you."

She looked up at him and caught sight of the clock on her bedside table. "Will it be quick? We are supposed to be there already. Are you going in your suit?"

"No, it won't be quick." He looked down at his trousers. "Do I need to change?"

Victoria sighed. "No. Let's go." She walked out of the bedroom and only paused at the top of the stairs. From here, she could see the full sweep of the staircase down to the hall. She had Charles to thank for all of this. Without his money, she never could have bought back her family home, Boscawen. Hearing his heavy footsteps behind her, she turned and smiled and held out a hand for him. Almost forty-one years to the day since they had walked together down these stairs on the night of their engagement party. Victoria shivered, remembering the expectant faces waiting for them at the bottom. Only one face hadn't been smiling.

"Tori, where are you?" Charles gave her hand a squeeze.

"Sorry, were you saying something?"

"Yes, something rather important. Don't tell me you didn't hear a word?" He frowned and his chins multiplied.

"Sorry, I was just remembering our engagement party." That brought a smile to his face.

"Forty wonderful years together." He kissed her. "Thank you, darling."

"A pleasure," she lied and collected the keys to his car. If they didn't leave now, they would be seriously late, especially if they had the misfortune to get caught behind a tractor.

Demi wouldn't let her mother down. She owed it to her memory, Morwenna had been so proud of her and the work she'd done here at Bottel and Lampard. Today of all days Demi could have used her mother's belief in her abilities. Her mother's death had been too sudden. How could her fit and able mother have just died? Swallowing back the tide of grief about to emerge, Demi stopped. This was not the best time to be thinking about it. Positive thoughts were required. She *would* get this job. She'd earned it by working hard and, of course, she'd loved it too.

Straightening her skirt and crossing her ankles, she heard her mother's voice in her head, reminding her to sit with her shoulders back, not hunched, trying to hide what her mother had called her assets. How Demi hated them. Not only had they resulted in her being continually tormented by boys at school, she would never be able to look elegant. They attracted too much attention.

Josh, sitting opposite, looked relaxed. Unlike her, he wasn't in the watery glare of the sunlight making its way through the dirty window. She frowned. The architect who had designed this building had thought only of the appearance and not of the need for cleaning and fresh air.

It must have been a man just like Josh. Demi had been on a practical with him for a year and during that time she'd constantly had to fix his designs. He'd asked for help and she'd given it — although she wondered why she had, because at the end of the year only one of them would be taken on permanently. Josh was all about lines and appearance, not about the practicalities. And that was why *she* should get this job, because she looked at both and so her designs functioned on every level. This is what she loved.

He kept looking at her and then away. Who knew what he'd done while she'd been away for weeks on compassionate leave? She hoped he'd been a disaster because this job would solve one key problem of the moment. Money. Although she had earned at bit

11

during the practical, she had paid most of it to her mother for living expenses and the cost of the funeral had drained her mother's account. Morwenna's life insurance would eventually cover those costs but it hadn't paid out yet. Demi took a deep breath. It still didn't seem real that her mother was gone and she didn't want it to be, but it was. She couldn't afford to take anything but a full-time, well-paid job now. She wouldn't even have a roof over her head if not for her boyfriend, Matt. Demi bit her lip. Thinking about how dire things were wasn't going to put her in the right frame of mind for the coming interview.

A drop of sweat ran down her neck and she saw Josh's eyes follow it until it slid under the neckline of her blouse. It was too warm for the jacket she was wearing, but if she took it off she had no chance of anyone looking at anything but her cleavage, modest though her blouse was. They wouldn't talk to her but to her chest. It was easy for men. The worst error for them was a bad tie — and Josh's tie was a *big* mistake. It showed he had no taste. Surely they wouldn't give the job to someone who would choose to wear a large, pink-spotted tie with a green striped shirt and a suit in a Glen plaid? It was wrong on so many levels.

Her own clothes were a bit old, but expressed an understated elegance — or as close as she could achieve with her curves, she thought wryly. If she were the one making the choice she would pick the employee who performed to a higher level and whose dress sense showed a basic understanding of colour, shape and design.

12

Thunder rumbled outside and the sun disappeared just as the door to the HR department swung open. She couldn't help feeling that it was an ominous start. Her opponent smiled in her direction but avoided eye contact.

"Demi and Josh, come through." Demi stood, and in her head she imagined that she was taller than five foot one. The sooner this interview was over and she had the job, the better.

"Take a seat." The woman went to her desk and Demi sat far away from the window. She didn't need to melt further.

"First, I'd like to say thank you. You've both done a great job during your internships here at Bottel and Lampard." She smiled at them in turn. Demi laid her hands flat on her skirt. This was not going well. Josh *hadn't* done a good job; passable, maybe, but only because she'd helped him.

"It's been an honour to be a part of the team." Josh spoke and Demi cursed him as a brown nose. He'd done nothing but complain and try and get her to shag him the whole time. He was an arse, but he was smooth. She'd allow him that, but only that.

"As you know, we can only take on one of you at this time and it's been a very hard decision." The woman lifted her mouth in a smile, but her eyes told a different story. Demi knew what she was going to say by the way her glance fell on Demi's left hand. She'd let slip that things were getting serious with Matt and yes, they were, but she wasn't planning to start a family just yet.

"So, after consulting the whole team, the consensus was the job should be offered to Josh for the stellar work he did on the design of the bathrooms."

"But —" Demi began but Josh stood.

"Wow, thank you so much." He moved between Demi and the desk so that she couldn't be seen.

Demi stood and moved from side to side, trying to get past him. That was her design, not his. She needed to set this straight. He was claiming her work as his. She couldn't let this theft pass. "That design . . ." She went to the side of the desk.

"Ah, Demi, your work has been of an excellent standard but I'm afraid we only have the one position and Josh fits on every level. Of course, if you'd like to continue on as you have been we would be delighted." Again the woman's mouth lifted but that was all. "And I will write you a glowing reference should you decide to look elsewhere."

One of the firm's partners walked in. "Congratulations, Josh. Excellent work." He turned to Demi. "So sorry to see you go." He looked away, totally dismissing her. Then she realised. "*Josh fits on every level.*" How many times had Demi been asked to go to the pub after work and said no to get home to Matt. But Josh had gone every time. They knew him, or thought they did, and she was a world-class idiot who hadn't played the game.

Demi couldn't move. Josh was shaking the director's hand and he wouldn't look at Demi. He was a thief — but what could she do? If she protested she'd sound like a bad loser, and she would still be the loser . . .

14

A bottle of champagne popped open as the rest of the partners appeared. No one would make eye contact.

"Thank you." She would do this as gracefully as she could. It was what her mother would want, for Demi to be graceful and generous. She slipped out of the door while they were pouring the champagne.

Outside the HR office, she stopped and leaned against the wall. She'd let someone else take the job that should have been hers. Anger — with herself as much as with Josh filled her. This wasn't trying out for the school play. This was life. This was survival. Should she go in there and confront Josh with his deception? No. It was too late now. If she had done it straight away it might have worked, might not have seemed like sour grapes. It was best to let go. It was easier.

The receptionist came down the corridor. "Demi, so sorry they didn't offer you the job."

Demi's eyes widened. Everyone, not just the partners, knew already. Even if she went in and told them the truth they wouldn't alter their decision. They'd look like fools and no one wanted to do that, including her.

She wasn't right for the job, but a man who claimed other people's work as his own was? She went to her desk, head down and pulled out her umbrella and her laptop. She was out of here without a job and she couldn't help thinking it was her own fault. Her mother would be so disappointed. Maybe it was a good thing she wasn't around to see this. No, that could never be a good thing. Demi bit her lip then fled before she had to see anyone else's pity.

In the crush of people at Westminster tube station Demi fought with her umbrella but it wouldn't open. After a few more attempts she cast it into the bin and walked out into the rain. The umbrella was useless. Just when she needed the damn thing it refused to work. Rain flung itself at her from every direction like a rebuke for her stupidity. It slapped her face and drenched her suit. By the time she reached the middle of the bridge her feet were squelching in her shoes.

Pulling out of the flow of people across the bridge she leaned on the wall. She needed to think, to make a plan. The raindrops hit the surface of the river and after the initial resistance they merged peacefully, doing what rivers do, flow. *She* hadn't bounced; she'd just faded away and let that sod take credit for her work. Now he had a job and at best they would consider her for another practical. That bastard had claimed what was hers while she was burying her mother. And what had she said? What had she done about it? Nothing. She hadn't even tried to bounce before becoming invisible.

Turning from the river she joined the rest of the commuters. It would be a wet walk back to her boyfriend's but at least there would be wine waiting.

"Cheer up, love, it can't be that bad," the newsvendor on the corner said as he handed her a paper, which she held over her head and smiled back at him. He was right. It wasn't all bad. She had Matt.

As she walked she focused on things to look forward to, like moving in officially with Matt. She'd been living

16

there unofficially since she'd handed her mother's flat back to the landlord. She swallowed; she wouldn't think about her mum, not now. Instead she would think of Matt's delight when she told him yes and she would think about what she could do with the flat. It was all a bit dreary and grey at the moment, despite the designer paint — which was in a shade of lavender that appeared grey on the flat's north-facing walls. The furniture was big, black and leather, all meant to complement the bloody huge television. It wasn't simply masculine; it was without personality. Demi had always puzzled how a man who dressed so well and took so much care with his clothing choices could care so little for making his flat feel personal.

She smiled: this would all change now. With a coat of paint — which sadly she would have time to give it, and a few accessories — she could soften the flat and make it feel more "them". Matt probably wouldn't even notice the changes. He would just smile that movie-star grin and she would melt.

Thinking back to the HR person's glance at her left hand she wondered why she had let slip that they were getting serious? They were, of course, and Matt was certainly committed, but that didn't mean she was about to get married immediately and start pushing out kids. Her career was important and she was only just twenty-five.

Drenched, and desperate for a glass of wine and a hug, she stopped outside his flat. The lights were on which was unusual, but maybe Matt had come home early. Probably planning a surprise celebration. God, had she really thought she'd get the job? She was such a fool.

Well, they would laugh at what an arse she'd been. Laughter was something she hadn't done enough of recently, for obvious reasons. Seeing her friends at her mum's funeral had shown her how much she missed them all and the fun they had had together. Matt didn't like them, which was OK — well, sort of — but she must get out more. She loved him, but he could be overpowering. Standing at the door she frowned when she heard the music they had been listening to two nights ago. She hesitated. They had had too much to drink that night and she didn't want to think about what she'd done . . .

She turned the key in the lock and nearly fell over from the sound — boys and their toys or, in this case, surround sound. She put her bag down, hoping her computer had stayed dry, then tiptoed into the sitting room. The walls were empty of all ornament, just the big screen as centre stage. She closed her eyes, imagining it with just a few framed prints or a large oil painting. It would give the room the personality it deserved. Maybe when her mother's life insurance paid out she could treat him to that painting they had seen together. It would be good to say thank you for all the support. He'd been such a help as her world fell apart.

There were grunts coming from the speakers. She sighed and opened her eyes. Matt was watching porn again. She hated that. It had the opposite effect on her that he wanted it to have. Watching it made her go off sex. Her heart sank, but she came up behind him and

18

put her hands on his shoulders, but just as she bent to kiss his head, she froze. There, on the 50-inch screen, was her naked body.

"Demi, you're back." He grabbed her hand and pulled her down towards him.

She tried to pull back, shivering as her moans bounced off the empty walls. What had he done?

"Let go of me!"

He released her and stood up, blocking her view. She studied his handsome face. The smile that had always won her over now looked false.

"Just . . . just what is that?"

"Us, Demi. It's so sexy."

Demi closed her eyes. She felt faint. Grabbing the back of the sofa for support, she tried to speak but words wouldn't come out. How could he have done this? She'd said no when he'd asked. "How . . .?"

"My new phone."

She shook her head. "How could you?" He'd done this even though she'd said no, that she hated the idea. Didn't her feelings matter to him?

"Don't be a prude. It's great — really turns me on."

She shook her head furiously. "No!" Clutching her stomach, she ran to the bathroom and heaved.

"Demi, don't be like this! It's so great. You don't like me watching other women so now I'm just watching you." His voice sounded weird through the door.

She didn't answer, bathing her face, still shaking. He'd asked. She'd said no. And he did it anyway. He was happy, turned on. She was disgusted, used.

"Demi, come on. It's just a bit of fun."

The cold water soothed her flaming skin. She looked in the mirror and big sad eyes stared back at her. What was she going to do? How could she stay with someone she couldn't trust? He'd said he was disappointed but he wouldn't film them. Told her not to worry and she hadn't.

Opening the door, she pushed past him and switched the television off. Glancing around the room she saw it for the soulless place it truly was. She turned to Matt. He was dressed in chinos and a designer shirt, smiling despite what he'd done. He had no idea, no remorse. There was only one thing she could do: leave. She picked up her bag and her shoes.

"Demi, wait!"

She turned to look at him. "You just don't get it."

"No, *you* don't." The smile had left his face. "You need to grow up. It turns me on — really turns me on."

"I said no, Matt." She slipped her shoes on and her toes curled at the dampness.

"You didn't mean it."

"I did. I really did."

He reached for her and caught her wrist.

"No!" She twisted free and left. She could hear him calling her as she fled down the street, wondering what now? Around the corner, halfway to the tube station she dived into a coffee shop. A cup of strong espresso would help her think. So much for the hug she'd been expecting and drowning her sorrows in a glass of wine. What was she going to do? She scrolled through her phone and called Sophie.

20

"Hi, I'm on holiday. I'll be tanned and relaxed when I'm back on the 31st. Please leave a message or email me if it's urgent."

"Hi, Sophie. I'll send you an email but I don't suppose anyone has your key and I can crash at your place for a few days?"

By the time she'd gone through all her friends and finished two coffees, the café was closing. Now she stood on the pavement as the man locked the door behind her. All she wanted to do was go home — but she had no home. And the calls she'd made had proved that having a crisis before a Bank Holiday was seriously not good timing. Sophie was away, Maia was about to deliver her baby, and nobody else seemed to be home. Demi went through the phone numbers again. Who could she turn to? All she wanted was her mum. She fought back the tears that had begun to mix with the rain that was still falling.

She thumbed through the Gs and then moved back to them. Her grandfather. She pressed dial and waited. She had last seen him two weeks ago when she'd helped him to Paddington to catch the train back to Cornwall. It still broke her heart the way he'd squeezed her hand as he left. That gesture had remained with her when grief had overwhelmed her. He'd lost his wife and now his only child. It wasn't the way life was supposed to work.

"Hello?"

"Hi, Grandad, it's me, Demi."

"Demi, my lovely. How good to hear from you."

The tears began in earnest and she couldn't stop them.

Victoria turned the handle on the sitting room door and then paused, waiting for Charles to catch up.

"Don't think I'll join you for that drink. I just want to check something on the computer," he said, walking into his study.

"Fine." She didn't turn to watch him go but listened to his heavy tread across the stone floor. Her shoulders relaxed as she entered the sitting room. Charles had been edgy all evening, had kept muttering about having something they needed to sit down and talk about, that the car journey was too short. And now, when they finally had time, he'd dashed off to his computer, so whatever it was it couldn't be that urgent or important.

Victoria sighed with relief as she slipped off her shoes. At the drinks trolley, she poured a whisky. She would be able to finish reading today's papers in peace. Perhaps she should be more interested in what he did with his time and his computer, but the simple fact that he wasn't hovering around her or trying to become involved with her restoration of the garden was a relief. When he'd sold the bulk of his business assets a few years ago, she had despaired. He had no hobbies or interests. It was business or her and she didn't want any more of his attention than she already had. As the old adage said, "I married him for better or worse. I didn't marry him for lunch."

She opened the French windows, releasing the stuffy air into the cool evening breeze. Tonight Deborah

Smith's garden had looked glorious. Victoria was jealous, but Boscawen's garden would become magnificent again now that she owned it. The estate was almost whole once more except for the Dower House. Victoria frowned. She loved that house. Sadly, Boscawen could never be as it had been in her great-grandmother's or even grandmother's time. They would never be able to buy all the land back, but at least they had the wood, the orchards and all of the gardens. She was sure that Charles would buy the fields for her if the farmer would sell, but thus far it hadn't happened. She shouldn't be disappointed. At least the house and the main garden had been brought back under one ownership, hers. Well, hers and Charles's and that was the same thing. He had said right from the beginning of their marriage that everything that was his belonged to her.

She stepped out on to the terrace and sniffed the musky sweetness of the rose, New Dawn, just beginning to flower by the window. Although not a choice of her great-grandmother's, planting it had been the right thing to do. She was pleased she'd listened to her young gardener, Sam, on this choice. The Australian seemed to know instinctively how to garden which compensated for his lack of experience. He'd been working with her for two years and they had clashed so many times, but he was a definite asset. And he was a feast for the eyes.

Releasing the rose, she took a sip of the whisky and let the tingling fluid play across her tongue before swallowing. She had been trying to seduce Sam since he'd arrived but thus far he'd shown nothing but indifference. She wasn't used to men turning her down. In fact, she could only think of one other. She strode to the end of the terrace.

Summer would soon be here. It was the end of May and the Thursday before a Bank Holiday weekend. The roads would begin filling with holidaymakers and she was glad to be well away from it. Although beautiful, the Helford was far enough off the beaten track not to achieve the visitor numbers that the rest of Cornwall endured. For that, she was entirely thankful. The Helford was a place out of time and she loved it. It was in her blood and in her soul. She took a deep breath and released it slowly. It had taken a while, but now she could move forward.

It was well past ten. She half closed her eyes and before her in the twilight was the garden of her childhood. The structure was still there, but that was all. Wild in parts, bare in others, only the bones of a once magnificent garden remained. She shook her head. It was such a waste. All the work of the past lost to ineptitude, ignorance and vulgarity.

She and Sam had begun to set it to rights and resurrect the glorious garden of her childhood. In its heyday, it had been the envy of the county. Her great-grandmother, Edith, had brought exotic plants back from all over the world and under her care they had thrived here at Boscawen. To this day some of them had survived, but many had gone so wild that they had lost their beauty and others had disappeared altogether.

24

For years, Victoria had had to stand back and watch the garden deteriorate further. All that she wanted was kept from her until two years ago when financial difficulty had hit the owner and Charles was able to make an offer.

Now her dream was within her reach — if only Charles would loosen the purse strings. Trying to achieve her plans with only Sam and a few occasional boys would take years. It wasn't good enough. Charles had no idea what was required. In fact, she didn't think he listened to her. She laughed ruefully. Well, she didn't listen to him either.

She turned back to the house. It had taken a huge effort and a good deal of money, but she, with the help of a small army of decorators and builders, had repaired the damage done to it. Most of it was decorative and of course there had been nothing she could do with regard to the sale of its contents nearly thirty years before. Victoria would never forgive her sister-in-law for what she had done. Perry, her brother, had only been in the ground a day when the house and its contents had gone on the market.

Sadly Victoria's hands had been tied because Charles had just sunk all their money into a new venture a short time before. Impotently she'd watched the Tregan heirlooms disperse. Over the years scouring salerooms, Victoria had managed to reacquire some of her heritage but only a fraction. Why she bothered she didn't know. Sentimentality, she guessed, for there was no one to pass the house or its heirlooms on to. She was the last

Tregan of Boscawen. Her brother had died without issue and she was barren. She had failed.

Turning on her heel, Victoria went inside. The past was best left alone. She couldn't change it. But she could make the garden glorious again and leave something worthwhile when the last Tregan had left Boscawen.

CHAPTER
TWO

The tannoy blared. Demi stood, watching people heading off early for the weekend, secret smiles on their faces as they dodged the puddles where the roof was leaking from the rain. Of course there was rain — it was almost the Bank Holiday. She and her mum had planned a visit to Polesden Lacey on the Saturday when Matt would be visiting his parents. Demi swallowed. It wasn't a good idea to think about what wasn't going to happen now. She would think about what was. She was about to take the train to Cornwall to go and stay with her grandfather. It would give her a few days to think and to make a new plan. The sleeper was the only train available at this hour and it had solved her immediate problem of where to spend the night.

The guard blew the whistle and Demi hopped on with her shoulder bag. That was all she had to call her own. The rest of her worldly goods were either in storage or at Matt's and she was never setting foot in there again.

She stared out of the window as they pulled away from the station. This all felt so wrong. As the train made its way, the back of buildings passed by with the glimpses of other people's lives framed like television screens. It all looked so normal and her life felt so far from it. God, she missed her mum.

Resting her head against the glass, Demi pulled her jacket tight and closed her eyes. She was off to Cornwall. Goosebumps covered her skin and not just because she was cold and very tired. Today had to have been one of the foulest days of her life. The only one that had been worse had been six weeks ago when her mother had died with no warning and no farewell. Morwenna had been more than her mother; she had been her best friend. Tears welled. The mother-shaped hole in her life was big enough to swallow her whole. And if she were still here, Demi wouldn't be on this train in the middle of the night.

The train moved, rocking her. Was this situation she found herself in all Matt's fault or was it her own? He'd mentioned that he wanted to do what he had and she'd always said no, but had she been firm enough? Had he actually listened to her? She'd given way on so many of the things that he'd wanted to do, like not seeing her friends. Then two nights ago she'd gone along with the kind of sex he wanted and she didn't, but she'd been lulled by champagne and motivated by the fear that if she said no that he'd stop wanting her, stop loving her. The memories made her feel sick. Was she just biddable and gullible? Her mother would say she was timid. And what on earth was she going to tell her grandfather? The truth was just too sordid for words.

The cry of gulls carried on the early morning mist. People disappeared from the platform and very quickly she was alone. Her suit didn't keep off the morning chill. She shivered as she squinted into the distance but could only see the empty car park. Getting directions would be essential. She had no recollection of having been here, which was odd considering this was where her mother had grown up. Her grandparents had always come to London never the other way around. Her mother had been visiting her grandfather frequently of late. She had said that he had a few health issues, but that it was nothing to be concerned about. And it was only two weeks ago that her grandfather had been with her. He'd been a rock and she'd been a mess. It had been her first funeral. She hadn't gone to her grandmother's eight years before because her mother had insisted on Demi staying in London as it had been during exams.

She glanced around. He'd said it was only a five-minute walk from the station. A sign to the Maritime Museum was her only clue so she headed in that direction. Last night her grandfather had sounded surprised but pleased at her request for a bed. She was sure he'd thought the tears were about her mother and they were, of course, but there was so much more — the job and Matt and loneliness. She tucked a strand of hair behind her ear. It was hard enough to see without that blocking her vision.

A car honked. Demi had walked into the middle of the road. She waved an apology and dashed on to the pavement. She could smell the sea, but she still couldn't see much of anything. Surely she must come across somewhere that was open where she could ask for help? For all she knew she could be heading in completely the wrong direction. She sighed. This seemed to be the way her life moved. Of course, she was the one who let it go that way; she knew that. But she needed to stand up for herself now. She couldn't lean on her mother any more.

She walked right into someone. "Hey, look where you're going."

"So sorry." Demi steadied herself. "I'm lost. Can you tell me where Marlborough Street is?"

"Take the next left and the second right and you'll be on the right street."

"Thank you so much, and sorry again." The man headed off and Demi scolded herself. She must stop losing herself in her thoughts and focus on the here and now. Matt was over. Right now she needed to find her grandfather's house. She yawned. She hadn't slept well on the train. Every cough and snore from her neighbours had woken her from her light sleep. What she longed for was a bath then a hot cup of tea.

A shiver of recognition ran across Demi's skin as she reached Marlborough Street. It felt familiar. Turning around she wrapped her arms about herself. The street was deserted, yet she felt as if she was being watched. Glancing at the houses, no curtains twitched but she couldn't shake the feeling. She was being ridiculous. Extreme exhaustion was making her respond this way, that and still being in her interview suit which looked like she'd slept in it and worse. This was taking the walk of shame to new lows. She'd better find her grandfather's house before anyone actually saw the state she was in.

Number 52 was just two houses from where she stood. The blue door appeared freshly painted. She glanced at her watch. It was now quarter past eight, but Demi hesitated before she rang the bell. Her grandfather had said he'd be awake when she arrived but it felt so early with the mist just lifting. She heard someone cough loudly. It must be her grandfather. He'd given up smoking last year at her mother's request, she knew, but the hacking cough had not ceased. How Morwenna could have thought that it would after sixty-five years of smoking Demi didn't know. Her mother had been funny like that, so fierce in her fight for the right thing and yet almost believing in fairy tales. She had worked so hard for the homeless. Demi had always thought that when her father had died her mum must have buried her passion in her job and, well, loving Demi. As the waterworks threatened yet again, she forced herself to think of something else. But her thoughts weren't helpful. They said she was homeless now and all she wanted was her mother to fight her corner. No, not fight for her — to hold her, encourage her.

She pressed the bell and waited. The sound of her grandfather's cane hitting the floor got louder as he neared the door. She stared at the palm tree in the neighbours' front garden; it was almost Mediterranean. Why had they never holidayed here? Fear crawled along her skin, but it made no sense . . .

Her grandfather opened the door with a beaming smile. "Demelza." He looked her up and down and took in her bedraggled appearance but didn't say a word. Yes, she would need to sort something out quickly because she didn't even have a change of clothes to her name.

"Hi." He extended his arms, embracing her. She pulled back and looked up. He'd grown older in the short time since she'd seen him. "Thanks for having me to stay on such short notice."

"You've always been welcome." He kept looking at her as if he was expecting something to happen. She frowned as they walked through the narrow hallway, which was painted off-white, past the stairs through to the kitchen. "I haven't had breakfast thinking you'd be hungry after the journey and we could have it together." He smiled.

She gave him another hug. "That would be wonderful."

"Good. I've made a pot of tea. You'll find it out on the garden table. Go and sit yourself down and I'll be with you shortly." He leaned heavily on his cane. She noted the walking frame in the corner. Was that new? He'd only used a cane in London.

"Are you sure I can't help?" Demi glanced around the kitchen. It hadn't been updated since the seventies from the look of the laminate counters and the old cooker, but the walls were painted a sunny yellow, making it feel a happy place. The dresser that lined the whole of one wall contained blue and white china and it stood awkwardly in the confined space. It must have

32

been moved out of a farmhouse and somehow found its way into this small semi-detached house.

"You look like you haven't slept at all. Go and do as your father tells you."

She frowned at his use of "father". "Thanks." She slipped out of the stable-style door into the cool garden. Rubbing the goose-bumps on her arms, she looked around. It was oddly familiar, but it must be that she had seen a thousand small gardens in her studies. Or maybe it was her mother's vivid descriptions from her frequent visits of late. Sadly, Demi hadn't joined her on these. She'd been too wrapped up in Matt. She winced at the thought. Because of him she'd missed her friends and valuable time with her mother. And what had she received in exchange? A betrayal of trust and humiliation.

Victoria rolled over when she heard the tyres crunch on the gravel and looked at the bedside table. It was only six, the birds were singing and yet Charles was on his way out. Odd. He was not an early riser and she'd heard him go to his room at about two thirty.

She stretched and slipped out of bed. Standing at the window, she looked over the garden. A heavy mist shrouded everything including the ancient oak woodland. Yawning, she grabbed her robe and threw it on, although why she bothered she didn't know. She was alone and could wander through the house naked if she wished. She bent to inspect a new bruise on her leg. It happened so easily these days. It must have occurred when she was with Adam — or had she banged her leg in the garden? Thinking of the garden, she tried to remember if Sam was returning today or tomorrow. He'd been a bit vague about it. Or she hadn't been listening properly. Taking time off in the spring when the garden was at its most unmanageable wasn't ideal but what could she say. He was worth his weight in gold, if a tad too opinionated.

She padded down to the kitchen and turned on the kettle before finding a cryptic note from Charles.

Need to sort out a legal issue so have headed to London. Will ring later.

No doubt it was for one of the many charities he supported, not only with his money but his time. She didn't resent the time, but the money side did niggle a bit, especially as he was quite tight-fisted about the garden. With half of what he threw at the charities she could hire ten of Sam and the garden would happen in less than a decade.

Taking her tea back to the bedroom, she changed into jeans and an old sweater. Although it was apparent it would be a glorious day, the morning was cool. She would start in the kitchen garden rather than work in the house. The cleaner would be coming later, anyway. She closed Charles's bedroom door as she walked past, still puzzled by his early departure. What could be so urgent in London that he'd left practically before dawn?

Leaving her mug on the counter, she moved outside absent-mindedly, pulling a few weeds out of the bed of spinach. For breakfast she'd have an omelette with spinach, wild garlic and cheese. Stopping in the shed, she grabbed a pair of gardening gloves and set off to the woods for garlic.

The temperature dipped as soon as she was under the cover of the trees. The eucalyptus trees planted by her great-grandmother, Edith, marked the border of the formal grounds. Oak then took over as she followed the path further into the ancient woodland that separated Boscawen from the river. The ground was damp and the air both sweet and pungent as the late bluebells vied with the garlic. Victoria didn't stop to collect the garlic but walked on, drawn by memories. As children, she and Perry had known these woods so well. She had been the fairy queen and he the elf prince, her subordinate as he should have been. She was the elder by a year, but of course she was a girl and no one, especially not her brother or her father, ever let her forget that. She had a defined place in the world and being in charge wasn't it. Except when she was in the wood. And when younger she had been taller and stronger than Perry, who suffered from asthma.

Here, all these memories whirled around her as if the trees held them in their branches. Yet the place was silent, as though the mist caused everything to sleep. So much history trapped and so much lost . . . She reached out and stroked the bark of an oak. What would the trees tell her now? She put her ear to the trunk and listened. Only her own thoughts, regrets and sighs could be heard. The woods would not speak to her any more. They had not forgiven her nor had she forgiven herself. She walked on and came out on to the old stone quay. Once this had been the lifeline for the estate. Goods had travelled so much faster by water then and the Helford had been a great trading river, with Gweek being the hub for the many local mines including some Tregan ones. All of it gone now, in one way or another. She turned to the river.

It appeared still and low clouds clung to the surface. A fish broke the illusion and Victoria watched the ripples spread out across the water. It had been years since she'd had a morning swim in the Helford, but today the water called to her. She shed her shoes first and then her jumper, jeans and underwear. She draped them over the rusting iron relic of the old boathouse. It had once supported a structure that would have been here when her great-grandmother had brought her finds back from the Far East, Australia and Africa.

Standing naked, with her toes curled around the granite stones of the quay, Victoria assessed the water's height then dived in. Every nerve in her body contracted in protest as the icy water held her. She broke through the surface, gasping for air, but it was a few seconds before her body relaxed enough to allow a breath back into her lungs. In those few moments under the water she understood what it must be like to drown. She could see the light above but couldn't reach it.

Her teeth chattered as she began a gentle breaststroke out into the centre. The pull of the current on its way to the sea was strong. All appeared still except for her movement disturbing the smoothness of the water. Flipping on to her back, she looked at the mist hanging just above her, erasing the banks on either side. They were gone and the world had disappeared; it was just the river and Victoria. A lazy backstroke spun her around in circles as she watched a solitary shaft of light pierce the mist, catching the dust in the air.

She flipped over and cut through the surface with strong strokes, imagining the marine life below, startled as she swam above them. Her skin was tight with cold and tingling everywhere. She would have to see Adam today. Making love with him made her feel alive. In his arms — or in the arms of any man except Charles — she could forget what she hadn't done and focus on the here and now, the earthly richness of lust. John Donne's poem "The Bait" wove through her thoughts.

> *Come live with me, and be my love,*
> *And we will some new pleasures prove*
> *Of golden sands, and crystal brooks,*
> *With silken lines, and silver hooks.*
>
> *There will the river whispering run*

What were the words? Her arms cut through the water and something touched her thigh as another line slid through her mind.

> *Will amorously to thee swim,*

In her head, she still heard his voice reciting the poem. The whisper of his breath trickling down her neck and further still. What made that memory appear now? Was it the caress of the water on her body? The weightlessness?

> For thee, thou need'st no such deceit,
> For thou thyself art thine own bait:
> That fish, that is not catch'd thereby,
> Alas, is wiser far than I.

She shook her head, casting the memories aside and turned around. She'd swum further than she'd intended to, lost in the past, and she could see neither shore. Her landmarks of the quay on one side and the boathouse on the other were gone. Panic hit. She trod water, trying to get her bearings, but couldn't pick out a single thing. Would she end up as one of the river nymphs her grandmother used to tell her about? Or would she end up on the wrong side of the river without a stitch of clothing to her name? She laughed and, looking for the sun breaking through, began a slow crawl to her left. She wondered who would be her rescuer if she happened to land on the south side? How would she repay them?

Various scenarios played out in her thoughts before the solid stones of the quay appeared before her. She smiled wryly; no scenes of debauchery would be played out by the riverside today. Briskly rubbing down her skin with her T-shirt, she slipped her clothes back on. She had breakfast to make and she was hungry for so much more than breakfast. It was a shame that Adam wasn't here now.

She stood for a moment, staring at the river, watching the mist rise higher as the sun warmed the air.

Today would be beautiful. She turned and set off into the woods. Mist lingered here and she remembered thinking the trees looked like creatures about to step out and capture her. Her thoughts raced back to the many childhood games she and Perry used to play. Their days seemed to have been spent in these woods, rain or shine when they weren't away at school. Victoria bent to pick a bluebell and enjoyed the scent and the luminescent colour remembering another poem.

> *A fine and subtle spirit dwells*
> *In every little flower,*

It was a childhood one from Anne Brontë that her great-grandmother had recited to her after their walks in the woods. Victoria couldn't remember all of it, only parts. Turning the stem in her hand, she recited,

> *O, that lone flower recalled to me*
> *My happy childhood's hours*
> *When bluebells seemed like fairy gifts*
> *A prize among the flowers*

She inhaled the scent. Nothing captured it. It was as elusive as the fairies.

> *I had not then mid heartless crowds*
> *To spend a thankless life*

A *thankless life*. How true those words felt. He'd given her bluebells once as a sign of his everlasting love, not

39

knowing the fairies would steal it away. Victoria inhaled the fragrance. Blame the magic folk or blame the world. True love was lost and so was the wood until now. Always she'd been the one defending the ancient woodland from the invading forces and now she was again. Although she was neither fairy nor princess, she would make certain this was protected for the future. Her legacy would remain.

Perry had loved it too, but he quite stupidly married for love and not for duty. Her father had died the year before and was not around to make Perry hear reason. God knows she'd tried, but he wouldn't budge. Of course, she was used to that. Her father hadn't listened to her either. He hadn't seen the injustice of leaving Boscawen to Perry just because he was male. Her father's logic on this hadn't worked and in the end Victoria had been right. She'd married well, and had she inherited the house then all would have been fine. Boscawen wouldn't have suffered at the hands of strangers. She kicked a stone in the path and watched it disappear in the ferns. The scent of the garlic overrode the bluebells and she harvested some for her omelette. Her stomach growled in anticipation.

The new loggia appeared in the clearing air and Victoria took a deep breath. She was home now and she had a chance to at least make some things right. Other things could never be fixed again. She bent to sniff the honeysuckle on the old wall as she approached the formal gardens. All of that history was behind her and she must look to the future, to Boscawen's future.

CHAPTER
THREE

Two empty plates sat in front of them along with a fresh pot of tea. Demi definitely felt more human and her grandfather looked better too.

"So tell me what has happened." He looked over the top of his reading glasses. "Not that I'm not delighted to see you."

She turned her mug around in her hands. "I'm a fool."

He frowned. "I doubt that. In fact, quite bright, I'd say."

She half smiled. On his monthly visits to London when she was little, her grandfather had spent hours helping her with her maths even though it wasn't his subject. The teacher in him wouldn't accept defeat. He had found a way that helped her to learn and she'd eventually mastered maths and it became her top subject along with art.

"Thank you, but I have been a fool in so many ways. First, having been far too trusting and second, for just being thick."

He shook his head and reached out a battered hand to touch hers.

She swallowed. "In short, Grandad, I'm broke and don't have anywhere to live."

He raised an eyebrow. "That's very short and doesn't tell me what I need to know."

"With Mum gone, I lost my home. And although there will be some money from a life insurance policy when it eventually pays out, there's a hold-up." Demi shook her head. "I didn't get the job I wanted after my practical because . . ." She rubbed her temples. "Well, if I'm honest, I didn't get the job because I let someone walk all over me and own my work."

"I see. What of your boyfriend? He seemed eager to be helpful at the funeral." He pressed his lips together and she could see his disapproval.

Demi nodded. "He . . ." She paused and looked down at the scum on the top of her tea. "He turned out to be . . . less than promising." The vision of him sitting on the leather sofa watching Demi do things she had no idea were being filmed sickened her. She exhaled. She didn't want to break down in front of her grandfather.

"Are you OK, my lamb?"

Demi laughed dryly, thinking that yes, she was all right as much as someone who was the fool she was could be. "Yes." She ran her fingers through her hair.

"Be kind to yourself. You've been through a lot."

She reached out for his hand. He'd aged so much in the few weeks since she'd seen him. "You have, too."

He nodded. "These things take their toll, my daughter."

She straightened and looked closely at him. Had she just misheard him? She looked at the wisteria in bloom above them, thinking she must have. "I'm still so angry. Is that normal?"

"Yes, grief takes on many forms," he said as he poured more tea into her cup. "You have no choice but to live through all its stages."

Demi added a lot of milk but the colour of the tea barely changed. "I wish it would go away."

"Don't wish your life away. Give yourself time." He put a hand under her chin. "Be kind to yourself, as I've said."

She sighed. That was so hard to do when she'd been so stupid. Yet he made it seem like it was the most logical thing in the world. "I'll try."

"Do. And if you can't do it for yourself then do it for me." His lopsided grin nearly broke her heart.

Victoria scrubbed the omelette pan. What on earth could have dragged Charles up to London at such short notice? Not that it bothered her, of course, but she was curious. Taking her rubber gloves off, she sipped her coffee, noting that she needed to replace the flowers on the kitchen table and probably in the rest of the house. Her grandmother, Gladys, had kept a detailed diary of what blooms to use, and when, and where in the house they were best suited. Sadly that had been lost and Victoria could only go on her memory. When both Edith and Gladys had lived together in the Dower House, they had argued over plants. Gladys had always been cutting them with Edith endlessly arguing that they belonged in the garden and not in the house. Victoria smiled. Everything about the two women was so different. Edith, a Londoner, had come to Boscawen as a bride of just eighteen and she'd spoken so often to Victoria of her first glimpse of the house on her return from her honeymoon in Paris. The house was grand, but the garden — well, there had been none to speak of, just lawns and orchards. Creating the garden had been her contribution to the house. Her daughter-in-law, Gladys, on the other hand, had come from another old Cornish family. She loved the garden but she could never understand why Edith had roamed the world seeking plants. Gladys felt the ones they had were quite good enough and she didn't get on with foreign imports. Thankfully, Edith had lived long enough to make sure her daughter-in-law didn't destroy the garden she'd created.

Just as Victoria was heading into the flower room, she heard the landline ring. It wouldn't be Adam returning her call. He only ever used her mobile. She considered ignoring it and letting the answerphone pick up but in the end she gave in to the lure of her curiosity.

"Hello, Tori."

Damn her inquisitiveness. "Audrey."

"So pleased I've caught you. You haven't returned my calls."

No, she hadn't, and had she been less curious this would still be the case. "Sorry."

"Doesn't matter. I've reached you now."

Victoria picked up her coffee cup and sat down. She knew this wouldn't be a short phone call.

"So, Tori, how are you?"

Victoria rolled her eyes. She hated being called Tori by Audrey. It was bad enough by Charles. But with Audrey it implied an intimacy Victoria didn't feel towards her, despite their years together at school. "Fine. You?"

"OK. I've needed your advice for ages."

Victoria pressed her lips into a straight line. This would be worse than she'd thought. "What can I help you with?"

"I just knew you'd be the right person to talk to about this."

"No doubt I am since you've been trying to reach me, but about what?" She frowned. Her coffee was going cold. If this conversation went as past ones had done, she would need another cup at least. Victoria glanced at her watch and wished Audrey would get to the point of the interruption. She looked out of the door to the bees enjoying the flowers on the tomato plants. The vegetable garden had begun to earn its keep. Charles had wanted to put in a pool, but Victoria had resisted despite her love of swimming. It would simply be a reminder of what she'd given up.

"Tori, did you hear what I said?"

"No, sorry. What was it?" Swimming. She'd learned to swim in the river and then at school she'd excelled at it.

"Our anniversary trip to Rome."

Victoria frowned. "Good God, what are you asking me about that for? I'm not a travel agent."

"It's not how to get there — but you've spent so much time there. It's our fortieth coming up and I want it to be special."

Victoria sighed. "I haven't been to Rome in years."

"It's the Eternal City, it doesn't change so they say."

"Everything changes." Victoria took a deep breath. If she let this conversation go on any longer she would explode. "Audrey, let Hal decide. As you say, he's been there before and wants to take you. I have nothing to add to this."

"But you do. You spent so much time there in 1995. It seemed like months."

"I was taking a course and it was nearly twenty years ago."

"You must still remember it. You were so full of it. Don't tell me you're forgetting things?"

Victoria huffed.

"Sorry, Tori, I've upset you and I didn't mean to but we are all getting to an age where things don't work like they used to."

"Speak for yourself."

"I know you are in fantastic shape but come on, even you have reading glasses."

That she couldn't deny. She was thinking about eye surgery instead of always having glasses perched on the top of her head. "Just what is your point?"

"Forget I mentioned it."

"Look, the gardener has just arrived. Must dash." Victoria put the phone down before Audrey could witter on any further. The woman could talk for Britain and say absolutely nothing at all.

She picked up the phone again and dialled Adam. "Hello, gorgeous."

"Victoria. I was just thinking about you."

"Excellent."

"Not in that way."

She frowned. "Why ever not?"

"Because I just heard that Nansennen may be coming on the market and I wanted to pick your brains."

"Well, I'll forgive you this time. Nansennen is a fabulous property. I remember a party there one New Year's ages ago. What do you want to know?" She'd been eighteen and in love. The evening was magical, especially the frosted landscape. Of course, the downside had been the lack of central heating. It was so cold she'd worn long underwear on her bottom half beneath her strapless gown. He had looked divine in his dinner jacket. He'd put it over her shoulders when they snuck out on to the terrace in the moonlight to make their wishes for the New Year ahead. Somehow he'd made itchy wool feel sexy, but those hopes and dreams . . . they'd disappeared with the frost. She shivered.

"Well, it may be coming on the market."

"Have they hit hard times or is it just too big for them now?" The upkeep on these houses was enormous.

"Not sure yet."

"So you want me to wheedle out the info?"

"Something like that."

She smiled.

"Oh, and any other information you can provide."

"What do I get in return?" She ran her finger around the rim of her coffee cup.

"You'll have to wait until later to find out."

"Tease." She laughed and began to look forward to this evening.

Demi walked along Church Street and looked through the shop windows. The first stop would be M&S for essentials. She couldn't believe she'd had to borrow money from her grandfather for clothes for now, but there was little else she could do unless she wanted to increase her overdraft which was big enough. In a few days her final salary from Bottel and Lampard would come into her account and she would be able to pay him back. She passed a charity shop then turned back and went in, hoping they would have a few things in her size. The fifty pounds from her grandfather wouldn't go far when she needed everything from knickers and bras to shoes. Fortunately, some parts of her, like her feet, were small enough that she could buy things in the children's department, which might save a bit of money.

She flipped through, the racks, hoping to find something good, but she wasn't optimistic. Decent stuff seemed designed only for women who were tall and flat chested.

"Can I help?" A girl with a nose stud came up to Demi. She looked to be only a few years younger, but she was a lot more laid-back from her tie-died top to her torn jeans.

"Don't suppose you have anything that would fit me?"

The girl looked her up and down. "Actually, I think we might. Some stuff came in this morning that should work. The colours should be good on you too."

Demi smiled. Maybe her luck was turning. Well, she could hope.

"Here." The friendly volunteer handed an armful of clothing to Demi. "The changing room's over there. Give me a shout if you need a hand or a second opinion, but I think the purple and blue top will go with your colouring."

"Thanks." Demi put the stuff down on a chair and wondered where to begin. She stripped to her bra and knickers and avoided looking in the mirror. She had seen more of herself than she wanted to on the widescreen television at Matt's. Shutting her eyes, she tried to push the images away as she grabbed whatever came into her hand. It was a lovely wrap dress in soft greens — exactly the sort of thing that worked on her figure. She slipped it on. Aside from the hem, which needed fixing, it was a success. But there was no price tag on it. She frowned and hoped that it wouldn't be too dear. She needed to reserve some money for the M&S stuff.

Much to her surprise everything fitted.

"How's it going in there?"

Demi was just putting her suit back on. "Great. All of it fits, even the jeans, which is a miracle. I can never find any that do." But despite her words she handed back two sweaters.

"Brilliant. I'm usually right on these things." She held up the jumpers. "What was wrong with these? Perfect colours for you, with V-necks too."

"The sleeves are a bit tight." Demi frowned as she looked at the pile on the counter and glanced at the shoes. There was a pair of old converse trainers that looked like her size in the kids' section.

"Is something wrong?"

Demi looked up. "No, thanks." Things could be worse, she knew that.

"Try the trainers and there's a great pair of flats on the next rack. I'll bag this stuff up for you."

"You'd better wait. I'm not sure I can afford it all."

The woman looked at her, taking in the crumpled state of her clothes. "Get the shoes and then pay me what you can afford, whether it's a fiver or more."

Demi stood with her mouth open. She must look worse than she thought. "Are you sure?"

"Yes, this stuff hasn't been priced, but it was donated to help people. You need help right now, I can tell. It's a karma thing. When you can, you pass the karma along. Now, do those shoes fit?"

Demi nodded.

"Lucky you. I'm stuck with bloody size nines and no one ever gives decent ones away."

Demi opened her bag and pulled out the ten five pound notes that she had. She took out two.

"Just pay me five. Things can't be good."

Demi shook her head. Was this woman psychic?

"I am, sort of, but don't tell anyone."

Demi's eyes opened wide. Had she spoken?

"My name's Peta Rowse. And you are?"

"I'm Demi Williams."

Peta frowned but then smiled. "Welcome to Falmouth. Are you related to the Williams who live on

Penrose Road? God, I used to fancy one of them like rotten when I was in sixth form."

Demi smiled. "I don't know. I'm staying with my grandfather."

"That wouldn't be old Mr Williams the English teacher, would it?"

"Yes." Demi's eyes opened wide.

"I know him. Bloody brilliant he was, the old bastard. Worked us like crazy."

Demi frowned. Her grandfather had been retired for ages. How could he have taught Peta?

"He stood in for our teacher who got cancer and somehow he got us through our A levels." She leaned on the counter and looked out through the window to the crowds beginning to throng the street.

"What do you do now?" Demi studied Peta with her dread-locks and make-up free face.

"Aside from volunteering here? I work in a pub three nights a week and I'm completing my degree in fashion design."

"That explains the colours thing and the sizing."

"Not really; that's down to this feeling stuff I have."

Demi frowned. "OK. If you say so."

"I do."

Demi smiled. "Thanks for all your help."

"No problem. Things will turn around, you know." She stopped and looked hard at Demi. "In fact, it will turn around faster than you think. Keep your head."

"OK." Demi left the shop with her thoughts circling. Peta was mad but she had helped her so much. She would have enough money to get a decent bra. She required something that was closer to full-strength scaffolding.

Victoria went through the seed catalogue. She wasn't having any luck finding what she was looking for because so many plants had gone out of favour. She would have to borrow Charles's damn computer and search online. She ran her fingers over Edith's plant lists. She was so blessed to have these. When Edith had died and death duties had had to be paid, they had sold the Dower House and these had been shoved into the far recesses of Boscawen's attic while Gladys had moved into the gatehouse. The poor woman hadn't complained, at least not to Victoria's father. She'd lived happily there, watching the comings and goings of her family.

Thankfully none of the intervening owners of Boscawen had ventured very far into the attic. Today people didn't keep much in the way of paper records, but the past was preserved on faded pieces. Victoria made all her notes on paper and refused to do any more than was necessary on her phone or on a computer. Charles did all of their accounts online. He kept telling her that she must embrace it, but she couldn't see the point. She still preferred to pay her bills by cheque. Wasn't that what private banking was about? She flipped through the fruit tree catalogue on the table. In the autumn, they would need to begin to restock the orchards. Some of the trees remained but two apple orchards had been grubbed. She didn't think there was anything sadder than destroying productive trees.

Edith had filled Victoria's head with her travels. Love, duty and a shared passion had led Edith and Arthur Tregan to the Far East in search of new plants to make their garden together. Victoria sighed. Theirs had been a fruitful union. Before they set out for China, India and Australia, Edith had given birth to four children — three boys and one girl. She had more than done her duty. Victoria frowned. How could she have Edith's blood in her and be infertile? Even Victoria's mother had had two live births and countless miscarriages. Victoria hadn't even had the miscarriages. It was as if she had been wired incorrectly. But that too had been checked out during the course of all the humiliating attempts to reach the holy grail of a child, an heir.

Victoria picked up her gloves and set off out of the door. She would tackle the weeds in the bed by the south-west wall where the agapanthus were beginning to push up spikes containing their tightly wrapped flower heads. Already it looked as if it would be a good year for them. Maybe she should enter them in the Constantine Flower Show. After all, she'd been back in Boscawen for two years now and it was time to become part of the community once more.

As she stepped out of the back door, the landline rang. Victoria hesitated. What if it was Audrey again? She couldn't bear another long chat with her. She would let it go to the answerphone. She stood on the threshold looking at weeds that had invaded the courgette bed, waiting for the machine to pick up. She heard Charles's voice mutter something about staying the night in London to have dinner with Sebastian and he hoped that was OK. It was more than OK. She pulled her mobile out of her pocket and texted Adam. They could have a sleepover. She smiled.

CHAPTER
FOUR

Demi sat in a coffee shop nursing her tea and using the free Wi-Fi. First she sent off a congratulations message to Maia on the birth of her daughter. The pictures on Facebook looked adorable, well, if newborns were capable of that. No, what was wonderful was the happiness shining out of Maia's and her husband's faces. To think Demi had thought she could find that with Matt. She must be the worst judge of character on the planet. Trying to avoid thinking about Matt, she scrolled through the status updates, liking things as she went along, but stopped dead when she came to one from him. It was a picture of her from last week. She was smiling and holding up a glass as if to say "cheers". How on earth could he still be posting pictures of her? She wanted it off his page, but he hadn't actually tagged her in it so there was little she could do. If she unfriended him she wouldn't know what he was doing. She dropped her head in her hands.

Positive action was required, so she sent follow-up emails to both the insurance company and the lawyer handling what he called her mother's estate. It was hardly that and, as she fixed her typing, she knew she would have to face Matt at some point. Her things, including her desktop, were in his flat, in the spare room. As much as she didn't want to, she would need to make arrangements to collect them. The idea of starting again, completely free from the past, was appealing, but there was a huge investment in the computer alone. Also her mother's few pieces of jewellery were there too. Until she contacted Matt she had nothing — not her mother's things, not her desktop, and not her portfolio.

She pressed the button to compose an email. She had two to do. One was a grovelling letter to Bottel and Lampard to thank them for the wonderful opportunity that they had given her and to try and keep the door open. Not that she wanted to do that. What she *wanted* was to send them her sketches, proving that the work that Josh had claimed as his was hers. She couldn't see how it would help, but she might feel better. Nothing she'd done since her mother had died was right. Morwenna could not be resting easily. She sighed. Do something positive. Write the letter to Bottel and Lampard.

> *Dear Ms Jones,*
> *Due to unfortunate circumstance and the sheer stupidity of trusting a bastard with a warped sense of what was sexy and right, I find myself destitute and in need of the job you didn't offer me but you handed instead to a thieving jerk.*

Demi sat back and sipped her tea. God, it would be good to send such an honest email. Her mother had encouraged her to never lie and that was telling the truth. Well, it wasn't telling all of it. Demi had played her own part in her downfall.

I was too blinded by his good looks and money to see what a prat he was. I should have trusted my mother's instincts and not my own. I should have known from the start that he was a sleazebag. But on paper, and visually, he looked good. He had a great job and was clever. It wasn't easy to see that he was a deviant.

So when she passed away he thought I would loosen up my frigid tendencies' as he called them. He thought that I might swing more. Hah! I'd said no to threesomes and more. It was hard enough showing my body to him, let alone having anyone else see it, and now he'd filmed us — well, more me — having sex with him. And it was not vanilla sex. I had given in to his constant pressure and . . .

As she typed each word, Demi felt her stress levels rise. She could see what a fool she'd been. How many times had she heard "never do anything you don't feel comfortable with"? Well, with Matt that had gone out of the window very quickly. He wasn't satisfied with normal sex. He wanted to do everything he watched on his porn flicks. He'd told her she was stupid to be ashamed of her curvy body. In fact, as she thought about it, she realised that all he had ever treated her as was a sex toy, almost right from the start. It was no wonder she hadn't enjoyed it.

She deleted all that she'd written except the greeting.

I am writing to say thank you for the wonderful opportunity to work with such a talented team at Bottel and Lampard. Please keep me in mind if you find you need another architect in the near future.
Yours sincerely,
Demi Williams

She definitely preferred the first version, but she could just imagine the woman's face as she read it. The devil in her thought it just might brighten the woman's day, but the sensible Demi in her took over and sent the revised email, thinking about what she would say to Matt. Timing wise she couldn't just race back up to London to clear her things. She'd just arrived.

And of course there was a minor — not — problem. She had a total of four pounds fifty left after the clothes shopping and her cup of tea. That wouldn't go far at all, so she would look for a job tomorrow. There should be plenty of summer work here that she could do while she sorted out her life and waited for her mother's life policy to pay out. As she looked through Instagram to see what her friends were up to she realised that this was the only way she knew about their lives. Her life had been too wrapped up in Matt. Did her friends miss her? They had certainly said so at the funeral.

Taking a deep breath, she began an email to Matt.

Matt,

I won't go into how betrayed I feel. I'm sure you have a picture.

What I need to do is to work out how to collect my things. I appreciate that you will want them out of your flat quickly and I am in Cornwall with my grandfather at the moment.

Demi paused and shuddered as she pictured Matt, sitting there watching them being disgusting on the screen.

I really never want to see you again You are a completely vile excuse for a human. How could you film me without my permission?

Stopping, she deleted the last paragraph. That would not help at all.

So I would be grateful if you could hold on to my things for a short time while I make arrangements to collect them.
Demi

Running her hands through her hair, she wondered if Sophie could pick them up for her when she came back from Greece. She sent the email and checked her mail again. Nothing but an out-of-office reply from Matt. She took a deep breath, grabbed her bags, smiled at the woman behind the counter, and set off towards her grandfather's.

Rubbing her lower back, Victoria rose from her knees. She could just see Sam stripping off his shirt. She swallowed. He was magnificent. The garden work and his love of sailing kept him in top shape and the sun glistening off his back showed his muscles to gleaming perfection. She really must figure out a way to seduce him. She couldn't have such a specimen in her garden untested. However, it was almost six and Adam would be here soon so she would have to wait for another day to move her plan forward to get Sam Stuart into her bed.

She walked over to him. He was digging out what had been one of the many rose beds, something he was particularly keen on. He wouldn't accept that you couldn't grow roses in Cornwall or in old rose beds either. He'd gone on about mycorrihzal fungi and lots of manure. She was willing to let him learn by his mistakes because there had been a rose bed here before. But she'd put her foot down about his insistence on buying bare root roses. If she didn't personally know the rose then she needed to see them in bloom and smell the scent. It wasn't good enough to trust pictures and descriptions. They could lie. Last year, with a few exceptions, black spot and green fly had blighted all they had planted. But Sam wouldn't give up. He had persistence if nothing else — and he certainly had something else.

For the past twenty years, the bed had been nothing and the local farmer occasionally had sheep in this part of the garden. She shook her head, thinking of the glorious plants of her childhood, all lost. The people who'd bought the estate after Perry's death hadn't believed in gardening, they'd just wanted the house and its quay. Only the lawn and the border immediately next to Boscawen were kept up and by the time the house came on the market much of the land had been sold off. Now, bar two farms and the Dower House, which she suspected would never come on the market in her lifetime, the estate was complete. It was as good as it was going to get and now the real work had begun.

"Sam."

He stopped and stood straight, towering over her. She liked a man who could make her feel short. Charles certainly didn't. He was only five foot nine, just an inch taller than she was. Sam, on the other hand, must be six foot two. "Mrs Lake."

She frowned. No matter how many times she asked him, he refused to use her first name. Mrs Lake made her think of her mother-in-law and that was not pleasant. She hoped the woman was rotting, feeding the grass above her grave. "I'll put the manure on it and we should be able to bed in the first set of roses on Tuesday."

"Excellent." She let her glance linger on his flat stomach. She must get Adam to work out a bit more to help with his muscle definition. Her fingers twitched. "How was London?"

"Great. It was good to see my mate and London's always good for a laugh."

"True." Victoria studied his face. There were signs of good breeding in the cheekbones and full mouth. "By the way, why did you mark those modern apple trees in the catalogue?"

"Diversity." He slipped his hands into his pockets.

"Diversity? What, are we some sort of company?" She twisted her mouth into a disdainful smile.

"No, but we already have a selection of the older varieties that have survived. You need to diversify so that they are not all cropping at once. And it's better for the insects too."

"I want the garden as it was." She crossed her arms against her chest.

"That's all well and good, but the garden, in the past, fed almost a whole village and everything was used. Are you planning on selling the fruit or making cider?"

Victoria flattened her mouth into a straight line. He had a point. Not that she wanted to concede it, but she would consider it. "Fine, we'll discuss it later before I place the order. I need to clear the expenditure with Charles." She stopped and stared at him. "You haven't discussed this with him, have you?"

"No." He raised his dirt-covered hand to shade his eyes. "The garden is your domain, he says."

"True. And the bills are his." Victoria sighed. "Never mind."

"Mrs Lake?"

"Yes."

"Earlier I was checking to see if there were enough elder-flowers in bloom to make elderflower champagne." His mouth lifted into a sheepish grin. Victoria smiled at the reference to elderflower champagne. She and Perry

62

had made it every summer and the recent weather had been warm so the blossoms had already begun.

"I noticed that a few of the trees are encroaching on the kitchen garden wall. Left alone, they'll block the path, so I thought I'd cut them back a bit rather than dig out the new bed in the sunken garden if that's OK with you."

"Walk with me." He propped the spade up, picked up his gloves and followed. Thinking about Perry and Boscawen stopped the sway of her hips, which she would normally enhance when she knew she was being followed by a desirable man. "Sam, I know we've spoken a little bit about the history of Boscawen but maybe not enough." She came to the east side of the house and it was obvious that he had a point. Without some judicious pruning, the elder would take over. "But Boscawen means dwelling by the elder tree and that tree there, although not the original one, is the one."

He frowned. "Elder trees don't live that long and doesn't the house date from the 1500s?"

"It does, but there has always been an elder tree beside the house."

"Fair enough, they're native and grow easily."

Victoria turned to him. What was it about the young that they thought they knew it all? "This is Cornwall, Sam, and here we respect the land and its legends."

He tilted his head to the side and she could see laughter lurking in his blue eyes. He might well laugh at her, but she was serious, deadly so. "You do not cut an elder tree without asking its permission."

"What?" His look said it all. He thought she was mad.

"You need to stroke the tree and say 'Elder, elder may I cut thy branches?'"

"If you insist." He shrugged. Maybe she *was* mad but this was obviously something she wouldn't budge on.

"I do." She strode down the path to the offending tree and stroked its branches then turned to him. "It's more important than you'll ever know." Her hand froze when she saw a cut. "You've already started!" She swung round.

"Not exactly." Sam leaned away from her. He pointed to the side of the path. Victoria could see a branch had snapped off and that Sam had then made a clean cut. No doubt trying to protect the tree from further trauma. She closed her eyes, praying it wasn't too late.

CHAPTER
FIVE

The sun was hot on her back as she wound her way through the streets trying to find her grandfather's house. The sky was a clear cerulean blue and the gardens that faced the road were filled with roses just coming into their best. It was pretty and the cry of the gulls in the distance was pleasant. Views of the harbour appeared around every corner and she wondered again why they had never come here, why her grandparents had always come to them in London. She'd ask her grandfather when she could find the house again. How could she become so lost in such a small town? She could understand in London or Bristol but not in Falmouth.

She stopped at the junction of two roads. She hadn't a clue where she was. Nothing looked familiar. As everything sloped down to the harbour, maybe, if she went down to it, she could begin the journey again. The plastic bags she was carrying cut into her sweaty palms. She came to a dead end and was about to walk back up the street when she spied an alleyway. Looking around, she decided to take it.

The angle of the sun overhead cast it in deep shadow and as soon as she stepped into the alley she became cold, colder than she should be. She could see the sun shining 200 metres ahead, but she felt frozen to the spot. *Fear. Panic.* She ran through to the sunlight below and nearly knocked over a woman with a pram. "Sorry."

"No problem." The woman checked the child.

"I'm lost."

"Can't help. I'm just staying in that hotel there." The woman pointed to a tired-looking building. It must have been quite swish in its day, but that glory was well behind it. Demi shivered and saw a table full of cakes in her head.

"Are you OK?" The woman put a hand on Demi's wrist and Demi lurched back. The woman looked at the baby, "We're fine but it must have given you quite a fright!"

"Yes, thanks and sorry again." Demi took one last look at the building before rushing down the hill. She didn't stop until she recognised Peta from the charity shop.

"Hello, you," Peta said, smiling. "Where are you off to in such a rush?"

"Lost, I'm afraid." Demi shook her head. "I'm such a sad case."

"Yes, but I can help. Just call me your guardian angel." She held out a hand for one of Demi's bags. "So, it's Marlborough he lives on, isn't it?"

Demi nodded.

"It's just a short walk if you know the way." She led Demi through a little alleyway on to a residential street with tall townhouses, then up another alley and Demi recognised where she was.

"Thank you. I'd still be walking around town."

"Yes, you would."

"Peta." Demi stopped but thought she'd better ask. "There's an old hotel back there. Do you know anything about it?"

"What were you doing there? That's well in the wrong direction." She squinted at her and Demi felt awkward, wondering if the fear she'd experienced still showed. "Hmm. It's been down on its luck for years." She pushed her large sunglasses up on her head. "Tastes changed and people don't need the same thing. If people want luxuries now they head to boutique hotels like the ones in St Mawes."

"Thanks."

"No problem." Peta handed her the bag of clothes. "Look after yourself; get a map and say hello to your grandfather from me." She stopped then said, "Why don't you take my number just in case."

"Thanks." Demi put the number into her phone. "I don't intend to get lost again."

"No one ever does." Peta smiled and waved as she set off down the hill.

The answerphone was flashing when Victoria walked into the kitchen. Was it just Charles's message from earlier or had someone else called? She pressed play.

Hi Tori. Me again. You must still be in the garden. Don't overdo it. We have that party tomorrow night and we'll be standing again for hours. Anyway. Just calling to say I love you. My business here is finished and I'll be on my way early in the morning to avoid the traffic. I'll give Seb your love.

He'd give Seb her love.

She closed her eyes. *Come live with me, and be my love.* Victoria flexed her shoulders, pushing the voice out of her head . . . She had forgotten about the charity drinks in Truro. Oh well, she would hear some decent music. They had hired a good quartet to play during the reception. She switched the radio on and sounds of Mozart filled the kitchen as she pulled the gin out of the freezer and poured a healthy measure. She added a slice of lemon and a dash of tonic. One ice cube should do the trick. A sip confirmed its perfection before she went upstairs to shower. It had been a good day in the garden despite the incident with the elder tree. She knew she was too superstitious but growing up in a house like Boscawen had that effect. A night filled with Adam would rebalance the world.

Placing her drink beside the sink, she turned on the taps for the walk-in shower. The bathrooms were one of the things that Charles had insisted on sorting straight away when they had bought the house. He'd been right. Updating them to modern standards and putting others in had lifted the house without taking away from it in any way. She'd put her foot down in the kitchen, though. He'd wanted to go all sleek and modern, but to her that was the one part of the house that had remained true to its past. Actually, the whole working end of the house had.

She dropped her clothes into the laundry bin and stood by the window looking out on to the garden. Sam was still clearing weeds out of the flower bed. He was as relentless as she was when it came to the garden. He had the right mindset for it. Except that he wanted to modernise things too much.

He turned and looked towards the house. Victoria remained standing naked in the window, hoping he'd look up. She was still in remarkable shape thanks to all the gardening, and despite celebrating her sixtieth birthday two months ago, she looked better than most forty-year-olds. She raised her arm to wave at him, enjoying the feel of her breast lifting and tightening, but he'd turned away.

She walked into the shower and let the water pummel away the day's soil and muscle ache. As she washed her hair she thought with longing of Adam and opened her eyes to find him about to join her. They soon stumbled out of the shower, knocked over the laundry basket, and just missed her gin. By the time they reached the bedroom, the floor was covered with items pushed off the surfaces.

"Damn!" He limped but fell on top of her on the bed.

"What's wrong?"

"Just kicked a phone — but don't distract me."

She rolled over him, then straddled him. "Don't distract you? Oh Adam, I have every intention of doing just that."

★ ★ ★

"Hello, lamb. You've been gone longer than I expected."
He peered at her. "And you look all rung out. Tea?"

"Lovely. Thank you."

"Looks like you've caught the sun."

Demi peered at her chest, which was distinctly pink in the V of her blouse. She didn't have her mother's colouring at all. Morwenna had been just like her parents, tall and dark, whereas Demi was short and blonde. She assumed she looked like her father, but her mother would never say. In fact, she would never speak about her father at all. It was something that Demi had given up on asking about by the time she was sixteen. Maybe, she thought, her grandfather would tell her.

Putting her bags in her bedroom, she looked longingly at the tub as she walked past the bathroom. Once she'd had tea she would take a much-needed soak. She was tired in places she didn't know she could be.

"There you are, love. I've made some cake for us to have. That should sort you out."

In the heat of the sun, the wisteria had opened fully and the sweet scent surrounded her. "Thanks." Demi sank into the garden chair and thought she should be waiting on him, not the other way around. His limp was more pronounced and he kept wincing with the pain.

"How did you make out?" He sat down.

"Well, I ran into an ex-student of yours, a Peta Rowse. She says hello."

Her grandfather frowned but then a smile spread across his face. "Ah, she was one of the A-level students

I helped out with one year. All sorts of piercings, I seem to recall."

"Yes, that's her."

"A good student, if a bit unconventional." He paused, looking at the far corner of the garden. "Also a touch of a second sense about her if I recall correctly." He shifted in the chair then rubbed his hip.

"Yes. She volunteers in the charity shop and she was a great help. I walked away with a whole new, well, old wardrobe."

"Excellent." He took a sip of his tea. "Shift your seat around a bit — you're still catching the sun. You have to be careful with that fair skin of yours."

Demi did as she was told. "Grandad, was my father fair?"

He looked up from the piece of cake he was bringing to his mouth. "You don't know?"

"Mum wouldn't talk about him."

He put his fork down. "Well, that doesn't surprise me."

"Why?"

He took a sip of tea. "Did she tell you anything at all?"

"She said he was dead."

He raised his bushy brows. "Well, he isn't."

"What?" Demi put her mug down. This she'd never doubted.

Why would her mother lie to her? She'd emphasised honesty in all things.

"She may have told you that, but I saw him only two weeks ago."

Demi's hand shook as she poured more tea into her grandfather's mug. Her father was not dead. He was alive.

"You remember nothing of him?" He studied her.

Demi squinted as the sun moved around a bit more in her grandfather's direction. "Did I know him?"

"Yes, but maybe you didn't know he was your father."

"That sounds very odd."

Her grandfather stood and placed his hands on his lower back. "It *was* odd, and it was certainly not what we wanted for our only child." He turned and looked at her. "Wenna was always headstrong and determined to live life according to her own rules."

Demi laughed under her breath. How she and her mother had laughed about her rules. They were good rules and were only meant to keep Demi safe and they had. The few times she'd gone her own way she'd learned that she wasn't safe, so Demi had become happy to live by them.

"Your grandmother and I weren't too pleased when we discovered who her boyfriend was, but she was thirty-five. There's not a lot you can say — or rather, there is a *lot* that you can say, but none of it will be heard." He sighed. "Wenna was involved with a married man."

The phone rang and he gave her a loving look. "I must take that. I'm expecting a call from the GP."

Demi frowned. Why was he waiting to hear from the GP and why had her mother not told her that her father was alive? She rubbed her temples. There was only one conclusion she could make. Her father mustn't have wanted anything to do with her and her mother had been protecting her from that pain. She closed her eyes.

CHAPTER
SIX

Her grandfather walked back into the garden paler and years older than when he left to take the call. He sat down and Demi stretched a hand across the table, pushing all the questions bursting in her head aside. "Grandad? What's wrong?"

"It's to be expected."

"What is?"

"The operation on my hip has been postponed."

She leapt up then dropped to her knees in front of him. "No, you need it."

He placed a hand on her shoulder. "I'm old. Eighty-five next birthday. Some things are inevitable and delayed operations seem to be one of them." He coughed. "Of course, it didn't help that I missed the first one."

"What?"

"Yes, sad but true. Some days my mind isn't with me. Other days it's fine."

"No."

"Oh, well, nothing to be done about it so no sense in fretting either."

She thought of her mother. That must have been why she kept visiting him.

"Give your grandfather a hug."

She held him tight then pulled back. "What are they going to do about it?"

"Reschedule. I'm not a high priority."

"But that's not right." He clearly needed a new hip.

"Maybe not, but that's the way it is."

She hugged him again.

"Now, my lamb, we need to get dinner started or we will be eating beans on toast tonight."

Demi smiled. "What can I do?"

"You peel the potatoes and I'll put the chicken in the oven." He stood but still held her hand. "I'm glad you're here."

"I'm glad I'm here too." She frowned. He must be so lonely.

"Let's get dinner on and then we can talk."

She knew from years of experience that he wouldn't talk until he had done what he set out to do, so she set to, peeling the potatoes so vigorously she nearly took her nails off. Meanwhile, her grandfather seasoned the chicken and placed it in the oven. Her job took longer and he went about preparing the other vegetables in silence. The muscles in her shoulders became tighter and tighter. Her father was *alive*.

Finally, she put the pan of potatoes on the hob and went in search of her grandfather. He was in the sitting room on the sofa with a photo album on his lap. She turned on the overhead light. The sun had moved around to the west, leaving the room in semi-darkness, which was not helped by the dark wallpaper. A fresh coat of white paint would lift the room without the need to change anything else except for the dark velvet cushions. They too would need updating.

He tapped the space beside him and she lowered herself down. Her mouth was dry and swallowing didn't take it away.

"Your mother didn't know we had this." He let out a breath. "Your grandmother, bless her, felt that one day you would need or want to know." He shook his head. "She didn't agree with your mother and after your last visit . . ." He coughed. "Well, after that we always visited you in London and on Wenna's terms."

Demi ground her teeth together. "I don't understand."

"I'm not sure I do either." He shrugged and turned back to the first page of the album. It held a picture of a newly born Demi, fat, red-faced and with a thick crop of black hair. He turned to the next and she must have been a year old, dressed in a christening gown with white hair instead of black. Her mother held her and there were a few other people standing around. Demi only recognised her mother and her grandparents. The remaining people were strangers.

"Who is in this picture?"

"Your father and your godparents."

She searched the faces again. And then she froze. How had she missed it when she first looked at the photo? There was her father. She looked so like him. His eyes were focused on her and he looked happy. She put her finger on him in the photo and her grandfather nodded.

"So you knew him?" There was something about his face, aside from the resemblance to her own, that Demi couldn't place.

76

"I wouldn't go that far. I met him on a few occasions. Wenna would leave you with us some times and he would collect her from here."

She tried to read her grandfather's expression. "Why didn't they marry?"

He leaned back against the sofa. "Your grandmother knew more than I about their relationship." He reached out and touched the photograph of her grandmother on the side table.

"Why didn't he leave his wife if he loved Mum and me?"

"Your grandmother thought it was because he was Catholic."

"That explains why they didn't marry."

"Wenna was," he paused, "very independent. She had to find her own way. We all do." He smiled. "Children need to follow their own path. You can't tell them the mistakes they will make even if you can see them coming." He shook his head. "I knew this only too well from teaching — but it's hard to watch your own child."

She leaned closer to her grandfather and turned the next page for him. She must have been about three and she was on a beach, sitting in front of a sandcastle, which she clearly hadn't built. In the other picture on the page she saw her father holding her hand and taking her into the sea. There she was, smiling in her father's arms both of them wearing hats and sporting pink noses. He was so like her. Or rather, she was so like him. She traced his face in the photograph. The next page was full of pictures she had seen before. Her father was conspicuously missing from them.

"What happened between Mum and my father?"

He sighed. "They kept their relationship going for a long time."

"Then what happened?"

"I don't exactly know." He cleaned his glasses with his handkerchief. "Your grandmother knew more."

"I don't understand."

"Not sure I do either. I do know that it all ended when you were . . ." He paused and squinted out of the window. "When you were six, I think." He looked at her. "Around when your appendix burst."

She knew all about that because her mother had mentioned it, but she had no recollection of it. "It couldn't be associated with that, could it?"

"I'm sorry, lamb, it's all muddled up in my mind. Though I do remember you being in hospital and so very ill. We nearly lost you."

The timer in the kitchen went off and she could have screamed with frustration. Her grandfather pushed the book on to her lap and hobbled into the kitchen. Slowly turning through the pages of the album, she saw her past in a completely different way. She remembered none of what was in the early photographs. Surely, she thought, as she reached a page when she must have been five, she should remember, if not her father, then at least the holidays on the beach? Closing her eyes she searched through her memories and recurring dreams, but there were no blond men or beach holidays. But with this evidence in front of her, how could she not remember?

As she continued turning the pages, she drew a blank. It was as if she had been hypnotised to forget her early childhood, because she remembered things from their life in London, trips to the zoo and museums yet she had never seen a photograph of herself there. If she didn't have these pictures in front of her now, she would never have believed she'd spent time in Cornwall.

She stopped on a page where her hair was in plaits and she was wearing a pretty frock. Her father held her hand and they were both laughing. It was obvious from the body language that she'd known him well and felt at ease with him. What had she called him? Did she know that he was her father? If she had, how could she forget? She looked at the date on the bottom of the page, April 1995. She was six, nearly seven, years old. Surely she should remember. But she didn't.

The rest of the photograph album was more pictures of her and her mother, but none with her father and none in Cornwall. She closed the book and walked to the kitchen. Her grandfather must have the answers or at least some of them.

He was leaning against the counter pounding the potatoes. She hadn't allowed herself those in years. She looked down at her waist, her best feature. She supposed one night of mashed potatoes wouldn't hurt too much.

"Why don't you lay the table? I won't be too long with these." He grimaced and reached for the walking frame.

"Here, let me do that. You sit down."

"You've always been so bossy, Wenna." He shuffled across the room to lay the table and Demi stared at him, wondering if he knew he'd called her Wenna. She thought back to the days around the funeral. If he'd had a slip up then she hadn't noticed, which wasn't a surprise. They had both been lost in grief.

In moments, they were sitting at the table. She smiled, seeing her grandfather's happy face.

"It's lovely to have you here again."

"Thank you." She couldn't say it was lovely, though. It was odd. She'd been here but she had no recollection. She wasn't sure how, but it must be connected to her father.

Eyes. Giant, the Kowres. She shivered as images of her old recurring nightmare flashed in her head.

"Where is my father now? You said you saw him two weeks ago." Why hadn't he sought her out during all these years? Because it was clear from the photos that he loved her.

He gave her a wary look from under his bushy brows.

And suddenly she knew. Her stomach dropped. Two weeks ago was her mother's funeral.

"He was at the funeral." He leaned across the table and touched her hand. "I'm sorry. I should have said something." He shook his head back and forth. "I just didn't know how to and I wondered if you'd recognise him, but now I know you hadn't."

She forced her mouth into a smile. "It's OK. It tells me something but I'm not sure what."

"Wenna, I've heard he owns a big house on the Helford River now."

She frowned at his use of Wenna. "What's his name?" Her father was nearby. Should she go and find him? Her stomach turned at the thought.

"Charles Lake."

CHAPTER
SEVEN

A ringing sound woke Victoria. She rolled over but it didn't stop. It was the phone. Who the hell called in the middle of the night? She sat up. Something was wrong. Had to be. The birds weren't even up. She slipped out of bed and went to the phone on the other side. Adam was still sound asleep.

"Hello."

"Is this Victoria Lake?"

"Yes, and you are?"

"Police Sergeant Simon Glass. Can you please open your front door?"

Victoria's stomach clenched. Police at her door, at whatever godforsaken hour it was, was a bad sign, a very bad one. "I'll be right down." She picked up her robe and tied it about her waist as she swept down the stairs.

Moonlight pooled on the slate floor from the windows either side of the door. She turned the big key, slid the two bolts and pulled the door towards her. She noted the two uniformed policemen. This was definitely not good.

"Mrs Victoria Lake? I'm Sergeant Glass and this is Constable Billings."

"Yes, come in." Leading them to the sitting room, she switched on lights as she went. She glanced at her watch it was three thirty, the dead hour. The time in London when thieves broke into cars and houses. She shivered. "Please sit down." She sank into her favourite wing chair and crossed her legs at the ankles, aware that she hadn't a stitch on underneath. Her mother would be proud of her deportment. It was one of the things the finishing school had been hot on — while all Victoria had wanted to do was to study biology at university. She could still hear her father saying that a university education was wasted on women. They didn't need a degree to raise children.

"How can I help you, Sergeant Glass?"

"I'm sorry to have to tell you this but your husband, Charles Lake, is dead."

The air left Victoria's lungs. She knew it had to be that, of course, to bring the police here now.

"How?" Her voice was steady.

"An accident on the M5."

"But he wasn't due home until tomorrow."

"That may be, but I'm afraid that he was killed in a multi-vehicle collision on the M5 just between Bridgwater and Taunton."

She closed her eyes. Charles was gone. Her chest tightened.

"Victoria, why are all the lights on?" Adam walked into the sitting room naked. "If you can't sleep I know how to help."

She stood. "Adam, allow me to introduce you to Sergeant Glass and Constable Billings." Victoria watched the constable take in Adam's assets. They were certainly worth noting.

"I'll go and throw something on." He smiled and covered himself with his hands.

"Why don't you?" The constable raised an eyebrow as Adam sauntered away, looking between Victoria and Adam's retreating backside.

"And Adam is . . .?" the sergeant asked.

She could tell it bothered him that Adam was twenty-six and she was sixty. "My lover." Victoria poured herself a brandy and drank it in one go. While the liquid burned her insides she could hear Charles's voice saying that that was a waste of very good cognac. She poured another.

"Later today we will need you to go to Taunton to identify your husband. He was taken to Musgrove Park Hospital." The sergeant's voice was carefully neutral.

She nodded, not turning around, but cradling the cut crystal tumbler in her hands, pressing the edges into her fingers every time an image of Charles came into her mind. "Yes."

"Maybe your, er, *Adam*," The sergeant put extra emphasis on the name, "could go with you so you won't have to drive in case you're distressed by what you see."

"Thank you, Sergeant Glass."

"Here's my card in case you have any questions." Glass stood beside Victoria with it held out in between them.

Victoria took the card.

"We'll be off now."

"Was anyone else killed?" Victoria turned around. "Was he the cause of the accident?"

"One other fatality, and the cause is still being investigated. An inquest will be held in due course."

"Thank you."

Victoria heard them speak to Adam in the hall. All she could think about was how she hoped Charles hadn't been at fault. He would never have been able to forgive himself if he had been the cause of another's death. He was a good man and, oddly enough, she would miss him. The wind had picked up during the night and she listened to the leaves protesting. Her breath caught. The elder had taken another from Boscawen.

Victoria was about to pick up the landline to ring her mobile, which she couldn't find, but the handset rang. She frowned. It was seven thirty in the morning. She didn't need any more bad news.

"Hello." Victoria looked out of the kitchen door. Sam was walking towards one of the sheds. It was payday soon. Did that money come out of the joint account or Charles's? She assumed that his account would be frozen now.

"Tori. It's Seb. Is Charles with you? He was supposed to call when he reached Cornwall."

"Oh God, Sebastian, why the hell didn't he stay in London?" Victoria sank against the table.

"I know you like your trysts, but seriously, how can you want to keep a man from his own home?"

"Damn it, Sebastian, it's not that." Victoria took a deep breath. "Dear God, you don't know." They were best friends.

"Don't know what? I know that Charles cancelled on me at the last minute to go to a meeting and then said he would head back to Cornwall when he'd finished."

She closed her eyes. It was probably best he heard it from her and not someone else but how did she tell him? There was no good way. "He's dead, Seb." Victoria shook her head as she heard the intake of breath. "There was a pile up on the M5 and he died."

"Christ Almighty. May he rest in peace."

"Yes." Victoria sighed. What could she say? Nothing would make the situation any better. "Sebastian . . ."

"He was the best of us. I can't believe he's gone."

"No." That was true. It felt unreal or even surreal.

"Are you OK?"

"That's a good question. I don't know." She took a deep breath. "I'll ring you later today after I've been to Taunton to identify him officially. There's so much to do." She looked at the list in her other hand. She needed to find her mobile. It was where all her numbers were stored.

"You can't do that alone, Tori. I'll meet you in Taunton."

"I can do it alone."

"Don't be so stubborn. You'll need help. I'll clear my schedule and meet you there at what time?"

Victoria sighed. She wouldn't fight him on this. "Shall we make it around four? That will allow us both time to sort a few things out before we go."

"I'll take the train down so that I can drive you back to Boscawen. Pick me up at the station. I'll text you the train time."

"OK." Victoria needed to find her damn mobile.

"Call someone. You shouldn't be by yourself."

Victoria looked to where Sam had been working. He was gone. Adam was sound asleep upstairs. "I will. See you later."

Dialling her mobile, she listened for its ring. It wasn't on the ground floor. She hung up and walked upstairs. She needed a shower and a clear head. The shower was easy, but a clear head was harder. Despite crawling back into bed after the police had left she hadn't slept. So many thoughts had bounced around in her mind. Sadness and elation battled. She stopped on the landing and looked down to the hall. Finally, this was all hers and she didn't have to share it with anyone. So why didn't she feel better about it?

Victoria tied the belt on the blue silk dress. Her shoes and her handbag were on the footstool by the bed. She checked the mirror then grabbed two hankies from the drawer. She had no idea how she would react. How was one supposed to behave in this circumstance? No amount of social training prepared you to identify your husband's body in a morgue.

Her face appeared very pale. A bit of lipstick might help. Her pearls lay on the dressing table. No, she couldn't wear them today. She wouldn't be able to put them on without Charles. A lump filled her throat. She should be rejoicing that she was free, but that wasn't the emotion of the moment.

With a last look around the room, she dropped the lipstick into her bag. This morning she'd cleared up the mess that she and Adam had created last night. It had looked like a herd of cattle had been in the room. Placing her shoes on the floor, she put them on. When she smoothed her hands down her dress, she saw her phone peeking out from under the corner of the bed. How the hell did it get there? And why hadn't Adam heard it when she'd rung it this morning?

She picked it up and checked the screen. The battery was dead so she would charge it in the car on the way to Taunton. She'd already called Sebastian and informed him that she would be mobile-less so she wouldn't need to call him en route. He was due at Taunton at 14.55.

One last glance in the mirror then she set off. The day was glorious and it struck her that it had been a total waste of a perfect spring day. She should have been working in the garden with Sam, not making phone calls. Really, it had been tedious more than heartbreaking. There were few things worse than having the same conversation twenty times and what had been most annoying was batting off people's concern for her. She didn't know what she felt and their assumptions irritated her.

Double-checking that the front door was locked, she collected her sunglasses before walking to the garage. Once in the car a tap on the window made her jump and she nearly threw her phone rather than connecting it to the car. She lowered the window. "Sam. What can I do for you?" She'd told him the news about Charles earlier.

"Nothing. Just wanted to make sure you don't want me to drive you? I can't think that you've had much sleep and you must be exhausted."

Victoria smiled and placed her hand out of the window and on to his arm. "I'm OK, or as close to that as one can be in the circumstance. The drive will give me time to think undisturbed."

"Sure?" He frowned.

"Yes, and I'm meeting Sebastian there so I won't be making the journey back alone."

"OK." He stepped back. "I'm so sorry."

"I know, and thank you. I'll see you tomorrow." Victoria reversed her 4x4 out of the garage, hoping today wouldn't become any more bizarre.

Traffic had been heavy and Victoria hadn't had a chance to stop on the journey north. Sebastian stood on the pavement, looking his normal dashing self with an overnight bag in one hand and briefcase in the other. Although he'd aged and much of his hair was streaked with silver, he still had it.

"Hello." Sebastian put his bags in the back then climbed into the front seat. Before she pulled out, he leaned over and kissed her cheek, covering her hand on the gear stick with his. He gave it a little squeeze then let her concentrate on driving through the traffic to the hospital. Victoria appreciated the consideration, but missed the reassuring touch as the satnav chirped out instructions. She felt his scrutiny and wasn't surprised by it. They had known each other over forty years and there was so much water under the bridge between them.

Once she had pulled into a parking space at the hospital, she turned to him. "Thank you for coming." She paused. "This is tougher than I thought it might be."

"I knew it would be." He got out of the car, came around to her side and opened the door for her.

"Always the gentleman." She smiled as he held out his hand to assist her.

"Some things are worth maintaining. Shall we?" He led the way. Victoria's stomach twisted as she asked for the location of the morgue. Sebastian put a hand on her arm as they walked along the hallway. He held open the door while Victoria walked in and glanced at the people sitting there. Were they also here because of the crash? Everyone looked grim, but that was no surprise. Death was rarely a happy event. It should be for her, though. She was free from a marriage that she hadn't wanted, which hadn't had the intended outcome . . .

The woman behind the desk looked up. "May I help?"

"Yes, I'm Victoria Lake and I'm here to . . ." Words failed her.

"We've been expecting you. Take a seat and someone will be with you shortly."

Victoria nodded and looked around for two seats together. She didn't feel in control of this situation. She had been trained within an inch of her life on how to behave in virtually every circumstance, but there was a gaping hole opening up before her, one labelled the grieving wife. She knew, once upon a time, there were defined rules, but now it was as clear as the old glass in the greenhouse.

"Tori. Breathe."

She turned to Seb. He took her hand and led her to a seat. How long had she been standing in the middle of the room? She sat where he pointed while he went to the water cooler. She noted the confidence of his movements. He was in no doubt of his role today. He was the best friend, the stalwart who always appears when the going gets tough, the man of the hour. He smiled at her as he walked back holding two flimsy plastic cups. When had he become so accomplished? He hadn't always been. The first time she'd met him he'd been covered in spots and his voice alternated between tenor and bass.

"Drink this." He handed her a cup.

"Thanks."

"I can do this for you." His grey eyes were so serious. Lines were now etched on his temples and the furrows across his brow were permanent.

"Thank you, but I must; I owe this to him."

"I won't argue about that but it's not a requirement. I'm one of his many lawyers so I am legally able to do this for you."

"I know." She took a sip of the cool water.

"Mrs Victoria Lake?" A man with a clipboard in his hand stood by the reception desk.

She stood and her shadow was close by her side. Everything about her was tense. If touched, she felt as if she would shatter into a million pieces right here on the antiseptic scented floor. The man opened a door. "Through here."

Victoria shivered. The thin jersey of her wrap dress was made for the spring day and not the arctic temperatures needed to keep a body from decay. In front of her on a metal table was a large lump covered in a sheet. She recognised her husband without them lifting it. She had seen that shape in bed since she was twenty. It hadn't changed much.

The man placed his clipboard down and walked up to the table. Her limbs were leaden as she crept forward.

"Before I remove the sheet. I just want to say that there are facial injuries despite the seatbelt and airbag."

She frowned, reaching for Seb's hand as the sheet was pulled back. Charles's thinning hair was caked in blood. His nose was cut and broken and his full mouth was pale and the lips were gashed. His skin looked strangely bloated and the lines that normally crossed his forehead were gone.

"Is this your husband, Charles Lake?"

Victoria bit her lower lip. Was this Charles? Not as she knew him. Seb squeezed her hand. "Yes, it is Charles Lake, my husband."

The man pulled the sheet over Charles's head. "Thank you. Could you sign the paperwork at the desk and the body will be released in due course?"

That was it. Victoria still held tight to Sebastian's hand walking down the hall. That was not the end that Charles deserved. He had deserved to die peacefully in his own bed. He'd given so much to help other people. Life hadn't given him a fair deal at all.

CHAPTER
EIGHT

Seb paced the terrace, speaking on his mobile while Victoria poured them both a whisky. They had driven back in silence through the heavy holiday traffic and she had nodded off to sleep, waking as they arrived at Boscawen's gates. The image of Charles's battered face was the first thing she thought of when she saw the house. She shuddered. Picking up her phone, she remembered that she'd promised to text Adam when she returned home. He too had been worried about her driving. She'd seen Sam standing outside the gatehouse with a few people as they had passed. It looked like they were setting off for the evening. He had integrated well into the community. She'd worried about him when he first arrived, but she needn't have.

Am home. Vx

She pressed send and then went on to check her messages. There were quite a few and they all said the same thing. How sorry they were and how Charles had been taken far too soon. It was a tragedy. Which from their point of view it was, but from hers it really was not. She would miss him in her way, but now she was

94

free to do as she pleased in every part of her life. She smiled as she scrolled through the options on her phone. She had been expecting to hear from Peter's Garden Nursery regarding a plant she was seeking and she wondered if the woman had called in the morning before she'd found her phone and had left a voicemail.

She saw several missed calls, but then her heart stopped. The last call she'd made had lasted for an hour. It was to Charles's number and it had begun at six-thirty last night. But she hadn't called him, she couldn't have. She'd been with Adam in the bedroom.

She sank on to a chair. Somehow the phone must have been hit during their lovemaking and it had dialled the last number she'd rung, which was Charles's. Dear God, he'd heard them and he'd changed his plans and driven down. She closed her eyes, trying to imagine what he must have felt.

"Are you all right, Tori? You're as white as a sheet." Seb put his phone in his pocket and picked up the drink she'd poured for him.

She focused on Sebastian. Surely Charles wouldn't have listened. He would have hung up — but then, if he had, the call wouldn't have lasted that long. What had she and Adam said? How absolutely ghastly for Charles. "What time did Charles ring to cancel?"

"It was about eight, I think." He took a seat opposite her. "I've just had a call from one of my associates. Charles was with him until gone ten last night so he must have left London after that. He would have been totally exhausted, having made the journey in the morning. Getting behind the wheel of a car that tired was suicide." Sebastian swirled the one ice cube in his glass. "What on earth had he been thinking of?"

Victoria's heart raced. She knew exactly what he had been thinking of, her and Adam. If Charles had ever suspected that she cheated on him, he knew then without a doubt thanks to that call.

"Tori, are you OK? I know this is all a lot to take on board."

"Oh, Sebastian, you have no idea, none at all."

Her grandfather was asleep in his chair with the television on and the newspaper in his lap. Demi walked to the attic where she had some phone signal. She watched the line indicate it was downloading her emails. Silently she sent up a prayer that something good would arrive — like she had a job she could go to, or maybe she'd won the lottery. Of course, she would need to play the lottery to win it.

In clearing her mother's papers she hadn't found her own birth certificate or her mother's marriage certificate and now she knew the reason for the latter: it had never existed. But her birth certificate would be somewhere, even if it was just in the records office.

She typed in Charles Lake into the search box. He had a Wikipedia entry. Scrolling through, it was impressive from the list of schools attended to his degree from Durham. He seemed to be involved with a great deal of charity work. She frowned. What had happened between her parents? Rain began pounding down on the roof and she looked around and saw several nice pieces of furniture including two old Windsor chairs and a wooden chest. They didn't fit in with the rest of the furnishings in the house, except for the dresser in the kitchen. They all spoke of an older time in a bigger place.

A ping sounded and she left the emails to download while she read a text.

Hi Demi. Sorry I missed your call. If you still need a key let me know. Soph x

Well, she might need the key as soon as she decided what to do, but it was a long weekend so she should just enjoy it with her grandfather. His lapses worried her. She hadn't seen him much this year, thanks to Matt, so she didn't know if this was new. Her mother would have known. She rubbed her temples, trying to remember if Morwenna had said anything. It was weird having her grandfather call her Wenna. He'd never done it before and she didn't even look like her mum.

She switched to the emails. Her heart stopped when she saw Matt's name and immediately below it was one from the HR person. Her finger slipped between the two. She knew they were both going to contain things she didn't want to see. She opened the one she still had a small bit of hope for and read.

Dear Demi,
Thank you for your email. We will certainly keep your name in our files.

Although it stung a little reading these words, Demi hadn't dared to hope so the response wasn't a surprise. Tomorrow she would begin a job hunt in earnest.

Her finger hovered over Matt's email. She didn't want to read it, but she had to.

Demi,
I don't know why you're all bent out of shape. You know what I like and you're just a prude, in fact you're bordering on frigid. You need to grow up. I thought your mother's death had done that for you but clearly not.
I have bagged your things. I was about to take the lot to the charity shop, but you caught me in time. I'll hold on to the stuff for a week but no longer. Give me 24-hours notice regarding when you want to collect it.
Matt

Demi shook; she could feel his anger. Nothing in the email surprised her, but she had dared to hope he would apologise for the betrayal, the betrayal of trust and so many other things. But he hadn't.

Demi turned from the windows and sat cross-legged on the wooden floor. Dust rose around her and she sneezed. What the hell was she going to do? She scrolled through the other emails, looking for something from the insurance company or the lawyer. Without money, she was trapped. Somehow she would have to get to London this coming week. Sadly there was no other way, but to take a loan from her grandfather again. She hated it, but she had to go to collect her things if nothing else. She needed her portfolio. She couldn't apply to "proper" jobs without it. It was a circular problem, all revolving around money or the lack of it and her own stupidity.

Demi tapped the top of her boiled egg. She couldn't remember the last time she'd had such regular meals. Did her grandfather always eat this way or was it for her benefit? When she had come downstairs last night, he had been asleep in his chair. She had kissed his forehead then went to bed after she had thrown a crocheted blanket over him. She wondered if he'd slept in the chair all night, perhaps because the stairs were too much for him, but he looked fresh this morning and certainly better than she did. She had dark purple circles under her eyes from a night spent tossing, turning, and trying to work out what to do.

"More tea?" Her grandfather held up the pot.

"Yes, please." She looked around the kitchen. It would be fun to redecorate the house for her grandfather. She was sure he didn't even notice his surroundings. As long as things worked and were clean she doubted he saw them. After breakfast, she would cut a few flowers and bring them into the sitting room to brighten it. The proportions of the room were fine, but the dark walls and furnishings disguised all that was good about it.

"You look worried."

She raised her eyes to his and thought about lying. "I am."

"A problem shared is a problem halved."

"Maybe."

He handed her another piece of toast. She looked at the gnarled fingers and longed to sketch them. She would love to lose herself in creating something for a while.

"I'm worried about money. I'm worried about not having a job and I'm worried about —" Demi stopped. She was worried about what Matt would do with the video.

"I always thought you should have studied art in the first place, not architecture."

"That's another thing where you and Mum are different. She said I needed a skill."

He opened his second egg. "She wasn't wrong about that, but you could have studied art, become a teacher, had a skill *and* done something that you loved."

"I don't think she would have agreed."

"She was just trying to protect you, to make sure you could fend for yourself."

"I don't understand."

"Your mother always wanted more. She was always the brightest and quickest. She rose to the top in school."

Demi considered the mother she knew and her knowledge didn't fit in with the wanting more. Although thinking of all the suits Demi had taken to the charity shop, they had been the best in their day but they were very old. "Why did she change?" Demi asked, but she knew what was coming.

"You. The scandal that could have erupted."

"Why scandal? We're not talking the fifties. This was the nineties."

"There is a scandal, no matter when it happens, when there are marital vows involved."

Demi's protest died. He was right, of course. Her father was married. She was still trying to accept that her father lived, and lived nearby. She could bump into him in Falmouth at any time. Would she know him? Yes. She just needed to look for a masculine version of herself.

Of course, he would know her too. He'd seen her. She played with the broken bits of eggshell on her plate. He'd come to her mother's funeral but hadn't spoken to her. She replayed the service in her head but could only recall seeing him as she walked out of the church. He'd looked at her. Why hadn't he spoken to her? No matter how hard she tried she couldn't make the pieces fit.

"Enough about your mother. How can I help? I can give you some money if that's what you need. And you have a home here." He frowned. "Well, actually the home bit can't be true for long, sadly."

"What's happening to the house?"

"In view of my hip and the stairs and other things, I'm going into a care home. I'm just waiting to find out when."

"I see." She cleared her plate to the sink and squatted down by her grandfather. "Thank you for the offer. I should have my last salary payment in my bank by the end of the week and I'll pay you everything back." She took a deep breath. "No matter what I do, I need to go and collect my things from my ex. So although I don't want to, I will have to take another loan to travel to London and face the music."

"Do you want to tell me about it."

She sank into the chair opposite. "No, not unless I have to and that's up to you."

"I would never force a confidence, but remember, nothing is ever as bad as it seems at first."

Demi smiled at him and wished he was right, but she couldn't see an upside to this situation.

Victoria walked into the kitchen and paused when she saw Sebastian sitting there, working on his laptop. He was wearing a grey cashmere sweater over a white T-shirt. Salt and pepper stubble covered his jaw and his hair looked as if he'd been running his fingers through it repeatedly. It was a good look.

"Morning," Victoria said as she moved towards the counter.

"Indeed." He closed the lid of his laptop and stood. Still-powerful muscles lurked beneath the soft fabric of the jumper and she suddenly wondered if he worked at maintaining this fitness level or if it was just in his genes.

"Been up for a while?" She noted the empty cafetière on the counter.

"Yes. Somehow my phone had signal and emails arrived loudly about four."

Victoria laughed. "More coffee?"

"Definitely."

Out of the corner of her eye she saw him put his computer into his briefcase along with a pad of paper on which he had been making notes. He looked uneasy, as if being caught at work was a sin. Victoria smiled. Charles, until he had retired, had always been up early working and had continued into the small hours most nights. It was a by-product of both men's drive, but she hadn't seen it in Sebastian before. Mind you, when she'd seen him in past years he'd come only for a long weekend and hadn't brought work with him. But now he was here as a friend and as an executor of Charles's estate — *her* estate now. She plunged the cafetière and mentally began making immediate plans to hire more help for the garden.

"How are you feeling this morning?" He walked up to her.

She gave a dry laugh. "I've certainly slept better. All night long I kept thinking I heard the phone ringing and reliving all the calls that came in last night."

He touched her fingers as she handed him a mug. "I'm so sorry."

"Oh, Sebastian, don't. We both know that things haven't been right with Charles and me for a long time." She blew into her mug watching the surface ripple. "If ever. But we'd been together an awfully long time."

He stepped back from her. He knew all of that so why had she said it?

"I thought, with your permission, I'd go through Charles's study and begin sorting the paperwork."

"Of course." She turned to him. "Look, I know I'm a bitch and didn't deserve Charles, but I did love him in my way."

He looked at her as if he could see her heart and she turned from him. There was too much there she didn't want anyone to view.

"Tori, he loved you more than you'll ever know."

She turned to him as a shadow fell across his eyes. He was hiding something, She was sure of it. She longed to find out what. Once she could have read him like the headlines on a newspaper, but now, after years as a solicitor, he had learned the poker face too well. Those grey eyes looked so serious at present. The humour that usually danced behind them was absent, but then she wasn't surprised. His best friend had killed himself driving down to Cornwall to accost his cheating wife. Though of course, Sebastian didn't know the last bit, only she did.

Victoria stood with a tray in her hands leaning against the study door. Seb was on the phone.

"Yes, I'll be in London on Tuesday. Do what is necessary but be discreet." He replaced the receiver.

"Be discreet? How intriguing." She smiled. "Come, let's have these sandwiches in the garden. It's a shame to stay locked in a gloomy study on a glorious spring day."

He rose, and when she was sure he would follow her, she left the study and cut through the sitting room to the terrace. The wisteria had fully blossomed in the past few days and as she walked under it, the fragrance floated around her, intoxicating and seeming to promise happiness. If only she believed in such happiness. No, she was far too practical for that. Life was a compromise as she had learned early.

She placed the tray down then slid on her sunglasses. Days didn't come much better than this. It was a shame she would be heading back inside to sort funeral arrangements. The funeral would be in London. It would be easier with the number of people who would come as so much of their life had been lived there. Victoria sighed. Well, she'd have to go up there sooner or later to sort out Charles's serviced flat, end the contract, and get rid of Charles's things. Of course, she hadn't even made a start on that here yet. Some charity shop would be happy to have all his clothing. He'd been such a clotheshorse.

"Isn't it fabulous?" she said as Seb came and stood by her and they surveyed the garden together. The distant sound of a mower just reached them. "The first thing I'll do when everything is settled is hire more help."

Seb remained silent at her side, frowning. "Does this still mean so much to you, Tori?"

Her eyes narrowed and she studied his face, looking for clues to why he asked the question. She found none. "Yes, always has and always will."

"It's like everything else. It's just a passing thing." He shrugged.

"It's more stable than most. The house has been here for hundreds of years."

"Do you really want to devote all your time and energy to this?" He looked out on the expanse of lawn in front of them with a distant vista to the fields beyond.

Victoria's chest tightened and she turned away from the garden and towards him. "What else do I have?"

"Tori, you're only sixty. You could find love or devote your talent and energy to a charity."

"Hah!" She went to sit by the table where the sandwiches were waiting. "I love this house and this garden. They need me."

He joined her. "It's granite and greenery, nothing more and you have so much to give."

She laughed. "I love how, even after all of this time, you think that I have something to give. You, of all people, should think the worst of me."

"I never have and I never will."

"Now that sounds like a challenge. And I love challenges. How many ways can I let you down?" She paused. "I'll have to work harder at it." She laughed sadly. "Let's eat and see if we can pick a day for the funeral."

"Don't be like this. I know who you really are, even if you hide from everyone else."

She sighed. "Sebastian, the girl you knew is long gone."

CHAPTER
NINE

It was just over a week since that horrible night and now Demi stood again on the pavement outside Matt's flat. She took a deep breath, knowing she couldn't run from this, that she had to be strong. He should be there in a few minutes. She still had a key so she could just go in and leave before he arrived, but he'd made it clear he wanted to speak to her, which was the last thing she wanted to do.

She glanced at her phone then remembered to text Sophie who she was staying with tonight. She had spoken briefly with her grandfather when she'd reached Paddington. Thank goodness he wasn't one for long phone calls. She'd nearly blurted it all out to him over the phone. A pigeon waddled towards her and she watched the sunlight catch the opalescence on the feathers.

"Demi."

She swung around at the sound of Matt's voice. Her hands shook. Be reasonable. Be calm. Don't let him manipulate you, she instructed herself in mantra-like fashion.

"Matt." Her skin crawled. How could she have thought that she'd loved him?

"You waited."

"You asked me to." She looked briefly in his eyes then away. She didn't want to know what he was thinking.

"I asked a lot of other things and you didn't do them." He stood with arms crossed and legs wide apart. He was spoiling for a fight.

"Matt, let's not go there."

He moved to within an inch of her and she willed herself not to step back. She could be strong. She held her ground and he walked up the stairs. She followed, repeating to herself that she must not be a doormat. He was a manipulating bastard who had violated her trust.

Inside the flat, Matt dropped his computer bag on the sofa. "We need to talk."

"Really?" Demi stood still and waited. This could mean many things, but it usually meant he was going to use all his persuasive powers to change her mind.

"Yes. We do. You've been totally out of line."

"*Me?*" Demi heard her voice squeak and she flinched. That would reveal to Matt just how vulnerable she was and he didn't know half of the story. What would her mother advise right now? Be proactive. Now was one of the times she needed to be firm. "*You're* the one who crossed the line. Filming us — filming *me* — without my permission." Her voice kept rising despite her best efforts. "It's wrong, so wrong."

"It's not, and that's what I was trying to show you."

"No. You filmed us." Her stomach rolled over uncomfortably. "You did it when I had said no to you doing it."

"You should have agreed. You're so staid, frigid even."

"Frigid, am I? Well, it didn't look that way on the 50-inch television. Quite the opposite. How could you?"

"Because I love you and it turns me on."

She shook her head. "Why? Why do you need to look at a flat screen when I was there in 3 freaking D." Her face was flaming. "Your sense of what is sexy is so warped by what you watch on the screen that you needed to make us part of it."

"No. That's not why I did it. You're so hung up about your body that you won't be naked in front of me. I had to show you how beautiful you are."

"I was afraid to be naked in front of you because you made me uncomfortable. You focused on parts of me and not me as a whole."

"I love you." He sank on to the sofa.

"You don't." She shook. "You love what you thought I was and I'm not that. If you thought I would in any way agree to what you have done, you never knew me at all." How could she have spent two years dating him, sleeping with him, thinking about marrying him? He had never seen the real her — nor, it would seem, had she seen the real him. What he loved was her body or bits of it anyway. What she'd loved was the idea of him . . .

"I want the video deleted." She stared at him, not blinking.

"I knew you would ask that. Can't you leave me with something of you? Better yet, change your mind and stay?" He stepped towards her.

She froze. In some way, it would be so easy to stay. It would solve her problems for the moment. His face was all excited and her stomach turned because his eyes rested not on her face but on her chest. This was not what she wanted at all. He grabbed her wrist and she panicked. Wresting herself from his grasp, she said, shaking, "Delete the video and any others you may have taken that I don't know about." She walked around him towards his computer bag.

"OK, OK I'll do it." He grabbed the bag and opened his laptop. The background picture of her in a bikini suddenly looked filthy to Demi. How had she never seen before that he objectified her? He'd bought the bikini as a present for her and hadn't stopped pestering her until she wore it for him. She watched him enter his password and then access the videos. The more she thought about it the more horrified she was that this was on his work computer. It wasn't private at all.

He called up the file. "Just watch and you'll see."

"No." She shuddered. "Is this the only one?"

"Yes, I only got the new phone the day before."

Demi remembered the night so vividly. He'd bought champagne and cooked her a wonderful meal. He'd set her up. She'd thought it had been to make her feel better after having lost her mum but no. The bubbles were to make her less self-conscious. She cringed. She'd always held back from trusting him fully. In her heart she'd known she could never really be herself with him — why else had she set aside her friends, her mother, even — but she'd never understood why.

"Delete it now."

He pressed the trash button and looked at her as if to say it's done.

"Now empty the trash."

"You don't trust me."

She clenched her hands into fists at her side. "No."

He did it.

"Now reboot your computer." She'd looked all this up to be sure. She knew that it would always be there on his hard drive, but if he took these steps then, it would take a hell of a lot of work to get it back and that was beyond his skill level.

"Seriously?"

"I've never been more serious."

"Demi —"

"Do it!"

He did. That had been too easy, she thought. "Your phone now."

"Oh, come on, why would I leave it on my phone?"

"Why did you do it in the first place? You haven't uploaded it anywhere have you?" Her heart raced with the thought.

"No way!"

She believed him. In his job, he couldn't afford for his backside to be on public display. But she knew he would have backed it up. She went to the desk and pulled out his memory stick and external hard drive. He might not have backed up to these yet, but she had to be sure. He fumbled with his phone after he'd put the password in and she pulled it from his hands and within seconds she had found it and deleted it.

"You were never like this before."

"I never had to be but I do now." She handed him the phone and then the hard drive. Once this was done she would call a cab and get the hell out of this place.

Victoria put her bag and suit carrier by the back door. The day was overcast but bright. It would make the drive easier. It was three weeks since Charles had died and she'd left going to London until the last minute. Tomorrow was the funeral. It had all taken so much longer than she had expected with the inquest and the coordination required to set up a funeral so many people wanted to participate in, even though she'd delegated as much as she could.

She ran her fingers over the plans for the garden. She wanted the funeral finished so that she could focus on where her heart lay.

"All set?" Sam stood in the doorway.

"Yes, thanks."

"I'll make sure everything is fine here. Don't feel you have to rush back."

Victoria smiled. "I hate being away from the garden at any time but this is the worst time to leave."

"I can send you pictures."

She chuckled. "Not quite the same as the real thing, is it?"

"Absolutely not, but if you can't have the real thing it might help." She watched him look down at the order form. "I thought I suggested varying the apple trees."

"You did, but I decided you were wrong."

Sam put his hands into his pockets. "Look, Mrs Lake, I know you want to restore the garden that was here, but you need to look at it differently."

She was about to interrupt, but he continued. "This estate once housed and fed nearly a hundred people. At the moment, there are two of us. So unless you plan on developing Boscawen Cider or something else you need to reconsider the fruit trees. You also need to think of diversity." He leaned against the Aga. "Currently you have five orchards, roughly fifty acres, but not in peak condition. Last year the bulk of the crop fell to the ground. Most of the trees produce fruit at the same time. If you introduced a few new varieties, or even other local ones, it would help." He pointed to the order form. "The bulk of the orchard is already made up of Cornish Giant and Cornish Gillyflower, which are excellent, but with a greater variety the harvest could be spread. But I have to ask myself: what on earth do you need a commercial-size orchard for?"

Victoria pulled herself up to her full height. As much as he had a point there was no way she was going to listen to him. This was her garden and her money. She was going to restore the garden that her great-grandmother had created and her grandmother had loved.

"Before you do this, think. Staggering the harvest is a good thing. Introducing other varieties will strengthen the trees that are there, creating a biodiversity that is better for the existing trees and the new ones that come. And it's good for the bees which we need for pollination."

Victoria looked at her watch. "Just what are you suggesting?"

"Cut the order in half and add other varieties. You have no idea how many apples will be produced if you plant that many trees and you don't use the ones you have now."

"I want the garden as it was," she said.

"Gardens move on, Mrs Lake, and if your ancestors were here today they would definitely introduce new varieties. Just look at all the species that your great-grandmother planted that aren't even native to this country, never mind the original garden. Mrs Tregan was a great plantswoman and an innovator."

She pursed her mouth. Odd that he knew that, but maybe he'd worked it out from the garden that had survived. "You have a point. I'll look at it more closely when I return."

"Thank you for listening. The old varieties are good, but the new ones have a lot to offer. And I think you need to look at planting more pear trees too."

"Walnuts and pears, you plant for your heirs," she muttered softly. That was a phrase she hadn't thought of in years. Her great-grandmother had quoted it often when they'd walked through the orchards. "You know less about gardening than I do, Sam." Victoria looked at him closely and his glance fell down to the plans on the table. "I'll see you in a few days. Call me if you need me."

"Everything will be fine here." He looked up. "And I'm so sorry about Mr Lake. He was a good man."

"Thanks." Victoria picked up her car keys. There was something that had been on her mind. "And Sam, please promise me that you won't cut the elder trees without asking their permission."

He frowned. "You really don't believe that, do you?"

She sighed. "Once I only paid lip service to it, but twice in my lifetime I've seen the result of not asking permission." She looked out of the window. It didn't take much to call to mind the argument she'd had with Perry's wife, Julia. All Victoria had been trying to do was pass on the knowledge she'd gained from Edith and Gladys. "Both times the people died in cars. It's a bit too much of a coincidence for my liking."

He cast a sideways glance at her. She wasn't mad, she knew she wasn't, and she knew she was the one to blame for Charles's death if anyone was. But the whole thing unnerved her a bit.

"I promise, if it will make you happy, but I don't believe trees could in any way be evil."

"I agree with that, but the elder is a tricky tree." She thought of her grandmother Gladys's warnings and her great-grandmother had agreed.

"Travel safe." He smiled.

She picked up her bag and the order form. "I intend to; and Sam, thanks for all your help." She left him in the kitchen with the plans. Apple trees. Why did she want to restore the orchards? Did she need to have a reason?

CHAPTER
TEN

Victoria sat straight and rotated in small half circles in the swivel chair. Her ankles were crossed and the navy skirt of her suit fell inches short of her knees. They were still good knees. She hadn't had to resort to long skirts to cover saggy, baggy or non-existent ones like so many women. Sunlight fell through the tall Georgian windows, highlighting the delicate weave of the fabric in her skirt. Today London appeared at its best, which it hadn't in the rain that had marred yesterday's funeral.

She still felt the curious stares of the congregation, as if they were sitting here in the boardroom with her. Her facial muscles hurt from alternately fixing a polite smile or a saddened, lost look on it. She'd done her best to appear the grieving widow and, to be truthful, she *was* sad. You couldn't spend that many years with someone and not feel some affection for him. Well, you could, but she and Charles had muddled along quite well once they moved past the point of children. In fact, considering all they had gone through trying to have children, it was a wonder they could still look at each other, let alone feel any affection. That circle of blame still stung when she let it come into her mind. She was barren. Sleeping with countless other men without

116

protection had proved what she hadn't wanted to believe. Charles had a low sperm count, but he couldn't take all the blame. Victoria was sure that all her men hadn't suffered from that complaint and she had made sure she had sex with them when she was supposed to be ovulating. It was fun — but it had never worked.

In her mind, she could see the casket being carried up the main aisle of the Oratory. The organ had played something sombre that she hadn't recognised. She wasn't sure it would have been Charles's choice. He preferred a rousing hymn to that sort of drivel. Maybe she should have paid more attention to the selection of the music. The flowers had looked wonderful, though, but Charles wouldn't have worried about them. In fact, he would have balked at the cost, preferring the money to have gone to a charity.

Once the money was in her control and this farce of a will reading was over she could at least live a life that was true. The necessary deception had been fun, initially adding spice to all her liaisons, but the subterfuge had palled quickly. She longed for the relaxation of papers in bed and no need to clear the evidence away.

As she stood outside the offices of Crowther, Dunn and Roberts, in Manchester Square, Demi pulled at the edge of her jacket, which hadn't fully recovered from being soaked and slept in. She looked like a tramp in contrast to the building with its elegant, double-height windows. It had been designed to impress and it did. She swallowed, but the dryness in her mouth wouldn't go. Unfolding the letter, she read it again to be sure this was where she was supposed to be and that her father was truly dead, not the false dead that her mother had created all those years ago.

All this time he'd known she existed and yet it was only when he was six foot under that he chose to get in touch, via a formal solicitor's letter that commanded her to be at the reading of Charles Lake's will on the appointed day. It was luck she'd even received it since it had gone to her mother's. Thankfully Demi had stopped by to visit an elderly neighbour who had been collecting the post for her.

Why hadn't he spoken to her at her mother's funeral? Well, maybe not then, but a few days after when it wouldn't have been as much of a shock. So many times in the past few days she'd been on the verge of replying that she wouldn't attend today, but in the end curiosity had overridden the desire to tell him or, more correctly his solicitor, to sod off. He hadn't cared all these years so why should she do anything now?

However, she had little money left out of her last pay cheque. She hadn't found a job and was staying on the floor of Sophie's studio in Earl's Court. She would have to sign on if this went on much longer. And maybe this dead father of hers had left her something useful. He'd been filthy rich by all accounts. She'd read the obituaries online and they made him sound like a bloody saint. They hadn't mentioned the bastard child he never provided for, of course.

She folded the letter and placed it in her bag, took a deep breath and walked up the few steps to the shiny black door. The paint was so perfect it reflected the green from the trees behind her. She pressed the bell and waited. She could do this. Pulling herself up to five foot four — only achieved when she wore high heels — she looked into the camera as a woman's voice asked who she was.

"Demelza Williams."

"Please come in."

A buzzer sounded and Demi pushed against the door expecting huge resistance, but there was none. She nearly fell straight through and was trying to regain her balance as the receptionist smiled at her.

"Miss Williams, let me take you to the boardroom." The immaculate woman stood then glided on heels so high Demi wondered how she stood, let alone walked in them. Demi looked down at her own shoes. They were her best ones, her interview pair, but here they looked so tatty that she wanted to hide her feet as quickly as possible. The sooner she was seated with her shoes hidden the better. But the thought of lots of people around a big table had the colour draining from her face. She hoped there wouldn't be any confrontations and that it would all be simple.

They walked up four shallow steps and the clean lines and warm colours were relaxing. This, of course, was the intended effect. Everything was neutral but not bland. Expensive ink and wash drawings were simply framed. Then, almost without warning, they came to white-painted double doors made of carved panels. Despite everything designed to relax clients, Demi's palms were sweaty. The sound of the phone ringing brought the receptionist to a stop and Demi's heart did the same. She pushed her bag up higher on her shoulder.

"If you would just wait here a moment?"

Demi nodded, standing in limbo. She looked to the doors and then to the entrance where she spotted the release button. Escape was still possible. She could go, live with her grandfather and pull pints at some pub. But she knew that wouldn't work long term. He was moving into the care home soon. Maybe she could pull pints here in London, but for that she required a place to live which she didn't have. Sophie's floor was a very short-term solution and she had sent out her CV to five architecture firms in the hopes of finding something. No luck so far, not even an interview, but it was still early days.

"Sorry. Let me take you through." The receptionist had returned. She pushed open both doors and the conversation in the room came to an immediate stop.

"Sebastian, this is Demelza Williams. Fr. Paul has just rung — he is caught in traffic and will be here in about ten minutes." She turned to Demi. "Can I get you a coffee or a tea?"

Looking around the room at the openly curious faces, Demi thought a double shot of export strength vodka might be more appropriate. "Coffee, please, black." She sank into the nearest empty seat around the big oval table before anyone could assess her any more.

Victoria tapped her nails on the table, not sure why she had come early. Sebastian was making a big deal out of

120

this reading of the will and yet it was so simple. Charles had left everything to her bar a bit of money for his charities. She was sure he'd left a painting or something to his nephew Edward, maybe some of his wine to Sebastian and his vintage Aston to the priest who would probably flog it then give the money to charity anyway. This, of course, was a waste of a beautiful automobile, but she needn't worry about that, she had her hands and her thoughts full of ideas for Boscawen.

She looked at the five people currently here. The priest was late as always, no doubt caught up trying to save someone's soul. She shook her head and noticed the big belly on the man that ran the charity that Charles poured money into. Clearly it was going towards feeding him to excess. He should be using the funds to buy shirts that were sufficient to cover the vast expanse, then the rest of the world wouldn't be obliged to view his hairy stomach pushing through the gaps of his present one.

Sebastian was on his mobile phone and looking out of the large windows towards the courtyard garden. Even after all these years it still worked. She had planned and planted it for him thirty years ago when he and his partners had purchased the building. But looking at it now just made her separation from Boscawen worse. She needed to begin work there properly. Last night she'd sat in bed sketching plans until the small hours.

Now Seb placed a hand on her shoulder. She looked up and he gave her what was meant to be a reassuring smile, but there was no reason to reassure her.

Everything was falling into place. Tonight she would be back in her bed in Boscawen and tomorrow she would begin.

The doors swung open and Seb's über-efficient receptionist entered, trailing a dishevelled young woman. She reminded Victoria of someone, but she couldn't place it. The girl must have to do with one of Charles's charities. She looked at Sebastian, who was smiling at the shabbily dressed blonde.

Placing her hands on her lap, she watched the faces of the assembled people, especially the stranger. Victoria could read anticipation on their faces, but of course they didn't know Charles's will, only she and Sebastian did. They weren't getting too much. Although Charles had been muttering about changes to the will recently, it would only mean that he'd probably increased his favourite charity's share after a windfall he'd had from some investment.

Victoria turned to Sebastian, hoping that he would begin this farcical meeting. She was sure it could all have been achieved via letter, email and a phone call or two. This reading of the will seemed overly dramatic.

"So, while Fr. Paul makes his way here can I just thank you all for coming." Sebastian leaned forward and placed his hands on the table. They hadn't changed much over the years, just a few marks of age gradually appearing, and he was still sporting the tan he'd acquired in the days he'd spent at Boscawen these last few weeks.

"Will this take long?" the fat man asked.

"No more than an hour once we begin."

122

"Then let's get on with it, Sebastian. I'm sure Paul can just join in and you and I know the gist of the will anyway." Victoria sighed. "Right now I feel like I'm caught in one of those ghastly television productions of a whodunnit and a badly dressed inspector will arrive any moment."

Sebastian turned to her and his grey eyes looked weary. "Things have changed in the will and it's important that all the named parties are here, Tori."

Her stomach clenched. This didn't sound right. Charles would never have changed things without telling her unless they were just small and simple. "Nonsense. Charles would have mentioned it."

Sebastian frowned. "I won't say any more other than these changes are recent."

Demi took the coffee from the receptionist, thankful for something to do with her hands while she watched the haughty woman argue with the solicitor. He had kind eyes and looked as if he was very exasperated with the woman. Anyone would be, but she knew that this was her father's widow, the woman he wouldn't leave, the woman he'd abandoned her for. Victoria Lake was elegant to the core from the silver grey hair in a chic, sleek bob, to the navy Chanel suit. Everything about her was expensive. Looking down at her own clothes she slid her chair closer to the table.

The doors opened again and a priest walked through them. "So sorry I'm late but there was terrible traffic." He smiled at everyone in turn. The tension in the room eased except for that emanating from Victoria Lake.

She glared at the newcomer, who walked over and kissed her cheek. Demi was sure he whispered something in her ear for her mouth bunched into a pout of distaste. The priest straightened and walked to an empty seat beside Demi.

He held out his hand. "I'm Fr. Paul and you must be Demelza."

Demi blinked and shook his hand. How did he know her name? She knew no one in this room.

"Now that we are all here we can begin." The solicitor sat down next to Victoria. "For those of you who don't know me, I'm Sebastian Roberts. I've been Charles Lake's solicitor for thirty years and am now one of the executors of his estate along with Fr. Paul Boaden." He paused and looked at the people around the table. Everyone was intent, their eyes focused on Sebastian Roberts. Although he was still wearing his tie, he had taken off his jacket and rolled up his sleeves before sitting. This was not what Demi had been expecting at the reading of a will. But then, what had she imagined? She hoped she would receive something useful like money. Gosh, she could use that at the moment because there was still nothing from the life insurers. They said they were working on it. In the meantime, her indebtedness to her grandfather increased.

"Charles Lake was a wealthy man who worked hard to achieve his fortune, but he was generous to those without."

Demi raised an eyebrow. What? She and her mother had lived frugally to say the least. There was never any extra. Yes, they had had a lovely rented flat and she never wanted for clothes or food, but just saving up for her computers took two years stacking shelves on the weekends while she studied. He hadn't been generous with *them*. She looked at the expensive wife. He had been with her. Victoria's mouth was still in a pout of distaste and Demi could see that she didn't approve of Charles's generosity. If Charles was so good then what did he see in that bi — Demi stopped, that woman?

"So let's begin with the Education for Good charity that he founded to provide quality education for gifted but poorer students in Cornwall." The solicitor nodded to the plump man on the other side of the table. "Charles has added a further three million pounds to the endowment he has already set up for the provision of school fees."

"How generous." The man smiled.

Demi's eyes widened. Three million pounds. She glanced at Victoria, wondering if she would be upset, but Victoria was examining the large ruby on her ring finger. The stone captured the light falling in from the window and bounced red rays across the room. She watched the play of shades of red to pink across the walls while huge sums of money were bandied about. If she received a fraction of this, then she would be set up for life. The other people in the room, aside from Victoria Lake, sat up in anticipation and the sums read out were jaw dropping. Everyone was pleased, except Victoria. The frown that had begun to form with the second charitable bequest deepened with each that followed.

"These changes in the will were duly authorised and witnessed as of Friday, 23rd May, 2014." The solicitor stood and rolled his shoulders. Victoria Lake was very still. "Now we come to the more personal side of the will, so I would ask that Fr. Paul, Demelza, Edward and Victoria remain and the others may leave."

Demi could tell that wasn't an option. He was politely telling the representatives of the charities to go. And from their expressions they were pleased. One recipient pumped the lawyer's hand so vigorously that Demi thought his shoulder would dislocate. The receptionist appeared on cue and opened the double doors, swiftly escorting them out of the room. They should all be pleased. It sounded as if Charles had upped everyone's gifts.

Tea and coffee pots were placed on the table and Demi wondered what was going to happen now. She filled her coffee cup and noted the tension in everyone, especially Sebastian. He kept flexing his shoulders.

"Shouldn't we begin?" Victoria looked at her watch. By her calculation, Charles's generosity had diminished the estate by an extra ten million. It could take it, but if he had altered what he was giving the others here in the room, she might have to rejig some of her plans. She knew he would have left only a small bequest to Paul because he had taken a vow of poverty so there was no real point in giving him a lot — he would simply hand it over to the Church. Edward, on the other hand, could be an issue. Charles had muttered in the past that Edward was his obvious heir, but recently that had stopped and when they had last reviewed their wills five years ago the balance of the estate — truly the bulk of it — went to the surviving spouse. So even if he had increased his gift to Edward, she and Boscawen would be fine.

"Of course." Sebastian filled his coffee cup and added a spoonful of sugar. Victoria knew then all was not well. Sebastian never took sugar.

"When Charles, tragically, died three weeks ago he was in the process of revising his will and had reached the final stages. On the night of his death, he was working with one of my team until late and what is presented to you now is the result of that late evening's work." Sebastian looked at Victoria. "Before we begin I want to say that all the changes were duly finalised. I also want to make clear that on an estate of this size probate will not be swift. It will take some time to establish how much tax the estate will have to pay." He looked at everyone, making eye contact. "So let's start with the bequests to Fr. Paul."

"Fine." Paul smiled. Despite having known him since she was a teenager he remained an enigma to Victoria.

"Charles has left you his Aston with an account of one hundred thousand pounds for ongoing care and maintenance. He has also left you the small Constable study of Venice. These are given in trust and cannot be sold until your death."

Paul chuckled and Victoria frowned. She was rather fond of that little painting.

"Charles left me the small Italian old master painting of the Madonna and Child along with a case of 1960 port," Sebastian went on.

Victoria smirked. That had not changed at all. In some ways, she would have thought that Charles would have left his best friend more, but then again, what did Sebastian need? Nothing. Victoria turned to the little mouse in the bad suit. Why was she still here? Surely she was one of the charity cases.

"To his nephew, Edward, Charles leaves the lump sum of one million pounds and his grandfather's gold pocket watch."

Victoria relaxed her shoulders and leaned back into the chair. Her biggest fear, that he would leave part of Boscawen to Edward, had passed. She looked at Sebastian. His fingers worried the black fountain pen in his hand. She had watched him tick his way through a list, and couldn't read his handwriting from this angle, but she could see there was only one item left on the list. This would be her, she thought, but then there was still this Demelza Williams woman, sitting on the other side of the table.

"Finally, to the residue of Charles's estate, which after anticipated tax obligations is four million pounds in various investments and cash, and Boscawen."

Victoria frowned. Where was the rest of his money? Five years ago, when they reviewed the will there was twenty million pounds after he had done his charity bit. Only four million pounds in investments and cash? The interest on that at the moment would barely cover the estates running costs.

"This will be divided equally between his wife, Victoria Lake, and his daughter Demelza Williams."

Victoria couldn't breathe, almost couldn't speak. "His wh-what?" Her voice died. Charles had no children. *She* had no children although, God knows, they had done everything humanly — and at times it felt *in*humanly possible — to have children. When? How? Who? Charles had cheated on her? Or had he adopted this mouse? Victoria looked closely at Demelza Williams and saw that this child was not adopted. No, she was Charles's. The hair was the shade of pale blond that Charles had had at that age, the mouth was full and slightly pouty, and the skin was abnormally pale. In fact, Victoria wondered, why hadn't she noticed the resemblance as soon as the wretch walked through the door?

Charles had cheated on her, broken his marriage vows, and now he was giving Boscawen — or half of it — to his bastard. It was too much.

She stood and did the only thing that she could. "I contest!"

CHAPTER
ELEVEN

Sebastian glanced at her with tired eyes. "Charles anticipated that you would."

"What the hell was he on?" Victoria stared at the bastard, this Demelza Williams. Share Boscawen with her? There was no way she would let that woman set foot on Boscawen's soil.

Victoria turned from Demelza to Sebastian. He'd known what was coming and he'd known that Charles had betrayed her. "What happened to all the money, Sebastian?"

"It appears that he made a few bad investments in the last year, which was most unlike him, and a month ago he gave away a very large sum to a homeless charity."

"A what?"

"A charity supporting the homeless." Seb sighed. She could see dark circles under his eyes that hadn't been there two days ago.

"How much?"

"Five million."

Victoria did some quick calculations as she sat down. "Has anyone asked to see Charles's medical records?"

"Yes, we did. He saw his doctor at the end of April and, aside from his well-documented high blood pressure, he was fit."

Victoria thought about the pills he popped daily. Did they have any side effects on the brain? Because clearly Charles had gone mad, totally doolally. Even if he hadn't given half of her home to the bastard, she would struggle on what was left. Then there was all the extra money he had given to these stupid charities. She would have to claw that back. She, as his wife of forty years, was entitled to his money and to a comfortable life. She had not lived with him, slept with him and entertained for him for all this time to receive half of such a diminished pot that it was almost impossible for her to absorb it.

She turned to the mouse who, if possible, had gone even paler than she had been. Obviously this had been as much a surprise for her as it had been for Victoria. Unless, of course, it was an act. Victoria squinted at Demelza, bringing her into closer focus. How much guile lurked behind that bland exterior?

"I know that all this information is overwhelming, so I suggest we allow it to sink in before we take any further action."

Victoria glared at Sebastian. "Excuse me?"

He put a hand up. "Paul, why don't you take Demelza to the pub, and Edward, if you have any queries you know how to reach me." He paused. "I just need to remind everyone that nothing, of course, will be finalised until probate is complete and in an estate of this size it could take a while."

Victoria glared at Edward. He looked like the cat that had eaten the cream. One million pounds clear and a gold sodding pocket watch.

"Aunt Tori, let me say again how sorry I am about Uncle Charles."

Victoria bit her tongue and nodded. She had nothing to say to the weedy nephew. Just looking at him made her skin crawl. Could she contest his million? Maybe.

"I'll ring you tomorrow, Aunt Tori, grief can hit you in many ways." Edward said, leaving the room.

She watched Paul remove the problem, Demelza Williams. When had Charles betrayed her? Demelza looked about twenty-two, maybe a little more. She turned to Sebastian. They were now alone.

"How could you have kept this from me?" Victoria stood up and she noted how tired Sebastian appeared. He was wan under the tan and his eyes had lost their sparkle. Memories of another time came to her, of disappointment and of loss.

"I had to."

"I've known you since I was twelve."

"I know." He ran his hands through his hair and turned to her, his grey eyes filled with more sadness than she had seen in years. "But it's my job and I had to make sure that everything was legally correct. I am an executor of the estate. I am bound by law."

"Bound by law," Victoria sneered. "We could also add friendship and stupid loyalty." She walked to the window and looked at the garden. What the hell was she going to do? Where would she begin? "When did you find out about the bastard?"

There was silence.

"Dear God, you've known that long?" She fingered the pearls at her neck, which she'd had to ask Audrey to help her put on. "Were there others?"

"No."

"How old is this Demelza?"

"Twenty-five."

Victoria closed her eyes. That was when she'd forced Charles to have one more go at fertility treatments and they had barely been speaking to each other. She had seen forty looming and knew time was running out. But time had never been the problem. Her bloody body had been the problem. The same one that could have been an Olympic swimmer had her father not said it was a waste of time, that it wasn't appropriate for his daughter. Had Perry been athletic and in the same position then he would have encouraged him. But she had been born to breed and that was the one thing she couldn't do.

"Who was the mother?"

"A woman called Morwenna Williams." He shook his head. "I'm so sorry." Sebastian reached out to stroke her shoulder, but Victoria pulled back.

"You!" She shook her head. "It's bad enough to know that Saint bloody Charles broke his marriage vows and had a mistress but you, Sebastian John Andrew Roberts, you *knew*." She laughed bitterly. "Your betrayal is almost worse, but then I suppose I deserved both in your eyes." She turned away. She couldn't bear to see the look on his face. Placing her elbows on to the table and then her head into her hands, she tried to think clearly. The law would be on her side. But, and it was a big but, even if she clawed back the money from Demelza Williams would there be enough?

"Was this woman behind this change in Charles's will?"

"Maybe."

"The bitch." Victoria sat up. "Where is she now? Had he seen her every time he came to London?"

"No." Sebastian sat next to her. "It ended years ago."

"If that was the case then how could she be involved?"

"She died about two months ago."

What could she do? Yet again she was left feeling powerless. Bile rose in her throat. God, she hated her father still. But Charles was worse than her father. Every man she had ever loved in her life had betrayed her and now even Sebastian.

This was a dream and Demi would wake to find that she was broke and Matt had posted the video of her having sex with him on the Internet. That was the reality of her life. Being a wealthy heiress wasn't. The priest had been charming but had been called away. He'd asked her to wait here and Sebastian Roberts would join her shortly. Her thoughts circled around. She owned half a house and about two million pounds. *Two million pounds.* She'd thought her mother's life insurance of ten thousand pounds was a fortune.

Yet there seemed to be coded messages in everything that had been said. Everyone but her had understood the subtext. Like why had Charles left her half a house? Why couldn't he have just left her money as he'd done his nephew? Instead, she had to deal with his wife and that, Demi could see, was going to be an issue.

Her phone pinged. It was Sophie.

How's it going? Has he left you anything worthwhile like money? Sx

What should she say?

Yes. Tell you more tonight. Dx

She looked towards the bar to find the source of a burst of raucous laughter. She was outside all of this, but she felt as if she was being sucked into a whirlpool. It was a feeling she couldn't explain, but fear swirled around her. This legacy wasn't the good news it appeared on the surface. Below there were issues that would pull her down and that was the last thing she needed.

The solicitor walked in and stopped at the bar. He picked up menus and joined her. "I have it on good authority that the best thing on the menu is the bangers and mash today, although that won't do my waistline any good." He patted a flat stomach. "Now, Demelza, I imagine you have many questions but shall we order lunch first?"

She nodded. "Please call me Demi. I never use Demelza."

He frowned. "Well, Demi, what's it to be? Bangers and mash or toad in the hole?"

She didn't fancy either. "A Cheddar ploughman's, please."

"Good choice. I'll just go and order it." He smiled at her. "A glass of wine?"

She nodded. Wine might help her think.

"White or red?"

"White please, dry." He nodded and walked to the bar. What should she ask first? Questions about her father? What she'd heard about him today didn't fit with the picture of him she had from the realities of her life. And her father apart, Demi wasn't so sure about the inheritance.

"Done. Now, where shall we start?" He looked at her with moody grey eyes.

She cleared her throat. "I was just wondering that myself."

"What's the biggest question in your mind?" He leaned back against the banquette and she felt his scrutiny.

She opened her mouth to say exactly what was on her mind at that moment, which was — is Victoria Lake as big a bitch as she appeared? But thought better of it. "Tell me about Charles Lake."

"That's easy." He smiled. "I've known Charles since I was six. We went to primary school together and he defended me against a crowd of bullies. Charles was big for his age at that point. He hit one on the nose, who then ran to the teacher with blood running down his face." He shook his head. "When the teacher came out to find Charles, I tried to step in and take the blame, but he wouldn't have it and he never told the teacher why he'd hit the kid. He was sent to the headmaster and bore the detention given without another word about it." He sipped his wine. "That sums up the man he became. He was ruthless in business, but fair, and always looked out for those less fortunate."

She leaned forward. "That doesn't fit, though." She stopped, wondering if she should say what was on her mind, but his smile encouraged her. "He was a man who cheated on his wife and then didn't provide for his child." And hadn't loved her, she added silently. She watched him digest the information and she couldn't be positive, but she thought he was preparing a solicitor-type answer that would tell her nothing at all.

"True; on the surface that is indeed what happened, but as life has gone forward, I have learned that very often things aren't how they appear. In a way, like the story, I just told you. Charles was called a bully by his teacher and headmaster — and yet that was so very far from the truth. He was a defender, not the one doing the bullying."

Demi squinted. "Everything depends on your point of view. We struggled financially, I never knew a father's love, and Victoria's husband was unfaithful. These too are facts."

He smiled. "Yes, the world is mostly grey. But I must correct one thing. Your father loved you. You should remember that."

"I have no recollection of him at all." As she said these words, she thought of the pictures in her grandfather's photo album.

"I can tell you that you were always in his thoughts and that the pain of losing you haunted him."

"Not enough to do anything about it."

Sebastian laughed dryly. "It looks that way, but he was respecting your mother's wishes."

Demi frowned. "My mother's wishes?"

"Yes, it was her decision that Charles should not have anything to do with your life in any way. Charles, being the man he was, had to respect that because he chose not to leave Victoria."

And therein lies the problem thought Demi. Victoria must have had him right under her well-groomed thumb.

Summer

*Say not you know another entirely till you have
divided an inheritance with them.*

Johann Kaspar Lavater

CHAPTER
TWELVE

Leaning on his cane, her grandfather waited on the platform. A smiled spread across his face as Demi stepped out of the carriage. A kind man helped her unload all of her bags and boxes off the train. There were two large suitcases and three bin bags full of stuff plus her portfolio and desktop computer. That was her life except for the laptop bag slung over her shoulder. Nothing was left in London.

"Hello, my girl. I've brought the car. I thought we might need it and I can see we do."

"Sorry."

"Nothing to be sorry about. I can manage one bag, but I think we'll need a few trips."

"You're not to carry anything!"

"Nonsense. I may be moving into an old people's place, but I'm not an invalid yet."

Demi was going to argue, but then saw the look on his face and gave him the lightest bag. The station was now deserted so she felt they could safely leave things on the platform and together they walked to the car and she made him stay put while she went back and forth with her belongings. In the end, there was no room for her in the car and she walked to her grandfather's once she'd made him promise not to unload the car without her. It was obvious that his hip had deteriorated further in the three weeks she'd been in London.

She was thankful he was so understanding. He seemed to take everything in his stride but her move here had come too late to stop his transfer to the care home. If she had descended on him even two months ago, he might have been able to remain in his own home. But the wheels were too far in motion to stop. In any event, there were his memory lapses. She didn't know if these were just normal old age ones, or a sign of something more serious, in which case he would need more professional care. Then there was the fact that the landlord had relet the house and the tenants were moving in in just over a week.

Her grandfather, despite his promise, was trying to pull a bag out of the boot when she got there. "Stop!" Demi sprinted the last stretch. "You promised."

"I couldn't help myself — and if I can't lift it, how can you?" He stood back as Demi arrived, panting from the run.

"Good question — but I can." She took the handle from him, bent her knees and heaved the largest bag out.

"I can roll it to the steps." He looked apologetic and Demi just wanted to hug him. He loved her. He was trying to help and thank goodness he was here. Otherwise she would be homeless. She was such a fool, but now was not the time to dwell on that. Once a fool didn't mean always a fool. She could and would learn from her mistakes. She would trust no one and all would eventually be fine.

But right now she had to get everything out of her grandfather's car. Then she would figure out what to do. Who knew when she would receive her inheritance from her father, and the insurance company was still holding on to her mother's money. Sebastian had asked her to a meeting at Boscawen in two days' time. He seemed to think that a meeting on site would help things but Demi just didn't see how meeting on Victoria's ground was going to change anything. The woman hated her, which was fair enough in her opinion.

The more worrying thing was her grandfather's health and his move to the care home tomorrow. She wouldn't think about where she would live the day after that when she had to be out of the house so that it could be cleaned for the incoming tenants.

"Eat child." Her grandfather looked at all the food still on her plate and then at Demi.

"Sorry, I'm a bit distracted."

"I can see that, but eat your dinner and make my last night here a memorable one." He smiled.

"I'm so sorry."

"No need. Although the timing of this move could have been better." He passed the bowl of peas and Demi dutifully ladled a spoonful on to her plate. It was a delicious meal of roast lamb, roast potatoes and peas and there was a trifle sitting on the counter. She had to find a way to do justice to it and not just move the pieces around on the plate. He'd worked so hard to make it special.

"This is really delicious. Where did you learn to cook?"

He laughed. "Not from your grandmother, that's for sure." He glanced at the dresser. "My mother was a fabulous cook and worked as one so I learned from her."

"Is that where the dresser comes from?"

"No, your great-grandparents used to farm not far from here." He looked out of the kitchen door to the garden. "When your grandmother and I married they gave us the furniture to begin our new life."

"What a lovely gift."

"It was. Back then we were in a bigger house and I was teaching in north Cornwall, but by the time your mother was born we had moved to Falmouth and downsized." He nodded towards the dresser. "As you can see, it was a bit of a squeeze."

"So lovely though."

"Your grandmother hoped that one day she'd be able to pass it on to your mother, but Wenna had her own ideas."

"True, she did. Not that it would have fitted in the flat."

He laughed. "No, it wouldn't have. Not sure what to do with it now. Don't suppose you want it?"

"I'd love it but I have no place for it at the moment."

He smiled. "I hoped you'd say that. I spoke to one of my old students just in case you did and he will keep it in his garage along with the chairs in the attic if you

144

want them too. I can take a few pieces with me to the home to make it more personal, but otherwise I've sold everything here to the landlord." He took a deep breath. "I'm just sorry I had already promised to sell the car to my neighbour."

"It's fine." She touched his hand.

His face fell as it looked out to the garden. Everything was in glorious bloom. She reached across the table and took his hand.

"I'm sure the family moving in will look after it."

"Silly to be so connected to such a small garden but I do love it."

Demi sighed, wishing her mother were here and there was some way she could keep her grandfather in the house he'd called home for so long.

He stood, then stopped and looked at Demi. "Not that it's important, but your great-grandmother used to be the cook at Boscawen."

"The one you learned from?"

"Yes. I used to spend my summer holidays helping her in the kitchen."

"So you know Boscawen."

He nodded. "It's a special place."

"Tell me about it?" She put her fork down and studied her grandfather.

"Well, it's old. Part of it dates back to the 1500s and parts are very grand." He frowned. "I spent most of my time in the kitchen which desperately needed updating." He smiled. "You'll have to tell me if they've done anything, especially about the garden. I loved it. It was a magical place."

"I will do." She ate a mouthful of lamb. "Why do you think my father left me half of it?"

"Guilt would be my first thought." He stood up from his chair slowly. "But maybe it meant something to your mother and him for some reason."

She frowned. "Did he own it then?"

He shook his head. "It was sold to a stranger on the death of Peregrine Tregan in the 1980s." He sighed. "Funny how I can remember some things but can't remember others — like what I had for breakfast."

She came up to him and wrapped her arms around him. "We had porridge together in the garden." She kissed his cheek. Maybe the care home was the best thing until she had the money from her father and then she could find some place where they could both live.

CHAPTER
THIRTEEN

Victoria paced the kitchen. She couldn't believe she'd agreed to have a meeting here with the bastard. She was still reeling from what the lawyers' fees were estimated to be for contesting the will on so many fronts, so before she set forth on that path she was going to try and appeal to everyone's sense of what was right and just. It was not in any way correct that she, Charles's widow, should be left so little. If she could claw back the extra money from the charities, she could offer the bastard a lump sum and buy her out of Boscawen. Of course, Victoria would still have the problem of not having sufficient funds to fulfil her plans, well, at least not quickly.

Sam walked out of the kitchen garden and turned to the left. Victoria stopped pacing, thankful that at least she had enough funds to continue to pay his salary. And having looked closely at the accounts, she could just about continue to run the house and the cleaner. But there wasn't anything spare. She could afford to eat, but that was the least of her concerns. Boscawen wasn't cheap and she wasn't sure that she could afford the additional help she'd had recently in the garden, two boys who weren't without cost. She rubbed her temples. Why were they having this meeting now, when she hadn't heard back from the charities?

At the sound of the gravel crunching in the drive she smoothed her hair and walked to the front door. She had to make Demelza feel as unwelcome and uncomfortable as she possibly could. No, not uncomfortable — guilty. Demelza had no right to Boscawen, although Victoria had to admit that she did have a right to something from Charles other than his genes. She frowned. According to Sebastian, Charles had not paid anything for the child's upkeep and this didn't fit with the man she knew her husband to have been. For heaven's sake, he seemed to have been intent on paying for the education of every bright but poor child in Cornwall. And as the poorest county in the United Kingdom, that had taken a great deal of his fortune already. Cornwall had once been the richest of counties and now, like Victoria herself, it was on the bottom. How could he have done this to her?

She opened the front door. Sunlight streamed in and she knew she had to make this work. Somehow she had to save Boscawen. She didn't know why. Victoria had no one to pass it on to, but it was her legacy. The garden, planned and loved by her great-grandmother, was what she would leave to the world. The name of Tregan would be associated with all that was best in gardens, Cornish gardens. That was what she'd planned to tell Charles, that they would leave the estate to the National Trust or something to be a benefit for all. He would have agreed with that plan she was sure. It was charity, after all. Why had she delayed mentioning it?

She sighed. Now was not the time to dwell on the past. She had to make the future work.

She put a smile on her face and stepped out of the shadow of the door and on to the drive to greet her husband's child and her co-owner of Boscawen. Ice circled her heart at the thought, but she ignored it and kept walking to the car. Sebastian slid out from behind the wheel of the Jaguar.

"Good afternoon, Tori." He shaded his eyes with his hand, looking around. Victoria noticed Sam, with a wheelbarrow, clearing the bed below the plum trees espaliered along the wall. He had stopped to look at the newcomer.

Victoria's glance fell away from Sam and on to Demelza as she came out of the car. She was so pale, unnaturally so. Even Charles with his doughy skin had more colour than that. Did she never go out of doors? Her mouth opened and formed an O shape, then she fell and Sam rushed to pick her up.

"Good lord, what has come over her?" Victoria looked at the limp body in Sam's arms as he carried her into the drawing room. She knew Boscawen was impressive, but not that impressive. Of course, it would be overwhelming for one who hadn't grown up with it or anything like it — another reason why Charles's daughter shouldn't own half of it.

Demi shivered and a soft blanket covered her. Images ran through her mind — giants and eyes and her mouth tasted of stale ginger nut biscuits. She hadn't had that nightmare in years, yet here in Cornwall the images from it kept drifting into her daytime consciousness. But it wasn't the giant or the eyes that knocked her off her feet. It was the door. She knew that door.

When little, she would wake from the nightmare screaming for help. Her mother had told her the dream was from the time when her appendix burst. She had suffered terribly from the anaesthesia and an antibiotic and while she'd been medicated, her mother explained, Demi must have muddled images from films and books. These things had grown into her nightmare.

But now Demi knew that it wasn't something her imagination had created under the influence of drugs. It came from Boscawen's door. She didn't know how she knew it, or what the giants and eyes had to do with Boscawen, but her young mind had connected them and the terror she'd experienced then still felt real.

A cool hand touched her forehead and she opened her eyes.

"Hi. How are you feeling now?" a deep voice asked.

Demi blinked and she focused, staring into the most beautiful blue eyes she'd ever seen. "Um, not sure."

"That was quite an entrance." His Australian accent made her smile.

"Not intentional."

"I'm Sam, by the way." His eyes seemed to dance with silent laughter.

"Demi."

"I know. You look like your father in a way." He tilted his head to the side. "And you're the cause of all the drama."

She frowned.

"Only kidding. Sorry. Bad time to try and joke."

She smiled at his sorrowful expression. "It was, but I'll forgive you this time."

"Pleased to hear it. Now let me begin again on a slightly better footing." He grinned. "Do you always make such an entrance or was it nerves?"

She swallowed, her mouth still dry with the taste of ginger. "Thankfully just nerves." And the knowledge that somehow she'd been to Boscawen before. She didn't know how, but her skin crawled with recognition.

"What on earth was going through your mind bringing her here?" Victoria stood in the hall facing Sebastian.

"It's hers now too."

She crossed her arms against her chest. It was the only way to stop herself from hitting him at the moment. "Don't be so ridiculous! Boscawen can never be hers."

"Tori, you're being unreasonable and you haven't a leg to stand on legally."

She ground her teeth. "Why did you let him do it? You *know* what it means to me?"

"It was his to do with what he pleased, and he *has* provided for you."

She turned away from the pious look in his eyes. He could take the high ground. He had always done the right thing. Stepping back when she'd wanted him to fight. Always being the better man, the better person. In fact, the more she thought about it, the more she knew the reason Charles gave so much to charity was to try and be more like Sebastian. Charles had known, of course, where her heart had remained all these years and look where it had taken her — sharing her home with Charles's love child.

"Sebastian, you know as well as I do that there is no way to make this sharing of the estate work and Charles didn't leave me enough to buy her out."

"She has a name, Demelza, or Demi as she prefers. She is a good kid."

"She's not a kid but a grown woman. She even has," she paused, turning to glance into the room, "Sam eating out of the palm of her hand."

Seb grinned. "Jealous, are we?"

She squinted, trying to read the body language. Sam was on his knees beside the bastard where he had gently deposited her on Victoria's favourite chair. She had seen the look on his face when he'd scooped her up. He was smitten. How did it happen so quickly? To the best of her knowledge he'd not been involved with anyone during his two years in Cornwall. Not that he didn't have a social life, but there had been no one in particular. She'd listened carefully to the grapevine, but it carried nothing of note. And yet it was so obvious that he was falling under the bastard's spell.

"Tori."

"Don't Tori me! Charles had no right to give my home away or to put me in this precarious situation."

"You could sell and move to London."

She swung round with fists held tight to her sides. "All my life I have done what I was supposed to. Lived where I was told and left the place that I loved most

152

because I didn't have a right to it, and now you ask me to walk away from the only thing I have ever wanted?"

He spoke quietly. "I've only ever asked one thing of you."

"That's not fair." She released her fists. "You left."

"Not for ever. You knew that."

Victoria sighed. "It's history and this is now; this is *mine* now." She looked again into the drawing room and saw them speaking. Victoria accepted that she had to stop thinking of Demelza as the bastard, but she didn't want to. "Charles never understood me, but I had thought he understood what Boscawen meant to me. I clearly had that wrong, very wrong." Her shoulders fell and tiredness swamped her. She turned to look at Sam, who was still at the girl's side. He was young enough to be her son, the child she'd never had. Of course, so was the girl.

"Let's get this blasted meeting over with." Victoria marched towards the room.

Demi straightened in the chair. "Who are you, Sam?" She studied him, noting his tan. His hands were rough and there were dirt patches on his forearms. As she looked up she noticed a twig in his brown hair. She smiled.

"The gardener."

That explained the twig. "Do you like it here?"

He nodded. "It's a good place to be."

She glanced around the room, pushing away the déjà vu feeling that something bad had happened here. She rubbed her temples. Nothing made sense and she needed to have a clear head. Sebastian had told her that Victoria was hostile although she hadn't needed anyone to tell her that, and he had outlined Demi's options to her on the journey to Boscawen.

In the hall she could see Victoria and Sebastian talking. Their voices were hushed so she couldn't make out what they were saying, but the body language between them was confusing. One moment it was very formal and then the next they had moved closer together. One made a step forward and the other stepped back but sometimes not the full way almost as if they were dancing. She squinted, trying to figure it out.

Suddenly Victoria turned her way and caught Demi's glance. Demi froze. Forget a rabbit in the headlights, this was worse. The hate in that glance was lethal. She took a deep breath. There was a fight ahead and she needed to be strong. A small involuntary laugh escaped from her mouth.

"Are you OK?" Sam rested a hand on her arm. The contrast in skin tones was startling.

Demi looked away from the dark and pale. "Yes, I think so. What is she like?"

"Mrs Lake?"

She nodded.

"She's determined and a great boss."

Determined. Hmm. That was obvious as Sebastian and Victoria left the hall and came towards them. Demi turned away from them and studied the room. It was large, with four French windows opening on to a terrace filling the room with light. But heavy velvet curtains swamped the lines of the windows and while the furniture was good, the fabrics were bland. Good bones but no panache. Several possible styles could be used to make this room special, instead of country house meets the seventies. Having seen Victoria's Chanel suit she had expected a house that would be just as designer, but Boscawen, or at least this room, was tired. Surely they'd had the money to invest in a decorator if that wasn't Victoria's thing?

"How are you now?" Sebastian sat on the sofa.

"Better, thank you." She looked from him to Victoria. Her face was a composed mask. None of the hatred she had seen a few moments ago was visible.

"Good, then if Tori would sit and Sam . . ." He smiled at him. "If you'd excuse us, please."

"Of course." Sam gave Demi an encouraging glance then left the room after nodding to Victoria.

Demi watched him walk out of the door and wondered what came next.

Victoria sat in the wing armchair. It was just like her father's had been, even down to the brown velvet. She stroked the nap of the fabric. This was her house. It would not belong to Demelza. Her jaw clenched as she thought about Charles and what he had done, landing her with his daughter. When had he made that decision? She had asked Sebastian, but he had simply said that Charles had been doing alterations on the will up to the moment he left London. Had he done this because he had heard her and Adam? Were these instructions Charles's new or old?

"You've both now had a chance to digest the contents of Charles's bequest." Sebastian looked at Demelza and then turned to Victoria. Victoria had more than looked: she had dissected it to see if there were any cracks to exploit. When she'd found none she'd tried to wheedle out of Sebastian any possibilities and finally, when that failed, she had turned, at great cost, to a solicitor recommended by Audrey.

"It was his intention that the two of you should share Boscawen and that was why he left instructions to that effect." Sebastian paused and Victoria grimaced as she digested what he'd said. She needed to question him about these instructions.

"I'm aware this may well not be what either of you want."

Victoria looked at Demelza's pale face. She did not look keen or even vaguely interested in Boscawen and her full mouth was not quite pouting in the same manner that Charles's had when something displeased him. To think she had once thought that action sweet. Now she wanted to scream.

"I'm sure you are aware that you have only two choices." He glanced at each in turn. Victoria studied Demi. She was squaring her shoulders. "You can keep Boscawen and work together to run the estate or you can both sell."

Victoria read the girl's expression. She wanted to cut and run. It would be what Victoria would do in her shoes. It infuriated Victoria that, if she wanted Boscawen, she would have to let this affront to her marriage, to her person, to her soul have it as well.

Because no matter how Victoria had crunched the numbers she couldn't buy Demelza out. Even if she had been given the whole of Boscawen and the four million she would struggle to make it work.

"No matter which route you both choose, nothing can really be finalised until probate is complete and that will take a minimum of six months, more likely a year." He stood and walked to the nearest window. "Whether keeping it and working together, or selling it, you will both need to do your utmost to make Boscawen an attractive proposition for potential buyers. An estate of this size has limited options. Although it reaches the river, you can't build there as the woodland is protected." He turned to look at them. "This lessens the value substantially. You could, however, repair and improve the access to the quay for a start then possibly be granted permission to rebuild and extend the boathouse that once sat there."

"Damn it, Sebastian!" Victoria stood and looked at Demelza, who now sat like a frightened animal. "This is untenable."

"What do you want to do?" Demelza rose.

Victoria looked at her intently and her voice was deeper and huskier than Victoria had expected.

"I want Boscawen. I would have thought that was obvious."

"Without me."

"But of course." Victoria forced her mouth into a pleasant smile. Maybe she could be persuaded to just hand it over, guilty that she was receiving something she had no entitlement to. Victoria's nose twitched. It might not work, but it was worth a try.

"I don't want Boscawen." Demi's voice wobbled a bit.

"Excellent." Victoria smiled. This could be easy.

"So buy me out."

"Before you two go any further: you forget that nothing can be done until probate is completed and the taxman paid, so there is no point in having this discussion now. Today is about starting to communicate."

Demi looked at Sebastian. He'd been kind, but he was deluding himself if he thought there was any halfway ground on this. A brief look at property prices in Cornwall had revealed that the estate must be worth at least five million pounds. So her share was half of that plus the other two million, less what tax had to be paid. She wasn't sure what provision had been made for that.

It was more money than she ever even dreamt of, except the one time when she'd bought a rollover lottery ticket. Now she'd won a lottery she hadn't even entered. Whereas Victoria no doubt felt she'd been robbed. Of course, Demi had been robbed too, robbed of her father, robbed of time with him and of his support while growing up. Not that her mother hadn't been wonderful, she had. But all those years Demi had believed he was dead, he'd been living not far away in London — and that hurt.

"Sorry to interrupt, Mrs Lake." Sam stood just outside on the terrace. "But the delivery of trees is here."

"Trees?" Victoria frowned.

"Apple trees, the ones you ordered."

"Bugger!"

Demi's eyes opened wide. What on earth was Victoria doing buying apple trees? On the estate paperwork she'd been given it stated that there were five orchards. What on earth did she need more apples for?

"What should I tell them?"

Demi watched Victoria flush then cough before she spoke. "Have them put them by the barn and we can deal with it from there."

"Here's the paperwork." Sam handed it to her with a pen. The colour drained from Victoria's face. Demi wondered how much these trees cost. Sebastian had told her that Victoria would probably not be able to buy her out of Boscawen.

He'd also suggested Demi move into the house for the time being. Uncertain, she had brought a small bag with her, leaving the rest of her belongings in the garage of her grandfather's friend, along with the furniture he was keeping for her. But move in with the devil? She had a feeling that living with her housemate might be more like living with an angry tiger. Still, if she didn't, she had to find somewhere else pretty sharpish to spend the night.

"I approve of the selection of trees, by the way. Thanks for taking on board what I said." Sam smiled at

Victoria and Demi thought she'd bite his head off as she thrust the paperwork back at him.

Victoria swung around. "Demelza, why are you here? You don't belong here. Boscawen is my family home and you have nothing to do with it."

Demi grabbed the back of the chair she was standing by for support. The venom expressed in those words said so much more than get lost. Demi had been prepared for get lost, but Victoria made it sound as if Demi wasn't worthy, that in some way she was beneath notice, that she could be walked all over.

"Charles Lake — my *father* — left me half of this estate and I have every right to be here."

"He had no right! And a bastard has no right to inherit, never has."

"Tori, you are way out of line — and legally wrong."

"Piss off, Sebastian." Victoria swept out of the room and into the garden.

Demi sank into the nearest chair. She really might have to live here for the moment, but it didn't look as if it would be fun.

CHAPTER
FOURTEEN

The sun was hot on her back as Victoria strode towards the barn. She hoped that Sam had known which one she meant. Only one of them had a reliable water supply and those young trees would need a lot of water. What had she been thinking when she ordered them? Had it been an act of defiance?

She rounded the corner walking down the path between the house, the kitchen garden and the elder wood. It was clear where Sam had cut the trees back. The wood had always stood close to the house, bringing it good luck through the centuries. All the Tregans had been almost fanatical about the wood — except for Perry's wife, Julia. She had cut the elder wood and broken the pact between the trees and the Tregans. Even Edith and Gladys had agreed that elder wood was vital to the estate. They certainly hadn't agreed on much else. Victoria's mouth twitched, thinking of the bickering of the two women. Each told her different tales but in the end it was always about preserving the family and Boscawen.

The air was cooler in the cover of the trees. Despite the dry weather, she could still smell damp earth. Sunlight fell deep in the wood, capturing a butterfly in a shaft. It darted about the ferns that covered the ground. Why had she bought three hundred two-year-old apple trees at twenty pounds each? Six thousand pounds. Just a week ago, she wouldn't have thought anything of spending that amount. In fact, she hadn't. But now that was a vast expenditure of capital and it was just the start. She would need to hire in more help to plant them. It would be a backbreaking job for just two of them.

She grinned, thinking of the look on Sam's face. He was delighted she had listened to him and trusted his judgement. At the same time he had guessed the situation she now found herself in. In the past, she would have been the widow pushed into the Dower House as her great-grandmother and then her grandmother had been while the heir was installed in the main house. Now the Dower House belonged to another family and she and the heir had to share Boscawen. But it was ludicrous for anyone to expect her to live with her husband's daughter — to have to look at the embodiment of his infidelity every day. She may have slept with countless men, but she had never loved them. She had never betrayed Charles in that manner. She had loved him the best that she could in the circumstances.

She laughed. She should have divorced him once it was apparent that they couldn't have children. But Charles was Catholic — well, so was she, but it didn't mean the same things to her. She had converted to marry him, to marry his money. She had spoken the words and that was all. So divorce hadn't been on

162

Charles's agenda. He had been true to his faith and to his vows to her. Yet he had had a love affair that had produced Demelza.

Looking back, she thought they could have tried to get an annulment. She was sure she'd read that not having children was grounds. He'd gone against his beliefs to have all the fertility treatment and that demoralising experience was what really had driven them apart.

Now Sam stood with three hundred pots in front of him, trying to rig up some sort of sprinkler. If they didn't act quickly, it would end up as the equivalent of throwing the money to the east wind, which was just picking up and stirring the leaves on the trees in the orchard beyond. The field to the left had been an orchard in the past, but after the Second World War it had been grubbed. The trees were old and there was no outlet for the fruit. Other markets had taken over. By the time the sixties had rolled around, another orchard had been destroyed. All had changed.

"Mrs Lake," Sam said, "I'll have to head into Falmouth tomorrow morning to pick up the hardware I'll need to set up a watering system. Today I'll water each one by hand but even once they are in the ground they will need watering every day." He looked her in the eye. "I thought you were going to order for winter delivery."

She heard the accusation. It would have made much more sense. There was less for them to do in the winter. But late June, when the garden was at its growing best,

163

was madness. She was touched by madness at the moment. "I know. I haven't been myself recently."

"You won't be for a while." He squinted, looking out on to the field. "Have you called Adam?"

She shook her head. Her body tightened at the thought of him.

"He came by yesterday; you haven't returned his calls and he's worried."

She was being told off. She laughed. Her gardener was ticking her off. "Thank you for relaying the message." She smiled at him and walked away with one last look at her folly.

Strange noises came from Victoria's old bedroom. What on earth was happening? She marched down the corridor, frowning. The door opened as she took the handle. She walked straight into Sebastian who tripped and they both fell on to the bed.

"I think we may have been here before." Victoria rolled off him and on to her side.

"I think you're right." He looked to the window.

"Yes, you crept through it more than a few times." She smiled. "Sadly, the wisteria that you climbed is gone."

He stood up and looked down on her. "Good memories."

"Hmm." She sat up. "What on earth are you doing in here?" Then she noticed the bed she was sitting on was made. She stood. "What do you think you are doing?"

"Getting a room ready for Demi."

She wanted to laugh as they stood on either side of the bed. The last time she'd been in a bedroom with him had been years ago. She'd been drunk and had tried to get him to make love. He'd refused. Now they were standing over a bed he'd made for Demelza. As if she would let the woman stay in her house.

"Forget it, Seb. It's not happening." She walked out of the room, slamming the door behind her.

"Sebastian, I don't feel comfortable about staying here." Demi tucked a strand of hair behind her ear. She felt uneasy on so many counts. How could she say she knew she'd been in the house before? It must have been when she was very young. Had Charles brought her here? Why had this place featured in her nightmare?

"I can understand. But Tori's bark is worse than her bite."

Demi raised an eyebrow.

"Believe me, I know her." He gave Demi a rueful smile.

"How long had Charles owned the house?"

"Just over two years. Why do you ask?"

"It's just that Victoria is so attached to it."

"Ah, Boscawen had been in her family for generations until it was sold on her brother's death in 1984." He carried her bag up the broad staircase. That didn't explain how Demi could have been here before, but it told her why Victoria was so determined. And it meant her great-grandmother had worked for Victoria's family. Demi wondered if Victoria was aware of the connection.

165

Following Sebastian, she noted the grand proportions of the hall. Like the drawing room, the hall faced west, capturing the afternoon sun. She was sure the large flagstones would be warm if she slipped off her shoes and walked in bare feet. The front door was still wide open in welcome, but Demi knew there was no welcome here and that there never had been, not for her.

"Are you all right?" Sebastian stood halfway up the staircase.

Her skin crawled. Panic and pain filled her thoughts. She put her hands to her temples.

Sebastian touched her arm. "Are you still feeling unwell? You've had so many changes recently."

"It's not that." She took a deep breath. "Well, that might be contributing to it, but," she paused, "there's no way I could have been here before, is there?"

He looked away from her. "The house has been owned by other people as I mentioned."

"Of course." She tried to smile. She must be imagining things. Maybe her mother had been right and she had read something about a place like this. "Sebastian, one more question. Why didn't my father want me?"

"Oh, Demi, he loved you more than I can begin to convey, but life isn't simple." He shrugged and led her on up the stairs. When they reached the landing, Demi stopped to look down. The walls were trapped in a Victorian time warp, painted dark burgundy, so the hall was bright enough at this time of day but in the evening it would be terrifying.

"Did you know that Charles came to my mother's funeral?"

He stopped. "Yes."

"Do you know why he didn't speak to me?"

"I . . ." He looked down. Victoria had entered the hall and kicked off her shoes. Demi watched as she picked a wilted bloom off the flower arrangement on the console table. Spikes of deep purple buddleia set off the rich green of the laurel, but the beauty was lost in the dim burgundy of the walls.

"I know he planned to speak to you but it hadn't seemed the right time."

"Oh."

Victoria looked up and exchanged glances with Demi. There was pure hatred in the older woman's eyes and Demi could understand why. Her father had cheated on his wife and now she was forced to share her home with his child.

"Sebastian, what the hell do you think you're doing?" Victoria's clear-cut voice rose up to them.

"Just taking Demi to her room."

Victoria had begun to walk up the stairs, but stopped and placed her hands on her hips. "I told you no, earlier."

"Victoria, you have ten bedrooms."

"No."

"Fine, but she stays tonight." Sebastian sighed.

"No." She crossed her arms.

"You are behaving like a toddler."

Victoria stood her ground, staring Sebastian down. Demi wouldn't want to cross her, but just by existing she was doing that.

"It's my home and I don't want her here."

Demi came up to Sebastian and whispered, "I'm happy to leave. I'll try and find a B&B."

"Leave it with me. Why don't you take a walk in the garden? It's really beautiful."

Sebastian went down the stairs with her, providing a shield from Victoria's killing glance, and Demi slipped out of the door into a scented heaven.

All along a tall stone wall a bed was filled with roses. The colour began with deep blood red and, as the bed moved away from the house, the colour softened to pink fading to white. She stepped closer and bent to inhale the fragrance but stopped to check that she wasn't being watched. It was so odd to see the doorway that had featured for years in her nightmare currently bathed in a golden glow. It looked beautiful, not like the entrance to a house of horrors. She must have seen the house featured somewhere and now she needed to find a way to separate these feelings of dread from the reality.

It was a glorious June evening. As she turned down the drive, she saw the flash of purple-blue in the distant woods, late bluebells. Her breath caught and she remembered her grandmother's warning that she must never pick a bluebell or the fairies would steal her away. Eyes. Woods. Fear. Her mouth went dry.

She fled along the drive, leaving the house behind until she came to a track. The sound of water running and someone singing badly drifted towards her. It was a Beatles song and Demi was pretty sure the soloist was Sam. She could hear his Australian twang and it sounded so welcoming.

168

Kicking a stone, she made her way down the track until she saw him near a barn, watering tub after tub of Victoria's apple trees. To the left of her the field was already full of fruit trees. Why on earth did she need more?

"Hi." Sam waved.

"That's going to take some time."

"Tell me." He rolled his eyes. "Want to help?"

"Sure."

"Can you fill the next bucket and so on?"

She nodded and set to work, trying not to be distracted by his arm muscles rippling. He was so fit. Matt, who prided himself on being in shape, was weedy in comparison. His appeal also had something to do with the tan and eyes the colour of the bluebells she'd just seen. Sam looked, well, healthy, for lack of a better word. Demi swallowed. She wasn't sure she should be admiring him, but he was gorgeous and she was allowed to look.

Water began running over the edge of the bucket she was filling.

"Slacking on the job already?" He took the full one from her and she laughed.

"Yes, sorry, boss."

"So you're an heiress?"

Demi placed the hose into another watering can. As she let go of it to stand straight, it writhed and broke free, spraying them both with water.

He laughed. "Hey, that tells me."

"No, it's not that. I haven't given it a lot of thought." She wrinkled her nose. "Well, not quite true. It's all too complicated and I don't think it will stick. Victoria is contesting the will."

"Hmm. Did you know Charles?"

"No." Demi moved the hose to the next one, making sure it stayed put this time. "Again, that's not quite true either. I'm told I knew him when I was little, but I don't remember."

"That's a shame. Mr Lake was great." Sam wandered off and watered another tree. Demi stuck the hose into another bucket and picked up a full one, meeting Sam halfway.

"Thanks."

"This is going to take forever. Will you have to do this every day?"

"Yes, but tomorrow I'll buy the things to set up a watering system, whether it's a sprinkler or a leaky hose." He tilted his head and grinned.

"A leaky hose? Is that the latest in technology?"

"Very effective, if primitive. All afternoon I've been figuring out how to manage it. I'm not sure what was on Mrs Lake's mind when she ordered these trees to be delivered now. We'd spoken about a November or December delivery."

Demi bent down and read the description of the tree on one pot, which said the fruit produced large quantities of juice. "Apple juice?"

"More like cider." He looked to the orchard behind. "They used to produce a good cider at Boscawen and it was pretty continuous right up until the Second World War."

170

"Really?" Demi looked at the trees in front of her. She knew it was an orchard, although the trees weren't in straight lines but a bit haphazard.

"Yes, in fact, going way back, they would have paid part of the labourers wages with cider."

Demi smiled. "You know a lot about it."

"Not really, but I find it interesting."

"The history or the cider?"

"Both." He smiled. "The history of the place adds to the appeal."

"If she has all these trees already what on earth did she want more for?"

Sam shrugged. "I'm not sure. But she wants to restore the garden."

"This isn't the garden."

"True, but Mrs Lake is very attached to Boscawen."

"That I can tell." Demi rolled her eyes. "But so many more trees will produce so many more apples."

"These trees won't produce large amounts of fruit for a few years. And the ones she has aren't enough to make a truly commercial yield."

"Do you think she wants to make it commercial?"

"Good question." Sam wandered off with two full buckets and she filled more. Before long they had finished the task.

"Thanks for the help."

She smiled. "It was good to do something. I suppose I'd better head back to the house to find out if they have killed each other and if I need to find a B&B for tonight."

"No need for that. I can give you a bed."

Demi stepped back. She wasn't used to such forwardness unless it had strings attached.

"There are two bedrooms in the gatehouse," he went on, "so I've plenty of room."

Did he have an ulterior motive? No, she didn't think so. He was just a genuinely nice guy. "That would be kind, Sam. Thanks."

"Well, you own the place anyway." He grinned and she laughed. She supposed she did, after all.

"Let's go and get your things." He checked the tap was fully off and led the way along the track. Demi followed a few steps behind, wondering what Victoria would say about this new arrangement.

"Just what are you playing at, Seb?" Victoria glared at him. He had a lot of cheek to think that she would let Demelza Williams stay.

He placed Demi's small suitcase down. "I'm not playing at anything. She has every right to stay here."

"No, it's wrong, it's wrong on so many counts." Victoria studied his face, looking for clues to his thoughts but yet again he was wearing his poker face. "Are you trying to hurt me?"

"Never. I am simply doing what is right. Demi is Charles's daughter and he clearly stated that he wanted you two to share this house."

"Why?" She shook her shoulders. "He wanted to hurt me. He wanted to rub my nose in the fact that I was the barren one."

She turned back to the flower arrangement. This morning it had pleased her, but right now she just

172

wanted to throw it against the blood-coloured walls. She'd wanted the walls painted white, but Charles had insisted on returning them to the colour they had been when he had first come here to collect his younger brother, Perry's friend. That meeting had changed her world and obviously his.

"I don't think that was his intention. Charles was never vindictive, you know that."

"Hah. Maybe he'd come to it later in life." She thrust her hand in her pocket and played with her mobile. What had Charles heard? Would that have made him change his will? Adam had arrived about six thirty. Charles had cancelled his meal with Sebastian and worked on his will with someone then drove down.

"What were the most recent changes to the will?" Would Charles have taken Boscawen away from her in anger? Surely he'd known about the men. In the early days, she'd been discreet but as time passed, she'd become careless, not worrying who knew. She hadn't wanted to hurt Charles so much as she had gone beyond caring.

"What makes you ask that question?"

"Well, I last saw Charles's will five years ago. There was no mention of this child."

"There was always provision for her."

Victoria swung around opened her mouth but then closed it. Of course, Charles would have provided for her. "And this he kept secret from me. Can you tell me what the provision was back then?"

"No."

She balled her hands into fists. Five years ago they hadn't owned Boscawen. "You've mentioned that he left instructions for you. Just what were these instructions?"

"Sorry, client confidentiality."

"He's dead." She raised her eyebrows.

"It doesn't change anything."

"It changes bloody everything!" The man was just too frustrating, standing there having all the information she wanted and he wasn't playing. In fact, he hadn't played with her in forty-one years.

CHAPTER
FIFTEEN

Sam insisted on carrying her bag as they walked down the drive to the gatehouse. Demi shivered. The large rhododendrons were mostly finished but a few bright red flowers remained.

"You OK?" Sam's blue eyes showed concern. "You're cold."

"It's cooler than I expected after the heat of the day."

"Yes, a dampness fills the air here, making it feel colder. It's not much further to the gatehouse."

She glanced out of the corner of her eye to make sure there wasn't anyone watching them. Had Victoria followed them down the drive to make sure she was as far away as possible? The woman was a bitch. She had reason to be angry but did she have to be so nasty? It was hardly Demi's fault that things had turned out as they had.

"Is she always like that?"

"Who? Mrs Lake?"

Demi nodded as she noted some foxgloves by the oaks that bordered the small garden at the back of the gatehouse.

"No. She's always been a bit tricky and a bit of a hothead, but no, not nasty." Sam reached into his pocket and pulled out a large key. It looked to Demi as if this was the original lock from when the building was erected. She guessed it to have been in the late 1800s with its gothic windows and flourishes.

"Home." He held the door open for her and she opened her mouth in shock. The inside was sparse with white walls and sofas but accented by well-polished antique oak furniture. On the round table in the hall sat a joyful display of forget-me-nots with a few bluebells tumbling out. Demi stopped and stared at the flowers.

"I thought bluebells were protected."

"They are, but these late bloomers were caught in the mower by one of the boys and I couldn't bear to leave them lying on the ground." He touched a fragrant stem and somehow managed to turn one bell inside out without breaking it.

"Wow." She was struck again by how the colour of the flower matched his eyes, a blue purple.

"A skill my grandmother taught me."

Demi gave him a questioning look.

"She missed her native England and had bluebells planted in her Perth garden. When I was young, she told me that if I could turn a bell inside out without breaking it I would eventually win the heart of the one I love." He gave her a lopsided grin. "I remain hopeful but it hasn't happened yet."

She smiled. "I was warned away from bluebells. They are the fairies' plants. If you pick one, they steal you away." A cold draught ran across her neck as she spoke.

"Come in properly. You're chilly." They stepped into the sitting room.

176

"Oh, it's lovely." She glanced about, noting the pine plank floors covered with old rugs in muted tones.

"Thanks."

All the side tables and the desk were softly gleaming in the evening light flooding through the west windows. "Antiques?"

"Yes, I found them in the attic of Boscawen house and Mrs Lake told me I could use what I needed."

Demi glanced around again then turned to him. "I'm impressed. You have good taste."

"Not sure if I should be offended or complimented." He tilted his head. "Does your surprise mean that you thought I had appalling taste, or no taste, or it just wasn't the style you expected I'd have?"

She grinned. "The latter."

"Hmm. I wonder." He rubbed his chin in an affected manner and studied her. "I think you thought I'd have the leftovers of uni chic, for lack of a better description."

"What on earth does that mean?"

"Battered poster of Che Guevara and planks on bricks."

"It can be a good look."

"It can be for an eighteen-year-old, but much less so for a twenty-eight-year-old."

She laughed as she walked further into the sitting room. Here she was delighted to find more flowers tumbling from jam jars and coffee tins. The effect was perfect — a careless elegance.

Above the mantel hung an old coloured print of a schooner travelling down a river. From what little she knew, the scenery looked Cornish and the faded colours contrasted beautifully with the chunky dark frame. The whole look of the room felt colonial, but there was something else. It was the furniture. It looked similar to the pieces of her grandfather's that had been tucked away in the attic. Good solid country pieces; in fact, a bit more than that since they weren't rough but more sophisticated.

"Let me show you your room." Sam turned to the left and opened a door on to a small neat room holding a single bed. The walls, unlike the sitting room, were covered in cabbage-rose patterned wallpaper. It was enchanting and shouldn't work in such a small room but did.

"Intense, isn't it?"

"Yes." She reached out and felt the print on the paper, enjoying the textured surface.

"Everyone said to paint over it, but I couldn't."

"You were right." She smiled at him. "They were wrong."

"I'll leave you to unpack and then we should hit the pub. I think we've both earned a drink."

"Sounds like a great idea." She watched him pull the door closed behind him then checked to see if there was a lock on it and there was. It wasn't that she thought Sam wasn't trustworthy, but she barely knew him.

"You know you'll have to come to grips with this sooner or later, Tori." Sebastian measured the gin.

"No." Victoria accepted the drink that he handed her. "No, I don't. Why do I have to accept it?"

"Because it's airtight. Charles knew what he was doing."

She pressed her fingers against the cut edge of the crystal glass. Mild pain bit into her fingertips. When she released the pressure, blood rushed back to her fingers. She knew it was airtight, that was Charles all over, but that didn't mean she had to accept it. The only problem was the cost. Just asking a solicitor one question cost a fortune and Sebastian was one of the best available and he was telling her it was a lost cause.

"Trust me."

"Hah." She walked out to the terrace. Maybe she should have relented and let Demelza stay here. Because of her stubbornness Demelza was in the gatehouse with Sam and Victoria had seen the way he looked at her. How long would it take until something happened between the two of them if she stayed there? It would be a matter of days with young hormones involved.

"What's eating you?"

Lack of good sex, she thought, but turned to him and said, "Why did he do it? He could have settled a chunk of money on her and not given so much to the charities." She shook her head. "I know you know, Sebastian. And on that subject, why so much to the charities and what happened with his investments? It was unlike Charles to lose money. He was like Midas. If he invested in something, it flourished."

"I have to confess it has puzzled me." He leaned against the wall of the house. Golden light still hit the second-floor windows. The house had held up so well. Thank God that all the main work had been done while Charles had money. How was she going to make this work?

"I did ask his financial advisor for an accounting of sorts."

"And?"

"Well, that's the funny thing. He really couldn't say. He did say that Charles had seemed distracted this past year." Seb sighed. "I've reviewed his investments. All sound, but it looked like he took some risks back in April." He paused. "And it feels as if he lost his focus."

"You know why?"

He looked at her. "I might have an idea."

She clenched her teeth together. So like Seb to be silent. He should have fought for her years ago. That was all she had wanted.

She searched through her memories of the past year. Had Charles been any different? If he had, would she have noticed? Probably not, which said more than she liked about her treatment of her husband. Yet she'd done all that was required of her, including sleeping with him when he expressed interest, which of late hadn't been often, and it had been years since she had sought him out for sex. Sex. She must ring Adam. "He only made the changes about the house on the Friday in the late night meetings, didn't he?"

"Tori, I can't say." He looked away from her out to the fields. She knew he knew so much more than he was letting on and she needed to find it out.

"Loyal even now?"

"No comment."

"This whole friendship thing doesn't have to carry on after death."

He laughed. "Client confidentiality does."

"Always on the side of right." Somehow she needed to find out, because Charles must have heard her and Adam and, if he had, then dividing the house was his revenge.

"One can but try."

"Always the knight defending the side of right. Never been tempted to move to the dark side?"

"Oh, I've been tempted." His grey eyes never left hers as he spoke. Remembered passion ran through her.

Demi's muscles were already aching from helping Sam earlier. She was in no doubt why he was so fit. Gardening was hard work. Maybe walking to the pub wasn't a good idea but Sam said it wouldn't take long plus it was a beautiful evening. She looked up at him. He seemed to be lost in thought. "How long have you been working here?"

"Nearly two years." He turned to her.

"What's an Australian doing in deepest Cornwall?"

"I was at a loose end and the sailing's good." He slowed his stride down to match hers.

She couldn't comment about the sailing, but she knew the feeling of being at a loose end. Everything was up in the air and out of reach. "Were you a gardener in Australia?"

"No." He looked out over the hedge. She wondered what he could see because her view was of the hedge and the foxgloves in it.

Turning to her he smiled. "What about you? What do you do aside from being an heiress?"

She laughed. "Still not so sure about the heiress bit but I suppose you're right. Currently I'm an out of work . . ."

His phone rang and he slowed his pace. "Sorry, it's my mum." Demi tried not to listen but it seemed to be something about fruit trees.

They came to a crossroads as he hung up. Demi spun around and looked at the signpost.

"Are you OK? Sorry about that." He slipped his phone into his pocket.

"Not a problem — and I have a strange feeling I've been here before."

"Maybe you have."

She frowned. He was right. Her mother was from nearby and she might well have come this way with her before her parents went their separate ways or perhaps she'd even come with her grandparents. Was she making more of this than she should? She'd been to Cornwall as a child and she didn't remember it. Maybe because her mother was so upset by the split with Charles that she blocked it from both their minds.

"Not far now."

182

"Good." Her phone buzzed and she pulled it out. Matt's name flashed up on the screen.

Want you so bad it hurts. Come back. All is forgiven. We can make this work. xx

Her stomach clenched uncomfortably. Why wouldn't he just leave her alone?

Sam glanced at her. "You look a bit pale. All OK?"

"Fine, just not used to the walking, I guess," she lied.

"You'll need to get used to it living in the country. Nothing is right on your doorstep."

"Well, let's see how long I stick around."

"I hope it's for a while." He smiled then pointed. "There's the pub."

"Not a moment too soon for my feet."

He laughed. "I'll try and get us a lift back." The outside tables were filled and Demi's mood lifted as they walked inside.

"Hey, Sam didn't think you were going to make it."

"Miss darts? Not likely." He rolled his eyes and turned to her. "I never played the game before I arrived here and have only been on the team for a month."

A tall blond man came forward. "Hello, gorgeous, I'm Tom and you don't want to be with him. He's ugly, an Aussie, and crap at darts. I, on the other hand, am wonderful." He grinned.

Demi burst out laughing.

"What can I get you?" Sam was trying to frown at his friend, but not making a very good job of it.

"I'd love a glass of white, thanks."

183

"What type?"

Demi turned from Tom. "Something dryish."

"OK." Sam went to the bar. "Hey, Jamie are you selling the Cullen Sauv by the glass?"

"So, what's your name?" Tom moved closer and Demi stepped back, trying to decide if this was good-natured fun.

"Demi."

"Demi like the actress?"

"No, short for Demelza."

"Are you Cornish then?" He grinned.

"My mother was."

"Cool."

A crowd walked through the door led by Peta. This shouldn't have surprised Demi but it did.

Tom leaned closer and said, "The competition has arrived."

"Demi, great to see you here." Peta came straight up to her and kissed her cheek. "Your fortunes have changed." Peta studied her and Demi flushed. "Don't look so surprised. You and your inheritance made the local paper." Peta smiled. "I'm good but not that good." She looked around. "So where is this supposedly awesome team that we're going to slaughter." She turned back to Demi and said, "I only wish that I could see things like who wins matches and the like. I'd be rich."

Sam walked up to them carrying a pint and Demi's wine. He gave it to her and stood between her and Tom.

"Hi. I'm Peta."

184

"Sam."

Peta looked from Sam to Demi and then back again. "Hello, stranger, are you the ringer they brought in from Australia?"

"That's a good laugh." He shrugged.

"Excellent. I need a cider as I'm not driving." She went to the bar. "What ciders do you have?" She frowned looking at the options. "I should rephrase that: what Cornish cyders do you have?"

Demi noted Sam was listening carefully to the conversation. Peta was so pretty, if eccentric. They would make an interesting match.

"Hey, Sam, you're not buying the competition drinks? She gets better the more she has, not worse," Tom called from the other end of the bar.

"Thanks for the warning." Sam came closer to Demi. "Let me introduce you to the rest of the crew." He stopped halfway along. "Hi, mate."

"Sam."

"Demi, let me introduce you to Adam. A . . ." he paused, "frequent guest at Boscawen."

"Hello, Adam." Demi smiled at him. Adam seemed to be holding himself a bit apart from the rest of the crowd.

Sam took her hand and took her to where the team was gathering near the darts board. "Don't suppose you play?"

"Never."

"Well, there's always a first time for everything," he whispered in her ear.

CHAPTER
SIXTEEN

"Good morning, sleepyhead." A voice came from the other side of the door and Demi blinked, trying to remember where she was. Swirls of colour came into focus. She was at Sam's.

"Morning." Her voice sounded husky.

"Didn't think you'd want to sleep the day away and I'm off into Falmouth." The handle jiggled. "I have a mug of tea for you."

Demi leapt out of bed and released the lock on the door. She popped her head around it.

"Thanks." She held out her hand, keeping her body hidden. She was only wearing an old T-shirt.

"No need to lock the door. I don't sleepwalk and nor do I visit a woman's bedroom without an invitation." He tilted his head and kept his mouth in a straight line, but his eyes were smiling.

"That's good to know." Demi laughed at his attempt at an offended look. Despite his charm and his words, she would still be locking the door. "Can I come into Falmouth with you?"

"Was hoping you'd say that. How long do you need?"

She ran a hand through her hair. It didn't feel too bad. "Give me ten minutes."

"Shall I make you some toast?"

"I'm not really hungry yet."

"Sure?" He frowned. "Some say it's the most important meal of the day."

"I'm sure." Demi closed the door and took a sip of tea. At least when she was in Falmouth this morning she would have phone signal, she could go and see her grandfather and then she could chase the insurance company. She needed money of her own. On paper, she was rolling in it, but in reality she was down to ten pounds and needed to top up the credit on her phone. Maybe she could take out a loan against the estate. She would ask Sebastian about it.

After a quick shower she looked through the closet where she'd hung her few things. Putting on a sundress, she glanced out of the window to make sure she had the forecast right. Yes, there wasn't a cloud to be seen. She twisted her hair into a topknot then joined Sam by the front door.

"Morning again." He handed her a key.

She frowned. "What's this?"

"A key to the gatehouse. You won't be with me all the time so I want you to feel you can come and go as you please."

"Thanks." Demi swallowed. It was so kind. "I won't be relying on your hospitality forever."

"No worries. You're an heiress, after all, and will cast me off for some rich bloke soon."

She laughed. "But of course. It will be all fast cars and yachts in my future."

"Your chariot awaits you." He pointed to a beat up old 4x4 that had definitely seen better days.

In Falmouth, Demi left Sam and headed into the care home. Just one night in the gatehouse at Boscawen and she felt cut off from the world. Could it really have only been two days ago that her grandfather had moved in here? She asked the woman at the front desk if he was in his room.

"No, he's in the garden enjoying the lovely June sunshine." She pointed to a door and Demi walked out to her grandfather reading in the shade of a tree.

"Hello." She bent down and gave him a kiss.

"Wenna, how lovely to see you." He closed the book. "Just reading a bit of Dickens."

Demi sat on the bench beside him, noting the book was *Great Expectations*. "Well, what's it like here, Grandad?"

"Funny, I was going to ask the same of you." He smiled. "Not bad here, but the food isn't as good as mine."

"That would be difficult."

"True." He studied her face. "You look a bit tired. Don't you like the big house?"

"I'm not actually staying there." She grimaced, thinking of Victoria's behaviour yesterday.

"Didn't like it?"

"No. It's lovely but Victoria is . . ." she paused, thinking, "tricky, I think is the polite way to describe her."

"She has a bit of her great-grandmother in her, then."

"You knew them." She shook her head. "Of course you did."

"I told you, the family used to work the farm nearest the Dower House. Edith Tregan was a good but determined woman."

She crinkled her nose. Good and Victoria didn't belong in the same sentence. "I still don't understand why my father left me half of the house. He must have known it would upset his wife."

Her grandfather frowned. "Yes, I do remember hearing that they were childless." He turned the book in his hands. "He was quite besotted with you."

"Was he?" The pictures seemed to show that but it didn't fit with eighteen years of silence.

"Oh, yes, most definitely."

"Mr Williams, the physio is waiting for you." The care assistant held out his arm for her grandfather.

"Sorry, my lovely, must dash." He smiled. "You'll visit again soon?"

"Of course." She kissed his cheek then walked back out to the front to wait for Sam to collect her. She checked her messages and Facebook. More pictures of Maia's daughter filled her News Feed and sadly, according to Matt, they were still going out even though she had changed her status to single.

Victoria looked into Charles's study. "Seb, why are you still here? Don't you have a job to do?" It had taken days but he had cleared the top of the desk and the large leather sofa next to it had neat piles all over it.

"I can't see you taking the time to sort this." He looked up and smiled at her. Her heart stilled. Even now that smile still had power to move her. If she'd married him forty years ago would she still feel this way? Or would the tedium of marriage have killed the spark? Probably.

She put a mug of coffee on a mat. She wasn't sure why she bothered. The leather top was scarred with so many ring marks that you didn't notice the leather. "Fair comment. It would make good bonfire fodder."

He leaned back. "Much of it would, but I need to be sure there isn't anything of value in here."

"Shouldn't a junior be doing this?" She placed a hip against the desk.

He leaned back in the chair. "Probably, but somehow it would feel like a betrayal of an old friend."

"You and your damned loyalty. What did it ever get you?"

"Not you." He stood.

"That's history."

"Yes, ours." He stepped closer until he could stroke her hand with his with barely a movement. Memories . . . Once her whole world had stopped for him. Then he'd left to do his bit for the poor in Africa and she'd moved on, but where did it leave them now?

Her mobile rang. She took a step back and looked at the number. It was Adam. She couldn't keep dodging his calls yet longing for his body. Even she knew that life didn't work that way. She pressed the button. "Adam."

Sebastian picked up his mug and walked to the French windows. While Victoria listened to Adam express his sorrow and concern, she watched Sebastian walk away.

Sam and Demi had collected about twenty elderflower heads in the basket and were on their way back to the gatehouse. "So this is your second batch?" Demi asked.

"Yes, I was too eager with the last lot and bottled it too soon — and one of the bottles exploded." Sam took the basket from her.

She wrinkled her nose. "That must have been fun."

"That's one way to look at it." He gave her a sideways look as he pulled a key from under a geranium pot and unlocked the kitchen door. "The other way, of course, is that there was a sticky mess everywhere, including the ceiling."

"Nice." She looked around at the items he had out on the counter. "This looks a lot more technical than simple elderflower champagne."

"This won't be just any elderflower champagne — it will be mine."

"The explosive kind." She grinned.

"Funny." He grabbed a few of the bowls she'd seen him sterilise that morning.

"Can I help?"

"If you divide the flower heads up, after I put in the sugar we can fork them into it." He measured out the sugar.

"Fork?" She squinted at him.

"Yeah, use a fork to take the flower heads only and not the stems."

"Why?"

He lifted his eyes from the scale. "The stems add bitterness."

"This is a lot more technical than when Mum and I made it." When she and her mum had made it, it had always come out differently — well, variably would be more precise. One year it had been totally undrinkable. How they'd laughed.

He smiled. "I'm sure it is."

He went back to his task and she counted the flower heads out, making sure not to damage them. "I suppose you are planning to make elderberry wine too?"

His head flew up. "How could you tell?"

She pursed her mouth. "I don't know . . . maybe your attention to detail here."

His shoulders relaxed. "I suppose it's a bit of a giveaway."

"Does all of this really make much difference to the taste?"

He straightened after he'd finished with the sugar. "Yes. The smallest adjustments can really change things." He took a fork and a flower head. "This is what I want you to do."

She drew a deep breath. Those words sounded a little too close to what Matt has said to her too many times.

"Sorry, I forgot to say please."

She smiled and copied his action with the fork. Before long they were all done. "What now?"

He covered the bowls with clean tea towels. "We leave them for three hours then we add the rest of the ingredients."

"OK."

"Fancy a walk around your estate in the meantime?"

She laughed. "It hardly feels like mine. She won't even let me in the house."

"I'll make sure she doesn't see us then, if that would make you happy."

She grinned. "I'm only a *little* bit afraid of her."

He laughed as he locked the kitchen door behind them. "I'm not afraid of her now."

Victoria put the phone down. The cost was mounting as she investigated contesting the will and it looked as if there would be very little return for her investment, if anything at all. She sighed. She'd seen Sam and Demelza walk past the house and across a field. God, the situation was intolerable. Boscawen was *hers*. She went in to the hall, trying to form a plan. There had to be a way, but according to the solicitor no one was likely to think that she had been hard done by when she'd received what equates to possibly five million pounds.

When she looked at the figures, she could see that he had a point but when you considered that, as of the last will, she would have received over double . . .

Seb walked out of the kitchen.

"You." She clenched her jaw. He had answers and he wasn't sharing them.

"Hello, too." He gave her a lopsided smile. "I've asked Demi to come by for a bit of lunch."

"You what?"

"I've invited Charles's daughter to lunch."

"You think I'm going to prepare food for her?" Tension began in her toes and ran through her body.

"No, I would never assume that." He chuckled and went back into the kitchen.

"I'm not having her in the house."

"Too late." Sam stood in the hall behind her. "She's here with me."

"No!"

Seb appeared at her shoulder. "I'm just making sandwiches. Sam, why don't you take Demi to the south terrace and I'll join you in a minute."

He was always so bloody reasonable and now he was using his lawyer's charm to do what she said, but somehow also not do it. Victoria made fists then held them tight to her side. "Get her out of my house and off my land."

Seb touched her shoulder and she whipped around. "Get her out now."

She watched him send a look at Sam then he held her with both of his hands. "I know you are upset."

"Piss off."

"No, it's time you grew up, Victoria Rose Lake. Time to put past grievances behind you and embrace the future."

She pulled away, but he held tight, staring her in the eyes not flinching.

"You need to accept the situation you find yourself in and make the best of it." He released her. "All this rage does nothing but make you look a fool." He turned and walked into the kitchen. She stood, shaking. Had he just walked away from her again?

CHAPTER
SEVENTEEN

After yesterday's outburst Demi was stunned to be sitting here in Boscawen's kitchen. So her grandfather's guess had been right that not much had changed except for the atmosphere. She doubted there had been this much tension in here when her great-grandmother had been in charge. Demi looked down at the surface of her black coffee. Despite the cheery appearance of the kitchen, dread crawled over her. She couldn't place the source of it, but it might just be Victoria. Every time she looked up, Victoria's accusing glance burned into her. Yet a part of Demi's mind noted the kitchen was a fabulous place. The scrubbed pine table where she sat clutching the mug for dear life provided some distraction. The architect in her wanted to study the features of the kitchen from the huge granite lintel above the range to the row of Belfast sinks. Yet every time she looked to the left a draught circled around her legs raising goosebumps all over. Her nose twitched. She could smell ginger.

Sam appeared at the door bringing in the scent of fresh cut grass. Victoria frowned and Demi looked back down at her coffee again. She'd caught his smile and held it to her. Someone here genuinely liked her and wanted her around.

"Good. Have a seat Sam." Sebastian looked up from his computer. "Victoria, sit. Pacing around the table like a panther won't help."

She pulled out a chair opposite Demi so that every time she looked up Victoria filled her line of sight. This was intimidation at every turn and Demi was not going to back down, no matter how much Victoria pushed her. Not that Demi couldn't see Victoria's side of things.

"I've spent the past few days looking at the state of things here and what, if anything, you can do about it." Sebastian pulled out a notebook. "And I've consulted with Sam."

"Excuse me?" Victoria stood up again. She was like an edgy jack-in-the-box. "Sorry, Sam, you are a wonderful gardener but what business does he have in this, Seb? It's bad enough to have to consult with Demelza."

Demi clutched the mug until her knuckles whitened. It was the way Victoria spat out her name, making Demelza sound like some foul disease. Demi squeaked.

Victoria turned towards her. "What was that?"

"Call me Demi, please."

"Demi? What are you so little or so wan that you are half?"

"Tori." Sebastian's voice was controlled but held a threat.

"Demi is not a name. Demelza is a name the name of a village. Now, if your mother had named you

Demetra, meaning a follower of the Greek goddess Demeter who ruled over the harvest and fertility . . ." Her mouth lifted into something like a smile. "That would have been quite amusing in a warped way."

"Sit down, Tori," Sebastian snapped. "You're being a bully."

She glared at him, then at Demi, but she did sit.

"The options all involve cooperation so I am expecting everyone to behave like the adults they are." Sebastian looked at Victoria who frowned.

"Option one is to sell. The estate could go on the market at any time and next spring would be best. However, feelers could be put out now."

"No!" Victoria bit the word out. "I've waited years to have this house back and I will not sell."

Sebastian ignored her. "I've spoken with all the major estate agents and a rough price guide would be five and a half million. More could be achieved if the estate were broken up, selling off the gatehouse, the coach house, and the various farm buildings separately."

Demi glanced up at Victoria. The woman was seething. Demi waited for her to jump up and explode.

"They estimated that the value of the estate would increase by about one million if this were done. Of course, this could be a long-drawn-out process because the market for large estates swings widely."

He paused as if he was waiting for another outburst from Victoria.

"They felt the interest might arise more from commercial propositions than from private. One estate agent felt that Boscawen would make a fine luxury hotel as it has enough land to create a golf course, spa and deluxe self-catering cottages."

Demi leaned back in her chair. She hadn't been allowed to view the house, but from what little she had seen it would make a fabulous boutique hotel. However, it would need a facelift on the decoration front. Some harking back to the past with the furnishing was good, but right now with the dark paints and poor lighting no one would pay good money to stay here. On her first practical she had worked with an architect tasked with doing this on a house in the Cotswolds and it was then that Demi realised how much she loved the dual role of building design and interior design. If she could choose her dream job, that would be it.

"So option two would be to take on this project yourselves."

"What?" Victoria stood. A bell went off and she went to the oven to extract a tray. The scent of warm ginger filled the room. Demi's stomach rolled. Of all the biscuits that Victoria could have made, why did it have to be ginger ones? It was as if she knew Demi hated them.

"You want to develop the garden and restore it and that could be part of the process." Sebastian smiled at Victoria as she slipped the biscuits on to a rack to cool. "The house has never been your interest, it's always been the garden and the woods."

"All very well, but we don't have the money." She glared at Demi. "Even if I had what has been given to

Demi it wouldn't be enough. You're talking a major investment."

"I am. It would require both of you to be partners plus substantial investment from a bank or for you to bring in other partners."

"The council would never buy it."

"I think you're wrong there." Sam spoke quietly and everyone turned to him. "Jobs are desperately needed here. This project would create quite a few jobs, especially if you also went into the production of cider as well and if you made the whole operation as green and organic as possible."

"Cider?" Sebastian asked.

"Yes. Look, currently there are five orchards on the land. They are old but still producing well although in need of work. Nothing has been done with them for years except locals scrumping." Sam looked at each of them in turn and Demi realised that he was very engaged.

"This year there might be enough of a crop to begin to produce."

Victoria held the back of the chair. "What on earth do you know about cider?"

"About cider? Well it's about the skill of blending and the variety of apples you use, but in truth, not as much as I'd like." He took a deep breath. "I grew up in wine country and worked in vineyards." He looked away from Victoria, not meeting her eyes.

"This wasn't on your CV." Victoria paused. "In fact, your CV was distinctly empty except for sailing and surfing."

"I thought I'd be working in a surf shop or chandlers and then I heard you were looking for a gardener."

Victoria's eyes narrowed.

"I love working on the land." Sam shrugged.

"So you have some experience?" Sebastian asked.

"Yes, I've been involved in every step of winemaking. I grew up in Margaret River." He glanced quickly between Sebastian and Victoria but not at Demi. She wondered what other surprises he was holding back. He hadn't mentioned winemaking to her, but she knew about his keen interest in cider. Of course, it fitted with his painstaking elderflower champagne process.

Sebastian leaned forward. "How would it be a viable business?"

"I've been working through a business plan."

Victoria raised an eyebrow.

"And I think it would be in profit in three years. There's a whole push for local products and if you package it with a hotel and self-catering accommodation people might buy into it in a bigger way. They will want to take a part of Boscawen, well, Cornwall, back with them and that will help to spread the word to a wider audience."

"Have you got the plan to a stage where I can see it?" Sebastian made a few notes.

"Yes, it's on my computer."

"No bank will invest." Victoria picked up a biscuit and bit into it.

"You don't know that because you haven't tried, nor have you looked for investors." Sebastian turned his gaze to Demi and she squirmed. "You've been very quiet."

"She'll say no. She wants to take the money and run. She has no allegiance to Boscawen." Victoria brushed the crumbs from her fingers into the sink.

"Hello, I am here, and you know nothing about me. Stop talking as if I'm not here or I'm a child. Seriously, if you want to go ahead with anything, you need to change your attitude." Demi stood up and walked out of the kitchen and into the hall. It was about time she stopped being nice and trying to respect bloody Victoria's feelings. The woman had none — and judging by the way the house was decorated she lacked taste except when it came to flower arrangement. In every room that Demi had been in there had been a beautiful display of flowers.

The library must have been her father's study and even though she had no memories of him she could sense him in here. Books lined the walls and silver photo frames covered the surfaces. There were none of Demi, of course. But pictures of Victoria and his nephew more than made up for the absence. On the far wall was a beautiful modern oil painting of a Cornish landscape. She walked closer. The colours were so vibrant and the brushwork heavy yet energetic. Quick strokes defined fields and a headland. She smiled as she touched the impasto paint.

She walked out of the study and passed the dining room to go upstairs, which she hadn't done since that abortive attempt of staying there a week ago. Not that she was complaining about staying with Sam. However, this was her house too. And what was it about Boscawen that made her feel she'd been here before? It was impossible. The house had been owned by other people when she was young and she didn't believe in reincarnation, but that sense of knowing pervaded, along with fear.

Standing at the top, she looked down into the hall and longed to see it lifted from the darkness. If she half closed her eyes she could see the renovation complete and hear the appreciation of guests as they were welcomed through the front door, the front door that she knew so well but of course couldn't know.

She opened the first bedroom door she came to and was delighted with the proportions. If all the rooms were this spacious, the house would need only decorative changes. The furnishings were good but needed reupholstering. It was as if they were straight from the back of a saleroom and hadn't been touched except for the caress of a feather duster.

The outlook over the fields and woodlands was enchanting, but it wasn't until she reached the servant's quarters at the very top of the house that she saw the sea. In the distance, the dense woodland fell down to the river, which was spotted with yachts before it opened out to what must be Falmouth Bay.

Demi stood staring and her breathing calmed. Despite the distance, she could see the sun reflecting off the water. She wondered if she was imagining this as the boats appeared tiny, but the distance seemed to shrink the longer she stood staring at the water.

"Demi."

She jumped.

Sam touched her shoulder. "I didn't mean to startle you, just wanted to make sure you were OK."

"Thanks."

"Quite the view." He smiled.

"I had no idea Boscawen was so close to the water because the grounds feel so enclosed." She turned around and surveyed the small room she was in. "Do you know if the house is listed?"

"I don't think so."

She nodded as she wandered off. On this floor she could see the signs of when the building was added to and the formal front put on. Another set of stairs led to a few more rooms and here she could see evidence of fire damage, charred beams and scorch marks. She wondered when that had happened — but the structure appeared sound and the repairs weren't new.

A few steps led to a door that gave out on to the roof. From here she could see for miles. The land dipped down to the water and she could see many undulations in the landscape. It was breathtaking. If she were to live here, it would be at the top of the house, far away from the woods. The woods, which as she looked down on them, appeared almost like clumps of moss except where the pines had invaded on the edges. What lived in those woods? Fairies or something more sinister?

"Wow, I haven't been up here before. Spectacular." Sam spun around beside her. "There's a fantastic view of the woodland." He walked to the edge of the roof

204

and peered over the parapet. "You can see so clearly the definition between the scrub oak and the elder." He pointed and Demi reluctantly came to his side. She had always been fine with heights, but at the moment that wasn't the case. The world seemed to wobble and the trees blurred.

"The woods were once coppiced for the tin and copper mines but no longer." He paused. "Did you know this is one of the most ancient forests left in the UK? The Tregans have been the caretakers for a long time except for about thirty years. Looking from here I can see why it means so much to Mrs Lake." He turned to her and reached out. "Are you all right?"

Demi pulled away. Everything felt wrong, swimming. The whole experience of having been here before closing in on her. She bumped into the parapet and teetered.

"What the hell are you playing at?" Sam grabbed her and pulled her back, holding her against his chest. The sound of his heart racing pounded in her ears. She'd been caught. She struggled.

"Calm down." His arms closed tighter around her. She fought harder. Nothing made sense.

"What on earth is going on here?" Victoria's voice pierced the fog of fear in Demi's brain.

"A case of vertigo, I think." Sam spoke quietly. His hold loosened but not enough for her to break free.

"One should never walk on a roof without knowing you have a head for heights." Victoria laughed and walked to the edge where the parapet tapered to a foot high. Demi's stomach rolled over just thinking about it.

"My brother and I used to play up here all the time."
Sam stilled and he watched Victoria closely.

"Were you close to him?"

"Yes, very. With only ten months between us we were like twins." She smiled, and for the first time Demi saw her features soften, becoming beautiful instead of hard.

"You must have been devastated when he died." Sam was motionless after he spoke, totally focused on Victoria. Demi stilled in Sam's arms enjoying the experience. She straightened at her realisation.

"Yes, I was, but to be honest my father had driven a wedge between us long before that." She looked out to sea. "Who's the king of the castle always felt more real standing here." She turned to them. "Demi . . ." She paused making sure that Demi realised she was using her preferred name. "Your colour is returning. Sam, you can let her go so that she can breathe. I always find that breathing helps."

CHAPTER
EIGHTEEN

Demi sat in the shade of the gatehouse making rough sketches of her ideas for Boscawen. A car pulled up and Sebastian stepped out. He waved at her and she put her sketch-pad down. Earlier she'd begun to put together some mood boards for the drawing and dining rooms. Yesterday after their initial discussion she'd done one for the library, adding a bar of sorts to it and extending the terrace off it, which would allow for seating.

"Just wanted a quick chat before I left for London." He sat on the seat next to her and glanced at the drawing. "That's good, very good."

"Thank you."

He ran a hand through his hair. "Tell me how you feel about this possible business venture?"

Demi raised an eyebrow.

"Seriously. I want to know your thoughts. It's easy to let Tori bulldoze you and everyone around her."

"Does she even notice other people? The more I see of her I'm not surprised my father had an affair."

He chuckled. "Things are far more complex than you realise: Tori was never easy, but she was kinder many years ago." He looked into the distance.

"Why the change?"

"I could guess, but they would only be guesses."

She shook her head. "So you prefer to leave me in the dark."

"I'll just say that Tori isn't as tough as she seems. She has had to become that way."

She frowned. Victoria seemed pretty sure of herself and Demi couldn't imagine her being any less so. The woman had been born with a silver spoon in her mouth, as the expression went. She'd come from a wealthy family, had had every privilege, and then married a rich man. The woman had wanted for nothing. It was the exact opposite of what Demi had known. Not that she'd lived in poverty, but there had been nothing spare and she had a mountain of debts from student loans.

She looked at her sketch. It showed an understanding of what lay beneath the walls and even in her brief tour she'd noted the updated wiring, the plumbing, and had had a sense of what walls were load-bearing and which ones weren't. When they had put in the new bathrooms and updated the old ones they had done a clever job with the use of space. She'd been impressed and wondered who the architect had been.

"I'm off to London for a day or so to pull in a few favours and work on Sam's business plan so I'm not pressing you for an answer now, Demi. You haven't received enough information to make an informed decision yet, but I'm wondering if you have strong feelings one way or the other?"

"Are you seriously asking me if I'm willing to go into partnership with my father's widow who hates the sight of me?"

"Yes." His mouth twitched into a smile.

The sketch in her lap told one story, but the voice in her head told another. "I don't know."

"That's fair."

"I'm tempted by the task of turning the house into a hotel. It is a project I could sink my teeth into." Demi took a deep breath. "But I've no desire to spend any time with a woman who hates me. I could take the money and go and buy my own project to work on."

"Fair enough." He smiled. "You're like your father in many ways."

"How so?"

"He always looked at all sides of any decision before he made it and he never rushed one."

She thought about this, twirling her pencil in her fingers. "Why did he abandon me?"

Sebastian looked into the distance. "He didn't; that was your mother's choice."

"You said that before but it just doesn't make sense."

He looked out to the gate pillars and not at Demi. "An incident occurred and Morwenna made a decision that Charles couldn't do anything about. His hands were tied."

"He wouldn't leave his wife?"

"I'm sure that was part of it. I think it was the hardest decision he ever had to make, but Charles felt the vows he took were sacred and —"

"Hah, so sacred he was sleeping with my mother," Demi interrupted.

"True. People aren't straightforward are they?"

Demi thought about Matt. On the surface, he'd seemed squeaky clean but underneath there was another story. "No, they aren't."

"Keep an open mind about your father, Tori, and the project."

She pressed her lips together. He was asking a lot.

"Trust me." He smiled, and the lines around his eyes deepened.

She closed hers for a moment. Trust him. She couldn't trust anyone except maybe her grandfather. She needed to talk all of this through with him.

"At least wait until I have put a proposal together."

She put her work on to the table. "OK."

She walked with him to his car.

"What happens if I pull out?"

He leaned against the Jaguar. "Tori will have to sell."

"Do you know why Boscawen means so much to her?"

"No, not really — and believe me I wish I did." He slipped into his car.

She walked up to the open window. "One more thing."

"Yes?"

"If we go ahead . . ." She bit her lip. "I'd like to make sure I have some money set aside and not all poured into Boscawen."

He opened the door and climbed out. "OK. May I ask why?"

"It's just that my grandfather is now in a care home and, if possible, I'd like to take him out and get a carer instead."

210

"It's good to hear he's still with us."

"You knew him?" She frowned.

"Not really but we met on a few occasions." He smiled. "A lovely man — and I will include your request in the calculations." He got into the car again. "Maybe part of the coach house could be converted for him."

Demi nodded. "That would be ideal." She smiled. "One more thing." She leaned in through the open window. "My mother's life insurance hasn't paid out and I don't have a job. Is it possible for me to take out a small loan against the estate? It doesn't have to be much, but I don't want to keep borrowing from my grandfather and claiming jobseekers allowance seems absurd." She shrugged her shoulders.

"Of course. I'll look into it right away." He started the engine. She waved as he drove away then dashed back to her sketchbook and jotted down a few thoughts but she would need to take a closer look at the coach house and stables before she could do much more.

About to pick up the phone to ring her grandfather, Demi stopped. The papers in front of her seemed to be about Boscawen. She shouldn't be prying, but looking at these she didn't think Sam was a gardener at all. These were not the plans of an amateur. The costings and depreciations were those of someone who had run a business before or had a degree in business studies or maybe an MBA. He also knew an awful lot about soil, including its chemical breakdown. What had he said the other day about growing up around vineyards? Not much, and it sounded like Victoria had hired him on a whim. From the way she looked at him it might be because he was eye candy. Sam Stuart certainly was that — but what else was he?

If she was going into partnership with Victoria and relying on Sam, surely she was entitled to know a bit more about him? She moved the papers about and saw an envelope addressed to AST Stuart from Australia. What did the A and T stand for? And why did he go by his second name? She heard the water in the shower stop and she swiftly pushed the papers back into place on the table and decided to ask him.

Then she picked up the phone and called the care home. They had suggested that she didn't visit for a few days as her grandfather had a bad cold and she hoped he was on the mend now. The way his face lit up every time he saw her filled her with hope that the world was not all bad. It's not that she didn't know this, but at the moment it was weighted more heavily on the bad than the good. On the good side she had her grandfather. On the bad one, Victoria and Matt with his harassing texts and emails, which were coming on a more frequent basis. The undecided area was full of Sebastian and Sam. Demi couldn't figure out what Sebastian's motivations were. He seemed to be taking this loyal friend thing quite far.

Of course, she knew other wonderful people. Her friends from school and university, but they felt so far away at the moment. Thank goodness the gatehouse had Internet or she would be cut off totally.

212

"If you know your extension number, please dial it now," the automated voice droned. She typed in his room number. The phone rang then there were various noises until finally:

"Heh, hello?" He sounded a little muddled.

"Hi, it's Demi."

"Ah, Demi, my love, I just can't get to grips with this blasted phone. How are you?"

She sank into a chair and played with a pencil. "Me? OK."

"Just OK?"

"Yes, but things are improving."

"That's not what your voice is telling me."

She laughed. "Well, it's telling you right and I'm a terrible liar."

"That's not such a bad thing."

"Not so sure." She looked around to see if Sam had come out of the bathroom yet. "I think being a good liar can be a useful life skill."

"Why do you want to lie? That's a far more interesting question."

"Are you sure you didn't do psychology?" She smiled, thinking of her grandfather helping her with her schoolwork in the past. Only now did she understand that it had been less about her learning and more about building her confidence.

"Being a teacher for over forty years gives you certain abilities in that area, I'd like to think."

"True."

"So what's troubling you?"

"People." She leaned on the table.

"Always a variable. So why are they causing you heartache."

"I wouldn't go so far as that, but so far this inheritance from my father is complicated."

"They frequently can be."

She sighed. "Rather than just selling the lot they are thinking of starting a business and need me to be a part of it."

"Ah. Getting into bed with the enemy."

Demi frowned. She wouldn't want to get into bed with any of them. Well, that wasn't quite true, she acknowledged as she saw Sam dressed only in a towel head into his room. "Yes, in a way."

"No one can make you do anything you don't want to."

Demi sat up straight, thinking: they can trick you into it or deceive you into it.

"You've gone off into that head of yours, Demi," her grandfather said. "Go and take a walk in the lovely garden and think of your old grandfather while you are doing it. Maybe in a few weeks you can bring me around it or at least tell me all about it."

"That would be lovely. I'll call tomorrow — and you learn how to use the phone by then."

"Will do."

"I'm so pleased you sound so much better. Has the cold finished?"

"Nearly, another day and you should be safe to visit."

"Good. Love you." As Demi put the phone down Sam walked out of his room with the towel slung low about his hips.

"Sorry, left the clean laundry out on the line. Haven't got a stitch to wear."

He disappeared through the kitchen and Demi was left admiring the view. Whatever Sam was, he was definitely worth watching, so maybe she had something in common with Victoria after all. Demi laughed as she went to find the sketches that she had made of the outbuildings. This could be a really exciting project and although she had her doubts that it would come to fruition, part of her wanted it to.

A dead tree full of large black birds stopped Demi in mid step. She and Sam were giving Boscawen a wide berth as they walked through the twilight in silence. She had no desire to see Victoria after yesterday.

Sam followed her glance. "Eerie, aren't they?"

"Yes, are they crows?"

"Jackdaws."

"I wonder if they know the effect they have, perching on that tree of all trees."

He grinned. "I kind of think they must, because it's a regular hang-out for them." He climbed over a style and held a hand out for her. He led the way through a field that skirted the garden.

"Are those eucalyptus?"

"Yes." He smiled. "They remind me of home."

"Do you miss it?"

"A bit, sometimes, but the sea and trees help, especially the eucalyptus." He took a deep breath. "Do you miss London?"

Stopping, she thought about the energy, the noise and all the people. "I haven't thought about it until you asked me so I guess the answer is no." She laughed as they walked under the cover of the trees. Looking up at them, she enjoyed the scent of eucalyptus in the air around them. "I wouldn't expect them here."

"Imports. Victoria's great-grandmother was an avid plant collector and made two voyages plant hunting. She brought back seeds for the trees and many other plants including the agapanthus. Mrs Lake has her garden notes and planting lists."

"You sound envious." Demi studied him.

"I'd love to read them, but she holds on tightly to them." He frowned. "It's like a talisman of sorts, I guess."

"She wants to restore the garden."

"Yes, and she has a point, but gardens move on." He looked around him. "For me, just seeing the plants that have survived despite the neglect is fascinating and," he paused, "looking after the garden right now is like touching the past, getting to know the previous plantsmen, but you have to look to the future, to what's sustainable and manageable."

They stopped when they reached a kissing gate. Demi went through first, noting the cows grazing in the far side of the field.

"Is this part of Boscawen?"

"Yes, Mrs Lake lets the land to a farmer. I think this is where Sebastian was thinking the golf course would go."

216

"Oh." Demi looked at the rural scene in front of her and wondered if a golf course was a good idea. She had heard there was another one not too far away. How many courses did an area need? "By the way, why do you call Victoria, Mrs Lake?"

Sam stopped and looked at Demi. His head tilted in the manner she was becoming accustomed to when he was thinking. His eyes looked off into the distance. He was a long way from her and the cows were beginning to take an interest in them.

"Well, she's my boss."

"True, but if we go ahead you will be a partner of sorts."

"I hadn't thought of it that way." He smiled. The path wound through into the woods. She was hesitant but reasoned with herself that not much could happen to her when she was with Sam. The track through the elder trees widened and she moved beside him. Nothing looked familiar.

She pointed to barbed wire in the distance surrounding a clearing. "What's that?" Ferns grew densely but there was a clear path up to it.

"It's Men an Skawenn."

"And that is?"

He took her hand and ducked under a few low branches avoiding the barbed wire until they came out near a large stone with a hole through the middle of it. "This is Men an Skawenn. An ancient stone purported to heal children passed through the hole and," he paused, looking at her with a big smile on his face, "insure fertility to newly weds if they pass through it — naked."

She laughed.

"Laugh you may, but despite Victoria blocking it off, couples visit it regularly."

"Dear God, have you seen them?"

"What do you take me for, a peeping Tom?"

She shook her head. "That hole doesn't look too big." She pretended to measure Sam's shoulders and then the hole. "Not sure you'd make it."

"Is that a dare?"

She suppressed a smile. "Well, if you said you would do it without your clothes on I think it might be."

"And what do I get?"

She swallowed. "Applause."

"You're not going through?" He raised an eyebrow.

"Definitely not." She glanced down at her chest. "I'd get stuck and the indignity would be too much to live with." She walked closer and touched the granite, almost expecting a shock of some sort, but goosebumps were the only reaction. Sam stepped closer to her.

"Well, maybe if you marry me, we could come with olive oil and wiggle through together."

Her head shot up and her eyes went wide.

"It's tradition, after all, and the new owner of Boscawen should keep traditions." His eyes were dancing with laughter and she grinned. It was much tamer than many of the things Matt had asked of her. And she wasn't marrying Sam, nor would she be the owner of Boscawen for long.

218

★ ★ ★

Victoria looked at Adam lying beside her, with his arms tucked beneath his head and a smile on his face. Was something amusing him or was it just the contented smile post sex? Maybe both, she thought as she stretched. The sex had been good and long overdue but she wasn't satisfied. She'd climaxed but it hadn't provided the usual release. Slipping out of bed she stood and looked down the garden. Two people walked with their heads close together, Demi and Sam.

"Are you coming back to bed?" Adam kicked the covers off and Victoria noted he was ready for action again. Sadly, she wasn't. Her mind was elsewhere.

"No." She picked up her dressing gown and slipped it on.

"You haven't really been with me since I arrived." He stood and walked over to her.

"Sorry."

"No need to apologise. I'm just a bit worried." He stroked her hand.

She looked up. "Thank you for understanding."

"My pleasure, I only want to help and I can tell your mind is everywhere at the moment."

"That easy to read?" She raised an eyebrow.

"Not often, but at the moment, yes." He picked up his jeans and put them on then took her hand. "Let's go and have something to drink. Then you can decide if you want to talk about what's on your mind or just shag me again or both."

She laughed. "Sometimes you are far more mature than I give you credit for."

"I know. It's scandalous that you've only wanted me for my body." He kissed her neck. "Now tell me all about the plans for Boscawen? Are you giving me the sale of a lifetime or are you making a deal with Charles's daughter?"

She turned to him as they walked through the house to the kitchen. "What do you think I should do?"

"Do you really want to know?"

She nodded and let go of his hand.

"As much as I would love to be the one to sell it, I think the plan as you've outlined it has promise." He reached into the fridge and pulled out some champagne. "If you sell it, I think you will leave the area and me. Not good." He took the foil off. "However, I would earn a substantial commission and would be able to afford this." He lifted the champagne then removed the muselet. He turned the bottle slowly until the cork popped. "God, I love that sound."

Victoria laughed. She'd had to teach him how to open champagne properly so that none of the wine was lost. Now he was an expert. She handed him the glasses. "You were saying?"

"Yes, the pros of keeping it are that you will still have your home, there will be more jobs locally and you'll stay around." He filled the glasses. "The pros if you sell are, as I mentioned, money for me and you will have more time, which you could spend with me." He handed her a full glass. "Plus you might buy another place locally." He raised his glass. "Here's to you and whatever decision you make."

She touched his glass. "You'd like me to sell?"

220

"I didn't say that." He grinned. "But there would be more potential benefits for me, at least."

She laughed and took his hand. "Grab the bottle and let's go back to bed."

CHAPTER
NINETEEN

Three hundred trees to be planted. It had been a moment of insanity and now Victoria had to live with it. Sam held a spade and Demi had a tape measure. They were marking out the orchard and seemed to have it in hand.

Victoria needed to do something. Everything was on hold and good physical work would help. It had helped her great-grandmother deal with her grief. She had spoken of her loss so poignantly to Victoria, told her that only working on the garden that she and Arthur had created together had eased the pain of her loss.

Not that Victoria was grieving, quite the contrary. Finally, at the age of sixty she was a free woman. It meant that she should have twenty more viable years in front of her and then she could jump off a cliff leaving behind . . . leaving behind nothing. What would be her legacy? Once Charles had bought back Boscawen, she'd thought a restored garden would be her legacy but now that had been taken from her.

What had she been allowed to do? Precisely nothing. No Olympics, no Oxford, no children. She grabbed the wheelbarrow and moved to the nearest tub. With a big huff, she lifted it then pushed it to the first spot. Sam indicated his approval with a thumbs up.

Before long Victoria's back was aching and her hands were raw, but between the three of them they had set out part of the field. Tomorrow they would begin the hard work of actually beginning to dig the trees in. She leaned against the hedge, inhaling the sweet scent of the wild honeysuckle and avoiding the nettles. This was worthwhile work even if it would end up being sold to someone else. Orchards had a purpose and she needed to find one.

Demi bent to take a drink of water from the tap by the barn. She had dirt smudged across her nose and Victoria could see the young Charles. He too had those freckles across his nose. A twinge of guilt niggled in Victoria's conscience. She couldn't shake the feeling that he had done this because of Adam, yet he wasn't vengeful. Up until his death he'd been silent about not having children. He'd never held that up to her to show her who was truly the faulty person in their marriage. Of course, she hadn't needed to see Charles's child to see that. She had slept with more virile men than most women would ever dream of and no child had been produced.

A smile spread across her mouth as she remembered her many lovers. Adam came to mind. Although last night's sex had been good, she hadn't felt the lift it normally gave her. She didn't want to dwell on it especially when she was watching Sam strip his shirt off and take the hose from Demi to pour water over his head and down his torso. Did he know the effect he had on women? She could see Demi trying not to stare and failing dismally. There was something appealing about him and it wasn't just his beautiful body.

He turned and caught her glance. She didn't flinch. A slow smile crept across his face. It was a smile she had seen before but she couldn't place it. She must remember to take the fish oil pills for her memory because things had been slipping away more than they should be lately.

"Thanks for the help, Mrs Lake." He shook his head and water went everywhere. Demi laughed as the spray hit her. Victoria turned away and began to walk back to the house. She didn't belong with them.

It was the nineteenth of July and the big day had come. Victoria wouldn't admit to the nervous butterflies in her stomach. It meant nothing, she told herself, it was just a bit of fun. Standing back she looked at the agapanthus blooms. In the soft light of the tent the blue seemed to pulsate. She adjusted the four heads, pulling the one still tightly in bud forward. A sideways glance confirmed that hers were the best. Well, she thought so, and she hoped the judges would feel the same. None of the others were as blue, although one pale agapanthus had a larger head. She pressed her lips together. This shouldn't matter to her but it did. Finally, after years away she was home and a part of this community where she'd grown up. This was her first real outing into it. Last summer things had been too chaotic in the garden to even think about taking part in the Constantine Garden Society Summer Show.

Rows of tables were filled with so many different categories. She loved the entries from the children at the school who had created animals out of vegetables. She didn't envy the judges who would have to make a decision on that grouping.

"Victoria, how lovely to see you here." A woman she vaguely recognised strolled up to her.

"How are you?" Trying desperately to place the woman, a catalogue of names, faces and houses ran through Victoria's mind. But she came up with no matches as she headed out of the tent. Judging would be taking place soon and the show wouldn't open until two in the afternoon.

"Well, I've just become a grandmother and I can't tell you how delighted I am."

Victoria forced a smile. "Congratulations."

"We're over the moon." The woman walked with her outside. Victoria had hoped that leaving the tent would end the conversation but luck was not with her today. The woman waved at a man. "The judges are gathering. We're so pleased to have Boscawen's Sam as one of them."

Did Sam belong to Boscawen or to her? She'd hired him, but where did his loyalty lie? Which ever was the answer it meant that either he would have to abstain for her category or she would be disqualified and this whole thing would have been a wasted effort. Of course the other problem was that Sam despised — well, not quite despised, but disliked agapanthus. He regarded

225

them as weeds and kept telling her they grew everywhere in Australia. He saw nothing special in them. They had agreed to disagree. A bit like his obsession with roses. He didn't seem to understand that the clear air in Cornwall made them prone to mildew and black spot. They were hard work and generally not very successful. He was determined to prove her wrong. "Yes, he's very good. If you'll excuse me I have a few things to get done before this afternoon." She smiled. "Shall I see you later?"

"Of course." The woman nodded and bustled off. Victoria let out a long breath. Maybe this hadn't been a good idea. Going back and doing things that had always been done in the past seemed so right, but at the moment it felt a waste of her time and energy. But if she didn't do it this year then there might not be another chance for Boscawen to win with a Tregan as owner.

She stepped aside as the Constantine Silver Band arrived carrying their instruments. As a child, this had been one of the high points of the summer with cream teas, tombolas, music and flowers. Maybe you couldn't go back and today, no doubt, she'd find that out for certain.

"Victoria, so glad I've seen you." Jane Penrose who owned another of the big houses came to her side. She was in her late seventies but defied her age by being involved in everything. Victoria had always liked her.

"Jane, how lovely to see you."

"I know I've written but I just wanted to say again how sorry I was to hear about Charles."

226

"Thank you."

"Becoming a widow at your age is so inconvenient." She shook her head as they walked along listening to the band warm up. "Men seem to be in short supply." She winked. "Although you've never had that problem, I know." She laughed. "Adam's aunt handles the changeovers in the cottages for me."

"Ah." Victoria was slightly taken aback by Jane's cheerful openness.

"I'm pleased you've entered this year." She tilted her head in the direction of the tent. "I've always coveted your agapanthus. But we must have different soil because despite some judicious theft when the other people owned it, they've never produced that blue, the Boscawen Blue as I think of it."

Victoria laughed, remembering watching her great-grandmother pinch cuttings of plants she liked without asking for permission. Gardening could be a competitive world.

"Not sure if it's your thing or not but the book club is rather wonderful." She placed a hand on Victoria's arm. "You should join us — and do you still play tennis?"

Victoria nodded.

"Good, we can always use a spare player if you don't sell Boscawen, which I hope you won't." She leaned closer to Victoria. "It's good to have a Tregan back in charge." Jane was looking in the distance to where Sam was standing with the judges about to enter the tent.

"It's good to be in charge again."

"See you later." A small child who wanted to throw tennis balls at the coconuts pulled Jane away. No small child would ever ask the same of Victoria and no Tregan would ever be in charge again. She'd better take first prize this year. She might never have another chance.

"Talk later, Sophie." Demi looked at her watch. "My grandfather will be finished with his physio and I need to go."

"OK, but seriously, if Matt's that much of a pest you should go to the police or block the number if you can on your phone."

"I'll look into it."

"Missing you."

"You too." Demi sighed. She couldn't go to the police about Matt. That would be a humiliation too far. She went into the building and found her grandfather using his walker to head outside. "Hello."

She kissed him and they sat on the nearest bench. He looked tired.

"It's the big day tomorrow," he said.

She nodded. "I know and I don't know where this week has gone."

"What have you decided?" He looked at her. "Or haven't you?"

"I think I'd really like to do it but . . ."

"Victoria Lake?"

"Yes." She smiled at him.

"You should just have it out with her. You aren't at fault."

228

"I know that but I know so little else." Folding her hands in her lap she decided that her grandfather seemed more lucid today. "What happened between Mum and Charles? I really feel like something's missing."

He shook his head. "By the time we came back from Cape Town — we were out there visiting old friends — you were out of hospital and they were over." He looked into the distance. "Your mother was never the same after nearly losing you. That much I do know."

"So do you suppose me nearly dying broke them up?"

He grabbed his walker and pulled himself up. "I think better when I move. Let's walk a bit."

She strolled beside him through the garden. It was hot. Everyone told her this constant sun was unusual for Cornwall.

"Is the walk helping you to remember?"

"Your grandmother said it was your mother's guilt, I think."

"Her guilt?" Demi stopped. "That doesn't make sense. There's no guilt to a burst appendix or to an adverse reaction."

"Ah, but she wasn't with you." He walked on and spoke to the gardener. "Midday isn't the time to be watering."

"Where was she if she wasn't with me? You said it was during the Easter holidays."

"She was with Charles."

Demi frowned. "Where was I then?"

"The plants will suffer, Wenna, if you water at noon. I've told you that before."

Demi put her hand on his arm. "Grandad, I'm not Wenna, I'm Demi."

He blinked and she could see his eyes focusing on her. "Did I call you Wenna?" He sighed. "Must have been lost in my thoughts. Your mother never listened to my advice."

"Where was I when my appendix burst?"

He cleaned his glasses. "I wish I could remember. You see, we were in Cape Town. I can recall seeing agapanthus that reminded me of the ones in the garden at Boscawen but, . . ." He turned to her and continued, "I know I should remember, but I can't."

She hugged him. "It's OK. Maybe it will come back to you."

He smiled. "It might. Most things do, but usually when I'm lying awake at three in the morning." He took her hand. "I'll put a notebook by the bed in case it does."

"Thank you." She glanced at her watch. Peta was meeting her for a coffee so she had to dash. "Never mind about me. Before I leave, is there any word on the new date for the operation?"

"Not yet but they couldn't plan anything until I was completely healthy again after that cold which hung on for so long."

"Hopefully soon then." He nodded and she left him chatting with someone as she dashed out to meet Peta, wishing he would remember more. She had no other way of finding out.

★ ★ ★

The dining room was formal and neglected. Demi looked for cobwebs and dust but found none. Tired, summed it up. However, the mahogany table gleamed, standing out from everything else. The walls looked as if someone had slapped a coat of hunter green paint over embossed wallpaper. She squinted and she thought she could make out the outlines of bamboo. She had seen similar styles in old magazines in her grandfather's attic. After the furniture had been moved, she and a neighbour had cleared the loft of years' worth of magazines. She'd wondered why they were there in the first place, but she supposed it had something to do with her grandmother. They didn't fit in with her grandfather's interests. If time had permitted Demi would have spent hours reading them and garnering ideas from the past. Instead, they all went to the recycling centre.

Sebastian slumped a bit at the head of the table with neat piles of paper in front of him including several binders. Shadows beneath his eyes added to the weariness about him.

"Victoria, would you sit down, please." He looked at her and she stopped pacing between the windows.

"Fine." She took a seat at the far end of the table from them. Sam gave Demi a small smile.

"I have spent the past few days taking Sam's business plan and the idea of turning Boscawen into a deluxe resort to various people, including investors." Sebastian looked at them all. "Sadly they were not keen on the idea for many reasons but mainly because, despite the boom in interest in Cornwall, they did not see the growth potential without exploiting the access to the river and, as the woodland is protected, that isn't an option."

"So get to the point, Sebastian." Victoria's hands were clasped on the table. "We're back to square one."

"Not quite. I sat down with another friend who has invested in similar projects and he suggested a scaled down proposal." Sebastian pushed the bound papers towards them and Sam stood to take a set down to Victoria.

Demi looked at it, wondering how she really felt about this. She had walked most of the estate with Sam and they had begun the process of planting the apple trees — backbreaking work, but there was something satisfying about it — and she and Victoria had managed not to kill each other by simply not talking to one another.

"On the first few pages it states the obvious. The figures are not exact as probate isn't complete and Victoria is contesting on all fronts." Sebastian glanced up from the graphs in front of him and smiled. "But if Victoria and Demi pool their resources there is enough capital to begin to renovate the outbuildings into holiday cottages and also start the cider press. Sam tells me there may be funds available from the government to revitalise the orchards as well." Sebastian looked at each one of them in turn until he stopped at Victoria. "If another investor is found then you can convert the house to a high-end B&B and continue work on restoring the garden and the quay, giving the guests access to the river and the sea. Possibly even buying a sailing boat as other resorts have done."

"What do you mean, 'pooling resources'?" Victoria's face showed no expression.

"I mean taking the cash reserves of both you and Demi for the financial investment required for the building and acquisition of equipment and staff. Then combining the investment income to pay for the running costs, salaries and basic living for both of you."

Demi longed to shout no. Why should she help Victoria in any way? She hadn't even said thanks for the help with planting the trees she shouldn't have purchased in the first place.

Victoria studied the "little mouse" as she had begun to think of Demelza. It was obvious she was not happy with the idea at all and, with just a quick scan through the proposal, Victoria knew it wouldn't fly without more money, which would mean mortgaging the estate.

"Sebastian, even I can see that, on the off chance that we agree to work together — and that is truly in question — we are still short of money. At best, we would make it through the winter and we wouldn't have made anything as we would only begin taking in customers next season."

"Yes, another investor is needed."

She sighed. "You clearly stated that no one was willing to invest."

"I said none of the people I spoke to were, but I didn't say no one."

She leaned forward and placed her hand on top of the papers. "Stop playing games."

"I'm not. I just wanted you to be aware of the situation before I put the next proposal on the table."

"Then get on with it."

Sebastian passed around another sheet. "Here's my solution."

Victoria waited while Sam brought the update to her. Demi hadn't said a word. Did she even understand the proposals in front of her? No, Victoria was being unfair. Charles had one of the keenest business brains around and her mother, from what Sebastian had said, had been a champion of the homeless, a driving force behind one of the top charities. Demi must have a brain of some sort.

"As you can see from the paperwork in front of you, I've found someone willing to invest two million which is the minimum required."

"Dear God — it's you!" Victoria looked at Sebastian. What on earth was he thinking?

"Yes, I would become your partner, as would Sam, as you can see on the sheet."

"Why?" Victoria stared down the long table trying to read the expression on his face, but he was giving nothing away.

"You will obviously need time to think this through." He turned to Demi. "I've already run through this with Sam in detail."

Victoria scanned the numbers quickly. With the added funds it really could be accomplished on the downscaled model. But did she want to be partners with Sebastian, let alone Demi? Sam, of course, was another matter. She definitely would like to be a partner with him. There was also the question of what Sam was actually bringing to the table, because it wasn't money.

"It's now July; if the property is to be up and running for the start of the summer next year we need to make a decision very quickly so that we can seek the permissions needed and find the contractors to do the work. Of course, the cider production is under a completely different timescale." Sebastian turned to Sam.

"We should have a good crop this year but not enough on our own. However, I have spoken to other orchard owners along the Helford and we should be able to buy their apples, which includes the Manaccan Primrose and Tommy Knight. The additional varieties will improve the cider."

"You've spoken to people about this?"

Sam nodded. "If we're going to produce a commercial-scale artisan cider, we need more fruit and I also needed to know from local restaurants and pubs if they would stock our cider."

"I don't want answers today. I want everyone to study the proposal and come back to me by the end of the week." Sebastian stood and gathered his papers.

Victoria leaned back. Clearly she had missed something in her assessment of Sam. He wasn't simply a gardener and there was something he wasn't telling her, but had told Sebastian. He sat there looking like a beach bum. She closed her eyes and tried to imagine him doing anything other than working in the garden or messing with a boat and it didn't fit. Had her vision become so narrow? Yes, it must have. She turned to Demi. What was she made of? What made her tick? Victoria needed to find out and find out fast if she was going to be able to save Boscawen and leave any sort of legacy behind.

CHAPTER
TWENTY

Demi pulled Sam's 4x4 into the car park at the care home. One of the residents was deadheading the flower baskets in the front. She walked up to her grandfather's room when she didn't see him outside. It overlooked the large gardens. It wasn't big, but they had made it homely for him. He sat in a chair by the window with *Pride and Prejudice* in his hands.

"Hello, my lovely. I wasn't expecting you."

She rushed and hugged him. Tears threatened which was foolish. She had no reason to cry, but the pressure had been building. All the others were keen to press forward and part of her was too. She would love to design the revamp of the house and the conversion of the outbuildings, but she didn't want to tie herself to Victoria.

"Make us a cup of tea and tell me all the news." He placed his book on the side table.

"How are things?" she asked.

"Good. November third is the day for the new hip and with all the physio I should be dancing again once it's done." He laughed.

She placed the mug in front of him. "I'm so pleased."

"Me too." He took her hand. "But your world, unless things have changed, is upside down still."

"True."

"No decision yet?"

"The plans were formally proposed yesterday." She shook her head. "And one minute I'm sure I want to go ahead and then the next I want to run as far from Boscawen as possible."

"Not surprised."

"Why?" She frowned. With his connection to Boscawen she'd expected a different response.

"I would have thought that that was obvious: Victoria Lake."

"She's not a nice person from what I can tell, but . . ." Demi sighed. "I can't believe she's quite what she appears either."

"Few people are." He sipped his tea and looked out to the garden. "No one is, not even someone as straightforward as your mother."

She missed her so much. At this point Demi would have loved nothing more than to sit and drink copious quantities of tea with her and discuss what she should do. "Do you know how my parents met?"

"Through work, I believe."

She digested this information. It fitted with Charles's charity connection. Oh, she wished she could remember him. It was as if her life didn't begin until after her appendix came out. From the age of seven Demi's memory was sharp; in fact, photographic in much of the detail, but nothing from before. She would

238

have thought the pictures in the photo album would have triggered memories, but they hadn't.

"I'm trying to put it all together but I can't."

He reached out and touched her hand. "I'm not much help."

"That's not true." She sighed. "Why did Mum say Charles was dead?"

"I wish your grandmother were here. She might have known."

"Me too." She sighed. Telling Demi her father was dead didn't fit with the mother she knew. Was it for fear of Victoria? Demi could understand that, but not much else. "I get this weird feeling whenever I'm at Boscawen."

He looked up from his tea. "Yes?"

"It's almost like a deja vu but not really. It's more feelings than images."

"What feelings?"

Demi ran a hand through her hair. "Fear, mostly."

"I see."

"I don't. Why would I feel terror in Boscawen? There's no way I could have been there before." She looked at her grandfather closely. He was quite still. "Is there?" She stood.

He frowned. "I don't think so."

"Why don't I *remember*?" She sank down on to the edge of the bed.

"You were lucky to survive when you were ill. We almost flew back early because it was touch and go"

"Anything else?"

He closed his eyes and rubbed his forehead. "Ah." He opened his eyes and picked up the notebook from the bedside table. "Your mother was staying at a hotel, the St Petroc."

"The St Petroc?" That was the one she'd seen when she'd first arrived. *Cakes*.

"Yes. I'm sure about that. It was very smart. Charles liked it and we'd meet you there for tea." He smiled. "When they went out and we couldn't look after you they would use the hotel's childcare."

"Was I with the childcare when I fell ill?"

"I would assume so. But that's all I know."

"Nothing else?" She frowned.

"Are you all right, my lovely?"

"Fragments are all I have. Everything feels out of reach."

"Well, after you were ill your mother didn't want to let you out of her sight."

"That explains a lot — but did I get lost or something?" She took a deep breath, studying her grandfather and wondering if there was more he could tell her. He looked so tired.

"I don't know. Your grandmother may well have known more."

"Thanks for telling me what you have." She stood and kissed his forehead.

"I don't suppose this discussion helped you to decide what to do?"

"No, but it helped in other ways. If you think of anything else, let me know."

240

"Of course. What I do know is that your grandmother thought your mother never recovered from nearly losing you that day. Maybe she blamed your father for what happened to you, although I'm not sure why. And I think she might have blamed herself."

"I wonder."

A bell rang.

"That will be lunch." He pushed himself out of his chair. "Will you walk down with me?"

She nodded and watched him hobble to his walker. The hip replacement couldn't come soon enough.

"Don't have caffeinated coffee — your stress levels are high enough." Peta sat down at the café table with her.

"How can you tell?" Demi squinted, trying to see how she could know.

"I could say you had a black aura, but it is the way your shoulders are bunched up. So skip the coffee and go for a camomile or maybe a fresh mint."

"Actually, that sounds good." Demi stood ready to head to the counter to order. "What can I get you?"

"A double espresso."

Demi smiled. "Cake?"

Peta nodded. After studying the tempting array, Demi decided that Peta could use chocolate to go with her coffee, but she would refrain. Despite all the hard work planting the trees, she seemed to be putting on weight and that wasn't good. She was curvy enough.

After she had ordered, she looked at the greenhouse they were sitting in. A light rain fell outside, but it was

241

still bright. In the distance, she could see artist studios. This was a happy spot and she was pleased that Peta had suggested this as a place to meet.

"So why are you stressed?" Peta looked up from her phone as Demi returned.

"The future of Boscawen and also of several people rests on my choice."

Peta's eyes focused on Demi. "OK, let's forget them. What do *you* want to do?"

"I don't know."

"OK, what do you *know* then?"

Demi shrugged. "Your cake looks delicious."

"It is, and why didn't you get yourself some?" Peta asked.

"Trying to be good."

"Why?" Peta turned her head slightly, showing her displeasure before picking up her cup.

"If I'm not careful I'll become fatter than I am."

"Wake up, woman, you are not fat." Peta looked at her over the rim of her cup. "You are simply gorgeous."

Demi smiled. "And you are kind."

"Sometimes." Peta grinned. "Mostly not, though." She cut a piece of cake off and handed it to Demi. "Now, once you've eaten that tell me about your time with your grandfather today."

Demi frowned despite the delicious spread of chocolate across her taste buds. "We finally have a date for the surgery."

"Excellent." She picked up her fork. "Tell me more about what he told you. It's troubling you."

242

Demi refrained from asking how Peta knew. "OK, wise one, can you tell me why I feel I've been to Boscawen before and what happened just before my appendix burst."

Peta put down her fork. "No, I can't, but you were scared. I can't see why though."

Demi swallowed as random pictures went through her mind. Eyes, bluebells, giants . . .

Peta touched her arm. "Hey, come back from wherever you're wandering."

"Where am I wandering?"

"I'm not sure but . . ." Peta squinted out of the window at the rain. "There was pain and fear."

"I need to know why."

Peta sighed. "There may be simple and good reasons you can't remember."

"Because I can't remember — is that why you can't 'see'?"

"Might be or might not." Peta shrugged. "I can't control the damn thing. If I could, I'd be famous."

"You have no desire to be famous." Demi stole another bite of cake.

"And how do you know that?"

Demi grinned. "You're not the only one who can read people."

"For that comment I'm going to get you a piece of cake."

She put her hands up. "I don't need one."

"Oh, yes you do. You keep stealing mine!"

Demi laughed but when Peta left for the counter she went back to thinking about the gap in her memories.

"Now here's your cake. Eat that and stop worrying about the past. Talk to me about your future and what it's like living with Sam?"

Demi blinked. Peta was hard to follow sometimes, but it was good to have a friend here to talk things through with, even if it was one who plied her with cake. She enjoyed the dark chocolate, thinking about Sam and wondering how to answer the question.

CHAPTER
TWENTY-ONE

Sun poured through the windscreen. Demi watched the icing begin to melt on the cakes she was holding on her lap. She'd baked them yesterday when Sam mentioned he'd volunteered and she'd watched him take out two packets of cake mix. He had claimed that was what they expected from a bloke. She'd laughed and went straight to work. She'd forgotten how much she missed baking. It was something she and her mother had done together most Saturdays. Had Morwenna learned to bake from her grandfather's mother, Demi wondered? She'd have to ask him.

Sam parked the 4x4 and then opened her door. He took one cake from her and she managed with great care to hold on to the other and slide down from the seat. Normally it was a two-handed job to climb down so trying to do this with a chocolate cake in her hand was tricky.

"Well done. I'll walk down to the cake stall with you and then come back and get the other stuff."

Demi frowned. She was unsure about this regatta thing that Sam was intent on. But it was a cloudless day and she had nothing better to do. At the crest of the hill she looked down on a field decked out in bunting. It was a hive of activity. Where had all the people come from?

"Follow me." Sam led her through the crowds to a long table sheltered by a white gazebo. Already it was laden with baked goods of every variety.

"Hello, ladies. It's going to be a hot one this year." He handed over the walnut cake and Demi quickly did the same with the chocolate offering. Her cakes didn't look too bad but compared to some they really didn't measure up to the high standard on show.

"Baked these yourself, did you?" One woman smiled at Sam.

"Well, this year I had some help, Jane." He winked and tilted his head towards Demi. For some unknown reason, she went scarlet. He wasn't talking about anything but baking. She was far too sensitive.

"Oh, I bet that was fun. Did you lick the bowl?" Jane grinned.

"How did you guess?"

"Might have been there myself once." She turned to Demi. "Are you new to the area, like Sam here?"

Demi swallowed. "Yes, but not from Australia."

"Ah well, you're from Boscawen now, so like Sam you belong here. Welcome and enjoy the regatta." She turned to Sam. "Will you be racing?"

"Of course. Has James been training?" He leaned against the table.

"Yes, but only of the bending the elbow kind!"

"Pleased to hear it. See you later."

Sam took Demi's hand and they walked past the gazebos all offering something different from whack the rat to tombola. "It will all kick off shortly. I suggest you sit here on this wall in the shade until I come back with your hat and the bags."

She nodded, mesmerised by all the activity. The area was buzzing with happy people. She smiled, watching a child head out on to the quay where the loudspeaker was directing activity. The creek behind glistened in the sun and many boats were decked out in bunting with people in various costumes. The place was mad.

A woman with an eyepatch on and a stripy cropped top looked strangely familiar. It was Peta. She was on the arm of a man similarly dressed. Was Sam going to wander down the hill as a pirate? He'd make a good one.

"Away with the fairies?" Sam asked.

Demi jumped. "No, the pirates." She pointed to Peta.

"Aye, aye, me matey." He popped her hat on her head. "Let's go and get the boat."

"Boat?"

"Come on. You're gonna have a brilliant day racing."

"Racing? Are you out of your mind?"

He grinned. "Don't tell me you're afraid?"

"I won't tell you then." She took a deep breath. "I've only ever been on a ferry on the Thames."

"Today will change all that. It's not racing as you know it or you imagine it." He paused. "Trust me."

She took a few steps backwards.

He held out a hand. "I promise you, it will be fun."

She looked at him and then the boat. It appeared harmless enough and everyone else around was enjoying themselves. Her phone beeped as a text message came in. She flinched. It would be from Matt imploring her to come back to him. Taking a deep breath, she took Sam's hand and climbed on board. It wobbled and she fell on to a seat.

"See you have the hang of it already." He looked at a sheet of paper. "We don't have a race for an hour so let's go and get a drink."

"I won't eat one." Demi crossed her arms. She'd been fascinated watching the woman pry the oysters open and then loosen them before she handed them to the waiting people.

"Helford oysters are the best and you must at least try." Sam held out a shell on his hand. "I'll show you how it's done." He put his head back, tipped the oyster into his mouth, closed his eyes and chewed. Demi watched the signs of pleasure cross his face. She had to look away.

He touched her cheek. "It's OK. Mind you, it would be better with a crisp Picpoul de Pinet, or even better would be a Clare Valley Riesling."

"Too true," the woman said.

"I thought you weren't supposed to eat oysters in a month without an R in it?" Demi looked at the shiny glob in the shell. It was alive. She couldn't eat something that was alive, could she?

The woman smiled. "Mostly true but we know our oysters."

Sam handed over money for another one. "Now it's your turn — and remember, it's for charity."

248

Demi wrinkled her nose. She didn't think she could do it. Peta came up. "Just knock it back in one if you're afraid of it. Not everyone enjoys them quite as much as Sam here."

"But you miss out the sweet salty flavour if you do that." Sam turned to Peta.

"He's right," said the woman shucking them. "But if it's your first one then it's not a bad way to try."

"Be daring." Peta pushed Sam's hand holding the oyster closer to Demi.

"I don't see *you* eating them."

Peta grinned. "I had three earlier and I've just had chocolate cake. It wouldn't taste right."

"OK." Demi took the shell from Sam, feeling the ridges on the back of it. She raised it to her mouth and could smell the sea, fresh and tangy. Copying what Sam had done, she brought the shell to her mouth. It was at this point that she noticed the crowd who had gathered to watch. It almost looked like they were taking bets on whether she would do it or not. Her eyes met Sam's. His danced with laughter. It was a challenge.

Silently she counted down. Three, two, one . . . she tipped it in. Cold. Tangy. Sweet. It slid off her tongue and down her throat. She opened her eyes as the crowd broke out in cheers.

"That wasn't too bad, was it?" Sam smiled.

"No." Demi would have loved that glass of wine he'd mentioned. If they had it here now she might be tempted to try another one.

"Well done. There's a first time for everything." Peta laughed. "Now for your first race. Sam, I brought the boat round."

Demi laughed. Well, if she could eat an oyster and enjoy it then this racing ought to be a laugh. She watched the parent-child rowing race finish then said, "lead the way."

Closing her bedroom door, Victoria walked downstairs. She could hear Seb on the phone in the kitchen, his deep voice putting something in order. Everything hinged on Demelza's decision. Victoria could only hope that she had some of Charles's business sense, but going by his last few investments, maybe that wasn't what she should wish for.

The day was not as bright as yesterday with the remnants of a mist lingering in the air. More so than normal she could smell the sea. Gravel crunched under her feet as she walked to the long bed. The agapanthus blooms were at their peak. It was hard to believe that all these plants came from the few seeds that her great-grandmother had brought back from South Africa. Victoria smiled. Edith had loved telling her about the month they spent there, waiting for the ship to be repaired. Using the time she'd explored the flora and fauna and had seen these intense blue agapanthus. She'd had to have them so she'd pleaded with the owner and he had parted with some seeds. Her great-grandmother had nurtured those plants for ten years before they had bloomed and their bright blue heads and the eucalyptus were the most obvious legacies of her travels. When she had come to Boscawen as a bride of eighteen, it had been mostly a working farm with a few roses and of course the orchards.

Victoria looked behind her. A watery light hit the granite face of the building, making it softer. The house would have looked pretty much as it did now, down to the elder trees, although the one growing close to the corner of the house was not the same one. It was just an offshoot of the one Edith had drawn in her diary.

"Mrs Lake." Sam walked up to her.

"Please call me Victoria, Sam. If we are to be partners, Mrs Lake is too formal." She smiled at him. He was carrying a handful of roses, a mixed lot. She guessed from the array of colours and blooms they were from the back of the cutting garden.

"I saw they were invading the raspberry canes as I was fixing the netting on the cages and Mermaid weed was invading the path."

"Thanks."

She turned to the agapanthus again. Already over one hundred heads were in bloom and tomorrow more would be opening. Her loss to Tregarne Farm at the Constantine show still stung but hopefully she would win next year. She sighed.

"They've put on a good display this year." Sam smiled.

"Yes. They're special."

"I'll grant you they are a good colour." He bent down and pulled a stray blade of grass from the bed.

"Really?" She'd known them all her life and to her they were a sign of summer. It was tempting to look back to the past when things were clearer and the biggest decision had been to sail or swim or both.

"Yes. But that's about all I can say about them."

Victoria sighed. She might not be here next year to see them. The thought terrified her. If she didn't have Boscawen then what did she have? "Shall I take those flowers?" She held out her hand.

"You aren't wearing gloves and Mermaid is particularly prickly."

"I can manage." She smiled at him. The pain of the thorns was easy to take. The loss of Boscawen would not be.

"If you say so." But his actions belied his words as he kept them wrapped in his glove.

"Thanks. See you in the dining room shortly." Victoria began to walk away then stopped and turned to him. "Has she said anything to you?"

"No."

"Well, we'll know soon enough." She lifted the roses to her face and inhaled. She just had to hope — and that was the worst part.

Laughter. When had she last laughed? Adam was fun but not funny. Victoria had seen Demi and Sam laughing as they walked together down the drive with a conspiratorial air about them last night. They weren't lovers yet, but Victoria knew the signs. They were all there. She almost wanted to shout at them to get on with it. Their sexual attraction to each other was annoying, especially as things with Adam were interrupted now that Sebastian was virtually living here. He was ruining everything. Without him here she could have Adam move in. She still could, of course. It would be awkward to start with, but just because Sebastian was willing to invest money in Boscawen didn't mean that he had a right to live in the house. However, she couldn't boot him out just yet.

Victoria closed her eyes for a moment, savouring the scent of the lilies she'd brought in yesterday. Today she would hear Demi's answer. Everything hinged on it and so Victoria had tried to stay out of her way as much as possible. She knew Demi hated her. Well, it was mutual. How was she going to manage to partner with the manifestation of Charles's infidelity and fertility? She didn't know, except that she would do everything for Boscawen. It was what she'd been trained to do, but never given the opportunity until now.

"Tori, I've been looking everywhere for you." Sebastian was clutching a pad of paper. She walked to him. He was rested today and his eyes danced with his smile. The grey at his temples and laced through his hair didn't make him look older, simply more handsome. His eyes were intelligent, caring and sensual. Where had he put his passion all these years?

"I've drawn up plans B and C for you in case Demi doesn't buy in."

Victoria raised an eyebrow. "I thought you wanted me to be rid of this place?"

"Only if it makes you happy."

"Happy? What an interesting concept — and you must be the only person who has ever worried about my real happiness."

253

"Maybe."

She stepped closer until she could see the flecks of black in his irises. There was barely room for the air to flow in between them but he didn't step away. "What do you want, Sebastian John Andrew Roberts?"

"That has never changed." His breath caressed her cheek.

"You never took it when it was offered to you."

"It wasn't mine to take then."

She laughed. "You couldn't possibly want it now."

He leaned closer. "Try me."

"Hmm, I could be tempted but . . ." Victoria inhaled his fresh scent and noted the deep lines beside his eyes, those clever eyes. "But it's best to never go backwards."

"But did we ever go forwards or were we just suspended?"

There was a discreet cough. Sam stood in the doorway. "Mrs Lake, we're in the dining room."

"Thanks, Sam, and again, please call me Victoria." She stepped back from Sebastian. It was tempting to think of falling back into his arms, but that was past and they all needed to look forward with clear sight and no emotional commitments.

Demi stood at the bow window. One of the sashes was up and the scent of roses drifted in on the breeze. The sound of bees filled the air as they harvested a bed filled with lavender just below the window. Her chats with Peta were fresh in her mind. Her father's inheritance was found money and she needed to take a chance on whether it was to set off and go around the world or try and make something of a life here. Her life so far had been too protected. She wasn't fragile or stupid so she needed to grab it with both hands and make it her own.

The business plan made sense and it gave Sam an opportunity to prove himself — and this, more than anything else, motivated Demi. He seemed driven to take this chance and to build something here. She sensed something else at work too, but couldn't pull it out of him. Maybe he'd missed or lost an opportunity in Margaret River. In one way, Sam was an open book, but she knew there was more below the surface. He rarely spoke of home or his family other than to mention that he had one. In fact, he shared very little about himself except his enthusiasm for Cornwall, sailing, and making something lasting with the cider. She heard him speaking to Victoria and Sebastian.

A shiver ran down her spine as she turned and caught sight of a portrait of her father. She hadn't noticed it when she'd been in the room before. He wasn't quite smiling but there was a kindness in his eyes. He was the one who had placed her in this position, a position of power. What she chose to do would affect every one of them. She hated this. It was bad enough deciding whether to have a cappuccino or a latte.

She perched on the windowsill and closed her eyes. Right now she wanted to talk to her mother. How would she feel about Demi being here and, more importantly, Demi investing in Boscawen? It all came down to what did she want. She looked at her father's portrait. By all accounts he had known exactly what he'd wanted in life and gone for it. Every decision she'd made since she had been a teenager she had talked through with her mum. Now she had to do this herself.

Turning around to look out, she could see one of the long flowerbeds. At the moment it was a mass of deep blue agapanthus. Every morning there seemed to be more. The colour contrast with orange crocosima was stunning. It had been a joy to watch the garden come to life in the weeks that she'd been here. Would she be here to see the next stage? Did she want to be?

If she invested she could lose her father's legacy. But as she had never had money before did it matter? No. It would give her a chance to use her design skills and, if it was unbearable, she could leave, maybe without her money but no, she wasn't tied here forever.

CHAPTER
TWENTY-TWO

It was like having a child sitting at the end of the table. Victoria had the urge to go and find a cushion so that Demi didn't look so tiny. Although she knew intellectually that Demelza was Charles's and was the right age to be Victoria's own, she found it hard to accept. Charles had been so straight, so moral, so bloody missionary position, how could he have had an affair? And yet . . . well, Victoria knew why. Although she had always been there for him physically, had she ever been there for him intellectually or emotionally? Her infertility had driven a wedge into the small crack that had begun when he'd refused to play along with the tradition of Men an Skawenn after their wedding. He'd been afraid he would get stuck and be caught naked in a field. Victoria smiled. She'd gone first and slid through without any problem just as Edith and Gladys had. Victoria had asked her mother if she had done it. She'd never answered but had blushed. That told her everything.

Even Perry and his wife had done it. Not that they had been married long enough to produce a family. Victoria sometimes thought she should find out what had become of her sister-in-law. But then she really didn't want to know, and if she were honest, she'd behaved appallingly to her. It was something that still stung her conscience even after all these years. Victoria had raged at her for cutting the elder without asking its permission and therefore killing her beloved brother. She must have sounded like a madwoman. All those extra fertility hormones that had been pumped into her had played havoc with her brain. In some ways it had been no surprise when the "for sale" sign had gone up.

"Good, we're all here." Sebastian placed a pile of papers and what looked like more plans on the table. "I'm just going to grab the tea I've made and we can start."

"I'll give you a hand." Sam jumped up. Victoria could sense Sam's nerves. He'd put a lot of work into his part of the plan and she wondered why he hadn't raised it with her before. Of course she'd never given him the chance. If they went ahead Sam would almost be an equal partner from what Sebastian had been saying, although she wasn't sure how as all he had was some experience in a vineyard in Australia.

She frowned and turned to Demelza, who was ashen. Victoria looked about for the ghost she must have seen but the room was empty except for them. A fly stole in through the open window. It came across the table and hovered over the pile of papers at the end, then it moved down, pausing in front of Demi.

Victoria and Demi looked each other in the eye. Demi, for once, held her glance without flinching. The fly hovered between them before making its way back to the window and out into the garden. What had she seen in Demi's eyes? Was it fear or was it defiance?

A laden tray was placed on the table, Victoria turned. Sebastian had gone for the full works. Not only had he made tea but sandwiches as well and he'd even found cake. Did he think this would be a long meeting?

Sam poured tea and she smiled. She liked men waiting on her, especially young, good-looking ones. He knew just how she liked it too. She grinned. Adam might be able to come over tonight. She must ring him.

"Right. I have sourced some extra funding and rejigged the plans a bit." Sebastian handed out sheets of paper and Victoria pushed away the feeling that she was about to sit an exam. This wasn't a test for her. She'd done everything she could to save Boscawen. Adam had told her that word was already out that it would be put up for sale and several people were expressing interest. She had a feeling she knew who they would be.

"As you can see from the figures below we have an offer of another two million in cash from someone who wishes to remain anonymous but wants Sam to act as a partner in their stead."

"Who on earth?" Victoria asked. "How can we work with someone who would have such a large stake and not know who they are?"

"You and Demi would still be the main shareholders." Seb turned his attention to Demi. "We will need your answer today."

"I know." Demi put her folded hands on the table.

Good God, couldn't she see that everyone was waiting for her? Victoria rolled her eyes. This was so like

Charles. He had to have the last word, and in a way that is exactly what he had done by dying. He'd been angry and made a decision to rush down to catch her with Adam. He'd got the last word, but not the way he'd intended it. She slumped in the chair. She would have preferred a slanging match. Not that they had happened often but they cleared the air. It was funny, she had never thought about that before. It was after huge arguments that they had had the best sex and had the best conversation. Only during those times had she felt she'd known him. Most of the time he kept his thoughts to himself.

"Tori?"

"Yes?" She looked up.

"I asked if you had any questions about the revised figures in front of you?" Sebastian looked mildly annoyed but it was more the tone of his voice that crawled right under her skin. Why was he doing this? He had no attachment to Boscawen. Her father had never felt Sebastian or his family had been good enough. So when Sebastian had gone off to Africa to build houses, her father had set up a relentless campaign to marry her off to Charles.

"Sorry. I was lost in a thought." She looked up and saw that wretched portrait of Charles. She had hated it from the moment he had raised the idea. From the wall, he neither smiled nor frowned although she detected a glimmer in his eyes. Yes, he was laughing at her she was sure. Had he won? Had they been fighting and she hadn't noticed. How had she not known that he had had an affair? Had she ignored the signs? She pursed her mouth and ran her fingers down the figures. What burned most was that he might have given what little passion he'd had to someone else.

She laughed. How could she be jealous now?

"Is everything all right?" Sebastian asked.

Victoria saw the three of them staring at her. She composed her face. "Fine. You've made an addition error in column three. It should read 1,350,500."

Sebastian frowned as he looked at her. He was not amused but suddenly she was.

The figures on the sheet in front of her looked fine. How Victoria could have seen that the calculation was wrong was beyond Demi. Everyone was looking at Victoria and she appeared cool, almost too calm, knowing how she felt about Boscawen. Demi jumped up and opened another window. She stood staring at the garden. They were all waiting for her answer but as yet hadn't asked her. Should she blurt it out?

Turning back, she saw everyone staring at her. The urge to bolt out of the room was great. Demi wiped her hands down her skirt and walked back to the table.

Sam caught her eye. His glance seemed to ask if she was OK. He had so much riding on this. She gave him a small smile and sat down.

"Aside from the small error, does anyone have any questions?"

"The only question that anyone has is: is Demi in or out?" Victoria turned to her. Her face was a polite mask. Demi blinked, searching for some emotion but Victoria revealed nothing. Could she work with

Victoria? Working with Sam and Sebastian wouldn't be a problem, but Victoria would be.

"Well, yes, we all do wish to know." Sebastian gave Demi an encouraging smile.

"I'm . . ." Demi stopped. If she was going to do this then she needed guarantees that she would have a say even though she was the person who knew Boscawen the least.

"Yes?" Victoria raised an eyebrow.

Demi clutched her hands over her knees pleased that no one could see them. Her nails bit into the flesh.

"I . . ." She paused again. How did she say this? "I am interested in going ahead, but I have reservations."

"What reservations?" Victoria leaned closer to the table.

You. Demi slowly put her hands on the table. "I want my role defined. Nowhere in this proposal does it list my role."

"And just what would that be?" Victoria raised her hands in question as if she was suddenly Italian.

"I'm an architect and I've worked on a project not dissimilar to this, so I want to be the lead designer for the —"

"No!" Victoria stood.

"Sit down." Sebastian's voice was calm but held a warning. Victoria turned and glared at him. This was what Demi was afraid of, Victoria.

"Demi, I'm sorry." Sebastian stood.

"Well, that's my condition." Demi gulped in air. How could she have thought of going forward? "You can count me out then." She stood on wobbly legs.

"No, Demi, I meant that I'm sorry I hadn't consulted you or considered what you could bring to the project," Sebastian said.

She stopped halfway out of the door and turned. "No, most people don't," she said and walked out.

"What a little madam." Victoria leaned back in her chair.

"No." Sebastian put his head in his hands.

"She'll get over it." But as the words left her mouth, Victoria regretted them. She was behaving like a man, a man dismissing a pretty woman.

Sebastian looked up at her. "We have just made a huge mistake and you're saying she'll get over it. You've dismissed her from the start and I didn't even consider anything else but her share of the estate and the funds."

Victoria opened her mouth but Sebastian put a hand up. "We all need to apologise."

"What for?" Victoria didn't like this train of thought at all. Attack was what she wanted — but there was so much to lose. She turned to the garden. What would she have, if she didn't have this? Nothing.

"Excuse me." Sam dashed out of the door. Would he be able to make her see sense? How were they to know? She'd never said a word. Victoria stood and went to the window. The scent of lavender filled the air. She breathed it in, hoping it would calm her. Nothing. She would have nothing. She didn't want the money — she wanted Boscawen.

She walked back to the table. "Seb, I'll go and apologise."

"It may be too late."

She released the pent-up air in her lungs. "That's what I'm afraid of but . . . I won't forgive myself if I don't try." She pushed back the feeling swamping her. "You see, without Boscawen there is no possibility for me to leave my mark on the world, a lasting mark, that is."

CHAPTER
TWENTY-THREE

Demi walked out of the front door. Decision made, she should be breaking out the champagne and celebrating. She was free. Yet she sighed.

"Demi!" Sam called. He dashed up the drive to her. She debated whether to wait or just to continue walking, but that would be rude and he'd been kind. She stopped and he reached her side. "Sorry."

"What for?"

"For being a complete idiot and focusing only on my part in the potential redevelopment of Boscawen."

She looked up at him and tried to see if this was truth or just words to get her on side. She started walking again and he placed a hand on her arm. "Seriously, forget everything and just know that I'm sorry." She turned to him. His big blue eyes held no secrets. He was sincere and he was looking at her and not just bits of her.

"Thank you." She slowed her pace. The sun filtered through the trees making patterns on the ground.

"I've been so self-centred." Sam's stride matched hers. "You've been staying with me and I never asked what you did — or if I did I didn't listen. You see, ever since I came to Boscawen I could see and feel its potential. I'd heard a bit of local lore in the pub and it spoke of the cider they used to make and not just ordinary stuff but a really fine cider. That had been playing on my mind and I was going to present my plans to both Mr and Mrs Lake but fate intervened in a way I'd never imagined." He shrugged.

"Oh."

"But you're the one who's had the tough time, losing your mother, and then before you had a chance to find out about your father he was gone. No one has been considering you in all of this and that was, and is, wrong." He looked at her solemnly. "Repeating myself again, I am really sorry."

Demi's mouth lifted on one side. He looked like a small boy at the moment with his eyes gleaming yet all of him trying to appear smaller and contrite.

"Thank you."

He grinned. "That's better. Let's forget Boscawen for a moment and tell me about Demelza Williams."

She frowned.

"Big topic?" He tilted his head.

She let out a small laugh. "Small person."

"You're really hung up on this small thing." He stopped walking and looked her up and down. She flinched. "Perfect, to me."

Demi tensed inside. "Yes, a little doll." Her face twisted with the sarcasm.

"No, not doll-like at all, far too real for that."

She turned from him.

"I seem to be able to put foot in mouth with every sentence today. What I mean is —"

266

"Look, Sam, I can tell you mean well, but let's just leave my appearance out of this." She sighed.

"If we must." He was trying to keep a straight face but the corner of his mouth was turning up in a smile. She looked away.

"We must."

"Fine. What are your plans now that you aren't staying at Boscawen?"

She laughed. "Good question. I hadn't thought that far ahead — you see, I had planned to stay but there is no way I can do that now."

They reached the gatehouse and she took a deep breath. The air was filled with the scent of the climbing rose that sprawled through an ornamental cherry tree nearby. What was she going to do? She turned to Sam. He was studying her with sad eyes. She could see the loss of his dreams in them, but she wasn't responsible for him or anyone else. She was only in charge of her own dreams. Now all she had to do was figure out what they were.

"What if she says no?" Victoria walked round the dining-room table trying not to look at Charles's portrait. If she had something to hand she would throw it at him. It was all his fault!

"Well, we'll need to try and find another investor or two; failing that, once probate is finished, Boscawen will go on to the market."

"Noooo." She spat the word out but as the long syllable finished Victoria knew that was what would happen. And once again she was powerless to stop it.

The wheels were firmly in motion. Even if she were successful in contesting the will it would be too late to save Boscawen, to save those wretched apple trees she'd bought.

"I'm sorry, Tori."

She swung around. Those words — she'd heard them so many times in her ears. She should have said them to him but instead he had said them to her.

"There's nothing we can do, is there?"

"Realistically, not unless Demi has a change of heart." He pushed back the chair and stood. A few steps brought him closer to her. "I've tapped all my resources. I could find another million myself but that's just not enough."

They stood just inches apart. Old words echoed around them, except then they hadn't stood by the dining table, but on the quay, on a summer's evening with twilight just taking the day away. *I'm sorry, Tori, that I wasn't good enough.* He was older but the same man was there inside. Failure was written all over him.

But he hadn't failed either then or now. He had done his best for her. She'd done her duty then but what was her duty now? It had always been Boscawen. She looked into Sebastian's eyes and for a brief second years disappeared. Blood rose. *"Come live with me . . ."* Past whispers moved between them and the cry of a gull stole in on the still air.

Boscawen. That was her duty.

"I'll go and apologise to Demelza now. Then let's see where we are." Victoria stepped back and picked up her teacup. She sipped the cold liquid. Being lured by the sirens of the past would not create a future.

"You can try but we all made a huge mistake."

"True. Who knew she was anything but pretty?" As Victoria heard her own words she knew she had done what people had done to her. They had written her off as a well-bred chattel. Demi wasn't well bred but she was baby doll, pretty, with blue eyes and blonde hair. Why had Victoria assumed she hadn't got a brain or skills? Why had she fallen into the same role others had taken with her?

Placing the cup down she turned to Seb. "There's no time like the present. I will go and grovel and see what I can find out." She headed to the door. "You've said that she's homeless at the moment and that's why she's staying with Sam?"

He nodded.

"Good. There's the place to start."

Sebastian studied her with narrowed eyes. His face revealed nothing. Those memories of hers must have been lost fantasies, appearing like a mirage shimmering on the surface.

She closed the lid on her suitcase. Then the next thing was to strip the bed. Demi could hear Sam moving around, but didn't want to think about it. She'd called Peta and asked if she could stay with her for a few days. Distance from Boscawen was essential and it needed to happen as fast as possible. She'd almost said she would do it, just to give Sam his chance. But that would mean helping Victoria too and Demi definitely didn't want to do that.

The bedside clock said it was three in the afternoon and Peta was coming to pick her up at four. She could get the bedlinen into the machine for Sam. It was the least she could do. She stopped as she balled the laundry into her arms. The hair on her neck rose. Victoria. She was here. A tap on the door and Demi froze. What should she do? What on earth did the woman have to say to her? She freed one hand and opened the door. Victoria's hair was windblown which made her look less of the evil dragon that Demi had created in her head.

"Demi, I'm so glad I've caught you. Sam tells me you're leaving."

Demi frowned at Sam who was watching them from a distance. Had he called her? He stepped closer, appearing innocent, but Demi wasn't buying it. Why was Victoria here?

"Let me take those for you." Sam took the linen out of her arms, stripping Demi of her armour.

"Can we take a walk?" Victoria's voice revealed nothing. It didn't plead, it simply asked a polite question.

Demi squinted, looking at her watch. "A quick one."

"Excellent." Victoria strode out of the front door.

Victoria took a path opposite the gatehouse that Demi hadn't ventured on to before. It headed east into the woods. Demi walked slowly, watching Victoria stride swiftly ahead. The sun was still high but in the shade it was almost dark. Demi shivered and looked around. A bird darted in the underground and she jumped. This walk was not a good idea. She slowed even more and the gap between them widened. Sunlight caught the silver sleekness of Victoria's hair. She seemed fairylike yet threatening, the queen of this domain. As if sensing Demi's scrutiny, she turned and noticed the distance between them. She walked back, looking at Demi's flip-flops.

"Not ideal shoes for walking, but it's not much further." She smiled but it didn't reach her eyes. Victoria continued on but at a much slower pace. The trees began to thin and the path climbed up until they reached a clearing that was more a scar in the landscape. When Demi looked up she could see the river and Falmouth Bay beyond. Turning slightly, Boscawen came into view. Victoria strolled on until they reached a large stone. Ice crept up Demi's spine. It looked Neolithic, like a giant. She glanced around, noting the trees on the edge of the fields. Without a doubt she knew she had been here before.

"I used to come here as a child." Victoria climbed up the back of the stone. It seemed too tall to climb but Demi didn't want to stand beneath Victoria. She kicked off her flip-flops and made her way up barefoot. From the top of it the land seemed to wobble beneath them.

"I would pretend that one day this would all be mine. Of course, even then I knew it wouldn't be." Victoria sat down facing out towards the sea. Demi remained standing and slowly turned around, taking in the patchwork of ploughed fields, crops, cows and distant buildings. The wind was brisk and it lifted the hair off the back of Demi's neck. The rock beneath her feet was both warm and cool at the same time. How could she have been here before? Why did she think of this rock as the Kowres?

"Is this still a part of Boscawen?" Demi looked down on Victoria.

"Sadly, no. Charles wasn't able to buy this back."

"Are we trespassing?"

Victoria laughed. "No, this is listed and there has been public access here for years. No one knows for sure what it was used for but it came from nearby quarries, which have been mined since pre-history." She waved her hand behind her.

"Does it have a name?"

"The Kowres, the giantess. There's some local legend that she spurned her lover. First her heart turned to stone then the rest of her did. She is forever looking out on where he lived."

Demi's mouth went dry. The Kowres, eyes, fairies . . . Her heart rate picked up and cold sweat beaded on her bow. She needed to focus on something. She turned again and saw a beautiful Georgian house. It was more farmhouse than grand, or maybe the two had been merged along the way. It was the nearest structure to them. "Who owns that?"

Victoria sighed. "That used to be the Dower House for Boscawen. It was sold off to pay death duties when my great-grandmother passed away." She sighed again and Demi squinted, trying to see if that really was something like tears in Victoria's eyes. "It was a beautiful house but needs must and my father had no choice if he was to keep the rest of the estate together."

She pointed to a quay down on the river. "That was where the stone from the quarry was brought to be shipped off and . . ." She pointed towards the west. "The other quay dealt with the tin from the mines. Now they are just remnants of a lost world."

From this vantage point Demi tried to imagine the industry. It was hard; now it looked like nothing more than sleepy farmland and a yachting paradise.

"Why have you brought me here?"

Victoria looked up at her. "To apologise."

Demi stumbled and Victoria leapt to her feet, steadying her.

"You don't believe me."

"No."

"I can understand that." Victoria helped her to climb off the stone and they began walking back down the path.

"We are natural adversaries." Victoria spoke quietly. "You are my husband's . . ." Demi flinched waiting for the insult to come. "Daughter. And I was never able to have children." They turned left and walked through the woods on a different path. "Discovering you existed was not my happiest moment."

Demi swallowed. "I can imagine."

"I shouldn't have been surprised but I was."

Victoria went through a kissing gate first. A sign warned that they were now on the private property of the Boscawen Estate and must keep all dogs on leads and not stray from the clearly defined paths. In the distance Demi could see a ring of trees and barbed wire. Victoria tensed and remained silent until they had moved beyond it. Was it the same one she had seen with Sam?

"Is that . . ."

Victoria cut Demi off. "The elder tree stone or, in Cornish, Men an Skawenn." She walked faster, silently cursing Demi for noticing it. What on earth had persuaded her to come down this path? She hoped the Cornish would distract Demi. Victoria pressed her mouth into a flat line. Charles had refused and, looking back, he had been right. No special magic could have given her children.

They came out of the woods and the house appeared in the distance. Victoria tensed at the view. She had to hold on to this glimpse of Boscawen bathed in late afternoon sunlight. If she didn't convince Demi to take part in their plans then this time next year Boscawen would belong to someone else again.

The sound of huffs and puffs from behind told Victoria that she must slow down. She'd have to change tack if she was going to win — and she needed to win. Stopping at the gate she waited for Demi to reach her.

"I've always loved this view of Boscawen with the top just visible above the trees." She watched Demi's eyes follow the lines of the building. They were Charles's eyes and yes, they did reflect his intelligence. Charles had had a very clever mind, which had been one of the things that had attracted her to him somewhat. She must not forget that and, of course, there were times when he'd made her laugh. That laughter was the best bit and the fact that he had loved her, truly loved her. Although maybe that hadn't been true at all. She gasped as a pain seared through her chest.

"Are you OK?"

Victoria nodded. It was a bit late to have a broken heart. She half smiled at the thought. "So, as things stand, Demi, what we see in front of us is an ancient manor house that belongs to both of us." Victoria looked for reaction on her face but all she saw was wariness.

"We've been left a gift and a burden and I can quite understand that you may not see the gift side of it."

"You have no idea what I see." Demi pulled her shoulders back and Victoria kicked herself inwardly.

"True." Victoria gave a dry laugh. "Very true, I don't. But I do know that we have both been treated badly in this."

Demi's shoulders relaxed and Victoria continued, "You should have been left a legacy without conditions or connections. You should have been free to go and fly away from the father who abandoned you."

Demi blinked and Victoria could see she had hit a chord. "And I've been cheated out of my home, a home that had been taken from me before because I am a woman."

Demi turned to her and Victoria noticed that the wariness had disappeared. "So I'm asking myself what can we do?" She took a breath. "We can sell it and I lose Boscawen again and you gain the cash to fly away and go and do whatever you want to do, or we can

275

work together and make something out of what we've been given."

Demi's glance turned to the house again. Victoria tried to read what was there but couldn't. She didn't seem angry, more resigned.

"The way I see things is that you don't have a home at the moment and the way things are going I won't either." She turned away from Boscawen and studied Demi. The girl was really unnaturally pretty. Every feature was perfect, from the china-blue eyes and Charles's blond hair, swept up to show an elegant neck, to the curves most women would kill for, and all in a pint-size model. She would be so easy to dismiss — as Victoria had.

"Demi, I know nothing about you other than that you are the evidence of my husband's infidelity, which is not a good start, but it's the only one we have. Should we try and begin again and both of us look at the situation we are actually in?"

The blue eyes were neither cold nor welcoming. Victoria had no idea what Demi was thinking but she didn't think she could say anything else and then she remembered. "I also owe you an apology."

A flash of interest sparked in Demi's eyes so Victoria stumbled on, "I wrote you off and I, of all people, should never have done that. I'm sorry."

"Why you of all people?" Demi leaned against the fence.

"All my life I have been dismissed as just a woman, a well-bred breeding machine." She laughed bitterly.

276

"You, I imagine, have received the same treatment because you are so pretty."

Demi snorted. Not an attractive action but it told Victoria everything. She might not like this woman but they understood each other.

"So can we sit down and talk — really talk — about the situation we find ourselves in?"

Demi tilted her head to one side. Charles used to do the same and Victoria shivered. Normally this was when Charles would say no and Victoria braced herself.

"Maybe."

CHAPTER
TWENTY-FOUR

Demi pulled out a CV from the bottom of her computer bag and handed it to Victoria. Inside she was trembling but she remembered what her mother had said: no one can see inside. Only you know you are scared. Her voice was steady as she said, "Before we even begin to talk I think you need to know a little bit about me."

Victoria took the paper.

"Read it and then call me." She held Victoria's gaze and then turned and walked into the gatehouse. Her bags and Peta were waiting.

"Cool customer. You go girl." Peta smiled and then pointed towards Sam who was standing by the entrance to the kitchen.

Demi walked towards him. "Sam, thank you for letting me stay."

He grinned sheepishly. "That's fine coming from you. You own the place."

"True, but it never felt that way."

"What am I going to do without you to help with the trees?"

"You'll have to make Victoria work harder." She smiled.

278

Sam took a step closer to her. "What are you going to do?"

"Aside from travel the world drinking champagne?"

He nodded.

"Well, I think I'll go and walk along the coastal path and let my mind go blank while I absorb the beauty."

"Sounds like the beginning of a plan." He put his hand in his pockets.

"She's coming out with me tonight and I intend to lead her astray," Peta said.

"Be careful with her." Sam trailed the back of a finger down Demi's cheek. "I'm going to miss you." He moved closer. Demi held her breath. He bent down and kissed her lightly. She couldn't move, holding on to all the details, the strength of his hands and the scent of peppermint lingering in the space between his lips and hers.

Peta picked up two bags. "I'll just take these to the car."

Demi stepped backwards, not looking at his face. She focused on the muscles in his arms, the contrast of white T-shirt and tanned flesh. These were easier things than the look of loss she had glimpsed on his face.

"Demi?"

"Yes?" She looked up, a mistake.

"I'm sorry, and you need to do the right thing for you."

"Um, yes and thanks." She fled out to the car as fast as she could.

*　★　★*

Victoria didn't stop walking at the house but continued past until she reached the quay. An easterly wind blew down the river and with the outgoing tide created small white horses across the surface. She waved to the fishing boat on its way in with the usual parade of gulls trailing behind. Slipping off her shoes, she stepped on a slab of granite, its surface cool beneath her feet. She flexed her shoulders, not sure what to do. She had no idea what to think of Demi. Having read her CV it was no wonder she'd been livid at their dismissal of her. The qualifications were impressive. Audrey had been to stay at the hotel Demi had worked on and she'd said it was divine.

But Victoria still wasn't easy about this odd alliance that Seb had hammered together. A project, if she could even think of Boscawen as one, needed a single vision not one spread among four people.

Sam's interest was easy to see. He wanted to try his hand at cider making. She wasn't sure exactly why, but he was a young man and here was a great opportunity to be involved with a startup, to make something unique reflecting the heritage of the area.

Victoria paced. Nothing was clear. She stripped down to her bra and knickers and dived into the river. Her chest tightened, squeezing the air from her lungs. She broke through the surface, gasping. In jerky motions, she cut through the water until her limbs warmed up and it began to feel less biting. She checked for boat activity, but at the moment she had this segment of the river to herself. That was all she wanted,

280

Boscawen to herself. But she wouldn't have it at all if she didn't share, dammit.

When she reached the southern bank of the river, she stopped to look back at the woodland. The sessile oaks clustered close together, almost in clumps. The sun caught the leaves held on twisted branches and she didn't want to let it go. She wanted to be its caretaker, the last Tregan to hold Boscawen. To do that she would have to work with Charles's daughter . . .

The journey back across the river was hard and several times the waves slapped her in the face, filling her mouth and her eyes with water. It stung, but the pain was energising and her strokes became stronger until the quay was in sight. Nearing it, she slowed to a gentle breaststroke. Sebastian stood at the back of the quay, watching.

Too many years ago they used to meet here and sit until there was no light left in the evening sky, sharing a bottle of plonk that he'd bought in the village store. The memory of the sweet taste of the wine and the salt of the sea made her mouth water. Innocence, hope, dreams washed out with the tide pulling them both elsewhere.

As she climbed up the quayside, he stepped forward with a big towel and draped her shivering frame. He held her and the years slipped away. She was eighteen and he was twenty.

A twig snapped and his hands fell to his sides. He kicked something as he moved swiftly away from her. Victoria spied a bottle of wine. "You think of everything."

"Once a Boy Scout . . ." He shrugged as his words died away.

She threw her head back and laughed as she rubbed her body dry. Casting aside her wet bra and knickers, she pulled on her jeans, enjoying the feel of Sebastian's eyes on her body. Chills of remembered desire touched her skin as his glance lingered on her breasts. She stood straight, looking directly at him as she pushed her arms into her sleeves. She might not be eighteen, but time had been kind.

"Beautiful." His voice croaked.

"Thank you." Her cold fingers stumbled buttoning her shirt and his hand stilled hers, taking over the task. She watched them skilfully manage the fiddly job. When he'd finished, his fingers came under her chin and lifted her head.

"You're shivering," he whispered.

"Just readjusting to the temperature after the swim," she lied. His closeness affected her more than it should. It felt like someone had let an old genie out of the box. "Let's have some of the wine you've brought."

His movements were spare, nothing unnecessary, no flourish, just a job efficiently accomplished. "Hope you don't mind but I raided the cellar."

She smiled. "Not at all, that's what it's there for and if I'm not careful some of it will go off." She turned the glass, noting the mellow colour of the wine. "And that would be a sin." She smiled at him over the rim of the glass, inhaling the bouquet. "You opened this earlier."

"It needed to breathe."

"Always thinking ahead."

282

"Yes." He moved to her side and placed an arm around her shoulders. Warmth spread through her and the shivering stopped. They moved together to the side of the quay and sat down shoulder to shoulder. The sun was beginning to drop in the sky, but it would be hours before it would set.

"Are you sure you want to walk?" Peta leaned out of the car window.

"Yes. I need to think and this is the best way to do it." Demi glanced round at the path to the coast.

"You have your phone and it's charged?"

Demi laughed and pulled it out of her bag. "I have a charged phone. Thank you for worrying, Peta, but I'm OK. I just need to find some head space to think."

"Fine, but don't take too long. I have plans for tonight, remember."

Demi frowned. She just wanted to walk, think, then sleep.

"And no backing out."

"What time do you need me?"

"Seven. Don't be late."

Demi looked at her watch. It was five.

"You're right. There's no way you'll make it to Falmouth in that time with those clothes on and those sandals." She looked Demi up and down. "So I'll collect you at Maenporth at six thirty." And with the sound of stones flying Peta was off in her little car and peace descended. Demi began heading down the path beside the church, but turned back, going through the gate under the porch. The graveyard was peaceful and much larger than she would have expected for such a remote location. She couldn't be in a place like this without being aware of what she'd lost.

Reading the headstones without really absorbing the information, Demi allowed the sense of loss to swamp her. But then her mother's voice sounded loud and clear in her head, telling her she'd had enough wallowing and it was time to take action. Demi smiled and left the graveyard behind, saying a silent prayer for all the souls buried there.

The way from the church led to a set of steps. Below, the hillside covered in tall trees fell away to the glistening water that shimmered in the silence, and only when she ignored the sound of her heart beating did she hear the waves meeting the rocks that lined the headland. She turned to her left and the path twisted down under the canopy of trees. The air was cool, scented with eucalyptus, earth and pine. She climbed higher in this magic cave of trees, listening to the sound of her feet and the waves below.

The breeze was fresh once she came out of the cover of the trees. She shivered. Her clothes, as Peta had pointed out, weren't ideal for walking but that hadn't been her concern. It was the need for space. When she'd been sitting on the stone with Victoria, the one she'd seen as a child, and she had seen the sea in the distance, it had seemed far away and she had longed to be closer to it. Now, lifting her gaze, there was nothing but blue, green and grey broken only by a sailing boat and a tanker, open space with nothing holding it in. But, of course, that was just an illusion. She turned, tracing the shapes of the various headlands with her eyes. There was something almost sensuous about the round mounds before they fell into the sea below.

Demi set off towards Falmouth, letting her mind wander where it would rather than forcing it to make a plan. When she was struggling with a design, walking through Battersea Park had always provided the answer as long as she didn't *think* about finding it. It was something about repetitive motion and the vastness of the sky above.

Her ankle wobbled as she stepped on a loose stone. She'd better pay a bit more attention to the path and not just the view otherwise she would end up with a sprained ankle. That was the last thing that she needed at this point because Peta's flat was on the top floor in a townhouse.

A cormorant on a rock below stretched its wings, waiting for the sun and the air to dry them. It reminded her of the Batman sign calling for "help" — which right now was rather true. There was so much in her head from these haunting feelings of having been here before and the sense of fear. Those things vied with the confusion of just how to go forward. It was as if she was on a dance floor and the DJ kept changing the beat. As for who she was dancing with, she hadn't a clue. She turned to the view. On a nearby rock sat a clutch of gulls watching the horizon. What did they see? A school of fish below the surface or just the waves mesmerizing them in their regularity?

A large sailing boat came out of the Helford and tacked in front of the headland. Demi stopped to watch as they raised the spinnaker. She squinted, trying to make out the people, but they were just a bit too far away to see clearly. One of them reminded her of Sam. Sam. She knew so little about him. So, truthfully, it was no surprise that he hadn't known she was an architect. It was a conversation begun that they'd never finished. So, what did she know aside from the fact that he was a gardener, that he liked boats, and that he came from Australia?

Her phone pinged. She looked at the message from Peta.

Don't take too long. It's a longer walk than you think. Px

Peta knew, somehow. Demi laughed. She glanced at her watch; it was already six so she had better speed up and stop staring at boats and thinking about Sam. But despite her determination, he kept popping into her thoughts as she walked along. Rather than seeing the roll of the fields and the blue of the sky his smile kept coming into her mind. He was too good to be true. He had a great sense of humour, was a gentleman, was kind — so where was the catch?

Her phone sounded again. She wondered what Peta was going to tell her now? Maybe to stay clear of hunky Australian men with dimples.

Missing you, wanting you and hoping that now that you've had time to think you will know I'm right and you belong with me. We were so good. I still picture us together. X

286

Demi dropped her phone. Matt. Her fingers curled and her skinned crawled. She picked her phone up gingerly and placed it in her bag. The sooner she could get into the shower and wash away all thoughts of him the better.

CHAPTER
TWENTY-FIVE

Demi looked across the river in the twilight. She could hear music. "Are we really taking a boat over?"

"Yes, it's a big night and one of the best of the summer, I promise. Our lift across should be here in a minute." Peta checked her phone. They were late and it was Demi's fault.

Demi looked at the pub behind her. It looked quiet and inviting at the moment. The last thing she needed was a raucous night stranded far from her bed.

"No backing out. You need to have fun." Peta patted her arm. "Harmless fun."

She hated the way Peta knew things. From the moment Peta had collected her from the beach at Maenporth, she'd been treating Demi with kid gloves. All she'd said, when Demi told her about the text, was that Matt was an arse and not to judge all men by him. She accepted that Peta was right, but that didn't mean she truly believed it.

A motorboat appeared from the other side. "Here's our lift."

"Is this the ferry?" Demi squinted in the fading light.

"No. It's my mate, Fred."

"Hop on, ladies, the party's already well under way." He grinned at them as he held on to the pontoon.

Demi clambered on board and held on tight. She wasn't at all used to boats, let alone small inflatable ones.

"I wouldn't perch there unless you want a wet bottom." Fred's voice held supressed laughter and Demi relaxed. It was clear he knew what he was doing.

"Thanks." She cautiously moved to the middle of the bench and Peta plonked down beside her.

"Fred, this is Demi from Boscawen."

She opened her mouth to deny it but Peta again had sensed her decision even before Demi had vocalised it herself.

"Cool. I helped my dad do some work over there a few years ago. Fantastic old house."

"Thanks." Demi glared at Peta who shrugged while mouthing "sorry". "What work did you do there?"

"Oh, new bathrooms, wiring, heating, that sort of stuff. Basically gave it an update." He manoeuvred around a few yachts.

"Great job. Do you know who the architect was?"

"Yeah, Mark Triggs. Great bloke."

"He's done a wonderful job." She thought about the way the bathrooms had been integrated without disturbing the proportions of the rooms or damaging the sense of history.

"He's good. Knows his old houses."

Demi nodded and turned from him, studying the boats they were passing. She wondered if one of the yachts was the one she watched heading out this afternoon.

"Here we are, ladies." The noise had increased the closer they came to a pontoon on the other side. "The tide's still coming in so I'll be able to run you back until about two, but after that you'll have to find a bed on this side of the river."

"Don't look so hopeful." Peta tapped his arm as she stepped out of the boat, sending Demi careening into Fred. He steadied her and helped her on to the pontoon. She looked at the coloured lights and throngs of people. This was so not what she wanted to do tonight, but as she felt the pontoon tip with Fred's weight she knew she was stuck here until Peta was ready to head back.

"It looks intimidating, but seriously, it's great fun. Come on and let me introduce you." Fred pointed to the ladder leading up to a stone terrace. Demi peered at her dress. Jeans would have been a better choice.

Victoria stretched her hands up to release the muscles in her back and shoulders. The swim had been good but she was not giving her body enough attention. Too much focusing on other things and not enough time making sure she still functioned at optimum levels.

Right now she wanted Adam here. She picked up her phone. It wasn't too late and he might be home. Did she want sex enough to drive to Falmouth to get it? Her fingers hovered over the keys. Then she thought of his untidy flat and how disappointing their last session had been. She'd been stuck looking at his poster of The

Lord of The Rings on the wall. Surely at twenty-six you were past movie posters on your wall? It had put her off completely and she had taken no pleasure in his naked flesh.

She sent him a text. Sebastian was heading to London tomorrow about noon and she was meeting Demi at ten, just the two of them. She would need something after that meeting. Adam could be the reward or the consolation.

Meet me at Boscawen at one. Lunch is on me. V

She smiled as she pressed send, then stripped. She would get some satisfaction tomorrow and she would just have to wait until then. Sometimes anticipation made it that much better.

Peta pulled Demi on to the crowded dance floor. Bodies writhed, mostly in time with the music. The youngest looked about ten, the oldest about seventy. It was madness and she certainly wasn't in the mood to really let go. She'd met so many people tonight her head was spinning. Fred had been true to his word. He knew everyone; his brother worked behind the bar and right now his mother was looking a bit tipsy on the dance floor, inches from Demi. Peta pumped her hands in the air to the beat of the music and Demi went through the motions. She was having fun but she'd had enough. Thankfully the song ended and they slid through the crowds towards the bar. The temperature inside rose dramatically and the face paint of the bar staff was melting. The green scarecrow looked positively eerie with paint dripping down his face.

Someone handed Peta a bottle of wine and glasses and they wove their way out on to the terraces. Although still warm, it was not the melting temperatures of inside although there must have been a couple of hundred people. She peered down to the lower terrace as more people arrived, landing on the pontoon.

With hand signals she indicated to Peta that she was moving down closer to the water. Peta filled her glass up and continued chatting to someone who looked familiar. As Demi reached the bottom step she remembered it was one of the darts players from when she'd first arrived. How time had flown.

The water was high and the surface was a patchwork of bright, reflected colours. The music, although still loud, was muffled and lights shone out of most of the cottages in the village. It was an impossibly pretty scene. Across the river Helford Passage was visible and Demi thought about her decision again. Her home would lie across the river and this whole area would become part of her life. How would her mother have felt about it? Demi sipped her wine. It would be good to have either one of her parents to ask that question of.

"Escaping?"

She jumped. "Sam." She frowned. "Yes. I didn't see you inside."

"The darts team just finished at a pub down the road so we thought we'd come and join the festivities." He leaned against the palm tree growing in the terrace.

"It's wild up there."

He nodded. "Last year was my initiation. I think I slept most of the next day."

She glanced at his hand; he held a pint glass but it wasn't beer.

"Water. Learned my lesson last year and I'm in charge of the boat."

"Ah, so no silly dance moves for you." She tilted her head towards a woman wriggling away on her own at the end of the terrace.

"Not this year. Maybe next." He shook his hips with indecent ease and Demi swallowed. He lifted his hand in invitation but she just laughed.

"So you are staying at Boscawen?" Demi looked at him from under some hair that had slipped from the loose knot at the back of her head.

"Ah, good question."

"Don't you miss Australia?"

"I do. I miss my family but Cornwall is . . ." He stopped and looked up to the clear sky filled with stars. "Cornwall is for me."

"So even if you can't set up your cider business you will stay?"

"Yes. What do you plan to do? Travel the world?"

She smiled. "Tempting, but I'm not sure I'm ready for that just yet."

"No wanderlust?"

She smiled. "Not really, or I should say, not in a need-to-do-it-right-now sort of way."

"Fair enough." He looked up to the crowds of people. "I just wanted to say I'm sorry again."

She smiled. "It's OK."

"No, it's not. My sister would kill me."

"Well, I can't answer for that." She sipped her wine.

"So you're an architect."

Demi nodded. Not that she felt like one. Maybe after working on Boscawen, when she could use all her skills, she would feel she fitted the job title. Right now it felt like a big name for a small person.

"Have people always dismissed you because you're so pretty?"

She nodded. "Not sure about the pretty bit, but more about the blonde." Demi stopped and looked down at her chest. Those, too, she thought but didn't say. She smiled ruefully. "They've either written me off as having no brain or objectified me." She grimaced. That was the wine talking. She shouldn't have blurted that out.

"Ouch."

"There you are." Peta joined them. "You're with Sam so I don't need to worry." Peta smiled.

Clearly her second sight didn't work when she was drunk. Demi stored this away for future reference.

"Has she told you she's staying?" Peta leaned against Sam and gazed up at him in an unfocused fashion.

Sam turned to Demi. "No, she hasn't."

"Well, she is. We get to keep her."

"Peta, there you are," a tall man called from the terrace above. "You owe me a dance."

"Coming." Peta staggered up the steps, swaying to the beat of the music and fell into the man's arms.

294

Demi hoped she would stay alert enough to get them home.

"You didn't say." Sam spoke so softly that Demi almost didn't hear.

"I haven't, actually." Demi bit her lip. "Peta is jumping the gun."

"So you aren't?" He tilted his head.

"At this moment, looking out on the Helford, I can't think why on earth I wouldn't want to stay and be a part of this place, but tomorrow, in the cold light of day, it may look different. And then there is Victoria."

"Ah, I see."

"I wish I did." She let out a long breath. Sam knew what he wanted and she was jealous of that. She closed her eyes for a second. What she wanted right this minute was simple. "Shall we dance?"

He smiled. "Yes." He took her hand and led her through the crowds to the dance floor, such as it was.

CHAPTER
TWENTY-SIX

It was decision day. She was meeting Victoria this morning and on her way to Boscawen she allowed enough time to visit her grandfather. It was so early that he was still at breakfast. Demi spotted him seated with two women.

"Morning, love. This is a surprise, a lovely one." He smiled. "Meredith and Alice, I'd like you to meet my granddaughter, Demi."

"Morning dear," said Alice. "It must be important if you're here at this hour." She stood. "Come on Meredith let's go so that they can chat."

"Oh, but I thought it would be nice to meet someone new," Meredith said, frowning.

"You *have* met her. Now come with me." Alice led her away.

Demi sat down and cast her grandfather a glance.

"Sisters. Meredith isn't with us all the time but Alice is as sharp as a tack. She used to be a banker."

"I'm pleased you are making friends."

He laughed. "Friends, hmm. Being a widower I seem to be accumulating women at the moment."

She smiled.

"But there's only ever been one woman for me."

"I know that." Demi saw a clean cup on the table and poured herself some tea.

"Is it today?"

She nodded.

"You've made up your mind."

"I want to do it." She poured milk into her tea. "I know it's madness, but I can really see Boscawen converted properly and it will be an exciting project."

"I love the way your face lights up."

"Does it?"

"Yes." He sipped his tea. "It also means you'll be around here too."

She reached out for him. "Yes, it does."

"Are you sure you want to work with her?"

"No, not at all, but Sebastian and Sam are part of it and I do want to work with them."

He smiled. "I'm so proud of you. Your great-grandmother must be delighted."

"Do you think so?"

"Absolutely. The Williams were connected to Boscawen until I broke the mould by becoming a teacher." He picked up her hand. "And now it belongs to you."

Demi laughed. "To me and Victoria Lake."

"Well, we can't have everything in life," he chuckled. "Oh, and I remembered something."

"Yes?"

"There was a child kidnapped the day before you went missing. It happened here in Cornwall. Your mother initially thought that's what had happened to you."

"Why would she think that?" Demi frowned.

"Because of Charles's money. The little girl was the love child of a very wealthy man and I think the similarities really scared her."

"I see, I think." She ran a hand through her hair. "I wasn't abducted, was I?"

"No." He shook his head. "I'm sure you weren't. I'd remember that." He reached for her hand. "There's someone who looks like a taxi driver looking around the room. Would that be for you?"

"Yes." She jumped up and gave him a hug. "Love you."

"Love you too. Be true to yourself."

"Will do." Demi dashed away, wondering if there was more to her appendix bursting and a connection with her recollections of Boscawen. Maybe she could find the hospital records. But first she was off to do something exciting.

This morning would decide Boscawen's fate — whatever Charles's daughter decided. It was all in the hands of the bastard. What would Demi ask for or, more importantly what was Victoria willing to give up in order to keep Boscawen? She laughed. She'd already given everything, so what did it matter if she sold her soul again?

"Tori!" Sebastian called from the hall. "Demi's here."

"I'll be right down." Taking a last look in the mirror she smiled and descended the stairs. She would do whatever was needed to keep Boscawen.

Sweeping past them in the hall, she headed to the kitchen. "Morning. Shall we grab a cup of coffee?" she said, using her most charming voice, the one she'd reserved for wooing Charles's many clients and investors. Looking back, she'd worked as hard as he had making his fortune or, more correctly, making it even larger than it had been. She smirked. She had even slept with one or two to seal the deal. Not that it had been a hardship in either case, in fact, rather fun, and Charles had never known. Only lately had she become careless and look where it had landed her. Here in her kitchen with his daughter.

"Am I remembering correctly that you take your coffee black?" Victoria pulled three mugs from the cupboard, loving the look of surprise on Demi's face. Despite the tension at the reading of the will she'd noticed that Demi had asked for a black coffee.

"Yes, thank you."

"Sebastian, I'm assuming you'd like one before you disappear." She looked at him, watching her closely. He knew her too well. He saw the charm offensive even if Demi didn't.

"Mine's white."

"I remember." Cheeky bastard, she thought. She knew how he took his coffee and that he preferred his eggs scrambled dry. There was only one thing she didn't know because they had never made love. They had come close so many times but foolishly they had held back. It had seemed important at the time, more important to him than to her. She shook her head, casting out thoughts of their young bodies twined around each other. She didn't need distractions at the moment.

Sebastian moved to her side. "Behave," he whispered.

She opened her eyes wide and batted her lashes. "Always."

"Is there enough coffee for one more?" Sam walked through the back door.

"Of course." Victoria reached for another mug. She and Seb could have been so good together.

"Just wanted to let you know that last night I spoke with Tristan Trevillion of Pengarrock."

"And?" She handed him his coffee. She'd known Tristan's father, Petroc, such a handsome man.

"They have three orchards that don't produce enough on their own. So we could buy their crop and he mentioned that there were more apples available from Trevenen. With them we would be able to harvest enough this year to make a good start on creating a bespoke Helford area cider."

"A bit premature." Victoria glanced at Demi.

"Possibly, but whatever happens we need to do something with this crop and the future harvests." Sam took his coffee from her. "I have also sourced bees for next year."

"Bees?" Demi asked.

He inclined his head. "To insure the best pollination."

"Oh, I thought they just found their way on their own."

Sam laughed.

"There's more to the birds and bees and Sam obviously knows what he's talking about." Victoria cast him a sideways glance. She'd very definitely underestimated her gardener. The look on his face triggered a memory but she couldn't hold it long enough to place it. She picked up her mug and Demi's. "Right, Demi, let's leave them to it. Shall we head to the east terrace?"

Demi followed in silence and Victoria frowned. They walked through the morning room and out through the French windows. The sun was still dimmed by the sea mist that had arrived at eight this morning so it was warm and bright but not too hot. The wind remained from the east. The river would be restless on the outgoing tide. She remembered last night's swim and what followed, the companionable silence until the sun went down. Sebastian was keeping his cards close to his chest at the moment.

Victoria waved to a wicker chair and plumped the cushion on hers. She had put them out this morning, hoping they could have the discussion here so that whatever the result she could enjoy the beauty of the garden. The wall marking out this part of the garden from the sunken Italianate one beyond was covered with hydrangea serratifolia and the sunken garden was not much more than a relic of the past. A few structural plants remained, nothing else. It was on the to-do list.

"Thank you for the coffee." Demi looked over the rim of her cup into the distance down the drive. She turned her gaze. "What is that vine-like plant over there?"

"The white one?"

Demi nodded.

"It's a clematis." Victoria paused. "Do you know much about gardening?"

"Not a great deal. We didn't have one so I know what I learned from the parks of London." Demi put her cup down. "My grandfather is, or I should say was, a keen gardener."

"Was?"

"He's moved into a care home so his gardening days are finished, but it was a passion of his. He took me to the parks and pointed out the plants and," Demi stopped and looked about, "the planting, if that makes sense."

"Yes, yes it does. Is he not well?"

"He's eighty-four and needs a new hip and he was struggling to look after himself. My grandmother died eight years ago."

"Are you close?"

"Yes." Demi sighed.

"Where's the home?"

"Falmouth."

"Not far." Victoria sipped her coffee, watching Demi carefully.

"No."

Victoria stored the information away. This was something she could see that tied Demi here, whether she realised it or not. Demi's grandfather could be very useful indeed. "I read your CV with interest. You're a talented young woman."

Demi squinted at her. Maybe that was too effusive a start. "The sort of work you did on Milton House

302

seems to be exactly what we might need here." Victoria cast a glance behind her at Boscawen's solid east wall.

"Thank you for the compliment — and I know I have the skills needed, even if they haven't been fully tested."

Victoria sat back and looked at Demi anew. She'd have to play this carefully. Something had changed in the mouse and Victoria wasn't quite sure what it was — except that maybe she knew she held the winning card.

Demi took a deep breath. She knew what she wanted and all that was left was to lay it out. "I'm happy to keep my money and my share of the house in this new partnership." She paused, watching Victoria relax. "But only on the condition that I have full control and final say on the house and the conversion of the outbuildings."

Victoria gasped.

"As I mentioned, I know nothing of gardens or orchards." She picked up her mug with a shaky hand. She'd done it, and now she waited for Victoria's no. Victoria's obsession with Boscawen would never let go of the control.

"I can't see that working." Victoria sputtered the words out. "You don't have the experience."

Demi took a long breath. She'd expected this reaction. "You just mentioned that my CV is impressive."

"But you didn't run the project on your own — you were working with an experienced architect and you were just part of the team."

"True."

"So I couldn't possibly let you," Victoria clasped her hands together on her lap as she looked around at the house, "have complete say over the house and the outbuildings. You don't know the history. You could get something wrong." Victoria straightened her back "Besides, there is little that needs to be done to the house. It was repainted just last year and your father had all the electrics and plumbing updated." Victoria smiled but Demi looked into her eyes and saw nothing but steely determination. Well, she could play this game too; she had to, for her own sake. Staying without proper rights would be intolerable.

Demi placed her mug carefully on to the table. "I thought that's how you would feel."

"I'm pleased you can see my side. So we can go forward with you consulting on the house and buildings, but the final say will rest with me and the architect we've used in the past, Mark Triggs. He's very good and he works all the time with special properties so he knows what the council will and won't tolerate. You, of course, have no knowledge of Cornwall."

Demi swallowed. She'd thought about the planning issues and knew she would struggle with that, but she wouldn't go ahead without being in charge. She wouldn't be bullied again.

"We may well need Mr Triggs' local expertise — and I would welcome another architect on the project — but you are wrong if you think I will go ahead without full control." Demi stood.

Victoria opened her mouth, but Demi knew if she didn't leave now she would be worn down. "Think about what I said, Victoria. I will be a part of Boscawen if I have full control of the house and buildings, otherwise I will instruct my solicitor that I want to sell my share of Boscawen." Demi walked to the French windows.

She heard Victoria's chair move. "You can't!"

Turning, she looked at Victoria. "No, I can and I will." She fled as quickly as her wobbly legs would take her into the kitchen where she grabbed her bag and practically ran out of the door. She'd stood her ground but she would lose all the impact of being strong if she were seen shaking like a leaf. And that was exactly what was going to happen if she didn't get out of sight fast.

Victoria paced the terrace, clenching and releasing her hands. Charles's daughter had just walked out on her and Victoria was going to lose Boscawen again. She resisted the urge to scream. It would do no good.

She ran her fingers through her hair. What could she do? There was no way she could give Demi free reign with the house. As tasteful as that hotel that Demi had worked on was, for all Victoria knew Demi had simply been in charge of the loos. She didn't want Boscawen to look like an over-tarted-up example of what people thought stately homes should look like.

"What on earth happened?" Sebastian stood on the edge of the terrace.

"She's pulling out."

"What? Sam just told me she was in. She told him last night."

"Well, that has changed and she just walked out and will be selling." Victoria located the nearest chair and collapsed.

Sebastian sat opposite. "Tell me what was said."

"In short, she wanted total control over the house and the buildings."

"Yes."

"I said no."

Sebastian laughed, a big deep laugh.

"It's not funny."

"Oh, but it is."

"Go away, Seb. I don't need your warped sense of humour right now."

"I will, but I think you do. You're so controlling that you've thrown away what you have always wanted because you can't let someone else choose the paint colours." He chuckled. "You never learn, Tori. You're still fighting battles from years ago. You have no idea what you really want."

"Go." Victoria rose to her feet.

"Tori, maybe now is the time to let go and live your life. Grow up and let go of your father's dreams." She scowled at him and walked into the garden, leaving Sebastian alone.

But she could still hear his voice as she walked towards the elder wood. Was it really all just because she couldn't let go? Was it because she was angry with Charles? She kicked a stone in the path and watched it fly into the undergrowth. She touched a branch to

306

thank the tree for its presence here and the part it's played in the history of the house. Could she let Demi have control over the conversion of the house? Wasn't the plan to use the house as a hotel or an upmarket bed and breakfast letting go anyway? It would be filled with strangers, so why not let a stranger decorate it? As she walked, Victoria shoved her hands into her pockets and she realised she hadn't really thought this through. By making the house a commercial enterprise she was losing it in a way. She would no longer be able to slip downstairs in practically nothing at midnight for mint tea. She wouldn't be able to shag Adam on the dining-room table. She smiled and looked at her watch. The car she heard would be Sebastian's departing and in half an hour Adam would be here.

A gap in the trees appeared in front of her and sunlight caught the pollen in the air, creating a hazy circle. A small gust rustled the leaves and the dust circled around; the fairies were dancing and she longed to join them. Were they worried what would become of their wood? They might have to move to the oak wood, which was protected. Who would protect the elder wood? No one. Victoria stopped and turned round. She would have to let Demi have control of the house. What really mattered to Victoria was not the bricks and mortar of Boscawen but the land, the trees and the plants. The growing things of Boscawen needed her. The land was her birthright, not the house. She could do this.

CHAPTER
TWENTY-SEVEN

The water glinted at her from in-between the trees. Demi hadn't realised how close the river was to the house. When she was in Boscawen, unless she was on the top floor, she had no sense that they were near the sea aside from the odd gull screeching as it flew above. The woods held the house so closely that it seemed hard to believe the river ran past just a short stroll through the oak trees. Looking at the state of the dilapidated granite quay, Demi imagined it would have been bigger when it was built and there was the footprint of what must have been a boathouse of some size.

She sat on a granite slab on the edge of the quay. Adrenaline and its after-effects were still working their way through her body and she felt a bit nauseous. Below her the water was clear and she could see small fish darting about. The light breeze caressed her skin and she tilted her head back and let the sun warm her face. Closing her eyes she wished again that her mum was here with her. She wanted to share the beauty of the place. But of course her mother would have known the beauty. She'd grown up near here, might even have sailed on the river with Charles.

She opened her eyes. Had her father sailed? She knew so little about him, except that he had apparently loved two women and gave a lot to charity. The thought crossed her mind that he might have done charitable giving from guilt rather than goodness. She would need to ask Sebastian more about him. Somehow she didn't think Victoria would have much to say about Charles that was good because, thanks to him, Victoria was going to lose her home.

Or was it, more correctly, thanks to Demi? She hadn't been unreasonable in her request. From the painting on her father's wall she could see that he had an eye for colour, which told her that Victoria didn't. Yet that didn't fit in with the garden. What was planted and established was glorious as well as harmonious. Was that Sam's influence? Maybe. Parts of the garden were very mature and other's just beginning.

A boat motored past and Demi smiled, looking at the antics of the children on board. Summer holidays were in full swing.

Her phone pinged. She was surprised she had signal here on the river. It might be Sam checking on her. What was she going to say to him? His dreams would be crushed. She looked at the message — and shook. It was from Matt again.

I need you. I lie awake every night dreaming about you.

Bile rose in Demi's throat. This was getting out of hand. She deleted it, not sure what else she should do, noticing that her battery was almost dead. When she was on her computer and had reliable signal she would Google how to block him. Her old life in London seemed so far away and sitting here with the sun shining she never wanted to leave Cornwall.

The wake from the boat splashed against the quay and hit Demi's feet. The water didn't feel as cold as she expected. Her short trip in the various boats last night had left her wondering what the scenery looked like from the river in daylight. Last night, crossing with Sam, the sky had been filled with stars and lights had flickered like giant fireflies on many yachts moored in the river. It had gone one thirty when they had left and most of the houses were in darkness on both sides, just the odd light dancing from the hillside. It had been so peaceful, listening to the clinking of the rigging on the boats.

Demi stood and brushed down her dress. Why had she bothered to look smart for Victoria? It wasn't as if she was being interviewed. She *owned* half of this place.

Adam was peering into the remains of the sunken garden when Victoria walked back towards the house. His jacket was thrown over his shoulder and his shirt was unbuttoned one too far for good taste. In fact, with his dark colouring he could be Italian. Her lips twitched remembering her month in Rome years ago — the wine, the food, the architecture and the sex.

She snuck up behind Adam, pushed him into the garden and against the wall. Before he could speak she kissed him. She needed this right now — without words, without anyone asking anything from her.

In seconds she had his shirt off and was working on his belt, enjoying the heat of the sun on her back. She heard a strange sound and stopped for a moment, trying to figure out what it was. It wasn't Sam, so it must be a small animal of sorts. Adam pulled her sweater over her head and released her bra. She went back to work on his belt and zip and in seconds they were naked and she felt the rough stone of the wall against her back as she wrapped her legs around him. It had been too long. It was also too quick for her enjoyment, so when they fell to the grass she tried to tease him into action again.

"You don't talk to me for days and then you expect me to be hard again in minutes." He laughed.

"Hmm, yes." She ran a hand down his chest slowly as he took in deep gulps of air. He rolled towards her placing his mouth on her left breast and his hand on the right. Pleasure began to build slowly until annoyance set in as his fingers ignored her nipple and kept going over the same spot on the side of her breast. He'd stopped teasing with his tongue as well.

"Adam, pay attention."

"I am." He squinted into the distance.

"Nonsense. You've been worrying the side of my breast as if it's a rosary bead."

"What's that?" He frowned.

She pushed him off her and sat up. "Never mind."

He reached out and she backed away.

He sat up, his face serious. "Victoria, feel the side of your breast."

She raised an eyebrow. "Is this some sort of new thing that turns you on?"

"No, and I think you need to feel your breast. There's something there."

She sighed and shook her head. The grass was beginning to feel prickly and she could see from his intent look that he wasn't going to play any more until she had done what he asked. She touched her right breast and didn't feel anything. "There's nothing there."

He picked up her hand with one of his and with the other he felt her breast. "It's here." His fingers wobbled back and forth.

Victoria held her breath and her patience at the same time. He put one of her fingers right where his had been and then moved as his had done. "No!" The word slipped out of her mouth as the pad of her fingers detected a small round object.

"If you can't find it I'll find it again." His voice was very gentle, as though he was talking to a child.

"I've found it, but it can't be what you're thinking."

He stroked her cheek. "Probably not."

She looked away and her eyes filled. "It's just a cyst. I'm sure."

"Call the GP now and make an appointment just to be sure." He took her hand and helped her to her feet.

"There's no need." She looked for her clothes. They were scattered down the incline to the rectangular hollow.

312

"Victoria, call." He took her face between his hands and turned her towards him. "My mum didn't think it was anything either."

Her hand flew to her mouth. "Sorry."

"It's OK." He took her hand in his. "I understand you don't want to think about this, or do anything about it, but you have to." He pulled her into his arms. "I don't want to lose you too."

Victoria gasped then dashed away from him, grabbing her clothes as she flew to the house. This was all wrong.

Demi slapped her hand over her mouth, half stopping the squeak that came out. She carefully stepped backwards through the gap, trying to block out the image of Victoria having sex against the wall with a man who appeared to be less than half her age. In fact, she knew him. It was Adam. She'd had a long chat with him the night she first went to the pub.

Once she was far enough away, she stood shaking her head, willing the image to go away. Charles was dead less than two months and Victoria was having it off with someone Demi's age; well, near enough. She sighed and carefully walked along beside the concealing wall until it reached the safety of the main drive.

Still shaky, Demi walked on. She needed a drink but there was no way she could head back to the house. She might find them sprawled on the hallway floor. God, the woman was supposed to be mourning her husband, not shagging some young thing. Charles must be turning in his grave. She ground her teeth. What she'd seen and heard wasn't the act of new lovers. Victoria had been having an affair so she had no right to be all high and mighty about Demi's existence.

There was nothing for it but to walk to the pub. She grimaced at her sandals; they were not made for country lanes. But she hadn't expected the morning to go the way it had. She should have, though. How could she have thought that Victoria would let go of the control?

Now she needed to make a plan. Her mother had died three months ago and her father two. Her mother's insurance hadn't yet paid out but she did have the loan from her father's estate. She was living carefully, but what she wanted was a job, as she wouldn't be working at Boscawen. Her shoulders slumped. That most likely meant London again and she really didn't fancy it. There was also the possibility of bumping into Matt. Just thinking his name made her skin crawl. At least here in darkest Cornwall she was safe from him. She looked to the woods and wondered if safe was the right word. Maybe free would be a better choice.

She supposed she could get a temporary job in Falmouth for the rest of the season and maybe flat share with Peta until she had herself sorted. Then she would apply for proper jobs again and put her life back on track. But of course she needed to think of her grandfather in the long term. How would he handle her being away again? She pressed her lips together. She didn't like the thought of being too far from him.

The gatehouse appeared in the distance. Maybe Sam was back and she could beg a cup of tea. He had been so lovely last night, getting her back to Peta's as her friend had been intent on partying the night through. In fact, Peta hadn't made it home by the time Demi had set off this morning but she'd texted to say she was alive and well.

Reaching the gatehouse, Demi tapped on the door and called out, but no one answered. Her stomach had settled and she was now feeling slightly hungry but there was nothing she could do about it. She sat on one of the garden chairs and cursed herself for her stupidity. She should have gone back to the house, regardless, and asked Sebastian or Sam for a lift.

But she hadn't wanted to answer questions and her emotions had been veering all over the place. Rubbing her temples, Demi remembered the spare key. Would Sam mind if she raided the kitchen? No, he wasn't that sort of person. He was a funny mix — one minute all stereotypical laid-back Aussie and then next switching on this super-focused business persona. Who *was* Sam Stuart?

Her stomach growled and she walked to the back of the house. Under the geranium pot, she found the spare key. She would make a cup of tea and steal a biscuit while charging her phone so she could call for a taxi — these sandals would never get her to the pub without scarring her feet permanently. The beginnings of a blister on her left heel spoke of what was to come.

Letting herself in through the kitchen door, she noted the roses and cowslips in a Mason jar on the counter. A twinge of longing hit her. She missed living here with him. His breakfast things were washed and drying on the side. He was so lovely with his big blue eyes, his deep wicked laugh and his kindness. He could even dance, as he'd demonstrated last night. She downed a glass of water.

While reaching for a mug, she considered how close he'd come to kissing her last night when he'd dropped her at Peta's. Locating the digestives Demi nibbled one while brewing her tea. Her stomach lurched, but not from sickness. It was more her reaction to Sam. Just thinking about him moved her in a way that Matt had never done. Tucking her hair behind her ears she blushed at her thoughts. How could she trust anyone after what Matt, a man who swore he loved her, had done?

"Hello." A sleepy-looking woman in a large white shirt appeared.

"Hi." A digestive crumb stuck in her throat. The woman must be at least six foot tall with olive skin and tousled brown hair. Her long legs never seemed to end.

"I'm Rachel." She held out a hand.

Demi shook it, not quite sure what to do.

"Is there enough water for another cup of tea? I'm parched. Long-haul flights do that to you."

Long-haul flights? Oh, God. Was Rachel Sam's girlfriend? Had Demi misread Sam's actions last night? Thank God she hadn't kissed him. She turned swiftly and grabbed another mug. "Plenty of water."

"Thanks." Rachel was clearly from Down Under. Her voice held the same twang as Sam's.

316

"How strong do you like it?"

"Very." She smiled. "You are?"

"Sorry, Demi Williams."

"Ah, the new owner." Rachel sat by the kitchen table and stretched those limbs out and Demi tried hard not to hate her for them alone. "I've heard lots about you."

"Oh dear, that doesn't sound good." Demi grimaced. She laughed. "All of it was good."

Sam walked in and looked from Demi to Rachel and back again. "You OK?" he asked, squinting slightly at Demi.

She nodded.

"I was worried, the way you fled, and then I couldn't find you." He leaned down and kissed Rachel's cheek. "I see you've met my sister, Rach."

Demi's thoughts crashed. Sister. She looked between them. Aside from the fact that they were both tall, they looked nothing alike. Rachel's eyes were chocolate brown and Sam's changed from intense blue to almost purple at times.

He turned back to Demi. "I'm pleased you took refuge here in the end. I heard from Seb that you walked."

"Yes." She swallowed, looking between the two of them.

"Can I ask why? Last night you indicated otherwise." He tilted his head.

Demi's mouth twisted until it settled into a straight line as she thought about Victoria's reaction this morning. "I put my offer on the table. She said no.

Simple." Demi shrugged but her nose wrinkled as she fought the urge to cry.

"She wouldn't let you design the revamp of the house?"

"No, she would let me design it, but wouldn't let me have the final say."

Sam nodded. "She's like that, but you can get around her."

She shook her head. "Look, this whole thing was never going to be easy. I'm not sure my father had any idea what havoc he'd be creating when he drew up his will."

Sam laughed. "Charles Lake was no fool. I can guarantee you he would have known."

"Why?"

"He and I used to play chess a lot when Victoria was away. The man studied every move before he made it."

"So what happens now?" Rachel stood and filled the kettle again. "Any decent coffee about? Now that I've had my tea I could murder a long black."

"Second cupboard to the right of the sink." Sam pointed to it.

"Thanks."

"I don't know what happens now." Demi picked up another digestive as her stomach loudly proclaimed that one biscuit wasn't going to be enough. "I guess that the estate will go on the market and we all wait until probate is finished."

"Exciting times." Rachel poured the boiling water on the coffee grounds.

"That's one way to look at it." Sam smiled and Demi frowned. She would like a different type of exciting, like the challenge of redoing the house.

CHAPTER
TWENTY-EIGHT

Victoria crossed her legs and tried not to look at the mother with the baby in her arms who kept smiling at her. She should have gone straight to a consultant in London, but Adam had insisted that she didn't delay a second longer. So here she was, sitting in a waiting room with more germs than air. The vaguely familiar old man beside her kept coughing and Victoria wondered if she would die of consumption before she was seen.

Rain hit the windows in a worrying pattern, increasing her heart rate. Of course she was sure this lump was a benign cyst, but then she hadn't examined her breasts in a few months. There had been nothing there in April when she was sure she'd last checked. Could stress bring on cysts? Maybe it was caffeine?

The buzzer sounded and she was called. She stood and her hip caught. Dear God, she was falling apart as each minute passed. The receptionist gave her an encouraging smile as she walked by the desk. Thankfully the woman was the soul of discretion because the last thing Victoria needed at the moment was her health scare on the local grapevine. Currently there were only three people who knew.

The door was open and a smiling woman greeted her. "Mrs Lake, I'm Sarah, the practice nurse, and I'm going to check your blood pressure first and ask you a few questions before I examine you."

"I thought I was seeing the doctor?"

"You will, but as we squeezed you in this is the best way to keep everyone moving."

Victoria frowned. There would now be another person in the loop. Thank God Sebastian had headed to London yesterday so she hadn't had to put on a brave face for him. Adam had wanted to stay but his fear had been tangible. Her own was enough. Instead she had roamed the floors of Boscawen all night and ended up staring at the stars from the roof until the sun rose. It had been foolish. Now she was so tired she could fall asleep here, even with the blood pressure cuff squeezing the life out of her arm.

"Do you smoke?" Sarah asked.

"No."

"Drink?"

"Yes."

"How much?"

"The truth or a polite lie?"

Sarah smiled. "The truth."

"A gin and roughly a half bottle of claret a night."

"That's well over the recommended allowance." The nurse wrote a few notes down.

"Yes."

"Well, your blood pressure is on the high side of normal, but I suspect that could be nerves. Has it ever been an issue before?"

"No."

"Good. If you remove your top and bra, I'll be back in a moment." She pulled a curtain across the room, dividing it. Victoria heard the door open and close. She stripped swiftly and sat on the edge of the examining table. She should have gone straight to London where she was anonymous. Here she was the lady from Boscawen, the girl who grew up here and lost it all and was about to again. Last night she had stood by the phone picking it up and putting it down. In the end she had balled up the sheet of paper with Demi's mobile number on it. How could she grovel and say, yes, you can have control over my house, my home? She couldn't, so instead she walked the halls trying to imprint it all on her mind so that in future she could continue to do so.

The door opened and Sarah returned with her fingers wrapped around a mug. Victoria raised an eyebrow.

"It's the quickest way to warm up my hands." She put the mug down and washed her hands thoroughly. Victoria wondered if that wouldn't defeat the purpose but decided to keep her mouth shut.

"Shall I lie down?"

"Not yet. Stand and place your hands on your hip but keep your arms relaxed — I want to assess the appearance."

"Seriously?"

Sarah smiled. "Yes, now raise your left arm." Victoria did as she was told. "Now the right." Then Sarah put her hand, and yes, it was cool, on Victoria's shoulder. "You can lie down now."

The silence that filled the room as Sarah examined her breasts allowed Victoria's mind to envisage the worst as Sarah's hand kept returning to the spot as Adam's had done.

"Is this the lump that you found?"

Victoria nodded. "Have you found others?"

"The tissue around the side of the breast is uneven but this is the only palpable lump."

"What now?" Victoria let the words slip out. All she wanted to do was go back to her garden and stare in wonder at the violent red daylilies that had opened this morning. Their angry colour against the sky expressed the turmoil within her.

"I'll go and get Dr Gordon. Just lie back and relax."

Relax? thought Victoria. She had to be joking. Her hand strayed to the offending breast. Her fingers found the lump and worried away at it until the skin was sore. According to the clock on the wall Sarah had been gone five minutes. Victoria watched the second hand and laughed bitterly. The pride she had taken in her breasts was gone in an instant. Sarah hadn't said it was cancer, but her solemnity had. The subtle change in her voice told Victoria the truth. She didn't need Dr Gordon's opinion. She knew. She had cancer.

"I hear Trengilly is looking for bar and waiting staff." Peta put the sunblock into her bag. The day was baking and they were on Grebe Beach enjoying the glorious weather.

Demi wore a big white shirt over her bikini. It wasn't the skimpy one that Matt had bought her but one her mother had encouraged her to buy. Morwenna had said it looked far better on her than any of the tankinis she had tried on. Today she found that hard to believe. She hugged her knees and looked at the sparkling blue water. She pulled her hat down over her face. "That's a long way from your flat. How would I get there?"

"True." Peta pushed her sunglasses up her nose. "You could move back in with Sam. It's only about a mile and a half from the gatehouse."

Demi coughed. "Not sure how that would work at the moment."

"Things uncomfortable after you pulled the plug on Boscawen?"

"No. His sister Rachel is here."

Peta sat upright. "Do tell."

"She arrived from Perth yesterday."

"Tall, tanned and gorgeous?"

"Yup." Demi sighed.

"Take heart, *mon ami*, you're fabulous."

"Short, blonde and round?"

"God, you don't see yourself properly at all. You hide away the most fabulous figure in your burka." Peta cast a dismissive glance at the shirt.

"I burn."

"Wear bloody factor 100 then but don't be ashamed of your body. It's beautiful."

Demi swallowed and took a deep breath. She was not going to get emotional on a beach because of body issues. Why the hell had she agreed to come?

She glanced at Peta's perfect figure. It was boyish and slim. What Demi wouldn't give to have that lean figure?

"Stop it, stop it now."

"What?"

"Body envy. I know we all do it. Seriously, I would love some of your G cup, but we have to love what we have. My little Demi, you are perfect and most men's dream."

Demi flinched.

Peta put out a hand. "That was tactless. I'm sorry. Matt is an arse and for God's sake don't judge all men by him."

Demi opened her eyes wide.

"You think about it all the time. Let it go. Believe me, men can be arseholes, but they can be wonderful too."

Demi was about to refute this when the tone of Peta's voice hit her brain. Peta was in love. Demi tried to think who Peta had been dancing with when she'd left The Shipwrights the other night. But it seemed to her that Peta was dancing with everyone.

"So who is he?"

Peta smiled and picked up a handful of pebbles from her side slowly letting them slip through her fingers. "You'll see soon enough." She looked out at the water and Demi followed her glance to a motor boat making its way towards the beach.

There were four people in it, three of whom were men. Well, she supposed that narrowed it down a bit. As the boat came closer she recognised Fred and the other faces looked familiar, but she couldn't remember their names.

Before long Peta was on her feet and racing down to the water's edge to hold the boat then she dashed back.

"Grab your stuff — we're off to another beach."

"Another beach?" Demi frowned. She was happy right here where there were very few people. She'd be able to take a swim if she could face the cold water without loads of eyes staring at her. If she went off with this lot she would have an audience whether she wanted it or not.

"Come on, you'll have a good time. Promise." Peta grabbed her hand. "I'm not letting you stay and besides, how will you get home from here without me?"

"You have a point." Demi reluctantly picked up her things and followed Peta.

"Audrey." Victoria held the phone to her ear. Audrey was the last person she wanted to speak to and yet Victoria knew she was the one person who would know who was the best oncologist in the UK. Her husband, Hal, was a top neurologist.

"Tori, how wonderful to hear from you. You've been on my mind and I was planning to ring you tonight. How are you managing?"

Without warning Victoria began to cry, to blubber even, and not a word would come out.

"Dear God, Tori, I'm so sorry I've neglected you but I thought you needed space to deal with Charles's death."

She couldn't find the words to shut Audrey up about Charles; all she could do was cry. She put the phone down and blew her nose. That was unexpected, she thought as she washed her face with cold water. The phone rang. It would be Audrey.

"Tori, I'm so sorry. Shall I come down tomorrow? I've cleared my schedule."

"No." She blew her nose again.

"But, clearly, you need me."

"I do." Victoria swallowed hard. "I do need you, but I will come to you."

"OK." Victoria could hear the questions in Audrey's voice.

"First, who is the best breast man in London?"

Audrey gasped. "You want a boob job? Surely not."

"Not that type." She took a deep breath. "Cancer."

"No!"

Victoria heard something fall over in the background. "Audrey?"

"I'm here. Sorry. There is only one, Philip Perkins. Shall I call and see if I can get you in? Have you seen your GP?"

"Yes."

"Right. Leave it with me and take the train up. I don't want you driving."

"Fine." Victoria looked around. The house felt so empty all of a sudden. Part of her wished Seb was here to at least make some noise or simply to just be him, calm and reassuring.

"Are you alone?"

"Yes."

"Don't be. Where's Sebastian?"

"In London." Victoria stared sightlessly at the garden.

"Your toy boy?"

She looked down at the ruby on her finger. She slipped it off and put it by her keys. She must put it in the safe. "Not sure."

"Find him or anyone — I don't want you alone tonight."

"Fine. I'll see you tomorrow." Victoria put the phone down and poured herself a very large gin and tonic. She walked through to the empty sitting room. At this time of day she and Charles would meet, sometimes compare notes, sometimes just read the papers together. Now she was truly alone. But wasn't that what she'd wanted?

CHAPTER
TWENTY-NINE

Sam was on the beach by a barbeque while Rachel was wading in the sea, looking like the model she must be. Demi's stomach turned and it had nothing to do with the swell pushing them towards the beach. How was she going to survive a day on a beach with all these people who were strangers? This would be the day from hell. Thank God she'd brought a book and she could head off and seek some shade thanks to her over-white skin.

Rachel splashed through the waves to help them land the boat and Demi tried to stay out of the way as she was the only one who hadn't a clue what to do.

"Perfect timing. The barbie is just ready so we need the food." Rachel grabbed several bags and took them to the beach while Demi tried to climb out of the boat. A wave pushed in at the wrong moment and she went in with a thump, bag and all. The only thing that was saved was her hat, which went flying on to the dry sand. Rachel helped her to her feet and Demi looked down, horrified. Her shirt was now transparent and clinging to every curve. Not good when she preferred to remain invisible.

Rachel took her hand and helped her up the beach, rescuing the hat along the way. "Those rocks back there are hot as anything in the sun. Let's spread your stuff out and it'll be dry in no time."

"Thanks." Demi tried to pull her shirt away from her body but it kept clinging.

"Take it off. You'll be warmer, and here's my towel."

Demi couldn't take her shirt off but it was worse with it on the way it emphasised everything. She heard her mother's encouraging words in her head. If you act like you have confidence no one will know the difference. So she peeled the shirt off and Rachel draped it across a rock. Demi covered her body in the towel with what she hoped wasn't undue haste.

"You'll warm up in no time. You've got sunblock on, I hope." Rachel smiled. "You have the most wonderful skin, so creamy and smooth. What I wouldn't give for it."

Demi frowned and looked at the tanned limbs that went on forever.

"I've had terrible acne and still have issues with it. The sun does help but, of course, that carries other problems." She shrugged her elegant shoulders and handed Demi her hat. "What can I get you to drink?"

Demi watched with amazement as everything but the kitchen sink appeared as another boat joined them. "Wine would be lovely."

Rachel dug into a cooler and produced a bottle of rose. "Pink OK? This one's nice and dry."

"Perfect." How could Rachel be so relaxed? Unless she'd been here before she didn't know all these people yet she was completely at ease. Demi tried not to hate her and took a sip of the wine. It was dry as promised but hinted at berries. She took another sip. It was perfect for a barbeque on the beach.

"Good to see you here." Sam came up to her. "Sorry you took an unplanned dip in the sea." He grinned.

Demi laughed. "That's one way to put it."

"The only way. What do you think of the wine? It's from Rachel's vineyard."

"Wow, it's brilliant." Rachel's vineyard? Wasn't Rachel a bit young to own her own vineyard? "Sam?"

He turned to her, smiling. "Yes?"

"I'm confused." She frowned. "If this wine is from your sister's vineyard, just why are you a gardener?"

His smile widened. "That wasn't the initial plan." He shrugged. "It just happened."

She pushed her hair back and looked at him more closely.

"I have Cornish roots like many Aussies and I was here checking them out when the opportunity came up to stick around for a while." He put some sausages on to the grill. "Rach was doing such a good job, I wasn't required at home for a bit. She needed to be able to prove herself without her big brother being in the way."

"OK." She couldn't read his expression as the smoke from the fire billowed as the fat from the sausage caught. "I should go and help." She began to walk away.

"Nah, Rach has it in hand as does Peta. You can help me with the barbie though."

"Sure." Demi tucked the towel more securely and walked over to the fire.

He smiled. "Surely you're dry by now?"

"Not quite." She glanced down at herself, knowing it was a bad look. She must appear three times her size as the towel fell from her chest to her knees. As if reading her thoughts, Peta came up and handed her a sarong.

"A bit more practical for the assistant chef." She winked and held out her hand for the towel. Reluctantly Demi released it and reached for the sarong.

"It's as hot as it gets in Cornwall and here by the fire it's warmer. You don't need the sarong either," Sam said.

Demi looked up, dreading the expression she'd see. But he wasn't leering at her chest, he was looking into her eyes.

"Good point." Peta walked away still holding her sarong and Demi stood in her bikini for all to see. She would have to tough this out for the moment or risk making a spectacle of herself. If she just stayed quiet and held her stomach in no one would notice her and soon her shirt would be dry.

The taxi dropped her off in Portman Square and Audrey was standing on the steps waiting for her. Victoria would rather have faced this alone, but Audrey had insisted. She took Victoria's suitcase and they walked into the building together. At least Audrey hadn't hugged her, so she must be thankful for small mercies. Right now, as long as she kept her hands in fists with her fingernails just biting into her skin, she had a hold on her emotions. And that was something she was thankful for; that and Audrey's ability to get her an appointment with Mr Perkins so quickly. God knows what strings Audrey had pulled, but she was grateful. It was the not knowing anything for sure, but feeling she knew, yet she didn't that was eating at her. Her thoughts were all over the place. She cried at the drop of a hat so the sharp bites of pain from her palms worked to hold the tears at bay. She wouldn't worry why this was. It was a necessary distraction for her too morbid brain.

"Mrs Lake to see Mr Perkins." Audrey spoke to the receptionist, giving her a big smile.

"Just have a seat and fill out this form. He'll be with you in a few minutes." She took the clipboard and pen then led Victoria to the overstuffed sofa, which almost swallowed them. Victoria was pleased she had opted for a trouser suit today. There was no way to sit like a lady on this.

"Shall I fill it in for you?"

"No." Victoria took it from her and looked up briefly before saying thanks. She'd stopped the pain in her hands so those bloody tears pooled in her eyes.

Fortunately the form was short and more about insurance than her health history. But one question haunted her. Pregnancies. Her hand shook but she managed to complete it, silently thankful that their insurance was paid up until February. Hopefully the estate would be sorted by then so she could pay next year's premium.

Audrey took the board from her hands and gave it to the receptionist. She stopped on the way back to fill a cup with water. Victoria's mind jumped to the morgue at Taunton. It was not a good connection to make.

Audrey sat on the edge of the sofa clutching her knees. She wore a pretty wrap dress that covered her matronly bosom. A bosom, that although large and droopy, was probably safe because it had nursed four children.

"Mrs Lake." A tall young man spoke. Victoria looked at him and then Audrey. She nodded. He didn't look old enough to be out of school let alone a consultant. Victoria stood and shook his hand then followed him into his office. There was a printed email on his desk, probably from her GP. Audrey's skills knew no bounds. It must come from years of looking after a large family.

"I'm aware you are thinking the worst."

She raised an eyebrow. "That you are ten?"

He smiled. "Forty-five."

"Can I have what you're taking?"

"It's all down to good genes." He smiled kindly. "And on the subject of genes . . . is there a history of breast cancer in your family?"

"As far as I know, no."

"OK, that doesn't give us much to go on."

"True. My mother died young of a complication with pneumonia. I don't know what her mother died of and sadly there is no one I can ask. On my father's side, he died of old age and his mother lived until she was ninety-five."

"Well, then; I see you don't smoke, you've had no children and you enjoy gin and wine."

Her mouth went dry. "Yes."

"Shall I examine you and see if I concur with your GP."

She nodded.

"While you take off your shirt and bra, I'll go and get the nurse."

With shaky hands she undid her buttons, thinking that having a nurse present wasn't really necessary. But she supposed if one were as young and as good-looking, as he was it was a wise precaution. He didn't need patients throwing themselves at him. She laughed; in other circumstances she might have had a go herself.

He reappeared with a small dark woman with him. "This is Freda." She smiled at Victoria who felt exposed for the first time in her life. Instead of sitting with her back straight she rounded her shoulders.

"I know it's hard to do in the circumstance, but try and relax."

Victoria almost snorted at that but as his warm hand started feeling her breasts something inside shrivelled away.

"Are you sure you want another drink?" Audrey asked.

"Yes, I'm sure." Why hadn't Victoria opted to stay in a hotel, where she could drink herself to oblivion without the caring tone of Audrey trying to tell her she would have the hangover from hell tomorrow? Right now Victoria didn't want tomorrow to come. Her breasts hurt like hell as they had taken sample after sample. Offering her neck to a vampire would have been more pleasant.

"OK, you will eat something though, won't you?"

She nodded. They were seated in Audrey's well-appointed kitchen in Fulham. The back of the house was all glass, opening on to a big city garden that was just past its peak. A few roses remained and the hydrangeas were out.

"Go and do what ever you do in the evenings. I can feed and water myself."

"It might not be that bad." Audrey shifted from one foot to the other.

Victoria stared at her. "Let's not play pretend here."

"You could get a second opinion." A smile hovered about her mouth, not quite forming.

"He *was* a second opinion."

"The success rate for treating breast cancer improves almost daily at the moment."

"Audrey, go and leave me to wallow."

She wrung her hands together. "I'm worried."

Victoria laughed. "I'm in your house. The worse that can happen is that I finish this bottle of gin and wake up with a hangover."

"OK." She smoothed her skirt down. "I'll go and watch the news. Hal should be home about midnight."

"I'll stay out of his way." Audrey didn't move. "Seriously, I am not about to do anything rash. Go and find out what's wrong with the world." She left but kept looking back over her shoulder. Victoria resisted the urge to throw a tomato from the bowl in front of her at her friend. Audrey was only doing what a good friend should do, care, but Victoria didn't want anyone to care. She wanted to find oblivion in the bottle of gin and hope that she would wake up tomorrow morning in Boscawen and that it was all hers and she didn't have to share it with Charles's bastard. That was all she wanted. She poured another gin, ever hopeful.

"You don't mind if I don't come back now, do you?" Peta looked so hopeful. Clearly she was more than smitten with Fred. "Here are the keys to my car." Demi rolled her eyes. She wished she'd seen this coming and she wouldn't have enjoyed Rachel's wine quite so much. She'd take a taxi back.

"No problem, but you keep your keys. I'll catch a lift or grab a taxi from the Ferryboat."

"Sure?" Peta turned and looked longingly at Fred.

"No worries. I'll make sure Demi gets home." Sam came up and threw an arm around Demi's shoulders. "Just have one question for you? Does Tamsin know you're cavorting with her eldest?"

"No, and I confess that worries me." She turned and looked at Fred organising the boat. "But I think he may be worth it."

"Who is Tamsin?" Demi looked from Peta to Fred to Sam.

"My mum." Fred grinned. "An amazing, totally terrifying woman."

"Looks as if you'll be needing a hat, Demi." Sam winked and Peta punched him. He dropped his arm from Demi's shoulders and she shivered. The sun had gone behind a cloud, the breeze was cool and her shirt offered little protection.

He pulled a hoodie out of his bag and handed it to her. "It will be cooler on the journey back and you'll need this." He threw it over her shoulders. It smelled of rosemary, bonfire and his aftershave as she put it on. He picked up her bag and gave it to Rachel who was already on the boat. They were such a team, continually teasing each other. Demi was jealous; she wasn't going to deny it.

Sam took her hand to help her into the boat. There was nothing graceful about it as she struggled to climb on to the front of the dory that was bobbing on the incoming tide. Each time she thought she was about to make it, the bow tipped up just too high for her to get her leg up and on to it. Before she knew what was happening Sam had swept her into his arms and placed her gently on to the boat.

"Sorted." He grinned and she tugged at her shirt and his hoodie, both of which had ridden up above her waist. She could still feel where his hands had been on her thighs. She scrambled to take a seat, clutching her bag to her chest until Rachel handed her a life jacket.

"You're not used to boats, are you?" Rachel smiled.

"Obvious, is it?"

"A bit. You'll get the hang of it being around here I think. Sam is boat mad, always has been." She cast a glance in his direction as she lowered the engine a bit then started it. Sam gave the boat a shove out then jumped onto it in one fluid movement. He had no right to be so insanely fit. He picked up a life jacket, put it on, and nodded to Rachel who set off into Falmouth Bay at speed. She was clearly at home with boats too. Demi grabbed the rail and held on tight as the boat bounced over the swell on the way back into the Helford. Scenery raced past and Demi wanted to slow down so that she could take it all in. Although she had walked the coastal path on the north side, everything appeared different from the water. They skirted a green buoy marked August Rock and then Demi spied the church on Mawnan Shere tucked in the trees.

Before long they were past it and pulling up to Porth Navas. She helped them unload the boat and get everything into the 4x4.

"Thanks for the lift. I should be able to get a taxi from here."

Rachel frowned. "Taxi? Nonsense. We'll give you a lift, won't we, Sam?" She gave him a shove as he put the last bag in the back.

"But of course." He smiled.

CHAPTER
THIRTY

Victoria knew she was alive because she wanted to die. Everything that could hurt did, including her stomach, which had emptied itself repeatedly. Audrey had the good grace not to say I told you so. She fielded the calls, made appointments and was under pain of death that no one, absolutely no one, was to know that Victoria had cancer.

Of course, her mind said, there was no proof yet. The results of the biopsies wouldn't be back for days. Yet the consultant had booked her for surgery a week on Monday. That was nearly two weeks away. On that day they would cut her open and remove the thing growing inside of her. She'd never been able to grow a child but it looked like she was effective at growing cancer. The scans had shown tumour-like growths in both breasts and he felt they were aggressive. How rude. How bloody inconsiderate. Right now, when she needed to fight for Boscawen, she was knocked to her knees.

"I've brought you some broth." Audrey was trying to keep the reproach out of her voice but she wasn't quite capable of it. She placed it on the table beside the bed. "Seb called. I said you were in the bath and would ring him back later."

Victoria rolled her eyes. She never took baths. Never had done. "What did he want?" She rubbed her temples. The room was still swaying a bit. Maybe Audrey was right and she shouldn't have drunk the whole bottle, but what did it matter? Everything was uncertain. The surgeon spoke of lumpectomies and of mastectomies, leaving her with something or taking it all. And once her boobs were gone she would have nothing left. Boscawen was going, all Charles's money was in the hands of charities that didn't give a shit, and now her body was packing up on her. It was like a time bomb had been triggered and things were falling one by one.

Demi hopped off the bus and walked up to the care home. She hadn't seen her grandfather for a few days and she missed him. There was also the hope that he might have remembered more.

"Hello, Demi. He's out in the garden." Demi smiled at the carer and wandered out. It was overcast but still warm. She wondered if it would clear, but was grateful to be out of the sun as she'd burnt a bit yesterday despite the high factor sunblock she'd had on. In fact, she had a tan line of sorts on her stomach.

Her grandfather was in a wheelchair. This was new, but he was directing a young man who was down on his knees in the flowerbed.

"Demelza, my lovely." He pushed his hands against the arms of the chair then winced. "Sorry I can't get up — the hip has totally given way." She bent down and hugged him, seeing the pain twisting his normally happy features.

"Thanks for the tips, Mr Williams." The young man stood and moved to another flowerbed.

"Why don't we have a cup of tea?" her grandfather suggested and Demi swiftly moved to push the chair towards the building. She was about to head to the lift so that they could go to his room but he stopped her. "Let's go into the dining room. They make a lovely cup."

"Fine." She frowned. He'd been so independent but things had changed.

"Mr Williams, your usual?" A woman smiled at them as they entered.

"Yes, but for two please."

"Take a seat and I'll bring it over."

"I love sitting by the window." He pointed to a table. "You can pull a chair up for yourself then tell me all the news."

The woman brought a tray over with scones. She gave Demi an encouraging smile. Why hadn't they called her? The hip replacement wasn't scheduled for another few months but surely as he was now in a wheelchair that could be moved forward so he didn't lose all his strength.

"So how are things at the big house?"

"I'm not staying at the gatehouse any more." Demi looked away. She felt like an outsider in everyway. A wave of loneliness had hit after she'd been dropped off at Peta's and she'd watched Sam drive away. It hadn't

342

helped that Peta hadn't come home again last night either.

"No?" The furrows lining his face deepened.

"Let's just say things haven't gone to plan."

He placed a shaky hand on hers. "So what are your plans?"

"Good question. I need a job, maybe just a temporary one for the moment while I wait for things to resolve, and I'm thinking about doing a masters." Maybe with another degree people would take her more seriously.

"That's good. In what and where?" He glanced at her then out of the window. Was it fear she had seen in his eyes?

"Not sure but maybe here in Falmouth."

His face brightened. "Good."

That made everything clear. She couldn't move to London or anywhere now. He needed her. Just a short time of not visiting and everything had gone downhill. She must come every other day if not every one.

"Do you know the farm I grew up on was part of Boscawen?"

Demi leaned forward. "You mentioned it."

"I don't suppose it belongs to the estate now but my family were tenant farmers for generations."

"What became of the rest of the family?"

"We died out."

"What?"

His face crumpled with pain and Demi wasn't sure if it was his hip or his thoughts about his family. The lady who brought tea over came up to them. "Now that you've had a bit to eat it's time to take your pain meds, Mr Williams."

Her grandfather nodded and held out his hand. It shook, so much more now than when she had arrived on his doorstep in May.

The woman looked at Demi. "These will make him quite sleepy. Do you want to take him up to his room or shall I?"

"I'll do it. Thanks." She stood and wheeled the chair towards the lifts. He reached his hand back and covered hers. "I'm so glad you're near. I hadn't realised how lonely I was."

Demi swallowed, longing to wrap him in her arms, but managed to negotiate the lift and the chair instead. By the time she reached the nurse's desk her grandfather was asleep.

"I'll look after him." She smiled at Demi. "He so loves your visits and talks about you all the time."

Demi smiled back, stuffing the emotions away. She bent to kiss his cheek. Standing straight she looked at a woman watching her from two feet away.

She stepped towards Demi. "Hi, I'm Jane Penrose."

Demi took the hand extended to her, frowning.

"We met on regatta day at the cake stand."

"Now I remember."

"And so do I." She smiled. "I hadn't realised you were Hugh Williams's granddaughter, but it all makes sense now."

Demi stepped back. "Sorry, what does?"

"You, dear."

Demi shook her head. "You've lost me."

"So sorry, but you looked familiar. I thought it was because you look like Charles, but I hadn't made the connection to Morwenna." Jane began walking down the stairs and Demi, although feeling light-headed, followed.

"I'm sorry, Jane, can you explain what you mean?" Demi asked when they had reached the bottom of the stairs.

"Of course. Walk with me? I left my car down by the Maritime Museum. I have to drop into Trago Mills for some paint for one of the cottages. I hear they have a good offer on at the moment."

"Fine." Demi knew where that was and she knew how to get to Peta's from there.

Jane smiled. "Now, what was I saying?"

"My mother, Morwenna, and Charles Lake."

"Ah, yes, when I saw you at the regatta I knew you were Charles's daughter. The resemblance is uncanny, but I hadn't realised who your mother was until I saw you with your grandfather." She waved to someone on the other side of the road. "Then it came back to me."

Demi sighed. "What came back to you?"

"The agapanthus and how ill you were."

Demi stopped walking. "I know this may be clear to you, Jane, but agapanthus and me being sick doesn't make any sense to me."

"A very large lady walker brought you to Boscawen when I was digging up some agapanthus, some Boscawen Blue."

Kowres, eyes, and the doors of Boscawen.

"You were burning with fever and I used the spare key and let us into the house." Jane tutted. "The owners were away — well, they always were — and I checked on the house for them from time to time."

"What happened?"

"Well, I had the lady take you into the kitchen and press cold compresses to your head while I rang for the ambulance." Jane shook her head. "While I was doing that the woman had fed you ginger biscuits which only a few minutes later came back up with a vengeance."

Demi wrinkled her nose. "Who was the lady?"

"No idea; someone very tall, very muscular and foreign. Her English was limited but between us we did our best to cool you down until help arrived in the form of the police and the ambulance. I think the police gave her a hard time because of the poor kidnapped girl we were all looking for." Jane sighed. "All very scary, but I had no idea who you were then."

The museum was in front of them and Trago Mills to the left.

"Thank you for telling me. I had no idea what had happened back then."

"Don't see why you would. You were young and very poorly."

"It's funny, though, when I came to Boscawen I knew I'd been there before but couldn't see how." Demi smiled at Jane. "Thank you so much."

"Lovely, dear, and it's so good that Boscawen has another Tregan too."

"I'm not a Tregan."

"I know that, dear. His blue eyes gave him away. His mother's eyes."

Demi was about to ask her what she meant but Jane cut across the street through the traffic and she was due to meet Peta at the charity shop so she dashed down the road.

CHAPTER
THIRTY-ONE

Waiting for Seb to answer his phone, Victoria paced Audrey's kitchen. He'd left so many messages that she knew if she didn't speak to him he would come and find her. She was just managing to hold everything together, but seeing him would shatter it and she would fall to pieces.

Tonight she was moving into a hotel. Audrey's kindness just made everything worse. The woman was mothering her and Victoria had spent the past two days biting her tongue. A hotel where she could do as she pleased was the only answer.

"Sebastian Roberts."

"Hello, Seb."

"Tori, where the hell have you been?"

"I'm here in London, at Audrey's." She paused. "Needed to do a little shopping and meet with my solicitors," she lied.

"What on earth about?"

"Contesting and," Victoria rubbed her temple wondering what she could need at this point in time that she couldn't find in Truro, "shoes."

"Shoes? Seriously, Tori, I thought you were a better liar than that. And there is nothing that the solicitors can tell you at the moment. So the truth, please."

348

Why had she thought ringing would be the answer? "Routine medical check."

"Ah." Silence followed and Victoria wondered whether to jump in with something.

"Why lie about it?"

Damn. Damn. Damn. She took a deep breath. This was harder than she had thought it would be. "One doesn't normally talk about these checks."

"OK. Have you reconsidered Demi's offer?"

Victoria leaned against the counter. No, was the answer but she couldn't say that. He would want to know why, when Boscawen was always in her thoughts — except now, when killer cells were growing willy-nilly in her chest, and she couldn't tell him that. "Still thinking about it." She hadn't thought about it in days. Other things had taken priority.

The results of the biopsies had been positive, but they wouldn't know the full extent of the cancer until they operated. The surgeon was modestly optimistic and she really wasn't sure what the hell that meant. Modestly optimistic, huh? She had cancer and the surgeon was optimistic. She wasn't. Her body had turned traitor again. First it failed on the fertility stakes and now it was producing killer cells.

"Tori, are you there?"

"Sorry, what did you say?"

"When are you heading back down to Boscawen?"

She bit her lip. "Not sure yet. I'm just catching up with things here at the moment." She glanced about the kitchen for anything that would be a reason to end this conversation. "Have to dash, Audrey's waiting for me."

She put the phone down. Audrey was out playing bridge. She needed to finish packing, write Audrey a note, and leave before anyone could stop her.

In the hotel Victoria was greeted politely and then ignored. The room was plush and anonymous. It was just what she'd been hoping for. She needed to shop for things for Monday and she might just ring the number she'd been given for the cancer counselling. Counselling. She hated the sound of the word. She didn't need counselling, she needed information. But much of what she wanted to know was unknowable. She might just as well go to a fortune teller as she had done years ago at a fair. Boy, had that woman been wrong. She had said that she would marry her true love and be happy in the home she had always wanted. Hah, and now no doubt the same woman would tell her that all would be fine and they didn't need to remove her breasts. Victoria looked down at them. Hate filled her. How could some thing that had given her and others so much pleasure be so deadly? The surgeon had asked her if she would trust him. Trust!

She sank on to the plush sofa. He would only remove what he needed to, but wouldn't know what that would be until he operated. Victoria said the word aloud slowly as if she was just learning it. "Op-er-at-ed." Dissected and mutilated, more like. She pulled off her sweater and unclipped her bra. The daylight coming through the window wasn't flattering, but her breasts stared at her from the mirror almost pertly. She pinched each nipple until it hurt. A lover would never be able to take pleasure from them again. She slipped on to her knees. What would she have left when they were gone? What would she have to offer? She was nothing but a dried up old bag who would have scars where her breasts had once been.

Reconstruction? What was the point? She was a sixty-year-old widow. They had to be joking. She could just see the scenario. There she was about to proposition a lover and all that was visible when she took her clothes were two X marks the spots where two good breasts once hung. Sorry, mate, you'll just have to close your eyes and think of England.

Her phone rang. She glared at it but picked it up. It was Adam. She shut her phone off. She couldn't talk to him. The last time they'd had sex he'd found the cancer and that would stay with her forever, however long or short that forever might be.

"Grandad, do you know a Jane Penrose?" Demi sat down beside her grandfather. He was in his wheelchair reading, this time Chaucer. Once an English teacher, always a literature addict, she guessed.

"Lovely woman. Owns a manor house and big farm near Gweek. Why do you ask?" He wheeled his chair through to the garden and she walked slowly beside him. The flower beds had lost a lot of their colour with only the hydrangeas and crocrosima in bloom. August had begun hot and hard on the flora.

"She told me I was brought to Boscawen by a walker who found me, that she called the emergency services from Boscawen."

He frowned then his eyes lit up. "Yes, I remember now! You were found collapsed at the base of the stone Kowres." He looked at her. "You'd been on a nature walk with a group of children." He looked into the distance. "I seem to recall they hadn't noticed you were missing until they returned to the minivan in the pub car park." He turned back to her. "The police initially thought you were the other missing girl when you were found. You were both the same age and blonde."

"You remember." Demi touched his arm.

"Funny how you find me one piece of the puzzle and other bits fall into place. You were in such a bad way that they had had to tackle the infection immediately or lose you. They gave you a penicillin derivative and that nearly killed you." He shook his head. "By the time the police had connected your mother to you in the hospital it was all touch and go." He peered at her over his glasses. "Does knowing what happened help?"

Demi gave a dry laugh. "I'm not sure help is the right word, but like you said, one piece of the puzzle helps others to fall into place."

The bar was emptier than she'd have liked. It would have been better to be doing this on a Friday night, not a Saturday, but she had no time left. She perched on the bar stool and crossed her legs, revealing a stretch of thigh. There were two attractive men sitting in the leather club chairs to her right but too caught up in their own conversation to notice her. The bartender was handsome and might prove to be a good backup if other candidates didn't arrive.

Victoria was determined to have one more night of wild sex before she looked more like a trussed chicken than a woman. She wanted to feel the power of seducing a man and enjoying herself before she couldn't any more. Life would have been so much easier if she had been a man. She would have inherited Boscawen in the first place and men were at lower risk for breast cancer.

The door pushed open and a good-looking man of thirty came in alone. His shoes were good, the soles just the right thickness, not that tonight it would matter, but her father had always said you could judge a man by his shoes. They were polished, but not too much. He had a linen jacket thrown over his shoulder and his sleeves rolled fashionably up, something that would never have done in her day but now it was in. He was very fit. Lurking under the striped shirt was muscle. All good so far.

He looked her way and she smiled as she recrossed her legs. His glance trailed up her thigh to where the skirt had ridden up. Good. He's wasn't gay. She had fallen foul of that once with the most exquisite man. Tonight this one would be lucky. He would have the night of his life and so would she. This would be her last time having sex as a whole woman and she had every intention of enjoying it. She would be sure he did too.

Victoria lay naked on top of the sheets. He was asleep and she couldn't remember his name. His hair fell over his face and she knew that she had misjudged his age earlier. He was all of twenty-five and he had one hell of a sexual appetite. Sadly she felt it had been a little too schooled in the X-rated category so that he thought he was doing the right thing and had had to be corrected. In the end they met halfway. She was exhausted, but she couldn't sleep. She wanted him out of her bed now.

A lump formed in her throat and she longed for a loving touch and not a lustful one. His hand flung out and landed on her right breast and she glared at it. By Monday afternoon it might well be gone and, no matter what, there would be less of it. His hand tightened and she thought he was waking but no. He rubbed, and despite herself she felt the stirring of lust. She clenched her thighs together, then pushed his hand off.

It was over. She rose from the bed and turned the shower on full. They'd both had a night they'd never forget but right now Victoria desperately wanted to.

CHAPTER
THIRTY-TWO

Demi waved to the woman who had given her a lift then walked down the drive past the gatehouse to Boscawen. She'd had a funny message from Sebastian about Victoria having second thoughts. She'd tried ringing but no one was answering. Victoria was probably working in the garden so Demi decided to tackle this head on. After her time with her grandfather yesterday, she'd walked the coastal path again, asking herself what she really wanted. The image of Sam popped up first, but she pushed that away. The next thing was the vision she had for Boscawen. She could see so clearly the clean lines of the rooms once the clutter and darkness had been tackled.

Over dinner she had talked things through with Peta and then this morning she had had the message from Sebastian. It was fate. She must bring Victoria around. Maybe they could meet halfway. So here she was at Boscawen, but the front door was closed and there was no car in the drive. Odd. It was Sunday, so Sam was probably out on his boat or sailing someone else's.

The roses on the south wall were almost finished, but the agapanthus was in full magnificence. What had Jane called them? Boscawen Blue. They were so vivid against the grey stone. A clematis with large white flowers covered much of it, but the granite stone blocks could easily be seen. The blending and contrasting of the colours in the borders worked so well. Why couldn't Victoria do it in the house?

Demi walked through the gate into the kitchen garden. No signs of life. To be sure, she peered in through the stable door but all was tidy and the normal bouquet of flowers that adorned the big table was conspicuously missing. Where was everyone? It was eerie, even though she now understood the déjà vu feeling she'd had. She still didn't know what happened between her parents. She might not ever know.

The day was warm and Demi shed the light cardigan she was wearing. What should she do now? Sam and Rachel weren't at the gatehouse. Sniffing a climbing rose she decided to walk to the orchards and see how the new trees were coming on. What would happen to the orchards when the estate was sold? No, she corrected herself, *if* it was sold. There had to be a way forward. If she and Victoria could leave out the emotional baggage standing in-between them then they should be able to make this work. And Sam was so keen to get the cider making off the ground.

There was no breeze and sweat trickled down the back of her neck. Demi twisted her hair into a topknot and found a pencil in her bag to secure it. That helped a bit but her light dress was clinging to her. Who knew that Cornwall could be this warm? She turned off the drive and walked towards the barn in the cover of the elder trees. It was cooler, markedly so. A shiver ran up her spine as she heard a twig snap. She twisted around but could see nothing. Her imagination was running away with her.

In the distance she could make out the standing stone, the Kowres. She walked closer. The wind blew off the river and up the field and the grass moved in waves. The footpath around the standing stone was well worn. Touching the granite she thanked the Kowres for helping her. She would have died there had the walker not come along, that much was very clear. She looked up and smiled as she set off for the cover of the trees before she burnt in the midday sun.

Demi didn't recall that the stone was near the barn. She must have taken a wrong turn. Looking around she thought that if she turned left it would lead her back to the house on the route that she and Victoria had taken. So if she went on the path to the right it must take her near the orchards. She hoped.

Slipping her cardigan back on she walked slowly over the roots that crossed the path. The trees became thicker and there was less light making its way through the canopy above. The elder gave way to oak mixed with scrub pine and the odd eucalyptus towering above it all. Nothing looked familiar. The path led her down hill and the trees changed to only oak, dense and twisted. She pulled the cardigan tighter about her shoulders, trying to remember landmarks if she needed to retrace her steps.

Another snapping twig brought her to a halt. Listening closely, there was no other sound and total silence slipped around her, wrapping her in fear. Where was she? Run, was the only thought in her head, and she catapulted down the path until she broke free of the trees and there was the river, peaceful, bright and calming. She gasped for air and looked around. Across the creek she could see a house with beautiful large windows. She couldn't tell if it was early Victorian or Georgian from this distance, but it sat contentedly in the summer sunshine. People walked out, including a man in a suit. Demi squinted because the man looked familiar. Yes, it was Adam who, thankfully, was fully dressed.

A woman's laughter carried across the water. Demi leaned against the tree and watched the scene. A man held papers in his hand and the woman pulled out a tape measure. The house must be for sale. It faced west and there was something lovely about it. It was a happy place, unlike the woods behind her.

Looking over her shoulder she saw the sunlight falling through the trees, creating a mosaic on the path, but a shiver ran up her spine when she thought about the journey back.

Her phone vibrated in her pocket and she pulled it out. She'd missed a call from Sebastian but the light was still flashing. She hesitated. It could be another ghastly text from Matt. She hadn't had one in a while and hoped he'd stopped, otherwise she would have no choice but to block him. Thankfully she wouldn't have to contact the police. She'd learned she could do it from her phone and he'd never know she'd done it if what she'd read on the Internet was true.

She cast one last glance back towards the house in the sun, squared her shoulders, and walked up the path clutching her phone like a talisman. It wasn't much good for anything else as yet again she had no signal once she was ten feet from the creek's bank. If an axe murderer were lurking in the woods there was nothing she could do about it except to accept her fate.

Treading as quietly as she could, she listened to be sure there was no one else in the wood with her. Noises came from nearby, but she didn't see anyone. Her imagination created nasty scenarios, which was silly, and by the time she found the barn and heard voices her legs were shaking.

"You're right. If we use old brandy barrels the cider will benefit from the flavour." Sam was intently focused on Rachel.

"You could use whisky ones as well or even wine." She tucked a pencil behind her ear. In front of her was a makeshift table with papers spread across it. Demi tried to see what it was but she was too short. They hadn't noticed her arrival. Their heads bent together suddenly and Sam circled something.

"That's what we need."

Demi swallowed.

"You're right." Rachel held her hand in the air and Sam high-fived her. "So bloody clever — but then you always have been."

"Hi." Demi walked in, hoping it wasn't a bad time.

"Hey, Demi. Come and take a look." Rachel indicated she should come to the table. Architects drawings of the barn converted in to a commercial cider brewery were spread out. Demi looked at Rachel.

"Are you the silent investor?"

Rachel laughed. "Silent and me don't go together too well, but let's just say I'm a representative."

Demi looked to Sam. His eyes sparkled and he sketched down a few notes on the side of the plan.

"What do you think?"

Demi chewed her lip. The plans looked great, but why were they moving forward when it was clear that it wasn't going to happen?

"You're not sure? Is there something wrong with the drawing?" Sam studied her. "I'm sorry we didn't consult you, but we thought it might be best to use someone who'd done work on this type of conversion."

Demi shook her head. "No, that's fine. I wouldn't know where to begin on designing a cider press or whatever it's called. It's just that these drawings don't come cheaply and right now this isn't going to happen."

"Ah, I see where you're coming from." Sam's mouth lifted into a smile. His phone rang. He frowned. "Excuse me. I need to take this."

Demi's shoulders fell as she watched him walk out.

"Don't look so worried, my big bro has a plan."

Demi blinked. "You really don't look alike." Demi studied Rachel then turned towards Sam. They were both dark haired but Rachel had chocolate brown eyes and olive toned skin.

"No." Rachel laughed. "Sorry, we don't, and that would be because we are step-siblings. My pa married his ma and the rest is history. Two families became one." Rachel grinned. "And mostly it works. It all happened when Sam and I were tiny so we really haven't known anything else."

"I see." Demi remembered Jane's comment. She must have meant Sam — but why would she think he was a Tregan? Victoria had brown eyes.

"You feeling OK? Can I get you some water or something? You've gone pale."

"I'm fine."

Rachel studied her. "Most people who've never met us think we're a couple." She laughed. "In fact, in his last year of his MBA he used it a few times to stop someone hitting on him."

His MBA? OK, Sam Stuart really wasn't what he said at all.

"He was nursing a broken heart at the time. The bitch dropped him for his best friend and although he's well over it now, at the time I was a convenient shield when I moved to Sydney for a bit and people didn't know me." Rachel smiled but then spoke, "You still look concerned."

"Just trying to figure out how you think you can go ahead with this without Victoria and I making peace."

"Ah, well, Sam is dead keen on this project. More so than anything I've ever seen him work at before and that says something."

"Being keen doesn't make something happen."

"True, but I've learned never to underestimate him. He has a plan. I may not know what it is, but he has one I can assure you."

CHAPTER
THIRTY-THREE

A waft of incense greeted Victoria as she pushed the heavy door open. It was between masses yet there were still many people milling around. It had been Charles's funeral the last time she'd been here. She wasn't sure why she was here now except that she had an overwhelming urge to light a candle. Of all the rituals of Catholicism, this was the one that appealed most, the idea of piercing the darkness with the light of Christ and sending prayers to heaven — if there was such a place. She stood at the base of the statue of St Jude, the saint of lost causes, and wondered what to pray. She put a pound coin in the box for candles and picked up three. Three wishes — no, she would pray for Charles. Right now she missed him. It was something she'd never thought would happen, but his calm steady manner was just what she needed at the moment. He wouldn't have been too optimistic, but he wouldn't let her wallow in fear. It was fear with capital letters that was sitting uneasily in her stomach.

The future had always seemed so clear, but each step of the way it hadn't worked. A woman moved aside and Victoria placed her first candle and lighted it. That one was for Charles. Was she responsible for his death? Was that on her soul? She stopped. That way of thinking wouldn't help now. The next was for Boscawen. Could she pray for an estate? It didn't have a soul, but to her it did. Was it too at its darkest point? And finally the last candle was for her immortal soul. Immortal. She couldn't be more mortal or venial if she tried. Tomorrow morning they would take her to bits and remove the offending parts. What would be left? Was it worth saving?

She clasped her hands together. Fear. God, she was afraid and she was alone. The latter was entirely her choice. She had pushed Audrey away and no one else except Adam knew and she couldn't have his fear mixing with hers. Lowering her head, she prayed silently.

Dear God. If You exist, and I'm not sure You do, I don't know why I'm here except that I'm looking for comfort, for answers, reassurances, but there are none.

Words failed her and she turned to that which she knew by rote.

Our Father who art in heaven, hallowed be Thy name . . . I'm scared. I'm alone. I need You.

Victoria pressed her fingers against the tears wetting her cheeks. It must be the incense her eyes were reacting to. Her shoulders sagged.

363

"Tori." Sebastian touched her shoulder. She looked up. It couldn't be. He didn't come to this church. He went to Farm Street.

"Dear God." He pulled her into his arms and held her. Home, was all she could think as she wept into his shoulder. Slowly he led her to a dark corner away from other people and gave her his handkerchief. Once she had blown her nose and wiped her eyes he lifted her chin. "Tell me."

She shook her head. If she spoke she would cry again. He nodded and took her by the hand, leading her out into the bright, sunny morning as people flowed in for the next mass.

Demi pieced together the information that Rachel had revealed as she sat on the terrace at Boscawen drinking another one of Rachel's wines. So Sam wasn't a gardener at all. He came from a winemaking family — a very good one if this sauvignon blanc and the rosé were to be believed. And he was somehow related to Victoria if Jane was right. "You don't think Victoria will mind if we use the terrace?" she asked, looking round, somehow expecting someone to shout at her.

Sam walked out carrying a tray with salami and baby tomatoes. "It belongs to you too."

"I suppose so, but that fact has never really sunk in." Demi sipped her wine. "I mean, I don't remember my father so it all feels more than a bit unreal."

"Get over it." Rachel raised her glass. "This is yours. Use and enjoy it."

Demi laughed. "I'll try, at least for this moment."

364

"Good. Have we got something we can barbeque?" Rachel picked up a tomato.

"I'm sure I do at the gatehouse," Sam said. "I'll nip down there before I join you two hitting the wine."

"You do that." Rachel grinned as he vanished. "He's been well trained."

"I can see that." Demi's phone rang and she jumped to her feet. She'd never had reception here before. "Hello?"

"I'm pleased I've caught you. I've been trying to reach Sam." Sebastian's voice was gruff.

"Is there a problem?"

"Well, yes."

"Can I help?"

"Maybe." Sebastian was silent and Demi wondered what to say. "Actually, yes you can." She heard a door close. "Victoria is going for major surgery tomorrow. It's cancer, breast cancer."

"Oh no." Demi pressed the phone closer to her ear. "This is sudden."

"Yes. So can you tell Sam to keep an eye on things?" He paused. "I don't know how long she'll need to be in London. In fact, to be honest I don't know much but I'm trying to learn fast." His voice faded and she thought she'd lost the line but she heard him clear his throat. "In fact, Demi, I think it would be a good idea to have someone living in the house. Would it be possible for you to move in?"

Demi swallowed. Live in Boscawen — all alone? "Demi, are you there?"

"Yes, and OK. I'll do that but I don't think that will help Victoria."

He laughed. "I see your point, but I'll tell her it's protecting the asset."

"Not sure she'll buy that one, but happy to help you. Let me know if there's anything else."

"I'm sure there will be. I'll be in touch."

She sat down.

"Somehow I don't think that was good news." Rachel topped up Demi's glass.

"No . . . Victoria has breast cancer and goes for surgery tomorrow."

"How awful. Poor woman. I can't imagine facing that on my own."

"True, but at least she has Sebastian." And Demi realised as she said the words that Victoria really did have Sebastian. That man was head over heels in love with her.

Victoria opened her eyes. Where was she? Grey walls and spotted curtains. Not home. Shit! She remembered. She was alive. She blinked. Things were soft-edged and nothing hurt. That must be the drugs. She tried to look at her chest but all she could see were sheets covering her. Did she have breasts left? The surgeon said something to her before she went under, something about a gene.

"Hi." A nurse smiled at her. "You're awake."

Victoria opened her mouth but it was too dry. Tears started running down her face. Where on earth had they come from? They weren't going to help the dry mouth.

"Not to worry. Many people cry after anaesthesia."

"My mouth is dry." Victoria didn't recognise her voice.

The nurse glanced at the drip and tapped it with her fingers. "That should ease you but if you need something now I'll get you an ice cube."

"And a tissue." She tried swallowing. "Please." Fear struck her at the thought of moving her arms. She knew they would have taken the lymph glands so there would be stiches there, if nothing else. The nurse returned. She wiped Victoria's face and cleaned her nose.

"Thanks."

"Here's a cube."

"How am I? What's left?"

"You're doing well and the surgeon will be in shortly to see you now that you're awake. Your husband has been pacing the floor. He's been very patient."

Husband? Charles? She was alive, wasn't she? She closed her eyes. Oh Lord. Sebastian was here. She'd told him not to wait but he was a stubborn old mule.

"You look good and your husband loves you. All that matters is that."

"He's —" She didn't finish because the chirpy young surgeon came in, closely followed by Seb. She wanted to tell him to go away but the words wouldn't come out.

"Victoria, I'm here to tell you good news."

She raised an eyebrow or she thought she did. Nothing seemed to be working quite the way she wanted it to.

"Your lymph nodes looked good but they have gone for testing to be sure. However . . ."

Victoria held her breath. There was always a however.

"Both breasts were littered with small tumours so I've had to remove them and a substantial amount of the surrounding chest tissue to be sure that we have caught it all."

Gone. Chest. Caught. She closed her eyes and saw small lumps running around on short legs and the surgeon wielding a net.

He spoke on but she didn't hear what he was saying. They were gone, totally, utterly gone. She might as well be a man. Her breasts were all she had as a woman that worked and now they were in the bin or on the way to a lab.

"I felt that it was the best decision in view of the BRCAI gene. We don't want to take any chances."

"Sorry?"

He placed a hand on top of hers. "Don't worry. I'll go through everything with you tomorrow. Just know that things are good and get some rest."

Victoria blinked. Her eyes had filled again but she didn't want to cry. She wanted to scream. Why had Adam found the lump? Why had she gone to the doctors? She would rather be dead. Through her tears she saw Seb's head close to the surgeon's. This was wrong, so wrong.

368

CHAPTER
THIRTY-FOUR

Demi placed the vase on the hallway table and adjusted the spike of fuchsia so that it was more in balance. Victoria would have done something completely different but Demi hoped in some way that Victoria would be pleased. Sebastian had called and said that she was recovering well from surgery. She wasn't sure what that meant but hoped it was positive.

Taking one last look at the arrangement, Demi climbed the stairs. It was time she learned more about Boscawen. It was also a wonderful opportunity to take proper measurements and make more drawings. Even if it all fell to pieces the drawings could become part of her portfolio.

At the top she looked down, remembering the first time she had walked up these stairs with Seb. She hadn't a clue which room was Victoria's, or which one Sebastian was using, or which would even have a made bed for her to use tonight. If you owned a ten-bedroom house did you always keep the beds made in case guests stayed over? What a hell of a lot of laundry.

After dithering she chose to enter the one directly in front of her. The handle turned with a squeak. Inside the large bed was stripped and she knew this was her father's room. The walls were filled with an eclectic mix of paintings. She stepped closer to a large canvas, all in blues. It reminded her of the river with the bright clear sky above it. A simple "J" was painted in the corner in crimson. She stood back in awe. Her father owned one of Jaunty Blythe's paintings. That must be worth a bit. Not far away another bold painting shouted happiness in yellows and fresh greens — a headland in spring, at a guess, and then, in complete contrast, a pencil sketch of a nude but not signed. It might be Victorian.

Looking around she understood why probate might take a while. Just listing all the artwork would be a big task. She walked to the window. Her father's room overlooked the elder wood to the east and beyond it lay a field of ripe corn. The good weather had brought forward the harvest.

Reluctantly she left the room and tried the next one. This room had a double aspect and was twice the size of her father's. Victoria's scent lingered in the air and the wallpaper was pretty, if dated. Everything was in place and not even a dent disturbed the surface of the bedspread. Large cupboards lined the east wall. Victoria's bed was high and she would be able to see the garden while still lying in it. She must enjoy that. Despite their difficulties she wouldn't wish what Victoria was going through on anyone.

Closing the door behind her, Demi walked along to the next room. Again it was a generous size and overlooked the garden, but the dark wallpaper put her off completely. The house felt dreary except for her father's room with its white walls and colourful paintings.

She climbed the next flight of stairs. Here the rooms were smaller but brighter and she chose one with distant views to the sea. Hunting through various cupboards she found sheets, located the boiler that controlled the hot water for her bathroom, and unpacked the few things she'd brought with her.

Her phone pinged. She glanced at in case it was Sam or Peta or even Seb but it was Matt again.

I miss you. I need you. I want you so much it hurts. You're cruel. Why won't you answer me?

No, no, no! Answering him, telling him no, didn't work. She deleted the text then went to her laptop and followed the instruction to block him. Enough was enough. She should have done it sooner.

It was the day after the surgery and Victoria seemed to have drains coming out all over while the drip attached to her wrist was keeping the pain at bay. Outside, rain pelted down but she couldn't see the sky, only the red brick of the building next door. Was it raining at Boscawen? She closed her eyes. Did it matter?

"Victoria." The consultant walked into her room, looking bright-eyed and perky. She hated him.

"Hi."

"How are you feeling?" he asked.

"Do you really want to know the truthful answer to that?"

He looked up from the notes he was reading and smiled. "That good?"

"Yes."

He pulled up a chair. "How much do you remember of what I said to you before and after the surgery?"

"Let me see. You confessed undying love and you told me you removed both breasts and as much other flesh as you could get your hands on."

"Right, I see you took a few things on board." His mouth twitched. "You carry the BRACI gene."

"What does that mean?" She tilted her head.

"It means that you are at greater risk for breast and ovarian cancer."

"Wonderful."

"I know it is a great deal to absorb, but in view of the number of tumours we found I think you need to consider having a bilateral prophylactic salpingo-oophorectomy."

"What?" She frowned. "Does it sound better in English?"

"Risk-reducing surgery of the fallopian tubes and the ovaries."

"A hysterectomy?" She looked at the rain.

"Not quite, but that may be included."

"Is it an optional extra?" She raised an eyebrow then continued, "Basically, you want to strip everything that is female from me?" She turned and stared at him.

"It's a strange way to look at it, but in a way, yes. It will give the best prognosis for recovery."

"I see."

372

"I want you to think it over." He stood and handed her a few sheets of paper. "I've brought you some more information. Once you've read that I'm sure you'll have many more questions."

She dropped the papers on to her lap.

He touched her hand. "Things are good. You may not believe that at the moment but I'm sure the lymph glands were clear. That is a good sign. We will know for certain in a couple of days."

"Thank you." She swallowed, trying to get rid of the dryness in her throat and watched the consultant leave the room and Audrey walk in. *Good Lord, who let that woman in here?*

"You look well," Audrey said cheerily.

Victoria closed her eyes. She didn't. She knew it and Audrey knew it, so why lie?

"I brought you some of my hydrangeas because I know you must be missing Boscawen."

Victoria looked at the lacecap blooms, so delicate yet vibrant. "Thank you." It came out in a garbled manner.

"Hal and the rest of the family send their love." She sat on the chair that the surgeon had perched on, announcing her fate. BRAC1. Victoria had a time bomb ticking away inside.

"I won't stay long. I know you must be exhausted."

Victoria wondered what the point of this visit was. Audrey was clearly working herself up to say something. Why didn't she just spit it out?

"Thank you for all your help beforehand."

Audrey reached out and touched her arm. "But of course. It was nothing."

Victoria took a deep breath, waiting for whatever it was that Audrey had to say. She wished the woman would just spit it out. No doubt it was key words of wisdom that she had picked up from other well-meaning friends.

"I know this is an awful time to mention it, but Tori, have you updated your will?"

Victoria's eyes opened wide. She couldn't be hearing this? Was the woman on drugs of some sort?

"It's just that with Charles gone and his daughter around have you thought about what will happen to Boscawen?"

Thought about what will happen to Boscawen? That's all she'd been thinking about her whole bloody life.

Staying at Audrey's might have been the lesser of two evils but Sebastian had insisted. In fact, he had insisted on a great deal. She'd always known he could be relied upon to go and get what he wanted. She sighed: except when it came to fighting for her all those years ago. He had just let her go.

"Tea." Seb placed a cup next to her on the side table. His house was not what she'd expected. All these years and she'd never crossed his threshold until the night before the surgery. Not that she'd taken in much. She seemed to have spent the night in tears.

Now, looking with clear eyes, it was all clean lines and mostly modern art except for the painting that Charles had left him. That Renaissance masterpiece was hanging above the fireplace. Why had she never come here? Was that her fault or his? She pressed her lips together. Both.

"Comfortable?"

She gave a dry laugh. "You're joking?"

"No. If you are in pain we should let the doctor know."

She closed her eyes. It was so simple for him. How could she describe the pain of her sutures let alone the ache of her loss? She couldn't, nor did she want to. "It will pass," she lied. It couldn't pass. She was just a hollow shell, or would be when she went back into surgery again next week. She had to live through a few days here, living in the light of Sebastian's pity, then she'd made sure she was moving into a private nursing home where she could be miserable with anonymity. She still wasn't sure why she was bothering. Pre-emptive surgery for what? To keep her alive longer. Surely it would be easier all round just to die as there was nothing left worth living for.

Autumn

All heiresses are beautiful.

John Dryden

CHAPTER
THIRTY-FIVE

Demi's visit with her grandfather had been less than satisfactory. He was asleep when she arrived and asleep as she left. She turned through the gates of Boscawen. Sam had loaned her his 4x4 for the visits. She had to have a cushion under her to see properly when she drove it. There was one bonus though. The high vantage point meant she could see over the hedges into the fields and even people's gardens.

Now, looking over the hedges, she could see one of the orchards laden with fruit, glossy and red, weighing the trees down. The harvest would soon be upon them. And thankfully the cider barn was the one thing that had moved forward most at Boscawen. It was now almost finished. She couldn't believe the speed at which it had happened, including the planning approval. Of course it had been done easily because Victoria had been out of the picture at the time. Now she was coming home two months after she'd left.

Turning down the long drive to Boscawen Demi thought about how the sight of the front door of Boscawen had frightened her at first, but now that she knew more about the past it welcomed her. Of course, Victoria might not be pleased when she discovered that

Demi had been living in Boscawen for weeks. She bit her lip as she parked in the garage, grateful she was back before Sebastian and Victoria arrived.

Coming into the kitchen, she could hear Sam singing. She smiled as she popped her head into the flower room.

"Hello, beautiful." Sam stood, sorting a pile of cut flowers.

She flushed and focused on the arrangement and not on the look in his eyes. "They look great."

"Hoping to welcome her home."

"And soften her up?" She leaned against the wall, studying him.

He grinned. "Possibly, but Seb says he has kept her in the loop."

"Hmm." She put the grocery bags down on the table. She knew Victoria must have approved everything, but she might not have been in her right mind. Victoria's silence in these weeks had been deafening and Demi had convinced herself that Victoria would emerge a new woman after what she'd been through. Well, Demi hoped she would.

Sam walked past with a large vase filled with vivid blue hydrangeas. He glanced at the food she was putting into the fridge. "Not the only one trying to soften her return."

"Possibly." Demi closed the fridge door. "I will confess to being a bit scared."

"She's not really mean, just a hothead."

"To you she's not mean."

He frowned.

"I hope she's called Adam. He hasn't left any messages for her in a while." She folded the shopping bags. "He's seemed so sad."

"She shouldn't have been with him in the first place."

She turned around and fixed a stern look on her face. "Why? Because she's sixty and he's not yet thirty?"

"Actually no." He tilted his head to the side. "Because it began when Charles was alive."

"Oh."

"He wasn't the first either."

He left her in the kitchen as she seasoned the chicken and placed it into the oven. She wasn't sure if Sebastian and Victoria would have eaten or not but this way there would be food available.

"Hey, you left your phone in the hall. You have a ton of messages from Matt." He raised an eyebrow.

"Thanks." She took the phone and put it in her pocket.

"Who's Matt?"

She took a deep breath. "An old boyfriend."

"He seems keen."

"You can say that again." Her hand shook as she began pealing some potatoes.

He came closer. "It's a problem?"

"No, I blocked him but I must not have deleted all the messages."

He put his hand on her shoulder and she jumped.

"Demi . . ." The sound of gravel on the drive stopped Sam from saying whatever it was he was going to say.

She dropped the potatoes in a pot of water and dried her hands but sweat covered them almost instantly. As she followed Sam through the hall she wiped them again on her jeans. She couldn't greet Victoria with sweaty palms — it would give the game away. Through the open door she could see Sebastian helping Victoria out of the car. The sleek silver bob was gone. Her hair was now in a short pixie cut that made her look younger. That, Demi hadn't expected. In fact, she'd thought Victoria would be frail, but at the moment she looked to be in rude health. Demi braced herself as she walked out of the door.

"Welcome home." Sam leant down and kissed Victoria's cheek.

"Thank you." Victoria turned to Demi who stood by the door, moving from one foot to the other. "Are you the welcome committee?" Her face showed no emotion.

"Something like that." Demi forced herself to smile.

Victoria looked up at the building and then at Demi. "It's good to be back. I hear we are to be housemates?"

Demi glanced at Seb and then Sam before she said, "Yes."

"I suppose it was inevitable." She turned to Sam. "I see the agapanthus have finished and you've left the heads on for me."

"Thought I'd better, after last year." He smiled sheepishly.

She gave him a sideways glance. "What else do I have to look forward to?"

382

Sam helped Sebastian get bags out of the boot and Demi's glance met Victoria's. Was Victoria angry or resigned? Demi looked at the ground. Neither said a word and she didn't know whether to fill the void or leave it. "Have you eaten?"

"No, but I'm not hungry."

"Fine." Demi stood straighter. This wasn't going to be easy, that was clear.

"Have you changed anything?" An eyebrow went up.

This could go downhill rapidly. The answer was most definitely yes but it might not be the best time to broach it. "A few things."

Victoria strolled into the hall. Her glance travelled over every surface until it finally rested on the flowers.

"Nice arrangement."

Demi flinched. The arrangement was stunning and it certainly brightened the dreary hall.

"Thank you, Victoria." Sam put a bag down. "Not up to your standard but I tried."

Victoria's expression changed in an instant. She smiled. "It's truly lovely and thank you."

Cow. Demi bit her lip. That wasn't fair. Rather than retort Demi walked through to the kitchen. Whether Victoria wanted to eat or not the potatoes needed finishing.

Sam entered the kitchen. "Take a deep breath."

Demi turned to him and smiled.

"We need her on board to go ahead, even if we've managed to ring-fence the cider business."

"True." Demi pursed her mouth. "I know I shouldn't be angry but it was so bitchy."

Sam shrugged. "She's been ill."

"She was a bitch before." Demi slipped her hand over her mouth.

Sam laughed. "Well, you do surprise me."

"Me too. I was raised to behave better than that."

"Right, Victoria may not be hungry but I am. Need some help?"

She smiled her thanks. She really must get a handle on her emotions and focus on what she wanted to achieve and not get caught up in petty things. But something told her this would be a big challenge.

Victoria watched Demi walk away and wished she would just continue going, but Victoria knew that wasn't going to happen. Hell, she was even living in the house. For all Victoria knew Demi had taken over her room. She took a deep breath. No, Demi wouldn't do that. She was a nice person, Sebastian kept saying so, and Victoria was sure he was right. But every time Victoria looked at her she saw Charles, and with that came the guilt. She knew in her heart that Charles would be alive today if he hadn't heard her with Adam. It had never been his plan to drive down that night. It had been madness to turn around and do the journey again in the same day.

What she didn't know was if he was driving down in anger or in sadness. As she'd looked through Charles's revised will again and again she'd tried to find out. What had his intentions been? She knew that Seb must know the answer but was keeping it from her.

"I'll just take these up to your room." Seb stood close by her. "Are you OK?"

"Not sure is the truth." She half smiled and walked through to the sitting room where it was obvious that Demi had been at work. Large charts were propped up on the furniture and fabric swatches were scattered everywhere. None of it was in keeping with the house. It was clean and crisp and not how Edith, Gladys or even her mother would have done it. She inspected the first board, knocking it over, but then picked it up examining it more closely. She was behaving like a child. She'd known what she was doing when she signed the papers weeks ago. Putting it back in place, she acknowledged the work was good, very good. And sensitive to the age of the house, yet focusing on the need for commercial appeal.

Carefully placing one card on top of another Victoria sat in her favourite chair. She could do this if she could find the energy. The surgery and the chemo had taken their toll. It would return, they said, but they hadn't said when. The scent of roast chicken wafted towards her. Maybe she had been premature in saying she wasn't hungry. First she'd have a G&T and then maybe dinner. She looked at her watch. It was too early to eat but she'd become institutionalised while in the nursing home. Whether she wanted it or not dinner, such as it was, arrived at six thirty, just when she longed for a gin, which was not allowed. Instead they gave her another form of stew. She had never known you could do so much or so little with stew. Even if it wasn't one, it always tasted just like one.

Proper roast chicken with vegetables from the garden — now that was real food. But she wanted a drink first. As she pushed herself off the chair she saw Sebastian walking into the room with the ice bucket.

"You read my mind."

He smiled wickedly. Her heart rose then fell. She could flirt, but that was all she could do. She sank back into the chair as the realisation hit that she had nothing to offer except verbal play. It was a poor substitute.

"Have you had a look?" He indicated the boards about the room.

"Briefly."

"Well?" He handed her a glass. She frowned. It was a half measure.

"You haven't had a drink in weeks. Slowly does it."

"Party pooper."

"Yes, and you haven't answered my questions."

A hint of rosemary came drifting into the room. She was definitely hungry and she had forgotten what real hunger was like. The relentless diet had deadened her taste buds.

"True, but first can you tell Demi that I'm sorry and I accept her offer of dinner? It smells divine."

Sebastian rose and came closer. "You should do this yourself but as I'm sure that you're tired I'll let you off this time. She is a good kid."

"She's not a kid."

"I know, but she's a lot younger than both of us."

"I was a married woman by her age."

"Was that a good thing?" He paused in the door.

Victoria gave a dry laugh. "With hindsight, definitely not."

"Well then."

"OK, please go and tell her before she changes her mind about her offer."

She watched him leave then turned to the designs. Each room in the house was done. Grudgingly Victoria had to admit that it would suit the market they were aiming for but — no, no buts allowed. It was accept this or sell. Each and every lawyer she'd consulted had told her that contesting Charles's will would fail. Not one felt that her husband had short-changed her.

She picked up the design for the dining room. Demi had obviously found Charles's stash of paintings in the attic and planned to use them throughout the house. Most of the recent purchases were by local artists. Victoria had looked at his buying as a form of charity, his way of supporting the arts, but she was beginning to wonder if he had been a connoisseur of sorts.

The colour schemes all picked up the hues of the countryside and the garden. Demi had portrayed pictures of flowers in each room. In fact, she'd named all the bedrooms after some of the most common flowers in the garden toning each room to the shades of the plant.

She put it down. It was good, but it wasn't what Victoria wanted. She turned to the gin bottle. Despite what Seb had said she needed another. As she put the gin down, she saw property particulars on the table. The Dower House was for sale. Victoria's heart raced as she scanned the details.

Her fingers trailed over the pictures, remembering. The urge to own it and to be there again ran riot in her mind, but she had to accept that she didn't have £600,000 to buy a house even though it held her happiest memories. The only sadness had been when she'd gone to say goodbye to it. By then her great-grandmother had been dead a year and her father had found a buyer. The sale had paid the taxes and helped with hers and Perry's school fees. Why had her father been willing to send her to a good school but then not been willing to support her going to Oxford? She should have gone anyway. Damn, she should have done so much differently.

"All set. Demi says dinner will be ready in half an hour." He came up to her and tut-tutted while looking at her drink. He picked up the sales particulars. "You loved that house. I remember sneaking around there in the dead of night so that you could show it to me." He laughed. "That was after we'd been at Men an Skawenn trying to see if I could fit my shoulders through. I seem to recall you talked me out of all of my clothes."

A smile spread across her face. "I didn't have any on either."

"You were a tease."

"Yes."

"You said you wouldn't marry me unless I could fit through the stone as we wouldn't have any children otherwise."

She snorted. "You did fit through — just, but it wouldn't have mattered or helped. I was barren."

Victoria gritted her teeth. She would not crumple. It was in the past. It shouldn't hurt.

"It might have been different."

She laughed. "Seb, you know as well as I that it wouldn't have been." She walked away. "When I failed to fall pregnant with Charles I tried with so many others, just to be sure." She forced a smile. "I found I quite liked it and always hoped that one of them would make me pregnant."

"Don't."

"There is no sense in hiding from it now. Those days are well and truly over. Hell, I'm not even really a woman any more." She took a deep breath and as she released it they were interrupted.

"Hey, you two, dinner's on the table in the kitchen when you're ready." Sam called from the doorway.

"On our way." Her voice wobbled despite her best efforts.

CHAPTER
THIRTY-SIX

Slamming the cupboard door, Victoria was near to tears. Where the hell were the coffee and the cafetière? And the soup bowls were where the mugs used to be. She leaned her head against the cupboard. She couldn't do this. She just couldn't. This was *her* kitchen.

"Are you OK?" Demi asked.

"No, I'm not OK." Victoria turned around. Demi was standing with her tape measure in her hand and a pencil behind her ear, no doubt having just authorised some other change in the house.

"Can I help?" She walked fully into the room and put her things on the table. "I was going to make some coffee. Would you like some?"

Victoria's eyes widened as she watched Demi open the cupboard where breakfast cereals were kept not long ago and pulled out the essentials for coffee, took the mugs from another one.

"Was that a yes or would you prefer tea?" Demi turned around after she put the kettle on.

"What did you think you were doing?" Victoria asked.

Demi tilted her head and pursed her mouth. It was Charles looking at Victoria. She clenched her fists.

"Doing what?" Demi frowned.

"Rearranging my kitchen."

"Oh." Demi pressed her lips together. "Sorry, but I couldn't reach many of the everyday things without a step stool so I readjusted a bit."

"A bit?" Victoria took a deep breath. "Every cabinet is altered."

"I —"

"You didn't even ask, you just did it."

The kettle clicked and Demi poured the water on to the grounds. "Look, Victoria, you weren't here and needs must." She took a deep breath. "Besides, it will all be changed soon when the renovation starts."

"You are not altering the kitchen!"

Demi blinked. "Haven't you looked at any of the correspondence or the rough plans?"

Victoria pressed her mouth into a straight line. It had been one thing to review plans but another to be standing in her kitchen and accept that it was all to change.

Demi plunged the cafetière. "Coffee?"

"No, no. Forget the coffee. And no changes. None."

Demi put her hands on the table. "I don't want to argue with you, but you have agreed. Builders have been organised, plans approved, and it all begins next month."

"No." She couldn't do this. She couldn't have random strangers staying in her house. "I'm pulling out."

"What?" Demi's face lost all colour and she hadn't had much to begin with.

"I don't want to do this."

Demi stood there shaking her head and part of Victoria wanted to laugh but she couldn't. By saying those words she'd just said goodbye to Boscawen forever.

"You can't."

"I can and I will."

"You will what?" Sebastian came in to the room. "That coffee smells great. Is there enough for me?" He stopped and looked from Victoria to Demi and then back again. "What's been going on?"

"I'm pulling out." Victoria reached for the back of a chair. Despite the six weeks since the last operation, pain still ran through her when she was tired. She shouldn't be tired, though. It was morning and she was finally home.

"Demi, would you be kind enough to leave us." Sebastian smiled at her.

"Of course." Demi grabbed her mug and fled.

"Sit down, Tori, before you fall down and tell me what this is about."

She sank into the chair and watched him pour them both cups of coffee.

"Well?"

"I can't do this."

"Why?"

Victoria dropped her head into her hands. Why? "I could say because she moved the cafetière, but that wouldn't be the whole truth."

He smiled. "She's short."

"I'd noticed." She breathed in the aroma of the coffee. "Seb, I'm tired."

"Understandable."

"It's not that simple." She took a sip. "I thought I was fine with the changes for Boscawen." She looked out of the door to the vegetable beds. "But when I couldn't find the coffee I realised that I can't do this. Boscawen is mine or it's not mine. I can't do half measures."

"I see."

"Do you?" She shook her head. "I'm not sure you do. But I want out."

"So you know what all of this does?" Demi looked at Sam.

He grinned. "Do you want me to show you?"

"Might not be necessary." She sat on a cement wall.

"That doesn't sound good. What's up?"

"Victoria's pulling out."

He sat beside her and tapped the cement. "Just so you know, this will be the apple wash."

"Oh." She turned and noted the dimensions of the long rectangular shape running along the back wall. There was a large, top-hinged door opening above it at the far end and to her other side there was a conveyor belt leading to a tall machine. "I'm so sorry for you. I know the cider operation is a separate business and she agreed to that, but I can't see how it won't be impacted as she has a share in this too."

He shrugged his shoulders. "We'll manage somehow." Taking her hand he lead her along the apple bath.

"This is where the apples are pulped." He paused as he took her to where a tube came out. "We put the pulp into these trays and call it cheese."

She wrinkled her nose.

"Weird, I know."

She stroked the wood of the tray, noting the open slats.

"It's made of acacia wood and copper nails." He smiled. "Then when we have seven trays they go to the press." He walked across the barn still holding her hand. As much as she wanted to focus on the cider-making process all she was thinking about was his hand holding hers.

"Here it's pressed and all the juice runs down and is collected into a large vat." He turned and pointed to the other side of the barn. "Then into a fermenting vessel." He stopped. "You're not paying attention."

"I was, but not closely; fermentation."

He laughed. "We will let most of it mature for five or six months but of course we will have some for wassailing."

She made a face. "Like the carol?"

"Indeed. On Twelfth Night we will drink to the health of the trees to insure next year's harvest."

"OK." Demi wondered if they would be here for Christmas.

"It will be fine."

"I'm not so sure. Sebastian's with her."

He took her face between his hands. "Look at me."

She raised her eyes.

394

"Victoria has been through so much recently she is bound to be shaky, but she's a Tregan and she will do everything for Boscawen."

"A Tregan — and that explains it?" She frowned, looking at Sam's beautiful eyes. Jane Penrose had known who he was from his eyes. They were so distinctive.

"The Tregans look after Boscawen," he said.

"And this is what you are doing?" She tilted her head to the side and watched him.

He smiled.

"Why haven't you told her?"

He shrugged. "Good question." He ran a hand over the acacia wood tray. "Mum had mentioned that they hadn't parted on good terms and she knew her sale of the estate hurt Victoria, so I didn't think bringing it up would be a good idea."

Demi frowned. "She loved her brother."

"I know that now. But I'd heard from my mother how angry she'd been that my father had inherited the estate and she received practically nothing." He sighed. "Since you've been here she's spoken about him and it's been great to hear about my father's childhood."

"I can imagine."

"Sorry."

"No need to apologise. I did have time with Charles. I just don't remember it." Although she'd dreamt about him last night and it felt as if memories were coming back to her.

"True. Anyway, when I took the job Victoria spent much of the time cursing my mother and what had happened to the house and gardens in those years."

She chewed her lower lip. "Is your mother the silent partner?"

Sam nodded. "It's the last thing that Victoria needs to know."

Demi laughed. "Are you ever going to tell her?"

"When I feel the time is right." He took her hand and led her into the orchard. "It's almost time to begin to harvest."

Demi rubbed her lower back. She'd been collecting windfall apples for the last three hours and had begun to make a dent. Sam was working in another orchard, as were the two people they had hired to help. Peta was going to come by later and give a hand. The schedule had been accelerated by the hot dry weather and the storm that had blown through last night. It was good, but had caught them on the hop. Their focus had been on having everything ready to go in the barn. Rachel was project managing that side of things. She'd come back from Perth only just yesterday and for once didn't look too bright. The jet lag was hell but there was no time for that or anything else.

Readjusting her hat, Demi began again. In all her wildest dreams she had never imagined that she would be working on collecting apples to make cider. She dodged a sleepy wasp and moved forward, filling another basket slowly in the heat. What she really needed right now was to cool off. The path down to the small creek wasn't far away and the thought of the cold water was so appealing that even though she didn't have her swimsuit on she decided that a swim was exactly what she needed. The tide should be high and the creek was sheltered from view. The only property that overlooked it was the Dower House and that was empty. Adam mentioned that it had been sold when she'd seen him in the pub the night before.

Five minutes later she was slipping out of her clothes, glancing around to make sure no one was near. Then she laughed. This was truly madness and it felt so freeing as she tiptoed into the water with the light breeze caressing her bare skin. In the shade of the trees the water was freezing but against her heated skin it was bliss. God knows what anyone would think of her if they saw her at that moment, great white body against the dark green waters. A dragonfly whizzed past. Demi started but then watched it find a resting spot on a branch bathed in the September sun.

The only sound was the hum of a distant tractor. She crept further into the creek, up to mid thigh. Her body temperature had dropped significantly and she began to wonder if this whole thing was a terrible idea. What if someone came along in a boat? Maybe she should get out now.

The sound of a cough reached her and she dived in. There was someone watching her. She knew sound carried here, but that was close, very close. She broke the surface, gasping for breath, making sure her body was obscured from anyone's view. She searched the bank, looking for the peeping Tom, for it was definitely a male cough. Her heart raced as her body numbed. The water was bloody freezing and she would need to move or die of hypothermia. She began to tread water, hoping the culprit would show himself. How was she going to get out of the water? She couldn't stay in here forever.

She heard the cough again and Sam emerged out of the shadow of the path. Was he her peeping Tom? He didn't seem the sort at all. "I see we had the same idea."

She nodded.

"Do you mind if I join you?"

Demi gulped. What did she say? "I'm not sure." Her voice broke.

"Great."

He clearly hadn't heard her. He swiftly pulled off his shirt. Demi was mesmerised by the taut muscle of his stomach and her temperature rose as he undid his belt and began to remove his shorts. She turned away and went under the water to resist the temptation to see him fully naked.

She came up for air and found him only three feet from her.

"Just what I needed." He smiled. And the light reflecting off the surface of the creek played in his eyes. Her limbs turned to putty, which wasn't ideal when she was well out of her depth. She didn't want to dwell on the fact that they were both naked in the water not two feet from each other, but it was all she could think about.

A sneeze echoed across the creek as Demi began a breast-stroke away from Sam.

"Bless you," he called.

She stopped. "It wasn't me."

Sam looked around and his eyes narrowed on the oaks to the left of the path. He began an easy crawl through the water towards Demi. Within a foot's distance he whispered, "There's a man in the woods watching us. He's blond and about six foot. Do you know him?"

Demi's heart stopped. It couldn't be Matt. How could he have found her here? "I know of someone who could fit that description, but he's in London."

"This person is not dressed to be walking in a Cornish wood. He's wearing tan trousers and a striped shirt. It's like he wants to be seen."

That was Matt's everyday wardrobe: always smart, never dressing down. "It might be my ex then."

"Seems he's still keen."

She sighed. "That's putting it mildly."

"Shall I go and threaten him?"

She frowned. Although part of her loved the idea of Sam hitting Matt solidly in the face, it wasn't a good idea.

"Or better yet, let's give him an eyeful so that he thinks you have definitely found love elsewhere."

"What?"

Before Demi could say anything Sam kissed her. Not softly or tentatively, but with such passion her toes curled. Her skin pressed against his, with the water skimming over them, made everything instantly more intense. She knew she should pull away, but she had never felt this turned on in all her life. Every nerve ending was on overload between the sensuous feel of the water and the hardness of Sam's body. She wrapped her arms around his neck and her legs around his torso so she didn't drown. She kissed him back with everything that she was feeling inside. He groaned or maybe she did. The sensations swamping her were driving them to one thing.

"Hey, you two, stop the shag and get in here now!" Peta stood on the shore waving frantically. Sam groaned again, lessening his hold. Cool water slipped in between them and she gasped.

"You OK?" Sam's voice was husky and several octaves lower than his normal deep drawl.

"No, but I'll manage."

"Come on. This is urgent!" Peta called sharply.

"Bloody well better be." Sam released Demi but quickly grabbed her hand as he walked forward. She still couldn't touch the bottom so she paddled to keep her head above water.

"I'm serious." Peta put her hands on her hips. "I've been trying to reach you for an hour." Demi's feet finally touched the mud and Sam kept walking but Demi stopped. She was naked. She couldn't just stroll out of the water. He would see her; Peta would see her; Matt, if he was still hiding in the woods would see her — not that he hadn't seen enough of her. She would stay here until they left.

Peta didn't bat an eyelash when Sam emerged dripping water on to the shore.

"What's the urgency?" He didn't sound pleased and Demi watched Peta's glance take in all of him. She wanted to hit her but she too was doing the same.

"It's Demi's grandfather. He's been rushed to hospital and they've been trying to reach her and finally called me because Demi had given them my number as she's staying with me."

Demi went from crouching in the water to standing in a second. She moved swiftly, shaking off water like a dog and throwing on her clothes faster than she'd ever done before.

Matt stepped out of the woods. "Demi . . ."

"Dear God, not now! I don't know why you are here but my grandfather needs me." She turned to Peta. "Take me to him, please." The three of them ran up the path leaving Matt standing there.

CHAPTER
THIRTY-SEVEN

The first thing Demi wanted was a shower then a glass of wine and some food. It was after nine and, despite her hunger, the need to remove the dried salt from her body was utmost. She crackled with every step she took. She didn't want to dwell on what had happened in the creek but her skin tingled at the thought of it. Everything had slipped out of hand recently, which wasn't surprising when she thought about how hard they had all been working. It was intense and that, no doubt, had made what fired up between Sam and her happen. That was all.

The most important thing was that her grandfather was stable and would be fine. He had fallen and hit his head. He had concussion, had broken his bad hip as well as his arm but the doctor had assured her all would be well. She would be able to talk to him in the morning.

She stopped at the bottom of the stairs when she heard the sound of sobbing. Surely it couldn't be Victoria? From what Demi could tell the woman was made of steel, but Sebastian had left this afternoon for a meeting in London so that only left Victoria in the house. Demi walked quietly towards her father's study.

The door was ajar and she saw Victoria hunched over the desk. The sound of her crying was so painful that tears welled up in Demi's eyes. What should she do? Walk away and leave Victoria to grieve or whatever it was she was doing?

She took one step at a time, waiting to see if Victoria would stop and tell her to go away, but she didn't. What on earth could have made her so sad? By all accounts she hadn't really loved Charles so it must be something else. She put her hand out to touch Victoria's shaking shoulder but pulled it back. They had never touched, other than a handshake. But Victoria's pain was almost tangible . . . She reached out again, putting her arms around Victoria's shoulders. No one should hurt that much alone.

Demi wasn't sure how long she stood there, holding her, but eventually the sobbing slowed down to just gulps of air being sucked in and Victoria turned to her but didn't pull away.

"Thank you." Victoria managed between gasps.

Demi nodded. She had no idea what else to say. She would have loved to ask what had caused the storm but something in Victoria's expression told her that no explanation would be forthcoming.

Victoria's breathing returned to normal and she sat upright. Demi stepped away and straightened her very stiff back. She might change the planned shower to a bath. Her muscles had spent most of today in the wrong position.

"You look like hell." Victoria's eyes narrowed.

Demi's hand flew to her hair. She touched the straw-like pieces falling down her neck. "A bit of an odd day, really."

"Thought you were working on the harvest?"

"I was." She blushed. "But I was called away to my grandfather who's had a bad fall."

"I'm sorry to hear that. Is he OK?"

"Aside from concussion and a broken hip and arm he's fine."

"Interesting definition of fine."

"Life is a bit that way at the moment."

"Really?" Victoria arched her left eyebrow. "By the way, there was a good-looking young man here looking for you this morning. I sent him to the orchards. Did he find you?"

Demi felt the colour drain from her face. "Yes." She had forgotten about Matt in all the worry for her grandfather.

"You look like you've seen a ghost."

Demi grabbed the edge of the desk. Everything seemed out of focus. "It's far worse than a ghost."

Victoria got up and went to the drinks tray. She poured two cognacs and handed one to Demi. "Drink this. It's one of your father's best."

Demi gasped and Victoria hid her smile. At least the comment had brought some colour back to her cheeks.

"Now, tell me about this man and why you're not pleased to see him. He looked respectable enough apart from his tiny eyes." Victoria sniffed her own glass, loving the tingle the whole way down. "I've never

404

trusted a man with tiny eyes although I have slept with a few; always disappointing."

Demi didn't know where to look. This could be rather fun Victoria thought, but she wasn't here to torment the girl. Her caring touch had brought Victoria back from the brink just now. She'd never felt so low; even in the midst of all the fertility treatment never had she felt as worthless as she had when she'd found Morwenna's letter. How could she have lived with Charles and yet know so little about him? She took a sip of the cognac. Her affair with Adam had killed him one way or another because that phone call had triggered his actions.

She looked at Demi. He'd nearly lost her and that had almost destroyed him. It was the fear of losing Demi that had parted them.

Now his daughter was here. Victoria couldn't shake the idea that he had wanted Victoria to know his daughter. He'd had to give her up for her safety and for his marriage, which he honoured in spite of falling in love with another woman. Victoria squinted into the darkness outside. Did she really know what love was?

"Victoria, I'm sorry that Matt came here." Demi peered out of the windows as if she expected to see him. There was more to this than a normal lover's spat.

"What happened between you?"

"I . . ." Demi closed her eyes tight then opened them, assessing her.

"Look, Demi, I know I'm not an obvious person to confide in, but I'm another woman and to be honest I don't think it's possible that anything you could say or

405

have done could in anyway shock me." She smiled ruefully. "In fact, I doubt there is anything you could have done that I haven't." Victoria added silently she could add manslaughter to the list if she counted Charles's death — and she did, even if everyone else would dismiss it if she said it aloud.

"I ended the relationship with Matt after I found him . . ." Demi twisted her hands together.

"With another woman?"

"No, in fact I would have preferred that."

Victoria raised an eyebrow. She didn't have Demi down in the threesome camp.

"No, not that way. He'd been on and on about doing things that I didn't feel comfortable about and had told him no."

"Good, but I can see there's a big 'but' coming."

Demi nodded. "I'm such a fool. He's handsome, charming and employed. Compared to most of the men I met at school and uni he was a breath of fresh air." Demi took a sip of cognac and colour washed her face. Victoria had to admit the girl was beautiful, but she lacked all confidence and confidence was the sexiest thing. It was what made people stand out from the crowd. When had Victoria's confidence arrived? Maybe because of the swimming she had always had body confidence and that had been a good start.

"He backed off and I thought we were fine. He was very kind when Mum died and helpful with all the stuff that death entails and then I came home early one day to find him . . ."

"Watching porn?"

"Yes, but not other people. He'd filmed us without me knowing. He'd got me very drunk and, well, I did things I normally wouldn't." Demi sagged in the chair. "It was all there on the large-screen television."

"Jackass!" Victoria spat out the word. She felt Demi's pain. "Right, we'll make sure he isn't around. I'll call the police and have him arrested for trespassing on our land."

Demi's head shot up. "Thanks but — but I might have to explain."

"True." Victoria sighed. "Did he find you?"

Demi went scarlet. "Um, yes in a way." She looked out to the window again. There was more to this than Demi was saying, but in view of the fact that Demi was looking exhausted and, Victoria frowned, salty, she would leave it there.

"Why don't you take a shower and I'll warm up some soup for you?"

Demi rose slowly. "Sounds wonderful." She rubbed her back. "A bit sore from collecting the windfall apples."

"I can imagine. Take a bath and come down when you're ready." Victoria watched her walk away like an old woman.

Demi hesitated just before the kitchen door. She could hear Victoria speaking. At this hour it must be a phone call because she'd heard no one else come into the house. Demi didn't have the energy for any more heart-opening discussions. She couldn't believe she'd told Victoria what she had. However, in some ways it had been good to talk about what had happened. This obsession of his had got out of control. She doubted his witnessing her and Sam in the creek would have done anything but inflamed his desire more. She wouldn't dwell on what it had done to her desire other than make their relationship awkward. If that was what passion felt like, then she had been seriously missing out all these years.

"Thanks, Seb. See you tomorrow. I'll collect you from Falmouth."

Demi took the plunge and walked in, thinking it would be good to have Sebastian back. He was always so cool-headed about everything and it would be useful to have his help. No, it wouldn't, because to help would mean that he would have to know and she couldn't bear that.

"You look better." Victoria smiled. "Would you like a glass of wine?"

Demi nodded yes but then thought better of it. "Maybe not after the cognac earlier."

"Fair enough." Victoria poured herself wine and sat opposite where she'd set a place for Demi. Steam rose from the bowl and Demi took her seat, grateful to have someone else provide the meal. She picked up a piece of crusty bread and dipped it into the tomato soup. Victoria must have made it today from the glut of tomatoes in the garden. It was one of the things Demi enjoyed most about being at Boscawen, the joy of having home-grown produce, yet she'd never imagined that a city girl like her would love getting dirty with the plants.

"This is delicious, Victoria, thank you."

Victoria smiled over the rim of her glass. "What was your mother like?"

Demi's eyes widened. That was the last question she'd expected from Victoria. "That's a big question to answer." Demi dipped another chunk of bread. "She was strong-minded but kind." Demi smiled. "She was my best friend, but too protective."

"How do you mean?"

"Well, I was nearly sixteen before she let me walk to school on my own and always made sure I walked home in a large group." Demi tucked a tendril of damp hair behind her ear. "At the time I really didn't think too much about it, but looking back most of my friends went on their own from twelve." Demi looked up from her soup. "She never made an issue of it, but always had a reason to be with me."

"That makes sense."

Demi frowned.

"I found a letter from your mother to Charles," Victoria explained.

So that was what had triggered the sobbing. Demi blew on the soup, watching ripples push against the sides.

"Were you old enough to remember him?"

"I didn't remember him at all. I was stunned when my grandfather showed me pictures. It's as if there's a black hole in my memories."

"Hmm."

Demi tilted her head. "What do you know that I don't?"

"Quite a lot, I should imagine." Victoria raised an eyebrow then took a sip of wine.

"I'm sure you're right." Demi smiled. Victoria had a very wicked way about her that was fun.

"But, on a more serious note, I read something." Victoria ran her finger around the rim of the glass then looked up. "Something that worried me and concerned you — the split between your mother and Charles. I wondered how it had affected you?"

"As far as I can remember I had a normal childhood with a single mother who was a touch over-protective."

"I see."

"What do you see?" Demi's eye's narrowed.

"Maybe it's best if you read this." Victoria handed over a sheet of paper. "Before you do, I think you need to know that I found it with many newspaper clippings. I doubt you'll remember, but there was an awful kidnapping of the young daughter of a wealthy man, a business acquaintance of your father's. Not someone I knew personally. It didn't end well."

Demi looked down at the paper.

My dearest Charlie,
Your angel is sound asleep after another terrible
nightmare. They have been worse since we
visited my parents. I'd thought being in Cornwall
would help but she was like a different child,
sullen and withdrawn. Her nightmares since then
have become terrifying for us both and I am
going to take her to a psychologist who uses

hypnotism. I will do and try anything to help my Demi.

I cannot get back to sleep. In my mind I keep thinking how close we were to losing her and all I feel is guilt. She wasn't with us because I wanted time alone with you. I was selfish and it nearly cost me my child. And to think we had been with John Samsom, Vanessa and poor Abigail they day before she was taken. Had it been the following day Demi could have been abducted too.

I love you so much, but the more I think about it I know we cannot continue. I respect your decision not to leave Victoria. I understand all she has been for you and been through with you. So I will not ask you to do that.

Demi looked up at Victoria. What had she and Charles been through?

I wish I could say this was a noble thing on my part but it is motivated by the need to protect Demi. The kidnap of John Samson's daughter is all the newspapers are filled with and if people know that Demi is yours she will be at risk — you have more money than he does. I know we have been discreet but since she's been ill I have been haunted by the thought of losing her.

Demi took a deep breath. Now she knew. "Victoria, what happened to the child?"

"It was awful. I was away in Rome at the time and even the Italian papers were full of it." Victoria shivered. "Despite the ransom being paid the child was murdered."

"Oh." Demi swallowed. Her mother must have been out of her mind with fear. It explained so much but Demi just wished that Morwenna had told her the truth, but maybe it was too painful for her mother even when so much time had passed.

"Where did it happen?"

"Not far away, sadly. The child was with a nanny on a beach and they were both taken."

"Did they catch the people? What happened to the nanny?"

"Complete breakdown and eventually they did find the kidnappers."

Charlie, I love you with all my heart and I always will. I know that taking Demi from you will kill you, but it is for her sake and I know you will do anything for her. So I am asking you never to contact us again. I will tell her that you have died. It's the safest way and there will be no questions.

I want you to give all your love to Victoria and share your wealth to help others. I know you already do this, but do more. When you do I will know that you are thinking of Demi and me.

Goodbye, my dearest love. Do not try and change my mind. If you love us, and I know you do, then you will let us go.

Wenna xxxx

Victoria grabbed a glass, filled it and passed it to Demi. She placed a hand on her shoulder. "I'm sorry."

"What for?" Demi turned to her.

"For so much, but right now for your childhood. Charles and I should have divorced." She sat back down. "Charles was old school and lived by the maxim you made your bed you lie in it." Victoria sighed. "Your mother's letter showed me just how much that cost him, you and me."

"He loved you." Demi knew this, but wasn't sure how she knew it.

"In a way, but not the way he loved your mother and you." Victoria swallowed. "He was already successful and I had the breeding, and the connections that made me a good match — but I couldn't give him the family he so desperately longed for." She took a sip of wine. "It left both of us starved in different ways. Charles eventually found your mother and I — well, I kept sampling all that was on offer." Her mouth twisted into a half-smile. "The interesting thing is that neither of us knew the other had been unfaithful." She laughed dryly. "I didn't think he had it in him, nor was I looking. I was completely self-absorbed and living an almost separate life for a while and he had some idealised view of me."

"But you stayed with him."

"Yes, I did. I didn't see any alternative and well, to be honest, Charles's money got me the one thing I truly wanted, Boscawen."

"Oh." Demi looked at the kitchen ceiling with its thick beams. It was beautiful, but was it worth everything that Victoria had given up for it?

413

"It means a whole lot more to me than the bricks and mortar. It was my heritage, my soul. I can't explain how I connect to this place, but I am the last of the line of people who built it with sweat and blood."

"A Tregan."

"How do you know that?" Victoria's brow furrowed.

"Sam told me." Demi sipped her wine, avoiding Victoria's eyes. "So I can see what you mean."

"I don't think you do, but if I said it was like the manifestation of the people who put it here would that make more sense?"

"A bit."

"Charles understood what Boscawen represented for me."

"Did you love him?"

"Yes, in a way."

Demi wrinkled her nose. Didn't you either love or not? The phone rang and Victoria looked at the clock on the wall. It was eleven. She frowned as she picked it up.

"Oh, hi, Sam. Yes, she's here and she's fine." Victoria smiled at Demi and her heart sank. Sam. What on earth was she going to say to him? Victoria handed her the phone.

"Hi." His voice travelled from her ear all the way along her spine. "Just calling to check on you and to find out how your grandfather is?"

"He's as good as can be expected. Thank you for asking."

"How are you?"

414

That question seemed to be asking so much more, a bit like the barrage of questions she'd received from Peta on the way to the hospital. "Tired but OK."

"See you tomorrow."

"Yes. Bye, and thanks." Demi put the phone down and found Victoria watching her.

"You need sleep. We can talk tomorrow."

Demi nodded and went to clear up. There was so much to think through.

"Leave it. I can at least do this although not much else at the moment." Victoria smiled ruefully.

Demi stifled a yawn.

"By the way, I'm staying in the partnership."

"That's brilliant." Demi grinned. "Sam said you would."

"Did he?"

"Yes, he said you would because you are a Tregan and a Tregan would do anything for Boscawen."

"How very interesting." A slow smile stole across Victoria's face.

"Good night." Demi yawned again as she headed upstairs, thinking it might well have been the weirdest day ever. But it had fitted the final missing piece to her puzzle. Her father hadn't been in touch because he really had loved her that much. It was almost too much to understand.

CHAPTER
THIRTY-EIGHT

Victoria smiled as Seb walked towards the car. He'd had a haircut and looked perky. He slipped into the passenger seat and leaned over and kissed her cheek. "You're looking well. Is this your first time back behind the wheel of the car?"

She nodded. It was the least of her concerns. "I found Morwenna's letter."

He frowned. "I'm fine, thank you for asking."

"What happened?" Victoria glanced in her rear-view mirror before she reversed out of her space.

"Because Morwenna felt their relationship put Demi at risk, Charles never contacted them in any way again."

Victoria cast a glance at Seb. His eyes were focused on a point somewhere far away. "They never even spoke again?"

"Never. They felt any contact, any contact at all, would put Demi at risk."

"I see."

Seb placed a hand over hers. "Is she home?"

"No. She's with her grandfather at the hospital. He had surgery this morning." She paused in a passing place. "How did they manage an affair without me knowing about it?"

Sebastian laughed. "I would say they were discreet — but I would also say you weren't looking." He cleared his throat. "Your attention was elsewhere." Victoria turned and saw the pub ahead. "Some lunch?"

"Good idea." He smiled and Victoria pulled into the car park. It had been years since she'd set foot in here but now was as good a time as any. She had to go out in public again, even if she didn't want to. She looked down at her chest. The bra she wore provided the effect that something was there even if she knew it wasn't. She had considered not wearing it, but then people might actually look. She smothered the laughter rising in her. Once she had wanted them to look and now she wanted to be invisible. She had a great deal to adjust to because Boscawen was not a cloistered convent and was going to become a boutique hotel. It really would be best to make her first outing here with Seb at her side.

The pub was busy but they found a table. "Tori, what can I get you? I'm happy to drive the last stretch back to Boscawen?"

"All two miles?" She grinned. "I'd love a hearty red to go with the game pie I see on the specials board."

"As you wish."

She settled back into the chair, thinking that she might not do too much more today. Just driving into Falmouth and back and she was exhausted. The north wind was picking up and she would light a fire in the sitting room and curl up with a good book when they returned. She had to enjoy the empty spaces of Boscawen while she had them. As of next spring she would be moving up to the servants quarters with Demi.

"Victoria."

She swung around at the sound of Adam's voice.

"Don't stand up, please." He bent down and kissed her cheek. "You look well."

She studied him. He was a sweet boy and he'd just kissed her cheek as if she was his maiden aunt. Time can change things so quickly, she thought. The last kiss they'd shared had been one of passion. She noted the woman standing by the door. Yes, things really had moved on.

"Things are good." She put her hand over his and looked him directly in the eye. "And I can tell they are for you. Don't keep that lovely young woman waiting."

"Thanks, Victoria."

"A pleasure."

He grinned. "The pleasure wasn't all yours."

She laughed and watched him walk away as Sebastian came back with her wine.

"Wasn't that your lover?"

"Was is the key word." She raised her glass to Seb. "Those days are over."

"Sad?"

She sipped her wine. Was she sad? "In one way, but in another no."

"You're growing up."

"Don't sound so pleased." The corner of her mouth lifted.

"I'll try not to in future."

"Good, now tell me about these instructions that my late husband and your best friend left you." She looked over the rim of her glass.

"Hmm, client confidentiality."

"Enough of the bullshit. I know Charles and he was a man who planned everything. Why did he want to put Demi and me together?"

"I would have thought that would be obvious to you by now."

She swirled the wine in her glass. "No."

Seb ran his fingers along the handle of the knife and Victoria smiled. She'd always loved his hands. He looked up and caught her watching him. "As soon as Morwenna died he wanted to tell you about Demi."

She leaned back, then crossed her arms against her chest, missing the feel of what should be there. "He did mention he had something to talk to me about but never got around to it."

"Well, he realised he wanted — needed — to talk to Demi first. He knew she thought he was dead." He paused while their food was delivered.

"I can see that. But what am I missing?"

Seb shrugged. "I can't explain it but I think Charles knew something was going to happen to him. He lost heart when Morwenna died."

Victoria went pale. "Seb, when did Charles leave these instructions?"

"I found them in the post when I returned to London."

"When was the postmark?"

"Why are you asking this?" He put his fork down.

"I need to know, Seb."

"He must have posted them just before he left to head to Cornwall because it was postmarked Saturday."

Victoria pushed the game pie away and took a large sip of wine. "Tell me what it said — please?"

"Tori . . ."

"*Tell* me." She clasped her hands together on the table.

He sighed. "I can't tell you all of it."

"Tell me what you can. Tell me about Demi." But Victoria already knew.

"He wanted the two of you together. He wanted you to have his child, the one thing he was never able to give you."

Victoria sank back into the chair. It was hard to breathe. After hearing his wife with her lover he hadn't sought revenge but forgiveness.

Avoiding Sam wasn't going to be the option or the answer to her embarrassment about their swim. He was one of her partners and she would see him every day. She had to deal with it. As she walked up to the cider barn she hoped he was alone. If Rachel was there it would have to wait. As lovely as she was she didn't need to hear what Demi had to say, although Demi wasn't quite sure what that was.

The overhead lights reflected on the gleaming surfaces. Already the machines had been in full operation with all of the windfall fruit so far and the trees were still laden. Apples from the nearby properties filled the apple bay and the sweet yet sharp scent filled the air.

"Sam?" Demi walked further in but couldn't see him. His 4x4 was outside so he must be nearby. She turned around to head out when she heard a cough. Swivelling she saw Matt out of the corner of her eye.

"Matt, what the hell are you doing here?" She put her hands on her hips to stop them from shaking.

"You. I needed to see you." He stood slightly hunched with his hands clasped, looking contrite. "You've blocked me — you have, haven't you? — and I was worried about you."

Demi frowned. "I'm fine, thank you."

"I could see that yesterday. You've moved on."

She released a big breath. "I have." She wouldn't think about what had happened with Sam yesterday. Now was not the time. She needed to convince Matt to let go. "Matt, I've made it clear repeatedly that we are over, finished."

He took a step towards her and Demi moved backwards. She could feel the breeze behind her. She wasn't trapped but right now being alone with Matt was not what she wanted at all.

"I miss you so much." He reached out to her. "And I want to say sorry." He was only three feet from her now. She could smell his aftershave. Too many bad memories were associated with that scent.

"Thank you."

"Please come back to me, Demi. I love you." He cupped her chin and she tried not to flinch.

"But I don't love you. It's over."

He stroked her cheek with his thumb and her stomach turned in disgust.

"We were so good together . . ."

"No, that was never true. I was never interested in what you wanted." She stepped away from him. Now was not the time to send the wrong signals. "It's best you just leave."

"You don't get it, do you?" He lifted his phone and took a picture of her.

"It's over." She ground her teeth, holding her temper in check. "Delete that picture of me."

"Sure." She watched him do it, then he tried to pull her into his arms and she pushed him away.

"I mean it, go away, Matt. Go and find yourself a girl who likes what you do because I don't and I never did."

"You were never like this before."

"Maybe not, but I've grown up. Now go."

"Just one picture for old times' sake."

"No. We are finished. Finished, Matt." She balled her hands into fists.

His eyes opened wide. "You really mean it?"

"I do."

His face drooped. "If you change your mind . . ."

"I won't."

"Fine, then." He left the barn and she prayed that that was the last she'd see or hear from Matt ever again. Her legs wobbled and she sank to the floor and was there when Sam came in.

He helped her up. "Are you OK?"

"Yes." She was finally free of Matt.

"Who was that?"

"My ex." She smiled. "Now, truly ex."

"So you are free for a new relationship?" He stepped closer to her.

"I might just be."

He pulled her into his arms. "I'm very pleased to hear it." He ran his thumb along her bottom lip. "Shall we go and wriggle through Men an Skawenn?"

"Is this an indirect proposal so that this particular Tregan can get his hands back on Boscawen by any means?" Demi tried to be serious, forcing herself to frown.

"Hmm." He kissed her slowly. "It might be, or it might just be me trying to get you naked again."

Demi laughed. She loved Cornwall and she loved Sam.

CHAPTER
THIRTY-NINE

Victoria rubbed her neck. Although she'd been warned about the exhaustion that followed chemo she hadn't really believed that it would go on for so long, that she would be feeling this worn out. She rested her head against the window and closed her eyes. She needed her strength back. She was useless to everyone including herself without it. She picked up the black-and-white photograph on her dressing table. Why hadn't she seen it before? She traced the picture. It had always been a favourite. They were laughing together at his twenty-first birthday. She was married, but still happy enough. Taking the picture she went downstairs and out into the garden where Sam was instructing one of the young boys on how to prune the plum trees on the wall.

"Sam, can I have a minute?"

He turned and smiled. It had been there in the smile the whole time and in the eyes. He had Julia's eyes. What that said about her trying to seduce him was not palatable. Thank goodness one of them had known the truth. She sat on the bench by the kitchen door.

"You look like the cat who ate the cream," Sam said, smiling, and she handed him the photograph.

"Why didn't you say? You must have known I had no idea."

He studied the picture then turned to her. "I didn't think it was relevant."

She drew her eyebrows together. "How so, not relevant? You are a Tregan. This was your father's home."

"Was being the key word." He handed the picture back to her. "My mother sold it."

"Why did you come?"

"I think we all long to know a bit about our past."

"True." She studied his profile. "When did you discover that Boscawen was in your past?"

"Three years ago when Mum saw it in *Country Life*. She was scandalised by what she'd received for it and what it was on the market for." He shook his head. "She told me about selling it, knowing she had to provide for me."

"I owe her a huge apology."

Sam laughed. "I think maybe you do, but she did mention that she was only twelve weeks pregnant so no one but my father knew except her, obviously." He stood. "How did you find out?"

She grinned. "Demi told me."

"Really?" He tilted his head.

"She didn't say it directly."

"Then how?"

"She said, 'Sam says that you are a Tregan and a Tregan will do anything for Boscawen.' So tell me, Sam Tregan, is that what you are doing?"

"The name is Andrew Samuel Tregan Stuart."

"Andrew after my father?"

"Yes, and Samuel after my mother's father. And yes, that is what I'm doing."

"Thank you." Victoria stood and kissed his cheek. She wouldn't be the last Tregan of Boscawen after all.

Victoria reached the quay. It was too hot for early October and the air didn't move. She rolled up her jeans and sat on the edge, sticking her feet in the river. She longed to swim. It would build up her strength again but her swimsuit didn't fit her — obviously — and she wouldn't skinny dip now. That pleasure was of the past. How the mighty have fallen. She laughed sadly. She, who would have been naked in front of anyone, couldn't bear the sight of her own body now. It was scarred like a treasure field where they had taken out the jewels. BRACI. Thank you, genes. She now was an it. All her sexual parts had been removed to save her life, but was it a life worth living? The doctor had said she could have sex again after eight weeks, but surely he was joking. Who would want to have sex with her now unless she paid them and she didn't have money for that. All her funds were tied up in the development of Boscawen.

"Hi." Sebastian sat down next to her.

"Glad to see you've brought the wine again." She smiled.

"Sad not to find you swimming."

She laughed. "Don't have a swimsuit."

"Never stopped you before."

"It does now."

426

"Why?"

"You're joking, right?" She shook her head.

"No."

"I wouldn't want anyone to see this scarred body. I'd scare them to death." Her voice wobbled.

"Tori, you are a beautiful woman." He looked into her eyes and she turned away from him.

"Was."

"No, are. Your beauty hasn't changed."

"God, you're so wrong." Tears began falling. She brushed them away with her knuckles. Seb took her face in his hands and wiped away more tears with his thumbs.

"I'm not wrong. Tori, you are still you, with all your passion and intelligence. What made you beautiful hasn't changed."

She tried to shake her head but his hands stilled her. "Who would want me now?"

"Me."

"No, you wouldn't." She took his hands away and turned to the river.

"I have *always* wanted you. I never stopped."

Victoria sunk her teeth into her lip, trying to create another pain. It didn't do its job. "Believe me, Sebastian, you wouldn't want me now." She looked at him and could see desire in his eyes. No, that must be wrong, she was deluded.

"Oh, but I do." He traced her cheekbone with his thumb.

"Sebastian, I'm not even a woman any more."

"You are."

"No. There are big scars where my breasts once were. There's a line across my abdomen marking the spot where my barren womb once resided. I am empty, hollow, useless."

"No, you are smart, funny and oh so beautiful."

She shook her head. He wasn't getting it. Today she wasn't wearing the useless bra. She unbuttoned her shirt and pulled aside the fabric, revealing the scar tissue where her right breast had been. She watched his face and waited for the signs of revulsion.

He reached out and caressed the scars, then he leaned forward and kissed her. "It was never about your breasts or whether you could bear children, Tori. I was, and always have been, in love with *you*."

"No, you can't be. You can't want sex with this scarred shell."

"It was never about the sex." He paused and half smiled. "I lie; at twenty it was all about wanting sex but trying not to have it."

"See."

"No, I don't see. When I look at you I see the woman I love not the scars she carries inside and out."

Victoria swallowed. "You can't still love me, Seb. You deserve more."

"I want you and have never wanted anyone but you."

"You could have had me years ago." She flushed at the memory of the time she tried to seduce him, more out of anger than love.

"I could have had you then, but there was no point in having only part of you."

"But that is all you get of me now."

"No, I get all of you. You've had surgery. You are not lesser because of it."

"I . . ." Victoria couldn't speak. Sebastian covered her mouth with his. Memories and new emotions filled her. His kiss was tender but she could feel the passion just below the surface. They had kissed for the first time here.

He whispered against her mouth. "I love you."

"You can't." She pulled back. This was wrong. He couldn't love her. She looked into his eyes and they were telling her what his words and his lips had. "No, Seb, no."

"Yes, Tori, yes. I do."

Victoria pulled away and stood up. She didn't deserve his love. She was a bitch and now she was a damaged one.

He stood and took her hand. "Look at me." She studied his hands clasping hers. She had dreamt of their hands before, of them growing old with each other but that was after a long, fruitful life together.

"Look at me."

Slowly she raised her eyes to meet his.

"I love you, Victoria Rose. I always have loved you and always will. I have waited years to be able to ask you to marry me."

"No." Victoria's free hand flew to her mouth as Seb sank to one knee.

"Marry me and make me the happiest man alive, please?"

The please was her undoing. Tears streamed, embarrassingly so, down her cheeks.

"I'm waiting for an answer and I have waited a very long time; please don't make me wait any longer. Please say yes."

She shook her head. She couldn't do this to him. He deserved a whole woman. "No."

"Why?" He looked up at her with eyes that moments ago had been shining and now reflected the grey sky above.

"I'm broken."

"You are beautiful." He stood and stroked her wet cheek.

"You will be filled with disgust, not lust, when you see me naked."

"You will have to trust me on this." He kissed her. "Say yes and I will make love to you right now."

She laughed as she looked around at the cold granite below their feet.

"You're right, I would much rather take you to my bed in the Dower House."

She frowned. "Your bed in the Dower House?"

He nodded. "I thought it would be the best place for us to live because I couldn't see you living in the attic rooms of Boscawen while the public slept in your room."

She smiled. He knew her so well. Should she risk it? What if he rejected her? Was love really blind?

He leaned forward and whispered, "Come live with me, and be my love, and we will some new pleasures prove." She shivered.

"So you won't take me there and make love to me unless I say yes?" Her eyes danced and she put her hand on her hip.

430

"No, I won't. I have waited years for you to be mine." He smiled.

"I just hope I'm worth the wait."

He raised an eyebrow. "So that's my yes?"

"Yes."

"I know you will be." He pulled her into his arms. She was home at last.

Winter

A man can receive nothing, except it be given him from heaven.

John 3:27

Epilogue

Demi looked at her breath coming out in clouds in the freezing air. Although she was wearing her warmest coat and had abandoned her heels for wellies, it was freezing. The church hadn't been warm, but she had been focused on not tripping as she walked up the aisle, making sure that the bride was happy. And from the smile on her face the bride was positively radiant, if cold.

Everyone was huddled together near one of the oldest apple trees. Torches were lit to hold back the twilight. The newlyweds, the king and queen of the Wassail, accepted their crowns made from evergreens. The Wassail bowl, borrowed from Pengarrock, was filled with hot cider, Boscawen's first in decades.

Sam held the Wassail bowl with steam rising from it. "It's Twelfth Night and time for celebration. I'm going to ask the new Mr and Mrs Sebastian Roberts, our king and queen of the Wassail, to begin."

Sebastian raised the bowl. "Here's to thee, old apple tree, that blooms well, bears well. Hats full, caps full, three bushel bags full, an' all under one tree. Hurrah! Hurrah!" He took a sip and passed it to his wife.

Victoria laughed then said, "Here's to thee, old apple tree. Whence thou mayst bud, and whence thou mayst blow! Hats full! Caps full! Bushel-bushel-sacks full, And my pockets full too! Huzza!" Taking a drink, she handed the bowl to Sam.

"Now, before we all have a drink, could the king and queen take this toast and dip it in the cider then place it on the branches of the tree to say thank you and ask for a good harvest this year."

"There'll be some pretty drunk birds here about." Fred wrapped an arm about Peta's waist. "Not to mention the waste of the cider." There was a rumble of laughter in the crowd.

"Shh!" Peta jabbed him with her elbow. "Don't upset the spirits of the trees."

"Sorry." He kissed her cheek.

Demi watched Victoria and Seb place the sodden toast in the trees and Sam took the bowl and raised it high. "Here's to the apples, may we have a good harvest." He took a sip and passed the bowl to her.

"To the apples." The cider was warm and delicious. He grinned, taking the bowl from her then before he passed it, he whispered in her ear. "I can't wait to get you under the mistletoe."

"You don't need to wait for the mistletoe."

"Then I won't." He bent and kissed her and Demi could taste the sweetness of cider on his lips.

"Hey, get a room and release the cider, mate." Fred took the bowl from Sam, freeing his hands. Sam pulled Demi into his arms. Her grandfather, smiling beside them began singing the Cornish Wassail song and they all joined in as they walked back to Boscawen where the wedding feast was waiting.

Now Christmas is comen and New Year begin
Pray open your doors and let us come in
With our wassail, wassail, wassail, wassail
And joy come with our jolly wassail

Acknowledgements

A story has to begin somewhere and this one began in a character workshop taught by Sue Moorcroft at the RNA Conference in Leicester. I won't tell you exactly how, but we had to create a character from three details and from this Charles Lake was born. Thank you, Sue. Thanks to Beryl Kingston for the title.

When writing the first draft of this book, I knew agapanthus flowers were going to be important and I needed information on them. It was just before the Chelsea Flower Show which would have been the ideal place to find answers. However, I couldn't go. I mentioned my disappointment on Twitter and a woman I'd never met said, "Tell me what you need to know, I'm going tomorrow." Thank you Claire Maycock.

If I could pick a research assistant I don't think there could be any better than the wonderful John Jackson. When I despaired of finding the information needed he always came up with the goods. He's brilliant and simply one of the best cheerleaders around for those down days when I didn't think I could write.

It seems I can't write a book without a funeral or some legal problem. Thank goodness I have Anne

Rodell to run things past. As always, any mistakes are mine and not hers.

Writing is a magic thing. Yes, it's hard work but sometimes serendipity is amazing. One day I was looking for something to throw into the book and the wonderful people who tweet from Archives and Special Collections, Falmouth University and the University of Exeter, Penryn Campus threw Kowres into the Twittersphere and the rest is history. They also put me in touch with Matthew Clarke who set me straight on the Cornish for a standing stone near an elder tree. Their help added a special Cornish touch and I am grateful.

There are days when writing a book is the best thing, and then there are those when it's not. Unfortunately for her, Cesca Major happened to be in my neck of Cornwall on one of those bad days. Cesca and her mother had to listen to me rant about a book I couldn't figure out. I think I kept them stuck outside the wonderful Down By The Riverside Cafe for hours while I tried to work things out. It helped, and I am grateful!

By October panic had truly set in and the fabulous Jan Campbell came to my aid and cast an eye over Sam's and Rachel's dialogue to make sure I didn't get the Australian side of things totally wrong — and again, all mistakes are mine!

About the same time I knew I wasn't going to make it to Cornwall in time to finish my research in Falmouth. Sue Kinder came to my rescue with wonderful photographs so I could add the missing details. Thank you, Sue.

As Boscawen is on the north side of Helford I had to include a scene with oysters. I couldn't have Sam choose any old wine so I sought help on Twitter from the Wright Brothers who own the Duchy Oyster Farm on the Helford and several restaurants in London. Thank you, Wright Brothers, for the help.

Huge thanks to — Julie Hayward whose eagle eyes spot the story's faults and failings, Sarah Callejo is the best reader to give crucial insight, and, of course, I wouldn't be sane or able to write without Brigid Coady. She is the best critique partner ever.

My agent Carole Blake's calming influence and wise words keep me on course while my editor, Kate Mills, always sees how to make it a better story and pulls that story out of me. Thank you both, and thanks to the teams at Blake Friedmann and Orion for all they do.

Finally, as always, the biggest thanks go to my ever-tolerant family, including my parents, but especially to Sasha who lost most of her October half-term to editing my book! They are all wonderful and I couldn't do this without their understanding. But no writing would happen without the support and love of my husband Chris. He is the best.

Author's Note

As in past books, I have taken liberties with the landscape. I have moved granite stones and stolen legends from other areas, added quays and moved quays, not to mention creating houses and moving them. The area around the Helford River is filled with history and beauty. I am grateful for the inspiration that it provides.